The
GARDEN
of
LETTERS

Books by Alyson Richman

THE LAST VAN GOGH

THE LOST WIFE

THE MASK CARVER'S SON

THE RHYTHM OF MEMORY

THE GARDEN OF LETTERS

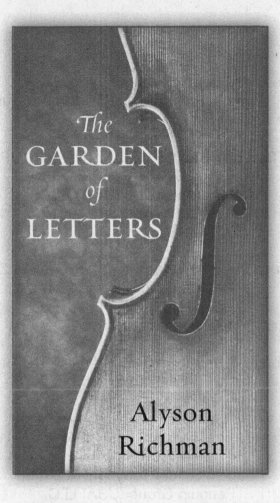

The
GARDEN
of
LETTERS

Alyson
Richman

**Doubleday Large Print
Home Library Edition**

B

BERKLEY BOOKS, NEW YORK

This Large Print Edition, prepared especially for Doubleday Large Print Home Library, contains the complete, unabridged text of the original Publisher's Edition.

THE BERKLEY PUBLISHING GROUP
Published by the Penguin Group
Penguin Group (USA) LLC
375 Hudson Street, New York, New York 10014

USA • Canada • UK • Ireland • Australia • New Zealand • India • South Africa • China

A Penguin Random House Company

This book is an original publication of The Berkley Publishing Group.

BERKLEY® is a registered trademark of
Penguin Group (USA) LLC.
The "B" design is a trademark of
Penguin Group (USA) LLC.

ISBN 978-1-62953-177-9

PRINTED IN THE UNITED STATES OF AMERICA

Title page art © iStockphoto.com/annedehaas

**This Large Print Book carries the
Seal of Approval of N.A.V.H.**

For Katia Galvetto,
who gave me Verona

For Zachary, Charlotte, and Stephen,
whom I will always love beyond the stars

"People have forgotten this truth," the fox said. "But you mustn't forget it. You become responsible forever for what you've tamed. You're responsible for your rose."

—A<small>NTOINE DE</small> S<small>AINT</small>-E<small>XUPÉRY</small>, **The Little Prince**

ONE

~~

Portofino, Italy
OCTOBER 1943

Her rucksack contains her life reduced to small pieces. Though their physical weight is inconsequential, everything she carries feels heavy to her. She tries to pull her skirt underneath her, but the wind coming off the bay is relentless, and the cotton billows around her like a parachute.

She closes her eyes and tries to picture herself being lifted from the deck of the boat, floating above in the cool air and looking down as the vessel moves across the water. Genoa, Rapallo, and the western coast of Italy look like a knife's edge against the water. From the boat, she can see the pale facades of the villas nestled into the cliffs and the century-old hotels that face the sea.

She has been traveling for days, but it feels like months. With a gray scarf covering her dark hair and her navy blue dress modest and unassuming, she could be any young Italian girl in her early twenties.

Her stomach is empty. She tries to forget her hunger by scanning her fellow passengers. The boat carries close to thirty people. Seven of them are German soldiers, along with a handful of grandmothers dressed in their widow black. The others are nameless men and women who all appear unremarkable to her.

Just as she hopes she appears to them.

Early on in the war, she learned how to lose herself: to appear plain, and not worth stopping in the street. She can't remember the last time she wore a brightly colored dress or her favorite silk blouse, the one with the white flowers. Beauty, she has come to realize, is another weapon, better packed away and revealed only when absolutely needed.

She instinctively cups her hands on her stomach as the boat approaches the dock.

She is surprised to find so many Germans there, as she had believed she was finally on her way to safety. She has spent weeks trying to avoid them, yet now here they are standing at the dock, waiting to check everyone's papers.

She feels her entire stomach turn. She takes off her rucksack and instinctively clutches it to her chest.

She stands up, her legs feeling like they may give out from underneath her. She takes her palms to her cheeks and gently presses the skin, so that the pallor of fear is replaced with color.

Afraid the soldiers might search too deeply inside her rucksack, she withdraws her forged papers and holds them to her side. She walks slowly behind one of the widows whose crucifix is so large, she hopes it might cast off a bit of protection onto her as well—or at least temporarily distract the soldiers.

She walks carefully across the deck until she finally reaches the dock. High on the hill, the white houses look like teeth. She sees bougainvillea roping over terraces and hibiscus flowers opening up like parasols to the sun. She inhales the scent of jasmine, but she is weakening from fear with every step.

"**Ausweis!**" The Germans are barking their orders and grabbing papers out of nervous hands.

Elodie is next in line. Her hand clasps her false papers. A few weeks before, she had destroyed the identity card that bore her real information. Elodie Bertolotti is now Anna Zorzetto.

Anna. Anna. She tries to concentrate on her new name. Her heart is pounding.

"Next! You!" One of the Germans grabs the papers in her hand, his fingers seizing them with such force that their fingers momentarily overlap. She shudders at his touch.

"Name!" the German snaps at her. His voice is so sharp, she finds herself momentarily freezing and incapable of uttering even the slightest sound.

"Name!"

Her mouth is now open, but she is like a muted instrument. She begins to stammer when, out of nowhere, a voice shoots through the air.

"Cousin! Cousin!" a large, barrel-chested

man shouts to her from the crowd that had congregated at the dock.

"Cousin! Thank goodness you've come. I've been waiting for you for days!" The man pushes to the front of the crowd and embraces her.

"She's with me," he tells the German soldier.

"Well . . . take her then," the soldier mutters as he reaches for the papers of the next person in line.

This man, whom Elodie has never seen before, squeezes her arm tightly and begins steering her through the crowd. He pushes people away so she can walk freely in his path.

He turns his head toward her and waves his hand in the direction of the hill. "This way," he whispers. "I live above the port, deep into the cliff."

She stands for a moment, frozen in her tracks. She can still hear the noises from the harbor: the Germans barking orders, the shouts as people try to locate each other, and the cries from tired children.

"I am not your cousin," she finally says to him. "You must be mistaken." She tries to speak slowly and clearly. She notices his speech is more proper than the dialect she heard on the dock. He speaks in an educated tongue. But still, Elodie wants her words to be received without confusion.

Her scarf has loosened, allowing her face to emerge from a sea of drab cloth. Like water receding to reveal a well-polished stone. Immediately, he is struck by the green of her eyes and the intensity of her gaze. He looks at her without speaking, then finally forms his words. "I know you're not."

"Then why? Why did you save me?"

She hears his breath, a whisper of air escaping from his chest.

"Every few months I come here and save one person."

She looks at him, puzzled. "But why did you pick me?"

He studies her face, reaffirming what he already knows.

"Why? It's simple. I choose the person who looks the most afraid."

TWO

~

Portofino, Italy
OCTOBER 1943

He asks if he can carry her rucksack for her. She tells him no. "I carry this myself." He does not push her. He cannot read her quite yet. He can only smell the fear on her. To him, it's the scent of a hunted animal. She is restless and suspicious. Her expression does not soften as they walk up the narrow streets toward his house. She focuses her eyes ahead and does not stop once to gaze at the unspoiled beauty of the village or the sea below.

He alternates from walking in front of her to moments of lagging behind. Sometimes he feels the betrayal of his own body. The swell of his stomach, the shortness of his legs, the foot injury that kept him out of this war. She is steps ahead of him, and he notices the strength of her body. The ribbon of muscle in her calves, the tightness in her hips. The firmness of her arms.

"We're almost there," he tells her.

She looks back at him and stares. He has seen that look—the vulnerable wanting to appear strong—countless times over the past year.

"You can trust me," he tells her.

Again she stares at him. One of the straps of her rucksack slips off her shoulder and she readjusts it.

"What is your name?" he asks.

She is so tired that "Elodie" nearly slips from her tongue, but she catches that word before it escapes her. "Anna," she says. "Anna Zorzetto."

"Anna. I am a doctor. The only one here in the village. I promise, you have nothing to fear from me."

His explanation seems to register with her, but she does not soften in the sunlight. He notices that the exact opposite happens instead, as if her body stiffens with his every word.

She tries to read him. The look in his eyes, the lines of his face that suggest both a sadness and an earnestness at the same time.

She turns her head back again, as if to look one more time at the port below. She is desperate to forget the sheer terror she felt only minutes ago, when she feared they might question her papers, or even worse, search her bag.

"Well," she finally manages to say, "I suppose I will have to trust you. I don't have any choice, do I?"

They walk deeper into the rocky cliffs, climbing a small, narrow path, passing over ancient stone walls that barricade a steep mountainside, before they arrive at a small archway covered in vines. Tucked within the jungle of flowers and thicket is a white house with a heavy door, the wood painted in glossy coats of green. She notices the lemon and fig trees and, again, the perfume of jasmine in the air. She feels dizzy. These are not the trees of her childhood in the north of Italy, with its crisp smell of pine and juniper berries in the air. Here she feels as though she has awakened from a dream.

The dialect is foreign. The skin more weathered, the clothes less refined.

How many days has it been since she has slept deeply? The fatigue inside her is paralyzing, and she is thirsty for sleep. Everything she does seems to require an inordinate amount of energy, compounded by the strain of trying not to appear tired and vulnerable.

Inside the house, he offers her a glass of water. She drinks it down greedily and he refills the glass. And, then, one more time. He goes into the kitchen and cuts her three pieces of bread. He spoons some honey into a bowl. He removes the stem of a persimmon and quarters it with a knife before scooping out the soft flesh into a saucer.

She takes only one spoonful of the honey with the bread even though she wants more. She takes only a little of the persimmon. She does not want to reveal the nakedness of her hunger. But the third glass of water, she finishes entirely.

"You are probably tired from your journey," he tells her. "I have a spare room, where you can get some rest."

He walks her to a small room with white

walls, painted tiles on the floor, and a window that overlooks the sea. The air billows through the translucent curtains, and the image reminds her of her skirt lifting in the ocean breeze.

"Yes, I need to sleep," she says.

He closes the door behind him, and she waits until she hears his footsteps down the hall. She notices the key in the door and turns it, hearing the lock click. Then, knowing she is finally safe, at least for the moment, she lifts up her rucksack to the bed and unpacks it.

The contents are both what one would expect and what one would not.

She takes out the first layer. The spare blue dress, her slip, and her underclothes. Then, the sweater from Luca, which she brings to her face and inhales.

Her heart pounds as she removes the second layer. A small toiletry bag that contains her toothbrush, a bar of soap, and her comb.

She next comes to her nightgown, then the small pouch with the amulet on a leather cord, which she cups in her hands. But then on the bottom of her rucksack,

she withdraws a book, so slender it could
be a journal. For a moment, she pauses.
She rests her hand on its well-worn cover.
Then, slowly and with great reverence,
she opens it. Inside this book is another
folded piece of paper. But it's not something written in a code that she doesn't
understand. Nor is she meant to deliver it
as she did during her days as a messenger for the Resistance. Instead, she un-
folds it to reveal a sheet of musical score.

   She closes her eyes and hears the song
imprinted on it.

How does one hear music? Is it the rhythm
of an unspoken language? An untranslat-
able code?

   Elodie hears the notes inside her head
like the movement of water. It begins in soft
ripples. She also hears the notes in color.
An ink wash of pale blue, or the glimmer of
white stone. Soothing at times, then escalating. Long, interconnected strokes that enter her in a wholly different channel. Not
through her mind, but in the deepest cavity of her belly.

   She closes her eyes and remembers her
cello back in Verona. The prestigious mu-

sic school where she carried her instrument every morning, in the black case nearly the same size as she.

She remembers holding the cello between her legs. Her knees two bookends against the lowest curve, one arm embracing the neck, while the other held the bow. With each stroke of her bow, her body coaxed the instrument into song.

But now, she merely takes the sheet of music to the bed and folds her hands over the top. She relaxes as the notes float through her. Sleep finally takes over her, until there is nothing but the melody of the notes inside her head.

Her parents had given her that first instrument when she was seven. For several months prior, she had gone to sleep hearing them discuss which instrument she would study. Her mother had wanted the flute, but her father had pushed for the violin. But Elodie had begged for a cello. She had first become enamored by the instrument's beautiful sound while at a concert at her father's school. The students had played the Dvořák cello concerto, and she sat there mesmerized.

On that walk home, she pierced the air with her own imaginary bow. She still heard the music in her head, every note lingering inside her. The dance of that cellist imprinted on every fiber of muscle and piece of bone.

The day she was finally given her first cello, and the sight of her father placing the dark leather case on their dining room table, were memories that Elodie stored inside her mind, each image like a single note connected to the next. She would never forget the sight as her father unsnapped the case. The instrument had been wrapped in a beautiful red scarf to protect the bow from scratching the varnish, and when her father removed it, Elodie gasped.

"It's a three-quarter size," her father told her as he handed the cello for her to hold. "When you get a little older, you'll play on a full size."

She took the instrument from him and, immediately, Elodie felt her heart begin to race. It was the most beautiful thing she had ever held.

"And the bow, Elodie . . ." Her father took out the bow and handed that to her as well.

"She is her father's daughter," Orsina

said, sensing that her daughter would have no problem once she learned the necessary techniques. "I can't wait to hear her play."

Elodie began her studies slowly, her father adamant that whatever she learned, she would learn correctly. The first thing he taught her was to caress her cello.

The ideal, he told his young daughter, was not to distort oneself. Instead, one needed to find a natural way to embrace the instrument. "You need to become one with it," he told her.

He took her hands and placed them on the top of the shoulders of the instrument. Then, slowly, he moved Elodie's hands alongside the cello's edges, allowing her to feel every curve.

The sensation of the wood beneath her palms was soothing. Each part of the instrument's construction evoked its own tactile response: the varnish of the wood, the length of the fingerboard, and the ridges within the scrolled neck.

Elodie's father showed her how to use her knees to secure the cello's tail into the floor to prevent slipping. He lifted her bow from the table. "A cellist holds the bow naturally, not like a violinist," he told her. And then he laughed and did a small pantomime, mimicking the awkward way a violinist gripped his bow, the left fingers rolling slightly, a technique that was used to increase the volume.

Over the next few weeks, she learned to make notes emerge from her cello. She began to feel her arms transform. No longer did they seem like two unremarkable appendages, but a part of her that had their own unique power. Like a bird's wings, they could lift and stretch. Her wrist, too, she learned to curl and extend, lending grace and beauty to her playing. She learned to wait. To take breaths. To hover her bow just above the bridge and then finally strike. She absorbed her father's instructions with an understanding beyond her years.

"A good musician must cultivate the art of interpreting," he instructed her. "The staves of the score are a road map. You read the notes, you play them as the composer dictates, but the emotion . . . that is what makes the music your own."

She looked at him wide-eyed and rested her bow on her knee.

"You must always listen to what your teacher tells you, then interpret it . . . demonstrate that you've understood far beyond just the playing. Do you understand, Elodie?"

Elodie nodded. "Even though you're young, I can tell you are gifted already by the way you sense what's hidden beneath the music." He walked over to her and took the bow from her hand, placing it on the music stand that was in front of her. Then, he took his daughter's hands into his own.

"When you were only a few months old, I held you in my arms. I looked at that beautiful face of yours and saw your mother's almond-shaped eyes, her perfect mouth. But I saw you had my hands." He opened her palm. "You have the same long fingers, the same wide expansion." He closed her hand again and brought the fingers up to his lips and kissed them. "You're destined to be a great cellist, because I can sense you want to bring your cello to life."

Just as her father anticipated, a special magic developed between Elodie and her cello. The instrument slowly became her, and she became the instrument. A unique bond that grew increasingly intense as her studies progressed. Sometimes when she held her cello, Elodie thought she could sense a pulse beating within its wooden cavity. It never occurred to her that it was her own heart she was hearing.

As she grew older, she was given a full-sized cello that her father had bought from a retired teacher at the conservatory. Made of walnut wood with a honey-colored finish, she practiced on it daily and her repertoire soon blossomed. She played the Brahms Cello Sonata in E major and the Vivaldi Sonata No. 5 with increasing emotion. She mastered the Tarantella, a piece that challenged her stamina, but she practiced it for hours until the notes were as clean and as bright as sunlight.

But just before her seventeenth birthday, only four months before her auditions to become a full-time student at Verona's music school, her father came home with an early birthday gift.

"It's a Venetian cello," he told Elodie. This time when the case was opened, the cello was wrapped in an enormous yellow scarf. Her father seemed to meditate over the instrument for a brief moment, as if he were offering a small prayer. Then, with a grand gesture of his wrist, he withdrew the material to reveal his daughter's newly gifted cello.

"It's extraordinary!" Elodie couldn't contain her excitement. She had thought the two cellos she had played on previously had been beautiful, but this one was truly magnificent. The instrument was unlike any cello Elodie had seen before. The varnish was not brown, but a striking red. A topaz-colored light glowed below its glossy coat, so that the cello appeared as though it possessed its own internal fire.

Elodie's hands fidgeted. She was desperate to touch it.

"In honor of your mother, it had to be Venetian."

Her father handed her the instrument and by instinct, Elodie began to caress it. Her hands moved across the edges and every curve, just as she had done with her first cello years before. Almost immediately, she could tell the proportion of this particular cello was slightly different. The bottom part swelled slightly, thus creating a more voluptuous shape. Even the carving of the

decorative scrolls seemed wholly different. As if the luthier responsible had been
motivated more by whimsy then tradition
when creating its flourishes.

"Papa," she said, still touching every part
of the instrument, as though she could not
quite believe her eyes. "This must have cost
you a fortune!"

"Its journey into our living room is a long
and complicated story," he said softly. "But
I assured the former owner that you would
care for the instrument as if it were an
extension of your own body."

Her father returned to the case. He
pushed aside the yards of bright yellow silk
and retrieved a long, slender bow made of
dark, exotic wood.

"The owner said it had to be played with
this bow in order to bring out the cello's full
beauty." As soon as her fingers took hold
of it, she remarked at its lightness.

"It feels almost weightless," she said.

She pulled herself to the edge of her chair
and began to prepare the bow. She first
tightened the hair, and then applied the
rosin.

Her father took out his violin and gave her
an A note so she could tune the instrument.

She craned her ear to her string and plucked. She closed her eyes and checked the note again. Only when she had tuned the cello to precision did Elodie begin to play.

Over the next several months, Elodie's playing became even more inspired with her new cello. She played with such intensity, such passion, that the mere trill of her vibrato caused her listeners to sense that they were in the company of a prodigy. Now nearly seventeen, her limbs had lengthened and her body had transformed into a woman, both lean and strong. Her father often invited his friends from the Liceo Musicale to listen to his daughter play, hoping to prepare her for larger audiences in the future.

She had both an acoustical and physically charming presence. When her arms drew the bow across the bridge of her cello and then pulled backward to sustain a single, long note, Elodie looked like a dancer. Professor Moretti remarked one evening that she resembled a swan, one capable of gliding across even the most difficult channel of music.

Every afternoon after school, Elodie opened up the case and pulled out her cello. "It doesn't sing until it's in your hands," her mother said one day, as Elodie began to play. She watched as her daughter rested her temple against the cello's long, brown neck. The amber waves of the instrument's varnish rippled in the sunlight, and the long shadow of the instrument's body stretched across the apartment's floor.

Orsina waited all day to hear her daughter play. It was like a thirst inside her. Her daughter's music brought beauty into her life. She still marveled that the child she created from her own womb had such a capacity to awaken things inside her. She had listened patiently as the girl first learned her scales, then graduated to arpeggios and more difficult études. Now she was playing full sonatas and concerti. Her daughter was on the cusp of adulthood, and Elodie's playing became more nuanced and a certain sensuality infused her music. Her fingers now moved with confidence, a nimble precision as they danced up and down the strings. Her bow alternated from long, ribbonlike strokes to gentle caresses.

THE GARDEN OF LETTERS

Elodie grew her hair past her shoulders, and occasionally, when she was fully engaged in the drama of her playing, her hairpins would come undone and her face would become hidden in a curtain of hair. But when her hair was pinned high and in place, she was a striking presence. She had her mother's china-white skin and Venetian green eyes. And when she performed, she appeared celestial.

"She is not only a gifted player," her father told her mother. "She also has a rarer gift in that she can hold the notes inside her head."

Her mother didn't seem to understand at first. "What do you mean, Pietro?"

"What I mean is that she has an extraordinary ability to memorize the musical score." He shook his head. "She doesn't get that from me, Orsina."

Elodie's memory was something her mother had noticed quite early on. The girl rarely ever needed to write anything down. She could also remember with great clarity what she had been wearing on a particular day, even several years after. She could read a book once and remember with ease its entire content without having to refer back to a single page.

"It's the Venetian in her," Orsina said. She knew that her daughter's memory came from her bloodline. Venetians had spent centuries navigating a floating city of mazes. One needed to remember pathways, landmarks, or even anecdotes of particular places in order to find one's way.

Orsina couldn't remember things that were written down like Elodie but she did have a strong visual memory, which she knew she had passed to her daughter. When the child was just four, she had directed Orsina home, telling her to turn left at the grocer, right at the park, and straight on the road with the gelato store in the front. She had smiled, knowing her daughter gave directions like her own mother had, and hers before her.

But Elodie's memory was even more astonishing than a typical Venetian's, and Orsina was happy that it would serve her daughter well in her music.

"This will set her apart from her peers," Pietro told his wife. "She'll be the one the professors want for their string quartets or for piano duets. It looks very impressive not to need to have the music in front of you when performing."

From the time she is ten years old, Elodie attends classes after school at Verona's Liceo Musicale, on the corner of Via Roma and Via Manin. By eighteen, however, she studies there full-time. Her lithe frame carries her cello case to the school's cloistered walls. Everything around her cast an impression. The blue-gray plaster walls, the stark practice rooms. The smell of dry leaves meeting moist air.

Her memory is like soft, red clay. A face on the street. The pattern of a dress. All that she encounters remains fixed inside her mind, like a web of permanent fingerprints.

She plays Vivaldi, Albinoni, Beethoven, Bach, and Dvořák, the music flowing through her, her body soaking up each note. Her body is just another part of her instrument. Her legs are strong like a colt's; her lean arms have the quiet strength of a dancer.

When she plays, she closes her eyes. She hears the fire. She senses the water.

Her bow is like lightning. Striking. Flashing. Touching down sometimes for just an instant, and other times moving back and forth like a saw. She does not play with any sense of fear.

Outside, the world is blackening with the encroaching war. She senses it like a shadow as soon as she leaves the classrooms at the Liceo or her home. The women in line for food at the grocery store, their hands clutching ration cards; the striking factory workers protesting on the streets. The black, billowing shirts of the Fascist police on their motorcycles. The fear that doesn't hang in a single note, but rather an intricate orchestration that is impossible for Elodie to decipher.

She is chosen to play in an advanced string quartet with three other students. Lena, a violist, is chosen as well. The majority of girls attending the Liceo Musicale play the piano or the flute. But Elodie and Lena are among the few girls who play the strings.

The two girls are opposites. Elodie, with her dark black hair, her sinewy body, and her green eyes. Her friend Lena looks more German. Her body is soft and curved. Her hair blonde, her eyes blue and round. There is a voluptuousness to the way she plays her viola as well.

They quickly become friends and learn to complement each other's playing. Lena laughs more easily and takes Elodie to the cafés to have espresso after class. She does not have Elodie's memory, though. Lena is like the two boys in the quartet as she needs to read the musical score. But on several occasions, her beauty is responsible for distracting their classmates.

"Franco was trying to look down your blouse today in rehearsal," Elodie teases. "It's a small marvel he didn't lose his place . . ."

"He's an imbecile." Lena snorts. "He wouldn't be able to open my bra even if he had three hands."

Elodie is amazed by her friend's quick tongue. It's such a contrast to Lena's angelic looks and the mask of demureness she wears through the halls.

Lena is critical, too, of Mussolini's alliance with the Germans. "Those swine," she calls the Germans. "The lowest from the gutter. You just wait and see . . . if we're not vigilant, we'll be like Czechoslovakia and they'll be steamrolling in here and ruling our country."

Elodie can feel the weight of eyes on them as her friend blurts out her feelings.

"You shouldn't speak so loudly . . ." she whispers. "You'll get us dragged into the police station with talk like that."

"What are you afraid of? The police don't see us as a threat. You're just a girl with a cello on the street. They're too stupid to even notice us."

Elodie looks around. What Lena said is true. The piazza is lined with women pushing baby strollers and a few men walking toward the post office. They are just two young girls carrying instruments, and easily blended into the scenery. No one takes notice of them at all.

THREE

~

Verona, Italy
APRIL 1943

As a child, Elodie fell asleep with music in her head. In the morning, she would wake and hear it, too. "Sleeping with the angels," is what her father called it when your dreams were accompanied by song. But Elodie couldn't remember a time when she didn't hear notes while she slept. Her father played long into the night, when he thought the house was already asleep. Softly and quietly, he played a nocturne, or occasionally a quiet romance.

He always stood near the tall paned windows that overlooked the street, his white shirt slightly unbuttoned, his violin tucked expertly underneath his chin.

His playing was the lullaby of her childhood. She knew when he played Mozart that he was savoring good news, when he was nervous, he played Brahms; and when he wanted forgiveness from her mother, he played Dvořák. She knew her father more clearly through his music than she did through his words.

Like her, he spoke very little. It wasn't that he didn't have thoughts or feelings. If anything, he had too many of them. He didn't have a quiet head. He felt things too deeply. Music had become a tonic for him early on in his youth, and he had learned to play three instruments expertly: violin, cello, and piano.

Elodie's mother, Orsina, was not a musician herself, but had fallen in love after hearing him perform.

He had been invited to play in her native city, a labyrinth on water. A place where in winter, the fog merged with the sea. Orsina's father knew the feather of every bird and made a living from all things ornithological. He traveled three months a year to places as far away as Africa to collect rare

plumage for his hat store, a jewel box known
to the city's most fashionable at the corner
of San Marco's Square. Ostrich, peacock,
and yellow and blue parrot, every journey
brought home a trunk full of feathers, each
one more exotic than the last.

Orsina couldn't forget the sight of her
mother's beautiful bed, laid out in feathers.
Silky plumes layered in abundance; a
feather coat of turquoise, lapis, and green.
It was her mother who took her father's
extravagant bounty and transformed them
into the beautiful hats that filled the windows of their store. Her narrow, tapered fingers were so delicate and nimble as they
sewed dozens of seed pearls, silk cor-
sages, and thin wisps of veil. Orsina learned
the styles early from her mother: cloche for
the ladies and the English tourists, broad-
rimmed for church and weddings, and the
flapper headbands with beads and white
feathers for those who liked to dance. In
her mother's workroom, there were always
tall stacks of fashion magazines her father
had sent from Paris so that his wife could
be kept abreast of the latest styles. Orsina
spent her days leafing through the pages,
dreaming beyond the lagoons of her own

childhood, to places like France, where there was a different kind of light. Cities where one didn't float but were beautiful all the same. She imagined them like confectionary sugar, air-spun and light as gauze.

Orsina had not expected that it would be a concert in I Gesuiti that would cause her to leave Venice. But her life took on another path, when one Friday evening, shortly after her twentieth birthday, her parents closed their shop early and took her to hear a rising young violinist play. It was at that concert that she found herself transported by music and entranced by the musician who played before her.

She and her parents walked that evening to the church, her father in a dark suit, her mother in a pale lavender dress; a cloche hat the color of plum blossoms framed her face. Orsina had chosen something wholly different; she wore her hair loose and a yellow dress made of the lightest chiffon.

As they settled into the wooden pews, the sounds within the church seemed to shift. Gone was the somber atmosphere of a Sunday Mass. It was as if the pale gray and celadon marble, with its intricate patterns and lace cut from stone, was electrified. Excitement and anticipation now filled the holy walls. No one glanced at their prayer books. Instead they all craned their neck to see the dashing violinist tuning his strings.

Soon he stood with his instrument at his side and smiled modestly as the church's cultural director proudly introduced him as the latest virtuoso from Verona. The audience clapped and Elodie's father began to play.

Elodie loved the description her mother often told of hearing those first notes.

"Like magic," she said. "I had seen feathers all my life, and his notes seemed like feathers floating in the air. Arabesques of movement that made my head spin." Her mother always gasped for air after remembering the moment so intensely, as the memory literally took her breath away.

"When he played a Beethoven Romance the audience was enraptured. Your grandfather tapped me on my leg and told me: 'You'll always remember this, the first time you heard genius!'

"But I already knew I would never forget it. I was completely intoxicated by the music." Orsina always smiled at this point and took another breath. "And I knew that the man who could create such beauty was the man I wanted to love."

At this point, Elodie's father would laugh and reach toward his wife's hand.

"I'm glad I've always played my violin with my eyes closed . . . Had I seen your mother in the front pew, with her dark hair falling over her shoulders and her eyes as green as tulip leaves, I would have forgotten every single note. I'm thankful I saw her only after I'd finished playing."

Orsina beamed. "I told your grandmother that I wanted to learn to play like that. But she shook her head and told me that such playing could not be taught. That is a kiss on the head from God.

"The line was so long to meet your father after that concert. The cultural director himself had to stand between him and the crowd." Her mother's black hair was now streaked with wisps of gray, but Elodie could always still see the young girl beneath whenever her mother laughed.

"I saw you right away, Orsina," her father said. The years melted away from his wife's face as he saw her once again standing there in front of him for the first time. The pale lemon dress, the jet-black hair, the sparkling eyes. He remembered with great sweetness how her hands trembled as she handed over her program for him to sign.

"He took me from my beautiful lagoon," her mother would now say, so many years later. "But I have no regrets." But sometimes, on very hot nights, Elodie could detect a wistfulness in her mother's voice. There was a parchedness, a thirst within her words. And when the summer bore down its horrendous heat, Elodie could hear her mother's words like an elegy, sad and full of longing.

"It's the dryness of the heat here. I'm not used to it . . ." Every summer brought the same lament. Elodie would watch sympathetically as her mother took a handkerchief to wipe her forehead. "I grew up surrounded by water. Inky blue. Green and black. We marked the seasons by the height of water, the mist, and the fog. As a child, my first memory was the touch of water. My first taste was the salt from the sea."

Elodie knew her mother had tried to fill her life with all things beautiful, and that she saw life through a unique prism. A pair of optimistic eyes. One only had to shift the

angle to reveal another facet, to radiate another beam of light.

She filled their house with flowers. Venetian vases the color of ribbon candy were
abloom with lilacs in the spring and roses
in the summer. She prepared comforting
food from her childhood: baccalá and polenta. Risotto steeped in squid ink and
Burano cookies, which her father had loved
to dip in sweet wine. But music she left to
her husband and daughter. The only time
Elodie ever heard her mother sing was
when she was alone in her bath.

Does everyone have a song? Elodie
wondered if even those not blessed with a
musical gift still had their own melody somewhere locked within. Her mother's voice
emerged only when she was shoulder deep
in water. It struck Elodie like the gentle hum
of honeybees, modest and sweet. It floated
over the steam of the bath. She saw her
mother's hair piled on top of her head.
Her long neck like a swan's, the angles of
her well-chiseled face. She sang songs in
Venetian dialect. Mostly love songs, but
occasionally she would sing one of the
melancholy ballads of the gondoliers.

But it was the latest French songs that

her mother seemed to love the most. Her affection for Paris had been the reason she had chosen a French name for her daughter. "Your name came to me like the notes from a harp," she would tell Elodie. And she would smile at her daughter, knowing that although she had never yet visited that other city of bridges and light, she had created something with its own sparkle and beauty.

Orsina believed that her singing was her own secret. Little did she know that on the nights when she excused herself to bathe, Elodie and her father would lock eyes. If they were practicing their instruments, at the sound of the heated bathwater being poured, they'd place down their bows. Then the two of them would sit back in their chairs and close their eyes. They did not rustle or even make the slightest sound. They just waited, like the audience at the conservatory, for Orsina's voice to come.

It emerged almost like a flute, her sweet voice floating through the door. Gone was any trace of parchedness. Orsina sang in a language her daughter didn't understand. But Elodie intuitively comprehended every melody. Her mother's voice reflected these subtleties in the same way Elodie interpreted her musical scores. Elodie now understood why Orsina had wiped tears from her eyes when she or her father played. She understood what it was like to listen to music created by a person you love.

FOUR

Portofino, Italy
OCTOBER 1943

"My name is Angelo," he tells her, and Elodie is immediately struck by the sweetness of the name.

Her sleep has refreshed her, and when she awakens, he is sitting in the small dining room. There is a long loaf of bread on the table and a small triangle of cheese. A carafe of wine and two glasses of water.

She notices the paintings on the walls. Small, simple scenes of the water. A fisherman and his net, and a white house against a sea of blue. She finds his age is difficult to estimate. His hair is still dark, but there are the first wisps of gray. He is paler

than the men she saw at the port. His eyes
are a soft, dusty blue.

There are books everywhere. On the
shelves against the walls. On the small coffee table, stacked in threes, with shells
placed neatly on top. She sees there is an
open book on the counter, placed front
down, as if he had stopped in midsentence.

The sight of the books conjures up memories of her first encounter with Luca, and
she finds herself wanting to cry, though she
stifles the urge to do so. But it snakes up
her throat and she pushes it down with such
intensity that she feels it twist like a tornado
within her belly.

He lets her eat in peace, and she is thankful that he does not need to fill the air with
words. In the silence, she hears only the
sound of his knife cutting against the plate,
or the snap of the bread as he breaks it in
his hands. The quiet wash of water as he
sips from his glass.

These are sounds that she can tolerate.
Their rhythm soft with a simplicity that
soothes her. She hears her mother singing
Venetian melodies in the distance of her

memory. She closes her eyes and tries to quell herself with another's song.

She wonders if this man sitting across from her realizes that her mind is elsewhere. That as she breaks her bread and chews it into bits and pieces and sips from her water glass, just as he does, her body is her cloak of deception. It occupies the space across from him, it mirrors his in the simple ritual of eating, but her mind is far away.

She travels through time and space. Extracting her spirit from her limbs, in the same way she used to pull music from an instrument that would otherwise have remained silent.

First and always there is the image of Luca standing in his bookstore. His dark hair and canvas smock with two sharp pencils in the front pocket. His fingers smudged with newsprint. The smell of paper. The dizziness from a chamber of so many words.

She tries with all effort to push these thoughts from her mind. Instead, she finds herself reaching for the small dish of salt, but her hands shake as she lifts it toward her. When she looks up, she sees her host has noticed this as well.

She wants to tell him that she is not shaking because she is nervous. She is beyond that. It's because her fatigue is bone deep. She wonders if that is how the elderly feel. So tired from the arc of their life, there is an almost instinctual urge to surrender. To finally give up and find rest.

After dinner, sensing she is still weary from her journey, he asks her if she would like to take a bath. He is quiet and respectful, giving her privacy as he shows her the door to the small room with the deep, wooden tub already half-filled with cool water.

She waits for him to bring her the kettle of hot water. Two more rounds will follow until the bath is sufficiently warmed, but the sight of the rushing water is a relief. She undresses with the door closed, and the simple ritual of removing her shoes and her skirt soothes her. She unbuttons her blouse and removes her slip and underpants. She does not look at herself in the mirror above the sink. She does not glance at the skin, now stretched taut and white. She places one foot in the water, then the other before she sits and pulls her knees to her chest. She closes her eyes and twists back her hair. Then, softly, quietly, thinking no one will hear her, she begins to sing. Not out of joy. But out of longing. Out of a desire for comfort. Just like her mother did, all those years before.

FIVE

Verona, Italy
APRIL 1943

From the age of eighteen, Elodie attended full-time classes at the Liceo Musicale, studying chamber music, music theory and later orchestra training. In the hallway, she would often pass her father, a professor there.

But she began to notice slight changes in him. A look of strain, of increasing agitation, had replaced his former peaceful expression. He had believed the Liceo to be sacred, one of the few places where Fascism couldn't penetrate. The saluting and the marches to show support for Mussolini, indeed all of Italy's politics, had, for the most part, remained outside its walls. But the anti-Jewish laws enacted four years before, forced out every Jewish professor from his position, and Jewish students were no longer able to enroll. Elodie remembered with great clarity the day her father came home enraged and related how Professor Moretti had been told he could not even retrieve some papers in his office.

Her father's reaction came flooding back to her the moment Lena mentioned to her that she'd been privately instructed by Professor Moretti since she was seven years old. Moretti's family had the apartment above Lena's, and the two families had been friends for years. It was Professor Moretti who first noticed Lena's musical potential, studying the young child's hands, the expansion between the fingers, and her unique ability to follow complicated rhythm patterns, and had encouraged her parents to nurture it. Over the years, through private lessons after his regular day of teaching at music school, Moretti had taught Lena everything she knew, from first learning to hold her bow to mastering complex chamber pieces. Even now, her parents paid for her to have private instruction with

him, giving him the chance to bring in a limited income to his struggling family, since
he could no longer work at the school.

One afternoon, after they had finished
classes, Lena looked particularly upset.

"What's the matter?" Elodie pressed.

Lena shook her head. "Things have become worse for the Morettis. They are prac-
tically starving. My mother tries to send
them some soup and what few vegetables
she can spare, but they are embarrassed
by the charity."

She paused and then whispered, "I'm
going to join Luigi tonight for a meeting."

Elodie didn't understand her. "A meeting
for what?"

Lena shook her head. "Of people who
want to stop all of this." She took a deep
breath. "Our country will be unrecognizable
in a few months. Just wait, Elodie; you'll
see."

"You're barely nineteen, Lena." Elodie at-
tempted to be logical. "You can't exactly
fight the Fascist army."

"Well, I'm certainly not going to watch as
my professor is rounded up with his family
and act like I'm blind to it."

"But you're not going to do anything that

could put you in danger, are you?" Elodie winced just imagining what the police might do to Lena if she were arrested.

"Danger?" Lena smiled and her eyes looked like firecrackers. "Well, no one will help me get false papers for the Morettis until I prove myself to them. That's why I've been helping them distribute materials. I hope to become a messenger for the group. That doesn't sound too dangerous, does it?"

Elodie looked at her friend, too shocked to utter a reply.

"How about you join me, then?"

"I wish I could, Lena." Her words sounded so weak, that as soon as she said them, a slight sense of shame came over her.

"It's just . . . my parents have such expectations for my musical career, and I don't have a stomach for danger."

Elodie could sense her friend cringing inside. She knew her answer, her evident lack of courage, was as repellent as the sound of broken strings.

As the weeks went by, Elodie noticed a transformation in her friend. Music was becoming less important to Lena, and Elodie sensed the difference first in her friend's

playing. There was no longer the same connection between her mind, heart, and instrument. Now Lena merely recited the
notes. The spirit she used to give to her viola was instead focused on her activities
for the early Resistance. Every afternoon,
she left Elodie after their studies and went
to the art studio of Berto Zampieri, one of
the group's members.

"I wish you'd come, too. Berto's sculptures are beautiful . . . sensual in a way I've
never seen before. Brigitte Lowenthal is
his girlfriend and muse. God, Elodie, if
you could see her! She has bobbed hair;
her features are so sharp, she looks like
a fox."

"Sounds like the opposite of you,
Lena . . ." Elodie raised an eyebrow. "If she's
the fox of the group, are you their kitten?"

"Hardly!" She laughed and Elodie noticed
how alive Lena seemed since she began
going to the meetings. "Really, they barely
even notice me . . . Brigitte's the one with
the dramatic story. She's the daughter of
one of Verona's wealthiest Jewish families.
They came here from Germany."

Elodie shook her head. "What you're describing to me sounds more like you're at-

tending an art salon, not an anti-Fascist meeting. Soon you'll be talking about music from the Liceo and playing chamber music for them."

"Don't be ridiculous! I'm just giving you a little background on some of the more interesting members. There are others, too, Beppe and many of his friends from the university, and a bookseller by the name of Luca who owns Il Gufo, the shop on the Via Mazzini.

"But we're all committed in our united goal to liberate Italy from the Blackshirts . . ."

Luca, Berto, Beppe . . . all these men's names that Lena was mentioning, they were all new to her.

"Of course, some of them are **communisti** . . . their satchels filled with the books of Marx and Lenin. They're even printing their own newspaper, borrowing one of the presses from one of Brigitte's contacts. But they're looking for other women to help them . . . we can move around more freely. No one thinks we're up to anything more than playing the instruments in our cases or going home to boil water for pasta."

Elodie walked home that afternoon by herself, her heavy cello case strapped to her back. She studied the men around her. The Black-shirts congregating in the corner, the police, and the young men smoking cigarettes in the café. She wondered if it was true that she was invisible to them. Her face was unremarkable, her body so slight that she caused no distraction.

I am invisible, she thinks. And suddenly, in a way that surprised her, she felt exhilarated by this transparency. It made her feel strong.

Elodie couldn't get what Lena told her out of her mind. Part of her was impressed with Lena's courage, while another part was concerned for her friend's safety. It was no secret what the Fascist police would do to her should she get caught. Their beatings and torture were a well-known threat to everyone in the city. Many people had simply vanished after being arrested, while others were sent back to their homes severely beaten, their scars a visible reminder of who was in charge of Italy. It was reason enough to stay away. That, and the fact that Elodie could only imagine how devastated her parents would be if anything happened to her.

For several days, Elodie found herself distracted by the knowledge of Lena's clandestine activities. Over dinner, her father, having sensed the recent lack of focus on her playing, tried to pull Elodie back to her music.

"Elodie, you need to devote even more time to your playing this year. You have to work harder than everyone else, even if it comes easily to you," her father told her. "You don't want people to accuse you of benefiting from the fact I teach at the school."

Elodie nodded her head, aware that she was clearly distracted by her conversation with Lena. "I know."

She tried to appear focused, but her head was spinning and the words of Lena kept resurfacing, like a song she couldn't ignore. She could feel her body moving and her voice responding to her parents, but her mind was truly elsewhere.

"You have a great career ahead of you. It may be a bit unconventional for a woman, your mother and I realize this, but you were born with a gift."

"Several gifts," Orsina added.

"Yes. I wish I had your memory, Elodie," he uttered. Pietro never ceased to be amazed that no matter how complex the score was, his daughter already knew her part by heart.

For several weeks, Elodie tried to refocus her attention on her music, but she continued to find herself distracted. Every Tuesday, Elodie and Lena would exit the school; Lena walked one way, to a meeting for the nascent Resistance, and Elodie would return home to quietly practice her cello and have dinner with her parents. But, still, she felt an increasing restlessness. Now everything that she saw on the streets seemed to be in high relief to her. The **Balilla** banner. The gangs of Blackshirts with their motorcycle brigades, threatening innocent people in the street. Terror was all around, if you opened your eyes and saw things clearly.

Her father, too, seemed to be increasingly angry when he returned home.

But it was the change in Elodie's playing, not her husband's behavior, that alarmed Orsina. There was an agitation to it that she had never heard before. A restlessness.

"Don't you hear it, Pietro?"

"We're all unnerved, Orsina. We're at war.

The Fascists are ruling the country. Mussolini is getting into bed with the Germans. My Jewish colleagues have been arrested; some have been transported to work camps. Why wouldn't there be a restlessness to her playing? Even fear!"

"But does she also seem distant at school?"

He sighed. It was clear he was preoccupied with something else.

"I saw Moretti near Piazza Erbe today. He was gaunt. I hardly recognized him."

Orsina didn't seem to hear him. "Do you think you could watch her after school . . . See if she's meeting anyone? What if she has a boyfriend we don't know about?"

"Did you hear what I just said, Orsina?" His whole face was twisted in disbelief, bordering on anger. "I just told you that a colleague of mine, Professor Moretti, looked like he was on death's door. God knows how his family is faring since he was forced to resign from school! What's the matter with you?"

His face was now rushing with blood. She could see small, blue veins swelling by his temples.

"Orsina, where has Italy's honor gone?

Has everyone lost their sense of decency?"
The striking of his fist against the table
sounded like a gavel.

Orsina fell quiet. The intensity of Pietro's
anger seized her. She had not meant to
sound unsympathetic to Professor Moretti's plight. She **was** sympathetic. More than
her husband could imagine. She, too, felt
betrayed by Fascism, but unlike her husband had learned to keep these thoughts
silent, for fear of someone overhearing her.
She always felt a wave of fear come over
her when Pietro voiced his true feelings.
How many people had been turned in by
their neighbors or friends, just for a better
job or a bigger apartment?

No, she hated the Fascist regime as
much as Pietro. It had been more than
twenty years that Italians had been living
under Fascism, but in the past five, it had
become unbearable. Now, when she sees
photographs of Mussolini in the papers with
his bald head and bulging eyes, ranting in
one of his speeches, it was hard to remember those first years of his leadership, when
everyone was so hopeful he'd return Italy
to its former glory. He spoke of a united
Italy—one of efficiency and strength—

where women were lauded for their contri-
bution to the family and the moral values
of the country. But Mussolini's insatiability
for more power overtook him. There was
his pursuit of Ethiopia, now for Greece. How
many mothers had seen their sons drafted
and killed for his territorial gains?

And if that wasn't enough, his alliance
with Hitler, passing over the Jews he had
previously promised were safe. He betrayed
these men and women and their children,
too. Orsina knew it all, even if Pietro thought
she was ignorant.

In truth, Orsina sympathized deeply. She
knew several Jewish families who were
struggling to make ends meet. She never
told Pietro that she often made extra tortelli
for Anna Bassani's family. Whenever she
arrived with her basket of food, she marveled at how Anna still managed to keep
her household so calm even with everyone
living in such close quarters and under so
much stress.

But at the same time, her daughter's
change in behavior was a new source of
fear and tension for her. And perhaps Pietro
didn't notice this change in Elodie, because his own behavior mirrored their

daughter's. Orsina detected the same agitation in his playing that she had heard in
Elodie's. They shared an impatience with
their bows, as if they couldn't wait for it to
strike hard on the strings.

The following evening, Orsina tried her best
to bring harmony back to her household.
Hoping to erase the memory of the previous night's outburst, Orsina cooked a full
Venetian banquet of Pietro and Elodie's favorite dishes: baccalá with polenta, a risotto
with squid and shrimp, and a cake seeped
in honey. After dinner, their stomachs full
and their appetites sated, Elodie and her
father went to the living room to rehearse.
Midway through, however, they were forced
to stop their playing because the Fascist
youth battalion in the square was so loud,
their cheering and drums rolling overpow-
ered every other sound.

    Pietro walked over to the window, where
below he could see more than twenty
grade-school boys dressed in their **Balilla**
uniforms singing "Giovanezza" and other
Fascist songs.

    "Agh, mini Fascists!" Pietro's voice was
filled with disgust.

Elodie walked over and peered down at the square as well. She could see the boys dressed in their uniforms, nearly identical to the grown-up Fascist police: the eponymous black shirt, the fez with the fasces emblem, the gray-green shorts and the bright blue kerchief, which was knotted around their necks.

They were Mussolini's little army, happy to have a chance to leave their homes for a few hours and make some noise.

"I can't hear a damn thing!"

"I know," Elodie said, placing down her bow. "How can they continue with such stupidity? Crying at the top of their lungs. 'Duce! Duce!' . . ."

Orsina stood in the middle of the living room, her hands fingering to untie her apron strings. "These boys should be in bed sleeping. Where are their mothers?"

"Their mothers?" Pietro laughed.

Orsina shook her head. She was grateful that she had a daughter. Every boy in Italy had to be enlisted in the **Balilla**, then onto the **Gioventú Fascista**. It was a governmental decree.

Elodie and her father tried to resume their playing, but the noise was unbearable. "I can't take it anymore! It's bad enough they've ruined the Liceo Musicale, now they're poisoning these children, too!" Pietro stood up and walked over to the record player. Underneath there was a small stack of records. He reached for one and pulled a black disc from its sleeve.

He placed down the needle and turned the dial to increase the volume.

The chorus "Va, Pensiero" from Verdi's opera **Nabucco** began to play.

"It's too loud," Orsina reprimanded him.

"Which do you prefer?" replied Pietro. "This or the sound of the **Balilla** downstairs?"

"You know the answer to that!" Elodie said confidently.

Pietro smiled. Then he dialed up the music even louder.

The next day, Pietro did not return home at his usual hour, and Orsina continually glanced at the clock near the dining room table.

"Your father is never late," she said to Elodie. "I'm becoming worried."

It was true. Her father was like clockwork. He had his coffee in the morning every day at the same time, left the house one hour later, and returned home each evening by six o'clock.

"I made his favorite risotto, and it will be ruined if he doesn't come home soon." Orsina stood by the pot and added one more cup of stock. She lowered the flame.

"I'm sure he'll be home any minute," Elodie said, trying not to share her mother's alarm. "He probably got stuck talking to someone outside school."

Forty minutes later, Orsina was sure there was something wrong. She had turned the stove off minutes earlier and the risotto was now a sticky mass.

"He shouldn't have played the record player so loudly last night." She sat down at the table and placed her head in her hands. "It was defiant. What if someone reported him?"

"I don't think someone would do that, Mother. It was only some opera music . . ."

Elodie saw her mother's back stiffen. Her face was so visibly strained with worry that she looked like a bridge of an instrument, with strings pulled to the point of breaking.

"Elodie . . ." Orsina said in the faintest

whisper. "People would report their neighbor for a few extra grams of butter."

Elodie looked down. She felt a wave of
shame wash over her. Shame that she had
been so naïve to dismiss her mother's worry
so quickly. Shame that she had not joined
Lena in a group that was trying to eliminate
the fear, which had now penetrated her own
family. And shame that she was now help-
less to find her father.

She found herself walking around the
apartment like a trapped animal that didn't
know how to make use of its nervous energy.

"You need to stop moving around so
much, Elodie." Her mother's voice strained
to emerge politely from a web of fragile
nerves.

Elodie tried to bring a small measure of
comfort to her mother by making some
coffee. She heaped two spoonfuls of the
chicory and added the water. But when
they each sat at the table, their hands
around the small porcelain cups, neither
of them could manage a single sip. They
sat there like two cats staring into the air,
each taking up space in the same room
without uttering a single word.

She and her mother sat at the dining room table for what seemed like hours. They didn't eat. They didn't drink. The only movement between them was when they both turned their heads to watch the clock.

They fell asleep where they sat with their heads on their arms, both waking at dawn with no sign of Pietro.

"I'm calling the police," Orsina said, shaking her head. She looked out the window to the piazza; the first light of the morning flooded through the room and Elodie squinted. "Something terrible has happened! I just know it."

Elodie didn't know how to respond. She was just as weak and as worried as her mother.

Orsina reached for the phone and dialed the exchange for the police. Elodie heard the excruciating sound of her mother's plea for someone to listen to her, desperately begging for more information.

"They told me nothing. They insulted me and told me to check the bars or the whore-houses," she said in tears.

Elodie reached to embrace her mother. "I just know he's going to come through this door any minute, demanding breakfast."

Her mother shook her head. "I pray you're right."

Two days later, after Elodie and her mother were besieged with worry and had received not a shred of information from the police, there was a faint rapping at the door.

When Orsina went to answer it, she discovered a very badly beaten Pietro, with one arm draped over the back of their neighbor, Giacomo.

It was clear by the way his right leg dangled that it was broken.

"Oh my God," Orsina gasped, covering her mouth with one hand. "Pietro!"

Giacomo helped bring him into the living room.

"I found him outside your apartment just a few minutes ago. They must have dumped him there and sped off."

"Who?" Orsina said in disbelief. She couldn't believe anyone could do something so savage to her gentle husband.

Pietro looked up at her with his swollen eye and bloody lip.

"Four Blackshirts in the **Squadrisiti** confronted me outside the music school as I was on my way home. They told me I was under investigation and took me to a place near the Roman theater. I think it was somewhere on Via Redentore where they interrogated me.

"They bound my wrists and covered my eyes. They called me a Communist. They said I had no loyalty to my country . . . that I've never worn a Fascist party pin on my lapel."

"This is sheer craziness!" Orsina cried. She looked to Giacomo and Elodie to agree with her, but both of them were transfixed on listening only to Pietro recount his story.

"I told them my only sin was that I played a record. I tried to tell them it was by Verdi . . . one of Italy's greatest composers." His tone, even through his wounds, was unmistakably sarcastic.

"I insisted I was not anti-Fascist. That I was only a musician, just trying to listen to my record.

"But whatever I said, they ignored my reasoning. They just kept beating me, and kept smashing me in the ear every time I mentioned music . . ."

"They are nothing but bloody savages!" Orsina cried.

"Orsina, please . . ." Giacomo whispered.

"We don't need them knocking on your door
again. Or heaven forbid, mine . . ."

Orsina tried to regain her composure.
"No, of course not."

"You should call a doctor for him," Giacomo suggested. "Do you have one you
can trust?"

"Yes, yes. Of course. We've used Doctor Tommasi for years."

"Good," he said. "Call him and take good
care of Pietro. Maria and I look forward to
hearing him play his violin again soon . . ."

"Giacomo, we are indebted for you bringing him home to us. What can we do to
thank you?"

"Nothing, Orsina. Just keep him safe and
keep him away from the record player." He
kissed her on both cheeks, then squeezed
her hands in his.

"I must get back to my family now." He
shook his head and lowered his voice. "This
is not the country of my childhood . . . to
beat an innocent man like this makes me
sick to my stomach. I fear for myself and
my children now."

Orsina nodded as she thanked him and
said good-bye. Once Giacomo left, she took
a deep breath and quickly locked the door.

SIX

~

Verona, Italy
MAY 1943

Since his return, Pietro remained bedbound. His foot was encased in a plaster cast and propped up on pillows by a diligent Orsina. He spent the majority of the day sleeping.

"He seems to sleep more than ever, Mamma . . . Shouldn't we be concerned he's not trying to walk around more? Doctor Tommasi even left crutches for him, but he never attempts to use them!"

Orsina shook her head. "Who wouldn't be tired after receiving such a beating? If a body is tired, it should rest."

Elodie was not convinced. "I know if I go two days without playing, my hands feel stiff. I think he needs to get up and move around."

"Let's give him a few more days, Elodie. It's only this week that those terrible bruises on his face have started to fade. Once he gets more strength back, we can get him on his feet."

Elodie nodded. "Maybe tonight, we can see if he can play his violin a bit. He doesn't need to stand to play. We can adjust his pillows and then do a small concert for you." She smiled and went to hug her mother. "It will be good for his spirits to get him playing again."

Elodie looked sideways to see her father sleeping in his bed. It was true that his bruises had begun to fade, but the brutality of Fascism was now more evident than ever, leaving permanent marks on her family's once-idyllic household.

Although she tried to remain as calm and helpful as possible to her mother, since her father's return, Elodie knew that she had been forever changed by this event. The sight of her gentle father being carried home by a neighbor, his body beaten beyond recognition and his leg dangling like a broken marionette—this was not something she could ever erase from her mind.

So when she saw Lena outside Guido's Café, Elodie seemed to have lost the meekness she exhibited the first time Lena had invited her to a meeting.

"When is your next meeting?" Elodie asked, unblinking.

"You're ready to join us now?" Lena questioned in turn. She was now staring at Elodie intensely, trying to gauge her sudden change in spirit.

"Yes," she said. "I've never been more ready. Just tell me when and where."

The next morning after she finished her coffee, Elodie did what she thought was impossible: She looked into her parents' eyes and told them her first lie.

"I will be late today, so don't wait for me. I don't want you to worry," she said, hoping that her parents would not ask for further details.

Orsina was still in her nightgown. A long black braid, with wisps of gray, fell over one shoulder. Even after a full night's sleep, she still looked tired.

"Of course I will worry, when you see what sort of animals are on the streets these days. What is going to keep you?"

Elodie took a deep breath.

"I need to practice a concerto with Lena. She's having trouble with her timing, and Professor Olivetti will have our heads if we don't get everything just right for the spring performance."

It was a complete fabrication on Elodie's part, but still something that seemed plausible enough. She looked at her mother to see if she had detected her transgression but Orsina seemed to have found the explanation credible.

Orsina sighed. "Don't stay out too late. And please, please be careful."

Elodie nodded and shifted her gaze. It had been easier to lie than she imagined. Perhaps too easy.

"Yes, Mamma. Of course."

Orsina glanced over at her husband, hoping he would express his own similar thoughts on their daughter's safety. But his injuries were so severe, he clearly hadn't even heard her and Elodie speaking. There had been a time, she thought, that he heard every breath, every whisper. But now he hardly seemed to hear anything at all.

That afternoon, Elodie and Lena leave their instruments at the school. They are dressed nearly identically: navy skirts and white blouses. Shoes with T-straps. Hair pinned behind their ears.

Lena tells her the meeting will occur in a small bookshop on Via Mazzini. It's a store that Elodie never even knew existed. The exterior is nothing but a small window front lined with books. Above the door hangs a black sign with the word **Libri** in gold letters.

Elodie wishes she had the security of her cello to comfort her. She is so used to her heavy armor that she hardly knows what her body feels like without it, almost as if she is missing a limb. She feels strangely weightless and her other senses are heightened. She hears everything around her: the sound of footsteps on the pavement, the sound of the birds in the air, the rustle of the leaves.

"Come inside," Lena whispers to her and points to the door. The small shop is lined from floor to ceiling with books. Bricks of color, Elodie thinks, as she looks at the walls. The spines protrude in an array of different shades. The leather volumes in red and brown, a few in forest green. The gilt letters of their titles glimmer like distant stars. A young man of around twenty stands behind a counter. He is tall, almost gangly, with a thick mane of black hair. His irises are deep amber. She has never seen an eye color like that before. Elodie immediately thinks of the gypsies who thread amber into necklaces, the prized pieces like fossils with bits of life trapped within. His face is beautiful and well chiseled, and Elodie reads it quickly like a sheet of music, taking in the angles and curves, memorizing the heights and plateaus.

The bookseller's hands rest on his desk. His long fingers are smudged with ink.

"Luca, I've brought a friend," Lena announces with confidence. Luca stares at both girls, but longer at Elodie. He says nothing at first, sizing her up with his eyes. Finally he wipes his hands on his smock and gestures for them to follow.

He takes them to the back room, and Elodie is first struck by the smell of fresh ink and damp paper. There are hundreds of pamphlets in tall piles. Someone is filling small satchels with them. The room is crowded, with at least thirty young men who all seem to know one another. They eye Elodie with suspicion as soon as she enters.

"She's my friend," Lena indicates right away. "She's a cellist, with a memory like you've never seen." She looks everyone straight in the eyes. There is a low grumbling in the room. Elodie hears it and begins to shiver. "You can trust her," Lena says without flinching. "You have my word."

Three women are in the room; one is unmistakably Brigitte Lowenthal. The sharp features, the expensive blouse. She scans Elodie quickly when she walks into the room and then turns her head to focus on something more interesting that concerns her. Elodie notices how she places an elegant hand on Berto's thigh. He has an artist's face, a sculptor's hands. In a flash, she can imagine with ease Brigitte naked on a daybed, Berto re-creating her flesh in smooth contours of clay.

Another woman is in the corner. Elodie hears the name Jurika mentioned. She is dressed in trousers and a button-down shirt. She looks at the two girls with even more suspicion than do the men. It is clear

from Lena's body language that she has
never seen this woman before, either.

"You should go over to the Catholic co-
alition, if you're interested in helping," she
tells them. "I don't think this group is for you."

Lena stares back at her. "I have already
begun fulfilling my duty here. Most of these
men are happy I can deliver anything they
give me."

"Lena's a good **staffetta**, Jurika," a tall
student in dark colors says in Lena's defense.

"And I've never seen you at a single meeting before," Lena challenges.

"I've been in the mountains in France
scouting, you little mouse." She stands up
and seems to draw the breath from the
room. "I don't suppose they teach you how
to hold a gun in music school?"

Elodie can feel herself shaking, but Lena
remains undeterred. On the other side of
the room, Brigitte turns a long, white neck
in their direction. She pulls out a cigarette,
which Berto quickly lights. Elodie sees how
her eyes turn from boredom to amusement
within seconds.

"No," Lena says as a smile spreads over

her face. "But since you seem to be the expert, why don't you come teach it there?"

The tension in the room instantly dissolves and everyone, including Jurika, begins to laugh.

"I like you," Jurika says, as she stands up. When she rises, she is like a torch; her powerful energy fills the room. The girls bask for a moment, pleased they've amused this female leader.

The girls are given satchels filled with the Communist papers for distribution. Luca walks them to the door.

"We'll see you two next Thursday at the same time. Now, get home to your parents."

"We're not little schoolgirls," Lena snaps. "We're old enough to be married!"

"And how old is that?"

"Nineteen," Elodie replies for her friend.

"Nearly twenty," Lena shoots back.

"Well," he says, smiling at both of them. "You now have two jobs then: Give out those papers and then go find a husband."

He walks over to a huge stack of flyers and lifts them, his arms stiffening from the weight. There is a flicker, like a branch of blue lightning, that runs through the veins of his neck.

Elodie and Lena open their arms and receive their parcels.

"Tell me," he says, "which would be a heavier responsibility? This or a husband?"

Lena is the first to respond.

"A husband, of course!" She let out an enormous laugh. "At least we can give these flyers away and then be done with them!"

The three of them continued to laugh until Elodie looks up and sees Jurika walking toward them. She says nothing to Luca, nor to Elodie or Lena.

With a quick, deft movement, she reaches into her pocket and withdraws a cap, which she immediately pulls over her eyes. Without a trace of femininity in her look or in her gait, she turns from them and walks out the door.

The next week, after having successfully distributed their pamphlets, the girls return to Luca's store.

When they enter, a little chime sounds from above the door. Luca is on his knees, uncrating a box of books. He looks up; his eyes pass over Lena then focus on Elodie.

"The two musicians," he says.

"The bookseller," Elodie answers.

Lena shoots her a glance, showing her surprise at Elodie's answer.

Luca stands up from his crate. He is taller than she remembered. He wears the same brown apron he was wearing the first time they met. There is a small notebook in the center pocket, a pencil behind his ear.

"I'm sorry. We weren't properly introduced the last time." He extends his hand to her. "Luca Bianchi."

"Elodie Bertolotti," she answers. She feels a tingle in her fingers as he grips her hand in his.

"Elodie?" A quizzical expression washes over him. "I have never heard that name before."

"Yes, it's French. My mother chose it."

"Is your mother French?" He smiles again. "We could use a French speaker. We're trying to learn as much as we can from the French Resistance."

Elodie laughs. "No, my mother's Venetian, and if you met her, you wouldn't think her a prime candidate for the Resistance."

"You might be surprised," he tells her. He raises an eyebrow and his voice betrays a

hint of flirtation. "We even have some gondoliers . . ."

Elodie nods, impressed. "I had no idea."

"Well, regardless, your name is beautiful. It suits you."

"Thank you," she says, blushing from his
attention.

Out of the corner of her eye, Elodie could
see Lena's eyes rolling.

"Well, this is all very interesting . . ." Lena
interrupts, "but we have a lot to report. Are
the others here yet?"

"A few are in the back, but we're still waiting for most of them."

He smiles at Elodie and she finds herself hesitating as Lena begins to walk into
the back room.

"Will you tell me what instrument you
play?"

She smiles, touched at his curiosity about
her. "The cello."

"Again, you surprise me." He lets out a
small laugh. "Such a big and serious instrument."

She feels the touch of his hand, a feather-
light sensation at the small of her back,
gently ushering her into the back room.

The men seem satisfied by Lena's reporting of their pamphlet distribution.

"We need to be saturating the university," someone suggests. "At least there, some are not afraid to fight the Fascists."

A few people agree, but others argue among themselves about where they can find more support.

Finally Luca stands up and says he has an announcement.

"Our head leadership has told us repeatedly it's essential we find new and innovative ways to deliver our messages. We have been clever in finding techniques to do that in the past. But the distances we now need to travel are getting longer. A simple bicycle run, with a piece of paper inside a handlebar, is fine for a short distance. But there needs to be something we can use that that can be transported longer distances, between cities . . ."

There is grumbling in the room.

"No need to discuss this between yourselves. You see, I have come up with an idea."

There are three books stacked in front of him. He takes the first one from the pile and lifts it in his hands.

"We all know what this is." Luca places his hand reverently on the cover. "For centuries, writers have used books as a way to transport their ideas and thoughts." He opens the book to its midsection. "But, actually . . . and I know this will surprise many of you, I think there are many other ways to use them for our cause, beyond just the stirring words that have been printed."

"In this book, I've taken a knife and cut out twenty pages from the middle. I then cut new pages, exactly the same size, that contain mock messages, and glued them inside so they merge seamlessly with the original pages."

He closes the book. "I'm now going to pass it around, and I want you to give me an honest answer if you would have noticed, upon first inspection, the new pages."

Silence sweeps through the room. Each person who touches the book and leafs through its pages is hard-pressed to identify the new ones that Luca has inserted.

"It's also possible to use a book as a way to carry a secret code.

In this book, you'll notice I have added some letters at the base of every tenth page. One could use letters, numbers . . . or even a combination of both, using this seemingly innocent object as a vessel of sending additional information."

Luca opens up the book and shows everyone how he had threaded the words **Il Gufo** through the book by placing one letter every ten pages. "This is a one-to-ten ratio, but it can be adjusted to one letter on every fiftieth page, or even every seventy-fifth."

Elodie can feel her entire body shoot with electricity as he speaks. When the first book Luca sends around the room reaches her, she places her hand on the cover just as he had, as if that gesture could somehow connect them.

The others react just as enthusiastically. "That's brilliant, Luca," someone shouts. Another person applauds his creativity in finding a solution. Elodie strains her ears to see if anyone isn't impressed. But everyone seems bolstered by Luca's ingenuity.

"I've saved the best for last," he finally says to calm the room. A single book now rests on the table before him, as the first two continue to circulate through the crowd.

He picks up a larger book, this one clearly heavier and more substantial. "I took this one from of a series of volumes I have stacked on those shelves back there . . ." He points to a tall wooden bookcase replete with several rows of large books.

He pauses for a moment before parting the center pages with his thumbs. The book opens like a large butterfly. On one side of the book, within the thickness of at least two hundred pages, is an expertly carved niche. And inside is a pistol.

"Clearly, this wouldn't be used for travel. The controls are too tight, but I think it's a good way for us to think about storing what guns we have. I can place several of these books side by side on a shelf in this very storeroom."

The room is now buzzing with excitement. Beppe comes over and pulls the gun from the cut-out pages.

Elodie cannot believe her eyes. She looks at Lena, who sits in her chair, too completely transfixed at what Luca has just shown her.

She turns to Elodie and whispers in her ear, "Well, he's certainly more than your average bookseller."

Elodie is speechless. But inside she is thinking the exact same thing.

SEVEN

~~~

Verona, Italy
MAY 1943

After the meeting in Luca's store, Elodie looked at books in a completely different way. Sometimes she would go to her father's bookshelves and pull out a book on nautical history or one on ancient Rome, and wonder if this couldn't be a perfect vessel for a message or a gun.

Luca's weapon had terrified her. She had never seen a pistol up close before. The most dangerous things in her parents' house were the kitchen knives. Even those she shied away from, preferring to set the table or stir the polenta.

Her life had been extremely sheltered.

She knew it was typical for Italian families
to protect their young, especially their
daughters. But she had grown up even
more isolated because of her musical gifts.
Her parents didn't want her to have any distraction.

But now a strange energy flowed through
her. Was it a motivation for revenge for her
father, combined with the passion for this
new group of people who were so dedicated to winning the country back from the
Fascists? Or was it simpler and far less no-
ble on her part? Had it begun the first time
Luca had looked at her? When he told her
that her name was beautiful? When he had
studied her face and told her that she was
full of surprises?

She could envision Luca with great precision. She thought of his full bloom of dark
hair, the chiseled features, and the amber
eyes. She had noticed the tendons in his
neck. Little ribbons of muscle, the blue
veins, just under the skin—reminiscent of
strings in the neck of her cello. What might
it feel like to slide a single finger on one and
feel the energy between their skin?

She heard the pattern of his voice, like
notes inside her head. The gentle rhythm

of his words; the escalation of his intonation as he revealed his idea of using the
books as part of their tactics.

She had been moved by the way he handled the novels. The respect for these objects that were so clearly precious to him.
It gave her comfort to know he appreciated
books as much as she loved her cello.

She fell asleep hearing a melody that
was new to her. She heard it in a palette of
colors. Rich like the varnish on her instrument. Deep red with long streaks of gold.

EIGHT

~

Verona, Italy
MAY 1943

There was a stirring in her body like she used to feel when she was first desperate to play her cello. When the music was so strong inside her, it was almost an ache, a hunger. Elodie told Lena that she was excited to attend another meeting, but what she didn't say was that she also wanted to go again because she couldn't stop thinking of Luca.

She rose early that morning and withdrew her cello from its case. When she played it, the notes now emerged with a sound that was foreign to her. She had learned from her father how the cello could sigh, weep, and make an audience cry. But this time, Elodie played with an intense longing. She could hear the instrument swelling and expanding as she pulled the notes longer and deeper. For the first time, desire infused her playing, a longing for something that was more than music. And as the music flowed through the apartment, Orsina awakened also hearing the difference in her daughter's music. It reminded her of the way Pietro performed that evening so many years ago when she first heard him play in Venice's I Gesuiti. When he played with a beauty that pierced her heart.

That morning, Elodie asked her mother if she could wear one of her dresses. The ones in Elodie's own closet suddenly felt childish, and she didn't want Luca to see her wearing her schoolgirl uniform of a white blouse and navy skirt. She wanted to walk into the bookstore in a dress like the one her mother had worn years ago, when Orsina first met Pietro. Pale yellow, the color of sunshine. Spring's first forsythia, golden and full of light.

Orsina welcomed Elodie's sudden interest in her wardrobe. She now connected what had caused Elodie's playing to change and was relieved to know it wasn't anything dangerous.

She opened her closet, her fingers drifting to touch each dress. Some of them contained memories that were secret to her and Pietro. A stolen kiss beneath St. Mark's Church, or the dress she wore the night he proposed. She could tell a hundred stories just by gazing into her wardrobe; her mind traveling back to the first time her skin slipped against the fabric. Beneath the fluttering hems was her red suitcase, the one she packed with so many of the same dresses when she left her home in Venice to go to Verona all those years ago.

This moment now with Elodie was a rite of passage, which she savored. It brought her back to her own youth, when she had stood at a threshold that soon brought her into a world of marriage and children.

She had thought that Elodie would enter this world a few years later than her peers. That her cello would distract her from more simple matters of the heart.

She watched as her daughter caressed the fabrics with her hand. The lemon chiffon, the red one with the grosgrain sash, and the one with spring flowers, which was Orsina's favorite.

"May I wear the yellow one?" Elodie asked. The first threads of maturity were woven into her request. A desire to push the boundaries and be a little less cautious, a bit more bold.

"Yes, of course," Orsina said, as she slid the dress off the hanger and handed it to Elodie. She smiled at the choice, knowing full well how a beautiful dress had the power to transform the wearer.

That afternoon at school, nearly every male student seemed to turn his head as Elodie walked through the halls. Boys who had never noticed her now craned their necks to get more than just a passing view.

"What's gotten into you today?" Lena asked her. "You look beautiful, but this isn't your typical outfit, that's for certain."

Elodie stopped in front of one of the tall windows in the hall. The sun behind her illuminated not just the beauty and angles of her face, but her entire being. She looked celestial.

"I just felt like a change today. I was tired of always wearing navy and white."

Lena nodded. She herself was wearing a very unremarkable gray shirtdress.

"You know, you can't attend a meeting wearing a yellow chiffon dress. The whole point is to not attract any notice."

Elodie's entire face fell. "Of course," and her voice began to shake as she tried to hide her own sense of failure.

"Well, yellow does become you," Lena said as she patted her friend's shoulder. "So next week, just stick to navy or gray."

That afternoon Elodie did not accompany Lena to Luca's bookstore. She knew her friend was right. Already, as she paced through the square, she felt eyes upon her as she never had before.

In the glass of the storefronts, Elodie saw her reflection. Her dark hair falling over her shoulders. The dress's long bow, loosely tied at the neckline, the path of white buttons from the top to the hem. There was a lightness to the material that she loved but that also made her feel vulnerable, and she wondered which was more dangerous—the transparency of a fabric or of a soul?

Elodie was certain Lena knew why she had chosen to dress that way. After all, as a fellow musician, Lena would have sensed the escalating tension between her and Luca.

She knew Lena was right, that she couldn't appear in the bookshop dressed like she was about to go to a tea party. She would stand out, draw attention to herself, and not in the way she hoped, but rather as someone who simply didn't belong. But still, Elodie couldn't quite convince herself to walk straight home. Instead, she found herself walking in the direction of Luca's store.

Her arm ached from carrying her instrument. For the first time, she considered her cello more of a burden than a beloved companion, and wondered if she was making a huge mistake.

Several times she stopped to catch her breath. Her dress became damp from perspiration. With both hands, she lifted the heavy curtain of hair from her shoulders and knotted it above her head.

When she arrived at the store, she stood outside the window and stared at the display of carefully arranged books.

She noticed her reflection cast in the glass. It was as if she saw herself as an apparition that could vanish at any second, no one ever noticing she had been there, floating against the display of the more permanent books.

She wondered what was happening inside the store, and whether Luca would ask Lena why Elodie wasn't there. She imagined Lena looking at him coyly and saying some witty remark about Elodie being over-dressed. She tried to push the scene out of her head, embarrassed by her folly. She could always return next week, she convinced herself. She would put the dress back into her mother's closet and return to her normal uniform. There would be no more walks through town in pale yellow chiffon. "That's the color of my parents' love story," she told herself. "Perhaps gray and blue will be mine." Elodie picked up her instrument and turned in the direction of home.

NINE

❦

Portofino, Italy
OCTOBER 1943

In his house, Angelo now has yet another stranger. He picks up one of his books while Elodie's in the bath and begins to read, hoping to find a comfort there. Looking at the novel, he knows that when he learns her story, it will be more complex, more heartbreaking than what is on the pages between his hands.

While she bathes, he takes the opportunity to examine the old wound to his foot. He leans over and unlaces his black shoes, rolls down his left sock, and sees the four toes and the small nub where the other one was blown off. An injury not from this war

but from the one in Africa—Mussolini's
quest for Ethiopia, which took place eight
years earlier. He knows what it's like to carry
hidden wounds. His is a wretched, blue
stump covered by a cotton sock. At night it
throbs. He feels the nerves of the toe that
is no longer there. Like the heart, it continues to beat despite all the sadness and loss
it endures.

After she has bathed and changed into
clothes, Elodie returns to the room.

She sits down. Her hair is damp and she
has now pinned it upward. She is all bones
and angles, while his wife had been an
abundance of curves.

"You like to read," she says. It's not said
as a question, but as an observation.

"Yes, very much," he answers.

"Will you read to me?" she asks softly.

The question startles him at first. It's not
something he had expected her to ask, but
it pleases him.

He picks up the book he had just placed
down and opens it. He begins to read.

The words are as much a comfort to him
as to her. They fill the space with sound.
These two people who know nothing about

each other are now entwined in a story that has nothing to do with either of them.

His voice, his inflection, even his pauses, all become a musical score.

He reads for nearly an hour, and Elodie inhales his words like air. She gets lost in Angelo's voice, the rhythm of his speech. She does not notice that his eyes are now weary, and that he rubs them in between turning the pages. It is only when she **hears** the fatigue slipping into his voice that she looks up and realizes how tired he has grown.

"You should stop now," she says, and as she speaks, he is struck by the first note of kindness in her voice. "It must be exhausting to read aloud for so long."

"I don't mind," he tells her. "It is nice to have an audience again."

She smiles, and a memory flashes through her mind of all the audiences she once played for. She sees the men and women in the crowd, their programs on their laps, their eyes focused on the stage. She remembers the sound of their clapping, like a distant thunder. Something from a lifetime ago.

She wishes she could tell him how much
his words calm her. That they are like a ver-
bal embrace. But she remains silent, thinking back to the last time she was read to
when she was in Verona. When books were
so much in abundance, Luca could spare
an entire crate just for the Resistance's
cause.

The light is changing in the room where
they now sit. Shadows are flickering on the
white walls. The window that faces the sea
shows the horizon. An ink-colored brush-
stroke, just hovering over the water.

She believed she would be safe in Liguria, near the Gulf of Poets, where, for years,
artists and writers had escaped from the
rest of the world, and in winter it was just
the villagers and the sea. But Elodie has no
sense of where she is.

"You have been extremely kind," she
says as she places her hands in her lap. "I
will not stay too long and be a burden to
you. I will try to get to one of the islands as
soon as I can."

Elba; Corsica; the islands farther west.
The three boys who preceded her all said
the same thing. The farther they go, the

safer they think they will be. They think they
can lose themselves in the sand, the blis-
ter of the sun. Angelo had helped every one
of them, asking for nothing in return. There
would always be another one, when the
house was too empty and the silence became too loud.

Elodie turns the key again and locks the
door of her new bedroom. The noise is
heavy and clunking, the sound of brass
against wood. She realizes Angelo will interpret this sound as fear on her part. But
that is not the reason she turns the key. She
does it not because she fears him, but because she doesn't want him to know what
she is carrying.

She knows he would not understand
the loose pages of musical score. He
would not have the ear or the breadth of
musical knowledge to understand these
notes on the page. Even if he could read
music, he would not be able read these
particular sheaves of paper like she can.
To her, the hurried way the notes are written, the shakiness in parts of the handwriting tell another story. She can detect

the fear in the melodies. But the amulet and the book are objects that connect her to Luca.

These are things she carries. The story of how they each came into her hand is still locked deep within the channels of her mind.

TEN

~

Verona, Italy
JUNE 1943

This much is certain: After Lena chastised her for wearing the yellow dress, Elodie wouldn't be asking to borrow her mother's clothes again. She returned home and immediately peeled off the dress.

"I miss hearing you play," her mother said gently. "Your father has been in agony all day. Won't you help clear my head with something beautiful?"

At first, Elodie wanted to resist her mother's maneuverings. She didn't need another person directing her actions, but her frustration caused her entire body to stiffen. She knew the music would be the only thing that could pacify her.

Elodie unsnapped the case, withdrew her cello, and settled into a chair. For a second, there was a silent exchange between the girl and her instrument, the privacy upheld through a curtain of her black hair. Orsina held her breath until her daughter finally lifted her bow.

She started with the main theme from the second movement to Dvořák's American String Quartet, and did not look up once to meet her mother's approving gaze. She played with her head to the side and her eyelids closed.

Orsina felt a sensation wash over her, as if she was moved by the current or pulled by an invisible tide. Within the poignancy of the notes, she sensed a plea for peace by the composer. She wondered if more people were exposed to beauty like this, would the fighting lessen? Would wars subside?

If only things were that simple.

She had been distracted all afternoon by the newspapers. The Allies had just bombed Sicily. She felt it in her bones: more bloodshed was to come.

She wondered if she could convince her husband to move someplace safer, perhaps to pack up the household and move back to Venice. She could not imagine the Blackshirts who had brutalized him finding their way among the canals and cloak of fog.

The time to travel from Verona to Venice was not terribly long, less than three hours by train. But since her parents' death, Orsina had difficulty returning to a place with so many memories. But the city still pulled her, especially during moments when she felt lost.

She had buried both her parents during the flu epidemic of 1918, just two years after she had married Pietro, and when she was five months pregnant. She had returned to her native city only to bury them, her heart heavy that she was forbidden to care for them while they were still alive because of the risk to her and the baby.

Pietro had traveled with her for the funeral, although he wished she had adhered to the Italian tradition of pregnant women being forbidden to attend funerals. But since her brother had died in infancy, Orsina was an only child and felt the full weight of her responsibilities.

The stench was horrific. Every day, boats traveled from the hospital to the cemetery to deliver the dead.

The island of San Michele, the city's ancient burial ground, was directly across from the hospital. Orsina had received letters from her father before he fell ill, detailing how the gondoliers had wrapped their faces with muslin as they were forced to ferry the dead.

The sensation of feeling like she was floating, which she felt most of her life there, had completely vanished. Now when they arrived at her childhood city, it felt like they were all suffocating. Orsina felt like she was sinking, being pushed into a cloud of blackness.

"We shouldn't have come," Pietro whispered to Orsina on the boat. He pulled a shawl over his wife's shoulders and wrapped an arm around her, drawing her closer as if to shield her from the invisible, infectious disease.

"How can a daughter not bury her own parents?" she protested. Pietro shook his head. He could feel his wife trembling. Her body was rail thin except for the soft swelling of her stomach. On top of the morning sickness, the stress of being unable to see her parents, to care for them as they were dying, had taken its toll.

"I won't abandon them to be buried by strangers in some mass grave."

He had weakly tried to put his foot down and forbid her from coming. But the sight of her crying and pleading with him had made it impossible for him to insist. Still, he knew that the frail and the weak were even more susceptible to infection.

"We must leave the same day as the funeral" was his only demand. "I don't care if we have to take a night train home, I will not have you sleeping there."

She nodded, her throat too tight from choking back the tears to talk.

That afternoon, they stood by the graves. The rest of the cemetery was filled with families all silently connected in a weary haze of funeral rites.

The priest in his dark robe raised the crucifix over both graves and recited the Prayer for the Dead. Two boys hovered to the side with oversized shovels in their hands, like staffs that seemed incongruous to their childish frames.

Orsina nearly fainted as the first shovel of earth fell upon her parents' black coffins.

On the way home, she did not stop crying.

They returned to Verona exhausted and Orsina took immediately to her bed.

For three days she slept, only waking occasionally to drink water and eat a few bits of boiled rice.

Then the fever began.

"It will be a miracle if she survives." The doctor stood outside their bedroom, looking grave.

Pietro, already pale and exhausted with worry, became chalk white. "She will make it. The baby, too."

"The baby?" The doctor shook his head. "Just try and care for your wife. Wash your hands. Keep your face covered. Get her to drink as much as you can." He snapped his leather bag shut. "The rest is in God's hands."

For days Orsina was on fire, her black hair wet with perspiration.

Pietro lifted his wife's head every two

hours, imploring her to take even a few sips of water. Twice a day he took a moistened sugar cube and placed it between her lips.

He had never been one to seek the mercy of God, but now he hung a crucifix over their bed and lit candles at church. He begged for his wife and child to be spared.

Five days later, Orsina's fever broke. She shot straight up in bed with her eyes suddenly alight with a completely different pain.

Pietro rushed into the room at the first sound of her cries. The linen in their bed was covered with blood.

He pulled the sheets away from her and saw her nightgown soaked in red.

She was hysterical, her hands pushing into her stomach. Her pain was excruciating.

"I'm going to get the doctor," Pietro told her as he lifted her in his arms and brought her into the bathroom. She did not answer. She did not need him to tell her what she already knew: The river of blood that flowed out of her no longer contained any life.

Orsina survived, but they had lost the baby. The tragedy hit them both so hard they could hardly speak.

Grief washed over Orsina like a dam breaking. There had been too much death to comprehend. World War I had just come to an end, and suddenly she found herself orphaned and having lost her first child, too. She hadn't even properly grieved for her parents, and now she struggled to come to terms with her miscarriage.

"We will try again," Pietro said, trying to soothe her. "When you feel ready."

She could not utter a single word, only the faintest sound. A whimper.

He looked at his violin case in the corner. The piano with its cover closed over the keyboard, the viola that rested in the corner near the window.

He had absolutely no desire to play.

That spring, he returned to Venice with Orsina to pack up her parents' belongings and place flowers on their graves.

The hat shop had been shuttered closed. Several months were owed on the rent, but the landlord had also died in the epidemic, and his wife, a longtime admirer of Orsina's mother's hats, had shown them some mercy. They had to clear out the shop by May.

A girl by the name of Valentina had assisted her mother in the shop for years. She had been caring for her own mother when Orsina's parents had fallen ill, so they hadn't seen each other for close to a year. But now that the sickness had left the city, Valentina had returned to help Orsina pack up the shop and sell off the remaining inventory.

The women spoke little at first between themselves, though Orsina did try and express her gratitude for the help. But slowly, as the days progressed, they became closer.

"What will you do now?" Orsina had asked.

"I hope to open my own shop."

The girl took one of Orsina's mother's hats and lifted it to the light.

"I will never have your mother's vision. But she taught me how to sew. To use judgment and proportion with the materials." She stroked a feather on one of the hats with her finger.

"I never saw an egret or ostrich feather in my life before I came to work here."

Orsina smiled.

"My mother loved to give a little flight to all her clients."

"Yes, she did." Valentina smiled.

"I wish I could give you everything. But take this and consider it my mother's blessing."

Orsina lifted a large box filled with spools of velvet and trimmings and brimming with silk flowers and feathers.

Valentina turned scarlet, embarrassed by the gesture.

"I can't take the feathers. They're too expensive."

"Yes, you can," Orsina insisted. "Use them like my mother would have. That will make me happy."

Pietro and Orsina left Venice the following week. They used the proceeds from the inventory to pay off her parents' debt. And before leaving, they visited her favorite church, Santa Maria dei Miracoli in Cannareggio, to pray for another child.

"I've managed to arrange a fellow musician to take over their lease," Pietro said. "Valentina will pack up the rest of your parents' belongings and store them until you're ready to go through them."

But by the next year, Orsina was pregnant again and neither of them, after the last two journeys, had any immediate desire to return.

ELEVEN

~~

Portofino, Italy
APRIL 1934

Although Angelo had been trained as a doctor he had loved hearing stories since he was a small child, and he knew every person in the world had something locked in his heart to tell.

His own story had begun against Italy's rocky coastline, and two women were sewn into the fabric of his soul. His mother was the first. The second was his first wife, Dalia.

He had met Dalia in San Fruttuoso during his final year in medical school. He had been on his way home to surprise his mother with a visit, when the boat he took

made an unexpected stop at the small
coastal village next to his hometown of Portofino. He walked across the beach, a carpet of smooth, flat rocks, and found a café
by the name of Fiorello Dolce only steps
away from the dock. There, Angelo had
stopped for a coffee and one of his favorite sweets, a **sfogliatella**, the triangle pastry with ricotta and orange zest tucked
inside. The heat, even for the port towns,
had been particularly strong that day. Hoping to get a bit of shade, Angelo had moved
his chair into the smallest square of shadow.
As he repositioned himself, he caught sight
of a figure dressed completely in white. A
girl of eighteen emerging from the entrance
of one of the stone archways, carrying a
basket of fresh lemons, many of them with
the stems still attached. She had pinned a
white gardenia blossom in her long, black
hair. Angelo was unable to take his eyes off
her from the moment he first saw her.

"Fresh lemons! Fresh lemons!" she
sang, as her feet treaded over the rocky
beach toward the café. Angelo's heart began to race. "Handpicked from my father's
grove!"

Angelo felt a sudden energy wash over

him. He took one last sip of his coffee, and his hand shot into the air.

"Signorina, yes, signorina, over here . . . I need some lemons!"

She walked over to him, a shy smile forming on her lips.

As she came closer, she appeared even more beautiful. He could now see her with greater clarity: skin the color of honey; eyes the color of Roman glass.

"How much for the whole basket?" he asked.

She looked down and counted the lemons. "If you take the full dozen, I'll sell it to you for five lire."

"That's far too little," he said, giving her his brightest smile. "Let's be fair, and you can sell it to me for eight."

"But that's too much," she said, trying to curb her urge to laugh. He knew she was amused that they were bartering in reverse. It was absurd. A buyer who was insisting he needed to pay a higher price, and she refusing to agree. But she wanted to be honest and fair.

He reached into her basket and pulled out one of the fruits. The fragrance of the lemons was intoxicating.

"I think I need to pay extra because their scent is so extraordinary. I have never smelled lemons this fresh."

This time, she allowed herself to smile fully, and when she did, he felt his heart quicken again. Her teeth against her rosebud mouth were as white as pearls.

"That's because you're from Genoa, where you can smell only the soot," she said. "Here, because we grow our lemons in our backyard, the very air is filled with their scent."

"What makes you think I'm from Genoa?" he asked.

"Oh, I can hear it in your accent. It's the pure Genovese. You sound proper," she said and laughed again.

"But you are mistaken," he said, switching into his home dialect as easily as a man taking off his work shoes for the day and slipping into a more comfortable pair of sandals.

She looked completely surprised. "What? I would never have guessed. Where are you from? Portofino?"

"Good for you!" He grinned, clearly impressed. "You're right."

"But you don't look like someone from these parts." She pointed to his linen suit and the shoes of hard leather, which had been meticulously shined.

"I'm studying medicine in Genoa and I'm on my way home to my parents," he said with a laugh. "I thought I'd surprise my mother with a basket of lemons and a visit from her only son.

"The next boat leaves in an hour," he said, glancing at his watch. "Now that I've bought your entire basket of lemons, won't you do me the honor of joining me for another coffee and any sweet you want . . ."

He stood up and took the basket from her, gently lifting it from her arms. Then, with a grace that even surprised him, he pulled back one of the café chairs and ushered her into its seat. He was normally awkward around women, yet this girl was so fresh and unassuming he immediately felt at ease.

"What will you have?" he asked. His own plate had nothing on it except crumbs.

"An espresso and a **sfogliatella**," she said, blushing. Angelo smiled and ordered her two.

He stayed with her all afternoon, missing the next three boats to Portofino.

"My mother isn't even expecting me," he said. "If I arrive before dinner or after, it won't matter. She'll still be surprised."

"My own family is expecting me, though," she said, her face still pink from all the attention he had showered upon her. "You have made me laugh all afternoon . . ." She pointed to the basket of lemons he had taken from her after they had left the café. She had commented that he looked silly walking with the basket looped through his arm.

"To avoid the village gossip," he told her. "This will look like I'm assisting you . . ."

"You are quite the chivalrous doctor in training. First you overpay for your lemons, and then you insist on carrying my basket." She giggled.

When she laughed, it sounded like the most beautiful music to him. As if God had captured sunlight and released it through her. He wanted to hold every bit of her between his hands. He wanted to cradle her face between his palms like a precious pearl, and press his lips to hers.

He noticed the flower in her hair had

grown limp and that the edges of the white petals had begun to turn brown. When she stopped and told him that she had to turn north back to her home, he reached to pull the flower from her ear.

"There should never be something wilting next to your perfect skin." Against the fence where they now stood were several hibiscus trees. He reached over and picked one of the brightest pink blooms and placed the new flower behind her ear.

As she went to touch it, her fingers met his for the first time.

"I wish I could bring you home to meet my mother tonight," he said, smiling at her.

"Now that would surely give her a surprise!"

"But she would be delighted . . . and, well, a bit surprised, considering you'd be the first woman whom I ever brought home."

"Bring her my lemons instead. Come back tomorrow and tell me what she thinks of them."

He had not wanted their fingers to stop touching, but eventually they fell away.

"Meet me at Fiorello Dolce tomorrow afternoon and tell me then," she said.

He knew his mother would lament his

coming and then leaving so quickly, but he couldn't resist the thought of seeing this woman again.

"It's a date," he said. "I will be sitting in the same spot waiting for you."

"And I will bring you another basket of lemons," she said, her smile curling like a ribbon above her chin.

His heart raced as he ran to make the last boat home.

Angelo arrived home later that evening and gave his mother the basket of yellow fruit.

"You bring me lemons?" she said, slightly confused. "Why? I can get them in my own backyard."

"But, Mamma," he said, "these lemons are special."

"Special?" She pulled one from the basket. "They are certainly lovely and fragrant, Angelo, but why are they so special? We have them here, in abundance. There was no need to waste your money on any more."

"Oh, but, Mamma, I brought these to you because they were handpicked by the woman I'm going to marry."

His mother placed her hands in her

apron. There was flour on her cheeks from rolling out the pasta.

"Marry?" she said, pressing her hands to her face. "Madonna! This is the first I've heard of this."

"Me, too, Mamma," he said, grasping her at the waist and lifting her. "But just you wait and see. You're going to fall in love with her as quickly as I did!"

"Oh, Angelo! This is craziness you're talking."

"No, Mamma. I am a man of science now. I know this for a fact. I made simple calculations on the way home. I will write her every day for the next year. Three hundred and sixty-five letters telling her how much I love her. The village donkey will get tired from carrying so many letters on his back."

She shook her head. "You must be hungry from your journey. You have given me enough surprises for today. Let me make you a little pasta. Your bones are showing."

She was a woman who did not take her apron off until she was just about to go to bed. The house of his childhood was full of the smells he loved: frying garlic, fistfuls of fresh basil, and the fragrance of olive oil. Like all the women of the region, his mother's love for her family was pressed with her very fingers into the dough she made every morning to roll out for pasta, every egg she picked from the coop, and each tomato she plucked from the vine.

She could make something wonderful out of almost nothing: focaccia out of a little flour and sea salt or a plateful of grilled sardines that glimmered in a puddle of oil and herbs. She would fry zucchini flowers stuffed with ricotta that she had made fragrant with lemon zest, and dust little fishes from the sea in bread crumbs and bits of grated cheese. For dessert, she used the fruit she had handpicked from her garden and served it alongside her **torte de miele.** When the children got older, their father would let them sip a little **sciacchetra**, the amber-colored sweet wine that made everything better and softer at the end of a long day.

She had given herself completely to the raising of her children. She had nursed one while spoon-feeding another. Angelo adored his mother. Seven children born to her, the first one when she was only seventeen. Angelo had been the fifth child, but the first one to graduate from school. Only his youngest sister still lived at home now, and there was already discussion of which village boy she would marry.

As he sat at the little table on their patio, which faced the sea, his mother brought him a plate of cold octopus salad. "Eat this," she insisted, while she went back to make him something else. He pushed a fork into the firm tentacles, each one shimmering with olive oil and lemon. He smiled. He loved eating, and he loved tasting the sea.

She returned a few minutes later with some warm ravioli.

"Mamma," he said. "I've missed you so while I've been away at school."

"Missed me? Then why this talk of an-other woman!" She stood over him and placed her hands over his shoulders.

"Mamma!" He put down his fork and smiled.

"Angelo . . . If you need to marry, why not pick a nice girl from here? Someone who we all know, instead of a stranger from an-other village."

He closed his eyes and remained serene. He did not pay too much attention to his mother's lack of enthusiasm for his decla-ration of newly discovered love. He had expected such a reaction from her. Instead, he let the memories of Dalia holding her basket of lemons, the curl of her smile, and the taste of his mother's ravioli, wash over him.

After he had finished eating, his mother sat down and pulled the basket of lemons up to her lap.

"Angelo. Angelo. My Angelo," she said, each articulation of his name punctuated by a sympathetic sigh.

She reached into the basket and pulled out a single lemon. The large, yellow fruit looked like a sleeping canary in her hand. She cupped two palms around its skin to warm it, then brought it under her nose and inhaled. "She has picked these with love, Angelo. I can smell it in the fragrance. . . ."

He smiled.

"Very well," she said. "You will need to tell your father tomorrow morning. He should be home early. The men have taken their boats out for some night fishing."

Angelo's father, Giorgio, was nearly twenty years older than Angelo's mother. He was a white-haired fisherman with a face like a piece of driftwood, but set alight by two marble-blue eyes.

Angelo had never known a time when his father was away from the sea for more than a day. When he wasn't on the water, he was down by the dock unloading his catch. As a child, Angelo had waited with excitement for his father to return from a day's work. He could tell if his father's catch had been plentiful just by the expression on the man's face. On good days, when Giorgio returned with his nets brimming with the ocean's bounty—fish with slapping tails and sparkling gills, baskets brimming with langoustines and spider crabs—he was radiant.

But on days when the seas had not been generous, the young Angelo could read his father's disappointment even before he saw the loose, empty nets.

This was when Angelo first started to read people's faces. To see hidden emotions in their eyes.

Happiness, sadness, anger, and frustration were easy to read in people's eyes. But he had been trained to look at what lay beneath the skin. Diagnosing a patient was

made through a series of observations,
each one connected to the next. So what
intrigued Angelo was being able to recognize someone who was carrying secrets,
struggling not to reveal their fear.

Angelo woke up early the next morning. He
knew if he timed things correctly, he could
see his father arriving at the docks and coordinate with one of the men to take him
over to San Fruttuoso.

"Papa!" he yelled, as he saw his father's
boat saddling up to the port. He waved his
hands above his head to catch his father's
attention.

His father looked up and returned a wave.
As Angelo walked closer to the boat, his
father called out his name.

Angelo smiled. "It looks like your trip was
a success!" He pointed to the full nets,
which were leaping with life.

"**Non male**," he said with a smile. His
teeth were like a piano of chipped and missing keys.

He reached over to embrace Angelo,
who was dressed in his best blue shirt and
crisp trousers. The salty smell of his father's

skin returned Angelo immediately back to his childhood.

"How is my doctor?"

"Not a doctor, yet, Papa."

His father shook his head. "Well, it's good enough for me! What a surprise to see you."

"Yes." Angelo smiled. "I wanted to surprise Mamma. I'll be home later tonight."

"Your sisters will be so happy to see you looking so well. . . ." He patted his son on his back.

"Tonight, Mamma is making dinner. But this morning I need to go to San Fruttuoso."

"Leaving, eh? You're home less than a night and already going someplace else."

"Yes. Just for a few hours. I was going to ask someone to take me over."

"What about your father? I have a boat."

"But you're tired, Papa. Let me ask someone who hasn't been out all night."

"I am never too tired for my son the doctor . . . What's in San Fruttuoso?"

"I have to meet someone, Papa." Angelo tried to remain vague.

His father shook his head, but then looked at his son more closely, a faint smile crossing his face.

"Meet someone?" His father smiled again. "Let me guess: It's a girl!"

Angelo nodded.

"Well, then," his father said. "What are you waiting for? Let's go!" He motioned for Angelo to hop into his boat. Angelo stepped into the center, making sure to avoid becoming tangled in the nets, which were piled high.

"Papa," he said, "I have to be honest, I wasn't expecting all this enthusiasm!"

His father grinned; the missing spaces of his teeth only enhanced his look of mischief. "Angelo," he said, laughing. "We should go . . . You don't want to keep her waiting!"

TWELVE

~~~~~~~

Portofino, Italy
APRIL 1934

The week Angelo was off from medical school, he traveled every day from Portofino to San Fruttuoso. Either his father or his father's fisherman friends became his ferrymen, dropping him off at sunrise and picking him up late at night. He always met Dalia in front of the café, bringing her flowers from his mother's garden. And she always carried a new basket of lemons.

He never told her he was aware that one of her brothers was always watching them. He knew he would have done the same in any similar situation involving one of his sisters. So he courted her as best he could

under the circumstances: telling her stories and making her laugh. Buying her an
espresso and a **sfogliatella.** But trying
nothing more than to hold her hand.

When the week came to an end and he
had to return to school, he promised to write
her every day.

"Might I have your address to write to you
when I'm back at school?"

She pushed her hands into her skirt,
showing him that she had no paper or pencil with her.

"I have!" he said resiliently. He put down
his basket and reached into his satchel.

"Tell me," he said lifting the pen to the air.

"It's simple," she said. "Dalia Orembelli.
We have our home and lemon grove just
behind the Piazzetta Doria Pamphili. Just
put my name on the envelope and write that
address, and the letter will get to me."

"I'm a good writer," he told her. "You will
see."

Her face did not have the reaction he
anticipated. He saw her eyes begin to
moisten, and a slight tremor rippled across
her chin.

Without her having to say another word,

he immediately knew what pained her: She couldn't read.

"Stop your worrying, Dalia," he said, taking a finger to gently move away her falling tears.

He could see the flush in her face, like a rose that deepened in color before him.

He took her into his arms to soothe her embarrassment.

"My **limonina** . . . You are not just beautiful. You are smart, too."

She lifted her face from his chest to look at him, and he saw his reflection in her watery eyes.

He placed a finger beneath her chin, whispering, "It isn't hard to learn. When I come back for Christmas, I will teach you. You'll learn to read through my letters."

And then he kissed her for the first time. Her brothers be damned if they tried to stop him.

She saved every one of his letters. And just as he had promised, one arrived daily. And although she could not read them, she did as he had instructed: She put every one in a box and waited for his return.

The box was simple, almost crude. A
wooden one that, as a child, she had re-
served for her most precious things. When
the letters began arriving, to make room,
she took out the small things she had once
deemed so special: the glass button, the
small sterling silver pin, and the tortoiseshell
comb, and tucked the letters inside.

And although she wished she could read
the words and understand what her love had
written, just holding them in her hands gave
her sustenance. She loved to look at his
perfectly rounded letters, the curve of his
script, the neatness of his lines. She thought
she could sense the content even though
she was incapable of reading a single word.

And so Dalia waited, counting the days
until he came back to her to fulfill his promise.

When Angelo returned, they walked up
to the top of the peninsula where the view
was most beautiful, and there under the
shade of a lemon grove he began to teach
her to read.

He wrote out the letters of the vowels and
the consonants neatly, and then once she
mastered their sound, they moved on to
short, simple words.

"Let's now see if you can begin with my first letter," he said, knowing that he had written it as simply but as purely as he could.

She took the little box made from cypress wood and opened the lid. The first letter he had sent was right on top.

She pulled out the paper from the envelope.

He could see her forming the sounds in her mind before working up the courage to actually say them. Gazing at her expression, Angelo knew that she could read the three words. The meaning of their simple beauty was floating across her face.

She smiled and turned to him, kissing him sweetly on the cheek.

"'I love you.' But that's too easy," she said, gripping his hand in hers.

"No, that's not easy at all," he said, staring straight into her eyes. "That's beautiful and rare."

Within months, she was reading with ease. Now when his letters arrived, she opened them and devoured every single word. He also began to send her books. Her head was alive for the first time with the world and its possibilities around her, and her heart beat faster every time she saw the postman walking up the street.

Her parents, now well aware of the courtship, were delighted that their daughter had charmed the heart of a soon-to-be doctor. They had so little money that a dowry was impossible, yet this young man seemed not to care.

"Do not worry, **limonina**," he wrote. "I only want a life and a family with you."

She counted the days until his next visit, throwing herself into her chores and reading the novels he had sent with little love notes tucked inside.

Then, a week before he was to return for the summer break, his last letter arrived with another sealed envelope enclosed. The front read "Please wait to read this with me."

A few days later, he arrived in San Fruttuoso looking more serious then she had remembered him. His hair was shiny and neat; he wore a pale blue shirt and white linen trousers.

In front of the café where they always met, she was dressed in a white peasant skirt and blouse. As always, she had tucked a blossom behind her ear, and her basket was full with fruit.

"You look different," she said as he went over and touched her arm. Inside she felt herself grow cold with worry.

"Let's go up to the lemon grove," he said. "Where are your brothers?"

"No brothers today," she said. "They are all out on the boats."

The two of them walked up the rocky path to their secret place. There, in the midst of the canopy of branches and fragrant lemons, she pulled out the last letter he had sent, still sealed in the envelope as he had requested.

It was written on heavy, handmade paper the color of natural linen. The edges were deckled and soft like a bird's feather.

"Now open it," he said softly. He noticed her hands were trembling.

She opened the small envelope, which had remained glued tight.

He saw her eyes register the words written within, and the gentle wave that came over her face, transforming it within seconds from a canvas that initially wore an expression of trepidation to one full of sheer joy.

She put down the paper, on which he had written, ever so simply, "Will you marry me?"

"Oh yes!" she cried. "Oh yes!"

She wrapped her arms around his neck, then took her finger to his heart and traced the words into his shirt. "I love you." Then she kissed him so deeply and pressed her body against him so tightly, he felt his very heart sealed onto hers.

They married four months later in the abbey in San Fruttuoso, his family climbing up the weathered stone steps up to the church in a single file. The smell of lemon blossoms and jasmine clung heavy in the air.

Dalia's mother had made her a gown from simple white cotton, and wove a crown of verbena flowers through the bride's long black hair.

That night, Angelo took her into his arms, and as his head fell onto her breasts, he felt as though God had given him his own perfect cloud to forever rest his head on.

He kissed every part of her. The pink raspberry of each nipple, the globe of each breast. Every part of her was a piece to be discovered. To be touched. To be tasted.

He began to move down the length of her. His lips, his tongue, gently sliding the narrow line that divided her rib cage. He could feel her heart beating like the wings of a hummingbird, so rapid he thought she might take flight. As she quivered and moaned softly with his every touch, he continued along his path of discovering his bride.

"Dalia," he whispered, as he lifted one leg over his shoulder.

"Where do you begin and where do you end?" he whispered into her skin. Her body was a map of hidden pathways each interconnected to make an exquisite whole. He took his fingers and traced the line from her ankle to her calf, circling behind her knee, then continuing up her thigh. He paused. He circled. He inhaled her, cradling her pelvis like a basket of fragrant blooms.

"My love," he said, and kissed her.

She opened her mouth like an orchid.

And he sealed her kiss with his lips.

Angelo now knew the answer to a question his classmate had once challenged him with: "At what point is a woman most beautiful? When you first see her body? Her heart? Or her soul?"

It was at that rare moment when you hold the woman you love in your arms and you see all three at once.

THIRTEEN

~

Verona, Italy
JUNE 1943

Elodie was not so beautiful that the other girls were jealous of her. She dressed so modestly, and her body was so slender and without curves that her only striking feature was the intensity of her eyes. But this was a benefit to her work for the group—a cloak of plainness that enabled her to walk undetected through the streets of Verona, not a single man lifting his head in her direction. For Lena, it was far more difficult. She was harassed constantly. The soft, protruding pillow of her breasts, the roundness of her hips, and the elevated shelf of her buttocks, were all physical attributes that made

her far more likely to draw attention. Aware
of this, Lena tried to dress as modestly as
possible, choosing primarily drab shirt-
dresses or the standard white blouse and
navy skirt. But still she caught the eyes of
the men who sat in the café calling out to
girls as if it were a sport.

Most of the other girls who volunteered
were handed books that contained small
coded messages, just as Elodie and Lena
had first been given. The others, who traveled on bicycle, were able to carry their
messages in other clever ways. The men
removed the rubber stops at the end of each
handlebar and inserted the scrolled paper.
The girls pedaled through the streets, committed to their delivery. They were never told
the content of the messages, even if they
asked.

"We're doing you a favor, by maintaining
your ignorance," the men told them. "We
can't take the risk that you might divulge
something if you are ever interrogated. It's
best to keep you in the dark."

The girls did not insist, and continued
to do as they were told. They reveled in
the excitement of having an assignment
for the cause, which contrasted so sharply

to the routine of their lives. At home, their mothers expected them to help with the laundry and do schoolwork. They felt a freedom, and even a sense of power, when ferrying secret information that needed to be delivered to help liberate Italy.

A few weeks later, the girls entered the back of the bookstore to attend one of the meetings, but arrived in the middle of a heated discussion. "We're hearing from our comrades that we should be expecting a German invasion by the fall and that we need to be prepared. Our men are starting to get ready in the mountains. We're going to start organizing delivery of guns, ammunition, and more supplies to them," a voice said from the crowd.

Luca agreed. "My brother's already scouting the mountains with Darno Maffini. Berto is arranging contacts in France. All of us here in the city need to be efficient and organized. They're counting on us to get them what they need."

A large, stocky man in overalls was standing in the front, trying to get his point across. "Yes . . . Luca's right. We need to start preparing before winter comes and access becomes too difficult."

"And what about men? There aren't nearly enough of us . . ."

"We need to think about getting more women involved . . ."

"Too dangerous!" someone barked back. "Would you want your own sister in the line of fire? Think about what those pigs would do to one of them in a holding cell."

Beppe, one of the key organizers, tried to settle the crowd. "Listen, we can't deny the danger. That is a fact. But we also know the women of Verona are fed up with war."

Someone in the background snickered. "They can gladly take their husbands, but not their sons!"

Beppe smiled. "Well, that's true. That's why they're getting angrier." He leaned over the crowded table. "But let's be serious. Our own mothers and sisters have been selfless for years in the name of Italy. But now they are becoming disillusioned. They see their conditions deteriorating. The milk and food for their children being rationed, their shelves nearly bare. Mussolini promised them a strong, united Fatherland, and they are tired of receiving nothing but empty promises for their hardship."

"Our own partisan, Jurika, in the mountains now, enlisted with us because her brother was sent to Africa and came back with an amputated leg and no money to provide for his family. He shot himself in the head, just so his mother and sister could get his pension. And the state tried to refuse him even that on the grounds of his suicide."

"We have two other women in our room today who want to help!" a voice shouted.

Elodie and Lena could feel all the eyes of the room suddenly turn to them. Brigitte Lowenthal wasn't in attendance and the girls were the only females in the room. It was Luca's voice that had pointed them out.

"These young girls want to save Italy as much as we do!" His voice was so impassioned, it gave Elodie goose bumps.

As everyone craned their necks to gain a view of Elodie and Lena, both girls blushed in embarrassment. Then Lena's strong voice filled the air.

"It's true. I would die for Italy! And my friend here saw her own father dragged from his house and beaten by the Fascists."

Beppe stood up and clapped his hands to silence the room.

"We will get the job done. We will get the guns to our men. We will sabotage the rails and intercept deliveries. We will find ways to be more cunning . . . one step ahead of them, even when we have less manpower. Let's put our heads together, make full use of our talents, and figure out how to stop this bloody regime!"

The room exploded with applause and cheer.

"They better quiet themselves down." Elodie looked at Lena, revealing her apparent alarm. "What if someone hears all the noise and reports it?"

But Lena wasn't listening. She appeared to have become completely enraptured by Beppe's speech.

"I wish he wouldn't wear those overalls," Lena whispered. "Otherwise, that's a man whom even I could cook pasta for at night."

Elodie smiled. The thought of Lena cooking pasta for anyone seemed comical.

"Maybe you should offer to play your viola for him. I think you'd have more luck winning his heart with your music than with your cooking."

Lena shot Elodie a bemused look. "And

Luca? Are you going to offer to play your cello?"

Elodie stared ahead, a thin ribbon of a smile crossing her lips. "I won't offer anything. But I will do whatever I'm asked."

Elodie and Lena found themselves increasingly busy as summer began, even without their classes at the Liceo Musicale. They would go every Wednesday to Luca's bookstore. Luca would always greet them at his front desk. If there were customers already in the store, he would wait until they had left before taking the girls to the back room.

"My music girls," he would say and smile. His smile lingered a bit longer on Elodie. "Too bad all your heart goes into your instruments . . ."

Elodie raised her eyebrow.

He laughed, drawing back the curtain of the storeroom that they knew so well from the meetings.

Elodie had yet to see the room without anyone in it, and she was surprised to find it now so still and empty.

They followed Luca to the shelves in the far corner, pushing past the chairs and leftover debris from the last meeting.

"I'm glad the two of you have passed the first round of tests," he said.

"Tests? What tests?" Elodie seemed confused.

"The last envelopes we asked you to deliver were actually blank . . . But you got them to where they needed to go, so now we know we can trust you with larger assignments."

Lena's face curled.

"Don't act so insulted." He laughed. "We do it with everyone."

"They just need to be cautious," Elodie said, touching Lena's arm. "It makes sense."

"I knew you'd understand the logic, Elodie. Thank you."

"Well, now that we've passed, what's our next assignment?"

Luca now stood on his tiptoes and pulled down two books from one of the shelves.

"Beppe prepared these last night, so they're all set."

He spoke first to Lena.

"Take yours to the bar on the northeast corner of the Piazza San Zeno. There will be a man reading a book with a green cover at the table in the back. Sit down. Order a drink. Finish it. He will come over to you,

place his book down on the counter, and
pretend to flirt with you. You will get up, take
his book seemingly by accident, and leave
yours on the table." He paused. "That's it.
Do you understand?"

"Yes," Lena replied.

"Repeat it back to me," Luca said to her.
"Slowly. I want to make sure you have
everything right."

"I take this book to the bar on the northeast corner of Piazza Erbe . . ."

"Stop!" Luca held up his hand to prevent
Lena from going any further.

"What's the matter? Didn't you say northeast corner of Piazza Erbe?"

"I said the northeast corner of Piazza San
Zeno!"

"Oh." Lena blushed. "I'm sorry. I must
have heard you wrong."

Luca tried to hide his agitation. "Try
again."

"I take this book to the northeast corner
of Piazza San Zeno. I go to the back and
look for a man reading a book with a green
cover. I order a drink. Finish it, and then
after a few minutes, I take the book he was
reading, leaving mine on the table."

"Yes. Exactly." He handed over a book with a red cover to Lena.

"Now, you." Luca looked Elodie straight in the eyes. She was mesmerized how his left one seemed to sparkle in the light and his right one seemed to absorb the shadow.

"You will go to 7 Via Fogge. It's a small tailor shop. The owner will be sitting in front of a sewing machine, making pillows. You go to him with the book in your hands, and tell him your mother sent you to ask how much it would cost to make three square pillows for her if she provides the fabric. He will tell you the price. He will then ask you the title of the book you are reading and whether it is any good. Tell him the title and mention that you wept during chapter thirty-three. After you finish your brief conversation, place the book down on the table next to him, pick up one of the pillows, and make some comment about its beauty. Then leave, pretending to have forgotten the book.

"Now, let's see if you got it right."

Elodie smiled.

"I will go to 7 Via Fogge. There, I will find a tailor shop. The owner will be sitting at a sewing machine, making pillows. I go to him with the book in my hands, and tell him my mother would like to know the price for him to make three square pillows for her if she provides the fabric. He will tell me the price. He will then ask me the title of the book I'm reading and ask me if it's any good. I will tell him the title"—Elodie lifted the book— "and mention that I wept on chapter thirty-three. After we finish our brief conversation, I will place the book down on the table next to him, pick up one of the pillows, and make some comment about their beauty. Then I will leave, pretending to have forgotten the book."

"Perfect!" Luca said exuberantly. "Perfect."

Lena reached over to touch her friend's shoulder. "What did I say at that first meeting? Elodie's memory is extraordinary."

The others in their group soon learned about her memory. The cellist. The slender girl with the black hair and green eyes. The girl who said very little but could recite anything back with razorlike precision. They marveled at Elodie's capacity to recite entire passages of Dante's **Inferno**, a whole chapter verbatim except for the three words that Beppe had changed for the sake of a code.

Elodie never forgot a single word she was told, even if it made no sense to her.

One time she was asked to remember a Lord Byron poem, but with every third word changed to one that didn't belong.

She did it with ease. Beppe slapped Luca on the shoulder and said, "We really got lucky with this one."

"Indeed," Luca said and smiled directly at her. His stare was both heavy and light.

She felt a strange desire to impress him. As if what she had already accomplished in her missions for the group hadn't been enough.

"Have you ever thought about having messages sent through music?" she pondered one evening. "If there is someone in the group who can read music, we can send things through code, like in cadenzas."

A cadenza was typically part of a concerto, written either by the composer or the soloist, in order to show off the soloist's musical virtuosity.

"You should ask," she said, looking at

Luca. She wasn't used to speaking up like this and could feel the fire and excitement rising in her and wondered if it was revealed in her own eyes.

She saw something shift in Luca's eyes, too. She saw he was intrigued.

Elodie felt exhilarated to be living in two worlds. In the morning and early afternoon, she was Elodie, the dedicated music student and devoted daughter. But in the late afternoon, she emerged in a new, more complicated role: a **staffetta** for Italy's early Resistance. Twice a week, she would leave the walls of the Liceo behind and attend a meeting with Lena. When she returned home, she would climb the stairs to her family's apartment, her cello on her back and her head full of Luca's ideas, but when she turned the doorknob and entered the threshold of the living room, she could hear the silence between her parents like a dart through her heart.

Her father had not regained mobility since his beating and still had to eat his meals in bed. One evening, Elodie convinced him to pick up his violin and try to play a few pieces with her.

The sight of him trying to play, only to find that his bruised and swollen fingers were unable to move across the strings as before, was devastating to watch.

Elodie began filling the air in the apartment with double the energy, as if she were now playing for her father as well. The contact with Luca and the energy of the early Resistance meetings also brought a new fervor to her playing. She now only wanted to play music that mirrored her internal energy. No more melancholy etudes or sleepy romantic nocturnes. She yearned for powerful, bold scores that made her feel strong.

She played with such passion that her mother often came into the room and just stared.

"You're like a match, Elodie. I'm afraid you might ignite your cello." Orsina was worried. "I hear changes in your music, Elodie." She paused. "It frightens me."

Elodie looked up from her instrument. Her eyebrows lifted and her gaze narrowed slightly. "I **am** changing. I feel that suddenly I'm seeing everything around me in a completely different way."

Orsina could feel the tension just beneath her daughter's words.

She studied the girl. She did look different. There was no longer that wide-eyed innocence in her eyes. She was reed thin. Angles where there should have been emerging curves.

"Elodie, there will always be evil in the world. We can't change that. We can only try and add a little more goodness. You are making us upset with this kind of talk."

"Am I? Because I have acknowledged that our country has succumbed to brutality? That thugs arrest and beat up my father for playing Verdi a little too loudly?"

"I want you to concentrate on your music! Not politics!" Orsina was shaking. "Elodie, you have a gift! Don't you know how special and rare that is! You mustn't let yourself become distracted . . ."

Elodie's back stiffened as her mother spoke. She could feel rage just underneath her skin.

Orsina took a step closer and as she placed a hand on her daughter's shoulder, Elodie winced.

"Elodie . . ." Orsina's voice was softer now. "Renata Santorelli said she saw you going into a bookshop the other day with your friend Lena . . . What were you doing there?"

Elodie looked her mother straight in the eyes and did not flinch.

"What do you think, Mamma? I went to look at some books."

Orsina shook her head.

"What, Mamma?" Elodie said, surprising even herself how easy it was to lie. "I can't believe it would upset you that I like to read."

FOURTEEN

~

Portofino, Italy
SEPTEMBER 1935

Angelo brought his new bride back home to Portofino and waited to hear from the government where he would be posted as a doctor. Portofino already had a physician in place, due to an early initiative of the Fascist regime that every village in Italy have one.

In the meantime, Angelo spent his afternoons reading the books on ancient history or seafaring adventures that he had bought during his time as a medical student in Genoa with money he made from a part-time job cleaning laboratory jars after class.

In the morning, he would wake beside

Dalia and feel the need to pinch himself. He couldn't believe that a perfect specimen of human beauty could also be blessed with a perfect soul. He would always try and wake before her, just to gaze at her, the soft brown limbs extending from the white of her nightgown, her long, black hair falling between the wings of her back.

He always greeted her first with his mouth, then with his hands. He kissed her everywhere: her cheeks, her neck, and his favorite spot behind her ear. He kissed the top of her shoulder, down the length of her arm. He took her fingers and kissed each one. Then after she had awakened in his arms, he'd unbutton the top of her nightgown, and cup her breasts, kissing each one, then lift her nightdress, to feel every inch of her warm, moist skin.

Dalia would smile like a kitten as Angelo cradled the back of her head with one hand while taking the other to caress the length of her long, tanned thigh.

They shared breakfast on a small, tiled terrace. Beneath them, ropes of flowers were resplendent in magenta and gold. Like a decorated gypsy, each garden seemed to have more flowers than the next. And the village's yellow church reflected against the hills like a second sun.

Later, Dalia would join Angelo's mother to prepare the family's meals. She would help roll out the pasta dough into thin sheets and drape them on damp towels on the table. Then, as Angelo's mother instructed, Dalia would take her basket and go to the family's garden to harvest the zucchini, tomatoes, and other vegetables in season.

If the seas had been generous that day, the two women would then sit on the terrace and scale the fish or clean the tiny squids. Angelo's sisters, who spent most of their mornings undertaking similar culinary preparations with their own mothers-in-law, would still find a way to come and spend some time with their mother.

Dalia seemed to blossom with each passing day. She continued to read the books Angelo handpicked for her. And at night, when the two of them were tucked into bed, he would take the novel from her dainty fingers and begin to read to her aloud.

Sometimes they were the latest novels in translation from America or books of poetry. But whatever Dalia was reading, it always sounded infinitely better when Angelo read it to her in his sweet and melodic voice.

"Mother told me today how you've budded like a flower in her heart," Angelo told his wife as he put the book down and wrapped her in his arms.

"She said she was skeptical a girl from San Fruttuoso could be happy in Portofino. She was sure you'd hate the tourists that fill the hotels in the summer. And how crowded the port becomes in the high season . . ."

"I have my jar filled with stones and shells from San Fruttuoso to remind me of its beauty," Dalia said, taking Angelo's hand in her own. "And that's all I need. I would be happy anywhere as long as I was with you."

"I know, my **limonina**. I know. Me, too," he said as he caressed her with his free hand.

"She also said you are both devoted and devout, two essential things in a wife."

"She took me to San Giorgio to pay my respect to the Madonna. She told me she had left an orange there three days before she learned she was pregnant with you."

Angelo smiled. He had heard this story many times before. His mother always retold it on his birthday. She loved to make him a cake with orange zest grated into the batter.

"And so did you go and also bring an orange to the Madonna?"

Dalia jumped on top of him and kissed him on the forehead.

"No, my darling. I brought her what had first brought us together . . . I brought her a basket of lemons."

Three months later, two important things happened. First, Angelo received notice that he was to be deployed to Ethiopia. Second, Dalia learned she was pregnant.

The letter instructing Angelo to report to duty for Africa had not been a complete shock. Many of his peers had been conscripted into the Italian army, as Mussolini declared his intentions of making a new colony in the desert to expand the Italian empire.

Thousands of Italian men had been drafted to fight Il Duce's war in Africa, and doctors were needed almost as much as soldiers.

"Two years, and then I'll be home," Angelo had told her, trying to remain optimistic. "If I fulfill my duty, I'm more likely to then get a position here at home. Doctor Pignone is nearing seventy now. Hopefully he'll retire by then, and I can take his place and we won't need to move."

Dalia began to cry. "I don't want you to go, Angelo. I won't be able to stand the separation."

"You won't be alone, darling." He tried to soothe her though inside his heart was breaking, too.

She was sobbing, her entire body shaking in his arms.

"My family will take good care of you. I will write every day, just like I did when I was in medical school. Your parents are close by, too."

She pulled away from him and raised her eyes to his.

"I'm late, Angelo."

He looked at her, puzzled.

"I think I'm going to have a baby."

"What makes you think that? How many weeks late are you?"

"Just three weeks. But I am pretty sure, now. Haven't you noticed a change in me?" She cupped her breasts to show that she thought they had become larger.

He smiled. He **had** thought they were a bit larger recently. But he had never given much thought to the reason why, only to the pleasure of the bounty.

Angelo felt both the joy at the unexpected news and the sadness of his departure.

"But you should have told me from the minute you suspected."

"I was afraid to put a curse on it. I was too happy. Everything seemed too wonderful in our lives. And now we've had someone put the evil eye on us."

"Don't be ridiculous!" Angelo waved away her concern. He had enough of this village superstition from his mother.

"You are healthy and strong. The baby will be fine. I will return and bounce him in my arms."

Dalia let him embrace her again. But a wave of uncertainty flowed through her, as if she had suddenly been engulfed in a dark cloud.

"Angelo," she whispered. "I wish I could be as certain as you . . ."

"Don't worry, my **limonina**," he again reassured her. But something inside Dalia haunted her. His words had failed to soothe her. She continued to remain unconvinced.

FIFTEEN

~~~~

Elodie and Lena were changing from girls to young women. Even Elodie, who had never seen herself as a siren, now felt she was being treated differently. The girls noticed that with the success of every mission, the men treated them with more respect. Lena now hoped they would help her get the necessary counterfeit papers for the Morettis.

No longer did the importance of a resistance group seem abstract. On the streets, people were more anxious than ever. The fear that the German army may invade at any moment was ever more palpable.

Berto Zampieri had just returned to Verona from a secret mission in Paris, where he met with members of the French Resistance. During a meeting in Luca's bookstore, he informed everyone that the Germans had already started deploying troops into Italy.

"We can't wait any longer," Beppe told the group. "We need to get organized. Establish our men in the mountains. Get the provisions ready. Make our connections with the villagers up there who will help us."

There was a rumbling through the room. "Quiet!" Luca bellowed. "Let Beppe speak!"

"Every one of you is valuable to our mission. We will be talking with you all individually over the next few days about how to best use your assets and connections to our advantage."

Lena looked at Elodie and raised an eyebrow. Her eyes were ablaze.

Elodie could see that Lena didn't seem nervous at all. On the contrary, Lena looked as though it was the night before Christmas. She was radiant and smiling.

Two days later, Lena met with Beppe in a café nearby. She came alone. "The men who have already gone to the mountains now need ammunition and grenades," he told her. He asked Lena if she'd be willing to undertake a mission.

He told her she could tell no one. They would give her a small shopping basket of vegetables with grenades hidden underneath. She would have to carry it several miles, past Fascist police who might ask to look inside her basket.

"You will not only risk death if you're discovered," Beppe told her. "Before they shoot you, they could do things to you that are worse than death." He looked at her with grave seriousness, never once blinking his eyes. "It is essential that you understand the risk before you take this on."

Lena looked squarely back at him. "I'll do it. Just tell me when and where."

A few days later, she was given the basket. On top, someone had put a head of lettuce, a cluster of tomatoes, and a loaf of bread. Underneath were eight hand grenades. The weight of the basket was substantial.

"Lena, you cannot let on that the basket is so heavy," Beppe instructed her. "You don't want some man to offer to carry it for you. I want to see that you can lift it now, without showing any physical strain."

Lena walked over to the basket and raised it. She was used to carrying her viola everywhere, so this delivery seemed quite manageable.

"I can do this," she said. "Just tell me where I have to go."

"You need to pass the amphitheater, cross the Piazza Bra, then take Via Roma to reach Castelvecchio. There you will cross the bridge, walk for several meters through the Campagnola area, until you find a park. Someone will meet you there. He will be sitting on a park bench reading a copy of the **Inferno**. You are to sit on the bench and place the shopping basket on the ground. After a few moments, he will get up and take your basket. You are to distract yourself by looking at the children playing in the playground. Do not look in his direction until he has walked away.

"He will leave the copy of the **Inferno** on the bench. You are to take that home with you and give it to me." Beppe cleared his throat. "Is that clear?"

Lena nodded. "Yes. I understand what I have to do."

"One other thing," Beppe said. His hand reached out to touch her shoulder, but she moved, and his fingers accidentally touched the skin below the short sleeve of her blouse. She shivered.

"Yes . . ."

"If they arrest you, they will interrogate you. And they will use brutal measures . . ." He didn't need to elaborate any further; she knew very well what they could do to her. It was beyond words.

"But no matter what they do to you, it's essential you don't give any information about who you are working for. Do you understand?"

"I will tell them the truth, Beppe." She looked him straight in the eyes and he felt heat pouring out from her, as though her gaze had the capacity to scorch his skin. "That I did this completely and wholly by myself and for Italy."

She walked with the bag for what seemed like over an hour. In agony from the weight, she did her best not to show the strain. Through the streets, past the amphitheater, along Via Roma, and across the Adige River. When she got to the third crossing,

Fascist police were there checking people's papers.

She stood on line with her basket. The lettuce was beginning to wilt, and the tomatoes were sun-ripened and fragrant from the heat. Below, the grenades were getting heavier.

She was wearing a light blue dress and her hair looked even blonder from the sun.

"Where are you going?" one of the police asked. He took a rifle and pointed it at her bag. He looked at her and smiled again. "And **what** do you have there?"

She smiled coquettishly. "What does it look like, Officer? Bombs, of course!"

He laughed and made a lewd gesture. **Bombe,** he said, the Italian slang for breasts.

But Lena didn't reprimand him. She gave him her heartiest laugh, which delighted him even more.

"You're a spunky one. I like that! Would you want to go to a movie with me sometime?"

Inside Lena was shaking, but she kept her arm straight with her dangerous package and her smile firmly on her face.

"Maybe," she said. "But I have to get this

to my grandmother before lunch. You'll have to catch me another time."

"I'll be here waiting," he said. She noticed that he winked at her as he waved her through.

Lena was unable to keep her latest mission a secret from Elodie. The story was too good not to relay to someone.

"When I told him I was carrying bombs, he just laughed!"

"Oh my god, you're just lucky he didn't take a look inside your basket!" Elodie gasped. She was shocked by her friend's brazenness. She could never have pulled off something like that.

"I had a backup plan, if he did that," Lena said, laughing. She took a finger and with a quick flip was able to knock the button of her blouse out of its loop.

"I would have leaned over and let him peek into something else instead of the basket."

Elodie shook her head. "I would never be as good as you under pressure . . . and I certainly don't have those to fall back on!" She pointed to her friend's generous cleavage.

They both laughed, before Elodie suddenly grew serious.

"We shouldn't take this lightly, Lena. We both know that had he not fancied you, you could have been discovered and shot!"

Lena looked at her friend and nodded. "Now that it's over, it almost doesn't seem real. It feels more like a dream. But you're right."

"I know I'm right," Elodie said. "I wonder if they're going to ask me to deliver grenades, or if they think I'm not competent enough . . ."

Lena looked at her friend. "Honestly, I think they realize you're capable of carrying more important things. Your memory is an enormous asset to them, and they fully realize that. Think about how they've already been able to give you with so much coded information."

Elodie smiled. "Who knew the Venetian in me would be so helpful . . ."

Lena raised an eyebrow. "What's the Venetian connection?"

Elodie shrugged. "I'm not sure. But my mother says if Venetians see something once, they never forget it."

SIXTEEN

~

Verona, Italy
JULY 1943

Elodie busied herself with her family while waiting for Luca or Beppe to call on her. Finally, the cast on her father's leg was removed and both Elodie and Orsina were shocked by the wrinkled flesh of his calf. The muscles had atrophied to such an extent that his leg was now as thin as one of Elodie's arms.

"You have to use those crutches . . . You must get around and move," Doctor Tommasi told him. "You won't ever be able to get back to the Liceo Musicale at this rate."

On the way out, the doctor chastised Orsina for not being more forceful with him.

"You need to make him walk a little each day. He'll lose all mobility if he doesn't get out of the bed."

Orsina shook her head. "I've tried, Doctor, but . . ."

"I know it's hard, but try and help him. He's lucky to be alive."

Orisna wiped her eyes. "I know you're right. I will work on getting him moving around as soon as I can."

"Good. That's what I wanted to hear." He kissed Orsina on both cheeks. "I'll come by next week to check on him."

"Thank you, Doctor. You've always been so kind," she said, walking him to the door. "I hope we'll all be in better shape when you come for your next visit."

The next day, Pietro moved from the bed to the kitchen table. Even without the cast, he still needed crutches.

To see her father in such a frail and weakened condition upset Elodie greatly.

"I hate seeing you like this," she said, coming over to where he now sat slowly reading the morning headlines. She began to rub her father's shoulders.

"Tell me, Papa, when do you think all this is going to end?"

"When they shoot Mussolini, that's when . . ." her father answered.

"Pietro!" her mother whispered, but her tone was severe. "Use a lower voice. I'll die if you're arrested again!"

"Let's hope the partisans get him sooner rather than later," he said as he placed the paper on the table. "Who knows what will happen in the next few weeks? There is talk they are going to close the Liceo Musicale."

"Is that true, Papa?" Elodie couldn't believe what she was hearing.

"If it becomes too unsafe here, yes, it is possible."

Elodie was in shock. And for the first time in her life, Elodie wondered if there was a place for music in all this chaos and war.

SEVENTEEN

~~~~~~

Verona, Italy
JULY 1943

It was Luca who assigned her next mission.

"I don't think I'm qualified to deliver hand grenades," she said, looking straight into his eyes.

"I would never ask you to do that, Elodie."

"But you and Beppe asked Lena to do that."

"That was different. And that was a test mission. We were trying to see how we might be able to get things past the controls. Maffini believes we have to start preparing for a German invasion. Lena was the right person for that job."

"And me? I'm the wrong person?"

He looked at her and smiled. She thought she saw his fingers inch toward her and then pull back.

"We have other ideas on how to best use your particular skills."

"How's that?" she challenged him.

"As you suggested, we've been trying to see if we could find a way to use music to hide coded messages. We are now working with someone who is an expert musician. Someone important. We want you to give him a message through a musical code."

"You want me to memorize it?"

"We'll actually need you to first help write it into the score—in the cadenza, like you said. You can visit him under the guise that you're going for a private music lesson, and then play the coded message for him. Then, when you're finished, he will comment on the cadenza, which you will say you yourself composed, and then you will hand him the encoded score."

Elodie felt her head rushing with blood.

"I can do this, Luca, and I want to do this. My only limitation is my curfew time. After what happened to my father, I can't travel too far. My mother would call the police if I didn't return home on time."

"I am fully aware of your constraints, Elodie. But only you can do this."

Luca's belief in her ignited Elodie's spirit and her body. Her skin felt so hot, Elodie considered asking him for a glass of water. But the thought of him leaving, even briefly, made her decide against it.

She couldn't remember the last time she felt so alive outside of a cello performance. She realized that Luca was telling her that she had been selected because of her talents. She heard his voice in the air:

Your gifts have not gone unnoticed here. We want to utilize your memory and your musical skills. We can't have our messages found or intercepted. The partisans in the mountains are relying on us to get their messages to their contacts in the city.

When she was with Luca, every one of her senses was heightened, as if she were interpreting a new sheet of music. She waited for pauses in their conversation, a moment of breath, when he might lift his head and their eyes might meet.

She wondered what it would be like to stare at his face at the different hours of the day. Would the colors of his eyes shift as the light changed, like in the ocean and sky?

"Elodie . . ." He said her name aloud. And when he said it, she felt her spine soften; her limbs felt almost weightless. His words were slow, as if he were trying to warn her that she would need to exercise caution. In his voice, she sensed concern.

"Yours will be a mission with a high level of danger. Part of me is hesitant to put you in harm's way."

"Like Lena?" she said, sounding serious.

"Lena's mission was different. What she was carrying was itself the danger. She held nothing within her mind. They would have arrested her and had her shot on the spot if she was discovered." Luca paused. "Your mission is different because **you** are different, Elodie." He stopped speaking and looked at her. A momentary silence passed, but the air between them ricocheted with its own energy. One single breath held by two sets of lungs. Elodie interpreted it like a pause in the music, a suspension of words instead of notes.

She could sense that he, too, was trying to remain focused. "You will not be physically carrying anything that could incriminate you. But you will possess essential information that we typically wouldn't entrust to a **staffetta**."

Staffetta, the Italian word for messenger. She knew it well by now.

"When you and I sit down to write this piece of original music . . . this cadenza, I will have to tell you things that the Fascist police would torture, even kill you for . . ."

Elodie maintained her composure, interpreting his eyes like a musical score. Yet Luca was caught between his awareness of their need to deliver this message and his concern for her safety.

"If this scares you, no one would blame you. No one expects beautiful, young women to die for their country . . ."

"What about plain women?" She laughed.

Luca smiled. "Elodie, you have a fantastic memory and musical talent. Two necessary things for this mission."

"You've never even heard me play."

"I will now," he said. "You and I are going to spend as long as it takes to get this done right. And the reward for me will be your performance."

Luca placed a "Closed" sign in the shop window so that the two of them could work undisturbed. He confided in her the details of the mission.

"We're trying to coordinate parachute deliveries of ammunition into the mountains from England. Typically, we'd transmit this information in invisible ink, with lemon juice, that gets heated over a flame. But a few other people have been caught recently, so we need to use a new method.

"You'll deliver a new cadenza each week, two nights before the scheduled drop so that the partisans will have time to prepare for it."

Elodie nodded. "I can do that."

"Yes. I'm fully confident that you can," he told her. "Yesterday, another **staffetta** delivered a book to me, which contains the key you will need to create the coded cadenza." He went back to the main room of the store and returned with the book.

"It's here somewhere," he said, leafing

through the pages. He seemed to find what he was looking for midway through.

"Here it is," he said, looking up to her. "It begins on page one hundred ten, and the instructions are written in over the length of every fifteenth page." He took out a piece of paper and began transcribing instructions for her.

"I obviously don't understand anything of what this means, but from one musical person to another, here is what it says: 'When the key signature of the cadenza changes from D major to D minor, that will signal that the coded information is about to begin. The first whole note trill after the key change will indicate where the drop will occur. If it's on an A, the drop will be in Zevio. If it's on an F sharp, it will happen at the top of Monte Comune. On a D, it will happen at Vigasio. Next, the number of sixteenth notes in a chromatic scale will indicate the time of the drop. For example, eleven such notes means the drop will occur at eleven P.M. Lastly, the amount of a series of triplets will indicate the number of ammunition boxes being delivered. Four triplets in a row will indicate four boxes and so on."

"Does this make any sense to you, Elodie?"

She was staring at him, wide-eyed. She could hardly speak. The key for the code was sheer brilliance.

"I understand completely," she said. "Whoever thought of this is a genius."

"Well, when you meet our contact, don't swell his head."

Elodie laughed.

"So we have a great deal of work to do, Elodie. I need you to pick a concerto that typically has room for a cadenza. This will maintain our cover. The selection is up to you, Elodie. You're the expert."

She was already ahead of him, trying to think of the next steps. She knew that even though this encoded cadenza would be nothing like composing a whole concerto or even a smaller étude, it would still require a tremendous amount of concentration.

"Give me a few minutes to think about this, Luca." Elodie closed her eyes and began to contemplate what would be the best choice. There were several she could pick from, but Haydn's Cello Concerto in D major seemed like the best choice. After all, several famous cadenzas had already been written for it over the years.

"I think we should go with Haydn," she finally said, and as she articulated the words, she knew it was the right choice.

"Before we start working on the code, will you play part of it for me?" There was a sweetness to his voice that was new to her.

She looked up and wanted to kiss him. There seemed to be invisible threads that were pulling her toward him. She hated being a girl and having to remain demure and without desire.

"Of course," she said. Although Elodie was feeling anything but shy, she still averted her gaze.

She stood up and went to unlock her cello from its case.

She saw his eyes focus on the instrument, which was shrouded in silk. She smiled, thinking back to the first time her father had revealed the instrument to her. She took her fingers and pulled off the material and reached to lift her cello.

"**Magnifico**," he whispered. The sight of the burnt red, glimmering cello was breathtaking, even to someone who had no musical background.

THE GARDEN OF LETTERS

"It's a Venetian cello," she said, and she again smiled thinking about her father. The men who had beaten him would suffer because she had now found a way to defeat them with the very instrument and bow her father had given her. She loved the poetic justice of that.

Luca remained silent, his gaze fully focused on Elodie and her instrument. She, in turn, directed her energy to tuning her cello and then adjusting its strings. She pulled out her bow and applied her rosin before sliding off the excess with a small cloth from her case.

Now on the edge of her seat, her legs open and her knees supporting the instrument, she looked at Luca one last time before closing her eyes.

In that small fraction of time, from the moment Elodie's eyelids shuttered closed and the moment she lifted her bow, Luca felt something shift between them. He sensed himself being drawn to her, pulled in by the very sound she created by sliding her bow across the strings.

She played with such feeling and emotion that he felt himself grow dizzy and his mind slip away.

The music, as it came, filled the space between them.

She continued to play with her eyes closed. Deeper and deeper she fell into the music, her bow lifting and then sliding over the strings, as the thought of him flowed through her. The piece was not intended to be played as an **appassionata**, but the passion came to her and she embraced it.

Only toward the end, did she open her eyes to see him. His reaction was of a man transformed. His mouth was open. His hair seemed to stand on end. He appeared to be lifting his arm out to reach her, but the limb was suspended in midair.

She returned to finish the finale. Her own hair had become wild and undone. This was the closest two souls could come to making love without touching. Through her music, this most sacred and intimate act, she had transmitted to Luca her own invisible code.

When her bow hit the last chord, her head lifted and her eyes opened wide. Luca was shaking his head from side to side.

"You are extraordinary, Elodie. Beyond

extraordinary. You are love, art, and God all combined into one."

He was the one who finally took the cello from her. After she had completed her playing, she sat there exhausted, as if she had lost herself for several minutes in a trance and had just awakened.

She was breathless. Her fingers were still grasping her bow, and her skirt was wet with perspiration.

"Let me," he said, standing in front of her. He stood there with his white shirt and his well-chiseled face; his hand reached out and fell upon hers. Their skin met at the highest point of her cello, where the neck curled like the top of a wave.

"How lucky I am to hear you play," he said again.

She felt herself warming again. In the darkness of the back room of Luca's bookstore, Elodie's skin was shining so much she could have illuminated the whole room.

⌒

They both knew they had to work with great efficiency because of Elodie's time constraints, and the two of them were fueled by equal amounts of passion to accomplish the task at hand.

Each one wanted to impress the other: Luca with his knowledge of crucial information that needed to be sent, and Elodie with her knowledge of music and composition.

Over the next two hours, Elodie was able to use the key he had been given to create the cadenza. Although it was almost atonal in parts, it would still pass as an acceptable cadenza by a student.

"I don't know how great this will sound. Will I still play it for this person, or can I just hand him the score?"

"It's up to you, Elodie. The guise, should anyone question you, will be that you're arriving for a music lesson, to see if perhaps he is willing to privately tutor you. But it would be impossible for even the most gifted musician to figure out this particular code acoustically, so no matter what, the musical score with the coded cadenza must be handed to him at some point . . ." He cleared his throat. "If this mission is successful, we hope to create codes that don't need the support of a written score."

"I understand," she said. "Anyway, playing it first would cement the credibility of the music lesson, just in case there are any meddling neighbors," she reasoned.

"Yes," he said, smiling. He was impressed with her foresight. She was starting to learn the pattern of one involved in a successful underground mission. Always think ahead. Always try to anticipate the threat before it actually happens.

EIGHTEEN

~~~

Verona, Italy
JULY 1943

On Tuesday afternoon, Elodie arrived at the bookstore, eager to learn the final details of her mission.

Luca appeared anxious when she arrived.

"Finally!" he said. "It feels like I've been waiting for hours to see you."

"Hours?" Elodie glanced at her watch. "I'm perfectly on time."

"You may be on time, but that doesn't stop the fact that there's so much to do."

He placed his hands down on the front counter. The black smudges of newsprint came off on the blotter. He noticed almost immediately the glare of his own fingerprints and quickly wiped them on his oilskin smock.

"Let's go to the back room." He went over to the door, quickly hanging a sign with a clock and adjustable arrows, showing he'd be gone and the shop closed for the next hour.

She led herself to the back room, which was now familiar to her, lifting the curtain and stepping inside. She was seized with excitement as she waited for him.

"You will not go by the name 'Elodie' for this mission," Luca told her. "We have given you a special code name."

Elodie knew that many of the partisans and higher-ranked people went by code names: Rat, Eagle, Fox. She had heard these men referred to during meetings, but who they actually were, she had no idea.

"And what will my name be?" she asked.

He looked at her with intensity. She even thought she saw his eyes narrow and then refocus.

"I've given this a lot of thought and come up with something that I think fits you perfectly: they're beautiful, they're focused, and always precise . . ."

"Well, go ahead then. Tell me."

"Your code name for this mission will be 'Dragonfly.'"

For the next hour, he outlined the plan. He wrote nothing down for her, but he spoke every word slowly, knowing she was more than capable of committing his instructions to memory.

"The man you will be meeting is called the Wolf. He is a retired music teacher in Mantua. He plays both the cello and piano and was a professional before the Great War."

"I wonder if he knows my father . . ."

"You will never ask that of him, Elodie. You are only to divulge your name as Dragonfly when asked. There is no need to tell him your real name and risk your family in these matters."

"You're right; I'm sorry. It's just that the musical world is so small."

"Small, yes. The world itself is small, especially when similar souls tend to gravitate toward one another. But the Wolf is significantly older than your father, and he also lives in Mantua. He lives on 17 Via Cesare Battisti, behind Santa Andrea. You will ring doorbell number three."

Elodie blanched. She wasn't terribly familiar with Mantua. There had been a few excursions to the city for shopping with her mother, but with the strain of wartime, it had been years since they had indulged in such luxury. She had also performed last year at the Teatro Bibiena in a joint effort with Mantua's Instituto Musicale. But she had never traveled there by herself. What she remembered of it was the sight of the city emerging majestically from a shimmering lake and its medieval fortress and stone towers. It was amazing that Mantua, which was only thirty kilometers away from Verona, seemed to her like a different world.

"Show up there tomorrow sometime after lunch. Tell your parents whatever you think you need to, but you'll be bringing your cello so they will not be suspicious if they think you're simply off to practice all day with a friend."

He moved the curtain to pass through, and she was struck by the light suddenly flooding through the room. She pulled up a hand to shield her eyes.

184 ALYSON RICHMAN

Her entire body was rushing with adrenaline. She wondered if he realized that behind her calm countenance, she was a web of live wires.

Elodie only wanted to appear calm and collected for Luca, so that he would feel their mission was in the most capable hands. So she responded to him simply and as succinctly as she could. "Yes, Luca. I understand exactly what I have to do."

Luca looked at her straight in the eyes, and she felt the heat burning off of him onto her own skin.

"Be smart, but above all, be careful," he said to her. She wondered if she was imagining this sensation she felt, the feeling that he didn't want her to go.

"Don't worry, I will." She lifted her cello and began to walk toward the door.

She felt his hand graze her arm and gently hold her flesh for just a second.

"I wanted to say one more thing, Dragonfly . . ."

"Yes," she said. Her eyes were burning now into his.

"Fly back to us safely."

NINETEEN

~~~~~~~

Verona, Italy
JULY 1943

Elodie left early the next morning, telling her parents she would be out all day to practice a quartet with Lena and two other students from school.

Her father sat in his robe at the breakfast table; her mother was in the kitchen getting more coffee.

Just as she was about to leave, her father beckoned her closer. He had always seen himself in his daughter. Her hands were his hands. Her musical ability, too, was from him. And he knew that Elodie had the capacity to keep a secret tucked deep within.

"Elodie," he said. His face was unshaven, but his eyes had a sense of life in them that had been missing since he'd returned from being beaten by the police.

"I want you to be careful . . ." he whispered, leaning into her.

She pulled back from him, startled by his warning.

"Elodie . . . no, do not speak . . ." He quickly turned his head toward the kitchen to make sure Orsina was out of earshot and then whispered the words: "Hasten thoughts on golden wings. Hasten and rest on the densely wooded hills."

It was from Verdi's "Va, Pensiero," the music responsible for his arrest. But the words of the chorus now floated over her like a blessing.

"Papa, I'm only going to   "

"All I did was play my record to protest . . . You were born with far more courage."

Elodie was taken off guard. Her immediate reaction was to deny that what he was insinuating had any truth. But before she had a chance to tell him he was mistaken, her father took a finger to his lip, then pressed it to hers, as if sealing each other to their shared secret.

"A musician always knows what's beneath the text. Let's speak of it no more."

She left the apartment in a hurry, her father's strange blessing still circling in her ears.

She tried to regain her focus. She told herself that, unlike Lena, she was not carrying anything that could incriminate her. She carried all of her instructions in her head.

In her cello case, she carried her instrument and the music she had written with Luca, which contained the encrypted code.

She looked at the clock on the church and noticed she had fifteen minutes to get to the train station. Within an hour, if there were no delays and no random searches, she would be in Mantua. From the city center, she would walk another fifteen minutes, until she found the Wolf's apartment.

At the train station, the Fascist police were examining identity cards. She calmed herself by silently repeating that she was not carrying anything dangerous. There were no bombs hidden in her cello case. Her clothes were not lined with gold coins.

She told herself she was simply a young music student, carrying her cello to a lesson.

At the train platform she stood with the other waiting passengers, her head down and fingers gripping her case. A man behind her tried to make a joke of the largeness of her instrument.

"It's nearly as big as you, darling. Did you buy an extra ticket for it? You better have, if you think you can put it on the seat beside you."

She wondered how to respond. She could tell him she had taken a train many times before with her instrument, and that she hadn't bought an extra ticket for the cello, because it fit quite comfortably on the luggage racks above.

But she decided just to smile back and keep moving.

On board, a policeman checked identity cards. The conductor directed people to the third-class compartments.

"Elodie?" the policeman asked with a smirk. "Is that Italian?"

"The name is French. But, yes, I'm Italian. One hundred percent." She lifted her head and gave him her brightest smile.

She sensed immediately that this was an unexplored power for her. She had never smiled easily, but now she wondered why she had not exploited this simple gesture before.

Within seconds, she noticed a change come over him. He met her gaze and smiled back.

"Well, then, have a nice trip, signorina."

She took her papers back and entered the train car, carefully placing the cello beside her.

In one hour, she would be in Mantua.

She rested her head against the window and felt the rhythm of the locomotive's wheels underneath her. She closed her eyes and began to dream.

Elodie recalled her specific instructions. "Take via Roma. You'll pass by Santa Andrea. Then, make a right at the corner with the shoemaker. The apartment is on Via Cesare Battisti. It's number seventeen. Ring the third doorbell. The Wolf will be expecting you."

She had shaken her head. "The Wolf will be expecting me?" As she said the words, she couldn't help but smile. "Maybe I should wear a little red hood?"

"Very funny, Elodie. But promise me,

you'll just play the coded cadenza for him and then leave."

She smiled. A year ago, if anyone had told her she would be traveling to deliver a message to someone called the Wolf and that she would also find herself attracted to a man who wasn't a musician, she would have said they were crazy. But she had discovered she could change from a young music student to a covert messenger in a matter of weeks, and she found Luca's confusion of all the musical terms charming.

The train had miraculously run on time, but Elodie's body was still seized with the possibility that anything could go wrong. Last year, she had traveled with Lena to perform at the Teatro Bibiena. But they had not traveled alone. Each of their families had accompanied them. They had all taken third-class seats, dressed in their best clothes. The hard seats didn't bother anyone, as the trip took no time at all.

Mantua was quite different from Verona, which had a Roman amphitheater, ancient crypts, and the famous house of Romeo and Juliet. But Mantua was steeped in Renaissance splendor. Surrounded by a moat of water, it emerged like a man-made fortress: salty gray marble and pitted cold stone.

She walked down the street and held her cello to her side so that it was aligned with her body. The instrument's heaviness soothed her, as if it were a shield offering protection. In the July heat, she began to perspire.

In the Piazza Sordello, she paused for a moment and gazed at the huge expanse of sky. Above her, a small army of birds dove through the air and then returned through the peaks of the Palazzo Ducale. Elodie felt her heart soar at the sight of a hundred fluttering wings.

She continued to walk straight, until she passed Santa Andrea; the instructions still engraved in her mind. When she made a left and arrived at the apartment number seventeen in Via Cesare Battisti, she stood for a moment in front of the large wooden door. There was a large, lion-shaped brass knocker in its center.

But she did as she was instructed and ignored the temptation to use it. Instead, she looked to the right of the door, found the third buzzer, and rang the bell.

As Luca had said he would, the Wolf did
not ask who was at the door, but simply
buzzed her in.

There was no elevator inside the building, just a long set of winding stairs that
wrapped through each flight of the building.
She mounted the stairs quietly, lugging her
case, her arm heavy from carrying the instrument so far.

When Elodie arrived at the third-floor
landing, she saw the door was already ajar.

She felt strange entering unannounced.
She placed her cello down on the floor and
knocked at the door.

"I left it open for you," she heard a voice
say from within.

Then, before she had a chance to answer, she heard the voice say flatly, "Please
bring your instrument and come in."

The first thing she is struck by is the sound
of music floating through the rooms. The
music is unfamiliar to her; a piece she cannot recognize. She strains to decipher each
note, searching for a clue as to the composer. But she comes up with nothing ex-

cept the beauty and sadness she hears woven through the notes.

She stands in the hallway not knowing if she should interrupt his playing to announce herself, or if she should continue waiting until he is finished.

Out of respect for the music and the musician, she decides to wait. She concentrates even more intensely on the music he is playing and tries to listen if there is some sort of code locked within it. But the only thing she hears is what she describes as a weeping of notes. A slow unraveling of a heart coming undone.

She stands there waiting in the hallway, imagining the Wolf with a face to match his melancholy playing.

The hallway of the apartment is long and dark. A tall mirror with an elegant table underneath is to Elodie's left.

She catches her reflection in the glass and immediately turns away. She does not want to see herself in her schoolgirl uniform. She does not want her mind to think of herself in childlike terms, but rather as a serious **staffetta** with a mission, someone entrusted to serve an important cause.

She is damp with perspiration from the journey on the train and from carrying her cello several blocks and up the stairs. She takes one of her hands and smoothes her hair and her skirt. She straightens her back. These are all movements she makes in order to counter the rush of adrenaline flooding through her. She takes a deep breath and tries to compose herself in the way she learned years ago as a way to banish her nervousness before a recital.

But this mission is far more important than a recital, and Elodie is fully aware of what's at stake. She forces herself to look again in the mirror, but this time she looks intently at the girl in the school uniform. She wants to make sure that every part of her— even if it is not how she feels—appears fully composed.

The music suddenly ends, and Elodie takes a few steps deeper into the hallway as she hears someone approaching.

"Hello?" She hears a voice from down the hall, as well as the sound of footsteps striking against the marble. "Yes, hello. Thank you for waiting."

Almost as a reflex, Elodie reaches down to retrieve her cello. She pulls it up straight, so it stands tall beside her, only a few inches shorter than her height.

She and her constant wooden companion wait together for the man called Wolf to show himself.

Suddenly he appears. He does not look as she imagined. With his playing, she imagined a small, dark man with somber eyes. But here before her is someone quite different: a tall man with white hair, a face that is both kind and grave.

He is wearing a pale blue shirt and white pants. He doesn't look Italian; his skin is pink, his eyes ice blue. If she had to guess, she would have thought him a Pole or a Russian, but certainly not Italian.

But he speaks to her in Italian. "I have been waiting for you," he says. "What do they call you?" He says these words slowly, as though he's waiting confirmation of her identity.

She cannot take her eyes off of him.

"I am Dragonfly."

A small smile crosses his lips, one that connotes a vague sense of satisfaction with her reply. "Yes, very good," he says and waves his hand for her to follow him. "Please, come this way."

The apartment is like a maze. Elodie follows him down a long hallway, where there are closed French doors. He pushes them open, leading her to a large parlor where she is immediately struck by the floor-to-ceiling windows that bathe the room in light.

There are upholstered chairs in striped silk. The walls are painted a soft coral, the drapes a heavy white silk.

"I have no real coffee," he says apologetically. "Only this awful chicory . . ."

She shakes her head and lifts her hand slightly, as if to apologize. "No, no. I am fine."

"A glass of water, perhaps?"

She considers the offer for a second. She is thirsty, but she doesn't want to accept any overtures of hospitality. She just wants to play the music, hand him the score, and get on the next train home to Verona.

"It's only water," he says, and smiles. Again, she is struck by the blue of his eyes.

"Very well then," she says. "If it's no trouble."

He comes back a few minutes later and hands her a glass.

"So, Dragonfly, are you going to play for me?"

"Yes," she says before letting the warm water run down her throat.

"And you're a cellist, as I am, too. Don't let my poor piano playing fool you." A smile crosses his face. She thinks she notices a flicker of recognition in his eyes. "From one musician to another," it suggests.

"Let's go to the next room. My piano is in there." He takes the glass from her and places it on one of the low tables.

She hesitates for a second and feels her body stiffen. They are like two animals in a cage, every one of their senses heightened as they each try to decipher the other's movements. Her grip on the handle of her cello case tightens, causing her fingers to whiten, and she sees his eyes glance from her face to her hands.

Inside, she chastises herself for exposing her fear to him.

"I am as old as your grandfather, my dear. There is no need to worry."

She does not return his smile, but keeps her face smooth, expressionless.

She cannot place any personal details about him. He does not look Italian, though he speaks the language fluently, and no object in the room reveals any particular background.

She hears the sound of his words in her head and tries to place his accent. But she realizes almost immediately why she can't: It's because he has none.

Immediately, she is struck by the intense color that saturates the room. The walls are painted peacock blue. There is a white marble fireplace to the left with a gilded mirror above, and to the right, a black grand piano. Small sofas flank the exterior wall. Underneath her feet, there is a carpet that looks worthy enough for a pasha.

"My favorite room," he says. "I'm looking forward to hearing you play."

He pulls out a chair for her and she sits down, placing her cello case at her feet.

As she looks up, she notices a small painting in a gilded frame above the piano. It's of a young girl with a red kerchief over her head. Her eyes are dark and piercing; her gaze is intense and unflinching.

"The painting," she says, motioning to the canvas on the wall. "Who is the artist?"

"Silvestro Lega," he says. He smiles. "Do you like it?"

"Yes," she says as she kneels down to open her case. "I like it very much."

He smiles. "I bought it for my wife many years ago."

"Your wife? Does she play, too?"

"Yes. But her real strength lay in her composing." He points to a large desk in the corner of the room covered with papers. "Her mind was a complicated labyrinth. Inside that desk is what I have left of the trappings of it."

Elodie remains quiet, unsure of how to react.

"Well," the Wolf suddenly says, his voice breaking the awkward silence between them. "I shouldn't have distracted you with such personal details. You have come to play for me, so let's hear it."

He sits down not at his wife's desk, but on a cane chair he pulled away from the wall.

"Please," he says, politely. "Whenever you're ready."

Elodie opens the lid of her case. Her fingers reach to find the instrument from the silk and velvet that protect it.

She proceeds to pull out her instrument, just as she has done so many times before. Her hand reaches for the neck, while the other one lifts the body. Elodie turns around to face this man they call the Wolf, and suddenly she sees a wave of shock come over his face. It is not the expression she expected to see.

"Your cello . . ." he stammers. His voice has suddenly lost its softness.

"Yes . . ."

"Where did you get that? How can you be playing on a Gofriller?"

"A Gofriller?"

"Yes." He is now straight in front of her, his hands caressing the instrument between them. Elodie feels her entire body shudder as if she is violated, even though his hands never touch her skin.

"Yes, a Matteo Gofriller. Where did you get this cello?"

She is not prepared for this barrage of questions from him. This was not in the plan she discussed with Luca. She is starting to grow faint, not knowing how much to reveal.

"It was a gift from my father on my seventeenth birthday. All I know is that it's Venetian." Her voice cracks. "Like my mother . . ."

His blue eyes now look up to her. The color strikes her as almost glacial.

She feels a wave come over her. She wants to push his hands away from the instrument, but he continues to map it with his hands.

"I have played this instrument once before. More than ten years ago, not far from this apartment. In Mantua." He stammers again, as if uttering the name of a ghost, both sacred and haunting: "Your cello once belonged to Enrico Levi."

"I don't know the name," she says.

"The family packed up and left just as things were getting bad here. Sold everything they had. Smart Jews, they were." He shakes his head. "I wish Levi had sold it to me instead of your father."

He steps back and looks at the instrument one more time. "Yes, I'm sure of it. I'm sure it's Levi's Gofriller cello." She hears the Wolf click his tongue before shaking his head.

"Such a young girl playing a Gofriller. Truly unbelievable . . . Remarkable, actually." He looks up at her and he smiles. "Have I frightened you in my excitement at seeing your cello?"

"No," she lies. "Not at all."

"To think it's been hidden away with you since Levi left . . ." He considers the fact for a moment before smiling. "It's rather amazing, actually. This little girl arriving here with a priceless instrument. Completely unaware she carries something of enormous value."

"I know it's valuable," she interjects. "My father told me it was a rare Venetian cello."

"Don't worry, Dragonfly. I'm glad you have the instrument. At least, I'm sure I will be once I hear you play it. It's a good thing you've kept it hidden away and tucked from view." He laughs. "After all, the death of beauty is overexposure. Everybody wants a glimmer of something kept secret, the feeling they alone have uncovered something exquisite and rare.

"Women are the same, Dragonfly. Don't ever reveal too much. That's good advice to follow. Even after this bloody war is over."

"I don't think I'll have that problem."

"Good," he answers. "Let's get started then. I'm anxious to hear you play."

Now he stands against the wall, the painting in the gilded frame like a flag above his left shoulder.

She takes a deep breath and sits on the

edge of the chair, places the instrument between her legs, and takes up her bow.

"Shall I strike the A on the piano for you?"

She nods her head. "Yes, that would be helpful."

She tries to regain her composure and focus by tuning her instrument. She positions her ear close to the string and plucks. She makes a few slight adjustments, then looks directly at the Wolf.

"I'm ready to begin."

"**Prego**," he says. "Please."

Elodie closes her eyes and begins to play the Haydn cello concerto.

The music is like a trance to her. Elodie's body stretches and elongates as she pulls her bow against the strings. Her cello rests against her chest like a shield; her arms are like wings. The elbows rising and falling, like a bird about to take flight.

As she plays the cadenza, she lifts her head for the first time to gaze at the Wolf's reaction.

The notes sound foreign and vaguely dissonant to her. Strange, almost modern in their lack of a familiar pattern.

Soon she finds herself approaching the

most important part of her playing. The first triple-stopped whole note starts on A flat, followed by twelve sixteenth notes.

With the key shifting and the tempo accelerating at times, she performs with such precision, to make sure everything is articulated just as Luca has instructed her to do. She cannot help but think of the irony of the situation. A cadenza is supposed to showcase the individual creativity and skill of the musician, but this one is only delivering a message from people whom she's never even met. Her sole purpose is to deliver the content.

After she finishes the cadenza, which is brief and furious, each one of the notes of the chromatic scale articulated in rapid succession, she dips back into the end of the concerto. It is like a wave that has crested and then fallen. She finishes slowly out of respect for the music.

She lifts her head and opens her eyes.

The Wolf looks not at her head, but straight ahead. At the door that is left slightly open. She can see that he is thinking about what he has just heard. That he is decoding something that has importance and relevance to not just him, but for many others as well.

She pulls the cello out from between her legs and gently puts it back in the case. She can feel her hair has become wild, and she smoothes it back with her palms, wishing she had some pins to twist it up and back.

He shakes his head, as if to commit the cadenza to memory before speaking. "That was very interesting, my dear, on many different levels." He pauses. "But I'd say we were lucky Papa Haydn wasn't in the audience to hear that."

She fidgets slightly, wondering if he is commenting on her playing or the atonal quality of the cadenza.

"May I have the score?" he asks her. He reaches his arm out toward her.

She had not used it to play but bends down and pulls it from the open case, her hand shaking ever so slightly as she hands it over to him.

He takes it and walks to his desk, sliding it into the top drawer.

"It wasn't meant to be beautiful," she says, in whose defense she does not know.

Afterward, he walks closer to her and his glacially pale eyes stare straight into hers.

"I am joking, my dear Dragonfly," he says, smiling. "In times like these, we need a little levity every now and then.

"Your interpretation of the rest of the concerto was superb."

She smiles and is surprised by the sense of relief that floods through her, not knowing if it's because her mission is now complete or because an accomplished musician has given her a morsel of praise.

"Thank you, sir," she says. As she stands up with her cello and scans the room once more, she sees there is a composition on the piano.

She can't help but be curious. "May I ask what you were playing when I arrived?"

She notices his eyes moisten slightly.

"It was the last thing my wife composed," he says. "She was in Paris when they arrested her."

"She was in the Resistance?" Elodie said the word in the quietest whisper.

"No," he says flatly. "She and Enrico Levi shared something in common besides just music. They both were Jews."

TWENTY

~

Verona, Italy
JULY 1943

Elodie returned home that evening to her parents' apartment, exhausted both physically and mentally from her mission. She merely picked at her pasta and told her parents that she wasn't feeling well, and that she might be coming down with a cold.

Her father did not eat his dinner, either. He lifted his head to look at her several times during the meal. She could feel his eyes on her, and their weight was not one of judgment or suspicion, but one that was harder to place, a silent acknowledgment offered only in the blinking of an eye.

Orsina, however, was not attuned to this silent language that flowed between her daughter and husband. She was tired and worn, preoccupied with all the political unrest surrounding them. Her once-idyllic household of music and simple routine had been replaced with the shadow of uncertainty. Her husband no longer had any strength and spent most of his hours in bed. She sensed her daughter was also increasingly preoccupied, and feared she was spending too much time in places she did not know and could not see.

After she cleared the dishes and put everything away, Orsina heated the kettle and started to fill the bath. The sound of the flowing water immediately calmed her. She undressed and slipped into the tub.

The arrival of her mother's singing floated into the walls of Elodie's bedroom and soothed her as well. She closed her eyes, and the day's events unraveled in her mind. She saw the long corridor of the Wolf's apartment, the room with the peacock blue walls, and the painting of the girl in the red kerchief. She could hear the notes of her cadenza sharp and executed with precision. But it was the music the Wolf had been playing when she first stepped into the apartment that filled the rest of her head. She fell asleep thinking of those haunting notes, and wondering about the woman who wrote them.

In the morning, Elodie offered to do the grocery shopping.

"Mamma, give me your list."

"My list means nothing. It's not what I want to buy, it's what do they have? If there are eggs, get eggs. If there's flour, get as much as they will give you. Here, let me get my rations card."

Orsina went into the next room and handed Elodie their weekly ration card. She also reached into her pocket and gave her daughter what few coins she had. "This may be enough. If not, be sweet to Flavio and see if he'll extend our credit for another week."

Elodie felt a wave of anxiety rush over her. "Mamma, maybe . . ."

"Stop. As soon as your father can return to work, things will get better. He just couldn't do his private lessons like he does every summer. But school will start in a month and he's insisting he will be well enough to

return by then." She squeezed Elodie's
shoulder. "Enjoy the last days of summer.
School will be starting for you, too, before
you know it."

Elodie walked outside the apartment and
headed straight to the little shop on Corso
S. Anastasia, where her mother bought
most of her groceries, like grains and the
other provisions. They hadn't had any meat
in weeks, so there was no use asking her
mother if she should get some. At the dairy
next door, she would bring the milk tin and
have it filled with the one-quarter liter allowed.

It felt good to devote herself to an hour
or so of simple errands for her mother. It
helped alleviate her guilt from deceiving her
parents over the past few weeks. It was a
relief to do this sort of menial, easy work
compared to the more complicated coding
for Luca. Here, all she had to do was wait
in line, rip off a coupon, get a loaf of stale
bread and a bit of coffee and sugar, and
come home. She let her mind relax for a
moment, enjoying the simplicity of standing in line with the other women, most of
them matrons, including the mothers of
some of her old classmates.

"Elodie!" Katia Segreti's mother chimed when she entered the store. "I haven't seen you in ages!"

Elodie smiled. "How are you? And how is Katia . . ."

"Good. Good. Well, as good as anyone can be during all this chaos. She got married in May. A good boy, Carlo Prescutti . . . do you know him?"

Elodie said she didn't. But, in reality, she knew him to be a bully and a notorious Blackshirt.

"Please send her my congratulations," Elodie said. Her eyes began to scan the shelves to see if there was anything she could bring home to her mother. But the store offered so little to buy. A can of tomato paste. A tin of sardines. A sack of moldy white onions.

Elodie waited until Signora Segreti had finished with her purchases and left the store before asking the shop owner to extend them additional credit.

Flavio was a kind man and said he could extend it by another week. "School's starting soon, eh?" he asks her. "I bet you're excited."

"Yes, yes. It will be good for both my

father and me to get back to our music,"
she told him.

"Give him and your mother my best," he
said. "I'm sorry I don't have more on the
shelves these days, but compared to our
boys out there fighting . . ."

"I know, I know," she answered. "We have
to be grateful we have anything at all."

They said good-bye, and Elodie went
next door to get what she could from the
dairy.

On the way home, she appraised her
bounty. In her bag, she had three eggs, four
deciliters of milk, one kilogram of flour, and
a sack of dried beans.

When she got home, her father was still in
his bathrobe. Her mother was standing behind him, rubbing his temples gently. There
was a grave look of worry on Orsina's face.

"What's wrong?" Elodie asked as she
placed the groceries on the table.

"It's his headaches. Your father says they
grow worse with each day."

"Can't we call the doctor for him?"

"I have! Who do you think visits us when
you go out to practice with your friend Lena
every afternoon?"

Elodie walked over to both of them. She touched her father's cheek softly with the back of her hand.

"I hate to see you suffer so much, Papa."

"Don't worry, my **tesoro**," he answered, his voice barely more than a whisper. He reached for her hand and kissed it softly.

"I'd ask you to play for me, but I can barely hear anything at the moment."

"I understand. How about I just sit here with you? Mother can rub your temples and I can massage your hands."

"No, no. Your mother can handle me by herself. Take your cello and go practice with Lena. I know the two of you have been working so hard these past few weeks. I'm proud of you and your dedication . . ." He managed a small, knowing smile through his obvious discomfort.

Elodie looked at her mother to see if she should in fact leave them alone.

"Your father is right, Elodie. You've already helped me by doing the shopping. Go practice with Lena. Just be home by dinner so I don't worry."

Elodie kissed both her parents on the

cheek and left with her cello. But she didn't go to find Lena. She went straight away to the bookstore, to see Luca.

When she arrived at Luca's bookstore, he nearly leaped up from behind the front counter.

"Elodie! I've been hoping all day that you'd stop by!"

She smiled.

He scanned the room. There was a lone customer in the back, looking at some books on naval history. Luca motioned with his eyes that they would need to wait to go into the back room until this customer had left the store.

In the meantime, Elodie put down her cello and took advantage of the opportunity to browse the shelves. She had hardly spent any time in the main storefront, as both the group's underground meetings and her time alone with Luca were always spent in the back room. But now she could see how charming the store really was. Around the perimeter were tall, wooden shelves bearing handsome leather volumes, and the light was soft and welcoming.

There was also something about the

smell of bookshops that was strangely comforting to her. She wondered if it was the
scent of ink and paper, or the perfume of
binding, string, and glue. Maybe it was the
scent of knowledge. Information. Thoughts
and ideas. Poetry and love. All of it bound
into one perfect, calm place. The shelves
lined with anything from Rome's ancient
history to photographs of archeological digs
in South America. Luca had stacked love
sonnets by Lord Byron against Francesco
Petrarch's unrequited love poems to his
muse, Laura.

And behind all of this bounty of knowledge and passion was a room that only a
rare few knew contained even more information. Like a clock whose dials and intricate mechanisms remain hidden from view,
Luca's bookstore was more than met the
eye.

Elodie looked at Luca with great admi-
ration as he gave the customer his change
and tucked his book inside a crisp brown
bag.

"**Ciao . . . Mille grazie**," he said politely,
as the man tipped his hat and waved good-
bye.

Luca walked to the door and switched

over the sign to signal he'd be back in a few minutes.

"Let's go," he said to her. "I'm so glad you came."

She took her cello with her and sat down at the table where, only two days ago, they had crafted the code and she played for him for the first time.

"Well, little Dragonfly," he said. "You accomplished your mission with great success! Our contact said you delivered our message, and also played superbly for the Wolf."

She smiled. "I felt like I didn't breathe the entire day yesterday." Blood was rushing through her, as the exhilaration of being so close to Luca and also hearing him say she had done a masterful job made her feel more alive than ever.

"Well, now you have some time to relax," he continued. "But in two days, we'll need to send him another message using the same code. I know school will be starting for you soon, but this second message is just as important."

"Whatever you need, I'll do my best to make the mission a success."

"Now, we must pray all goes well for the men in the mountains," he said. "I feel guilty that I'm safe down here in my little store while my brother and his men prepare to fight in the wilderness . . . And who knows what will happen once the weather turns . . ."

Elodie shook her head. She tried her best to sound like a good soldier. Solemn and serious, though inside her mind was spinning with other thoughts. She felt that her mission had made her more animalistic in a way. As if she now moved to pulses and rhythms that did not have an acoustical sound, but were sensed instead through instinct.

"Yes, we must consider ourselves lucky and pray that the autumn will not bring too much rain nor the winter too much snow." Her words sounded wooden and came out flat. Quickly, Elodie tried to light a bit of fire to her words.

"I suppose a bookseller's job is not affected by the weather."

Luca let out a small laugh. "Indeed, not."

"Was the store your father's?"

"Oh no!" Luca threw his head back and laughed again. "My father? He couldn't even read. Neither of my parents could. Nor could I until the age of ten. I actually taught myself to read."

Elodie looked surprised. "Really?" Suddenly the room felt bright as an energy was ignited between them.

"Yes." Luca nodded. "No one in my family, not even I, ever went to school. The fact is, I'm the son of a blacksmith. There were no books in my house. My father knew how to work only with his hands. My three brothers and I all helped him. We swept the floor and chopped wood, and my older brothers helped stoke the fire."

Luca cleared his voice.

"One day, when I was ten years old, a customer came into my father's shop with a book tucked under his arm. My father told him the iron set he had ordered for his fireplace would be ready shortly; he just needed another twenty minutes for it to cool.

"The man's answer startled me. Typically, customers got angry when their orders were not immediately ready. But this man seemed almost happy with the news.

" 'Twenty minutes, eh?' he said. 'Great. I'll just sit outside and read a bit.' The man tapped on his book and walked to the bench outside my father's workshop and I followed him.

"I watched as he sat down, looked up at the sun for a moment, and then opened his book on his lap.

"'What's the matter, little fellow?' he asked me. I was covered in soot, as my brothers and I always were.

"'Nothing,' I said shyly. He seemed to study me for a second, perhaps sensing the curiosity in my eyes, peeking out of the mask of filth, before returning to his book.

"I crouched by the doorpost for twenty minutes, watching as his face changed with every page.

"I tell you, Elodie, it was like watching an actor in a movie. The words he was reading made him smile, even laugh out loud on occasion. Then a few pages later, his face became serious and grave. His brow wrinkled, and his eyes were fixated on every sentence. Then, when my father called out that his order was ready, the man couldn't even respond until he had finished reading his chapter. That's how taken he was by the book's content.

"I remember that day as if it were yesterday because it was then and there I vowed to myself that I, too, would learn to read. I guess you could say I realized from an early age that there was a code locked inside each book, and I wanted to be the one to learn it."

"But then how did you come to own this store? You're so young!" Elodie gushed.

"Well, you have to understand, I wasn't busy like the rest of the children with any obligations of school. Once I started teaching myself to read, through mostly discarded newspapers, I saved all my money from odd chores to buy my first book. And eventually after several months, my collection grew. I then began to trade books with dealers. By the time I was fifteen, I had enough to sell books on the street from a cart. Five years later, having combed all the flea markets for secondhand books, I found a handful of rare editions that I got for a song and resold them for a bounty. I had a friend, Pelizzato, who used to trade books with me; we positioned our carts side by side in Milan. Eventually both of us had enough to open our first shops. He went to Venice and named his La

Toletta . . . and I started Il Gufo here in Verona."

Elodie was amazed. "That's incredible," she said. "You're a self-made man at the age of what, twenty-two?"

"Twenty-four," he said, smiling. He straightened his spine and pushed back his shoulders. "And I've cleaned up, too . . ." He patted his cheeks with both hands. "No soot! Just some occasional ink."

"And now instead of unlocking codes, you're creating them," Elodie said.

"Yes. Exactly. And we need to write another."

"I only have until dinnertime," she said. "Then I need to get home."

"Well then," he said looking at the clock, "let's get to work."

Just like before, the two of them worked side by side. Elodie now knew the key by heart, so it was easy to write the coded cadenza once she knew the number of sixteenth notes needed to relay the amount of guns being stockpiled, and the particular placement of the triple-stopped whole note so that she could inform the intelligence scouts of the location.

She worked deftly and efficiently. Once the code was written, she stood up and pulled out her cello.

"Let's hear how it sounds. I don't want to completely offend the Wolf's sensibilities again . . ."

It was strange how things had changed between the two of them. The first time Elodie played for Luca, she remembered the pangs of embarrassment and nervousness flooding through her body, before she was able to surrender to the music. Now, it just seemed natural to play for him.

She wasn't sure if it was the fact that he had just revealed something about his past to her that made her feel more connected, or perhaps it was their shared connection to creating the important codes. But regardless of the reason, this time felt different to her.

She picked up her cello and settled into her chair. In two seconds, her bow was at the strings, her body was like a dancer electrified. The music. The code. Her playing. She radiated like a starburst from her cello.

TWENTY-ONE

Verona, Italy
JULY 1943

Elodie's second mission to the Wolf did not evoke the same fear in her. She knew the route, she knew approximately how long it would take her, and she knew that the man was far less intimidating than his code name.

The day after she finished the code with Luca, Elodie woke up, tucked her white blouse into her navy skirt, and told her parents she would be out rehearsing with Lena, taking her cello with her.

She moved quickly and efficiently through the streets. She looked at no one. She made her face expressionless. The only thing she focused on was getting to the station to catch the early morning train to Mantua.

When she arrived at the Wolf's apartment building, she found the main door ajar. She walked inside and took the stairs to his apartment. Elodie placed down her cello case and knocked at the door. One minute passed; she remained outside. She pressed her ear to the door to see if he was lost in his piano playing, but again there was nothing but silence. Elodie knocked again.

She didn't know if she should remain on the landing to the apartment or return home. She decided to knock one more time. Shortly after, she heard movement. A shuffling of footsteps. Then a crash, like the sound of a vase falling to the ground.

"Hello? Who's there?" It was the sound of the Wolf's voice.

"I've come for my lesson," she said. She thought it unwise to announce herself as Dragonfly and call attention to herself, should any of the neighbors be listening.

Suddenly the door unlocked and the Wolf stood there, looking far shabbier than at their first meeting.

"Please excuse my appearance," he said, smoothing his shirt down with his hands. The top button of his chemise had been left undone, allowing a small tuft of white hair to peek through.

"I only got back last night and need to leave tonight again, so I'm sorry that I'm not better prepared for you."

She smiled. "Don't even mention it. I usually close my eyes anyway when I play."

"Yes. Indeed." He clasped his hands. "Let's hear you play then. I'm anxious to hear what you have in store today," he said. "Come with me."

They walked down the long corridor, where a shattered ceramic vase lay on the floor. "I'll get to that later," he said as he shuffled by. "I hate to lose any time while you're here."

"Thank you," she said as she stepped again into the peacock-blue music room.

"Same position as last time, then?" He went to get a chair for her. She scanned the room, glancing again at the painting in the golden frame above his piano.

The Wolf turned his head and saw the line of her gaze.

"You like that painting, don't you? I

noticed you staring at it when you were last here."

"Yes," she said blushing.

"I bought that painting many years ago, for my wife's birthday." He slid the chair underneath her, and she sat down.

"It's beautiful," she said. She reached down to unfasten her case.

"Not so beautiful, thankfully, that Goering wanted it. Mussolini's henchmen came here in '38 and took inventory of everything I had. I have friends who had Titians and Tintorettos, and all that was taken for Goering's personal art collection. I'm lucky I had given my wife something too bourgeois for his taste."

He smiled again as he turned his back to her and looked for a chair for himself. "Not that it doesn't have value. You could probably sell that today for a tidy sum—as you could, your cello . . ."

She pulled out her cello and brought it to her chest.

"Enrico Levi's Gofriller's cello. Unbelievable."

His eyes were firmly focused on her, and Elodie tried not to show her unease.

The Wolf let out a little laugh. "Don't

worry, Dragonfly, I'm not going to steal your cello away from you . . . It makes me happy that it's in the hands of such a gifted musician."

She knew enough not to smile. Even in her young age, she knew not to soften under the easy words of a man's flattery.

"Levi was a kind man. A generous soul . . . He was Mantua's best dealer when it came to fine, rare instruments. His showroom was just a few meters from the town center. A small door that once you entered, you could smell the scent of varnish and wood. Violins hung from the ceiling. Bows were pegged to the wall. Behind the glass, he kept his cherished Stradivarius violin. I once was at a salon where his son played the Strad and he played your Gofriller. To hear the two of them play! My God, angels were in the room that night!"

Elodie could almost see and hear the music wafting from the salon room he described. And, as much as she wanted to appear unmoved, she couldn't help but smile.

"I wish I could have been there," she said softly. Her hands, without her knowing it, were still covering her cello protectively. "I

suppose you don't think I do my cello justice," she said to him.

"No, I don't think that at all . . ." He narrowed his eyes slightly, as if to absorb her
into his mind completely. "Something about
you reminds me of my wife. She was older
than you when I first met her, of course. But
she had that same gaze. That fire underneath her eyes. So focused she was . . ."
His voice cracked slightly. She heard him
take a breath as if to fortify himself.

"When was the last time you heard from
her?"

"It's been over six months," he said. "I
begged her not to leave Italy. She was arrested in France trying to help her parents
and was then deported—I'm told to somewhere in Poland."

Elodie winced. She had heard from
Zampieri that there were members of the
French Resistance who were arrested by
the police and sent to work camps in Poland. No one ever heard a shred of information about them after that. It was a big,
vast hole.

"I'm sorry," she managed to say. "I heard
you play her music the last time I was here,

and it lingered inside my head for days. That's how good it was."

"She was a talent beyond words," he replied. "She played three instruments, traveled throughout Europe to perform, and composed much of her own music. I was a pedestrian next to her."

Elodie was about to offer another morsel of sympathy for him, but he suddenly grew conscious of the fact he was revealing too much of himself.

"Well, that's enough of me bellyaching to you. You are here for a reason, Dragonfly. What am I listening to today?"

"Boccherini," she said. "Cello Concerto in B flat Major."

"Boccherini, eh? I prefer Haydn."

She laughed. "Me, too, but it's a good piece for a cadenza."

"Well, begin," he said. He pulled up the pleats to his pants and sat down.

Elodie lifted her bow, closed her eyes, and regained her focus. She forced everything he had just said to her out of her mind.

The music was lighter and faster than the Haydn concerto she had played the last time. This time when she shifted the key into the cadenza and did the triple-stopped whole notes, her bow plucked like a fiddler.

There was a strange levity to the sound of the notes, which she knew contrasted with the importance of the encoded message.

She saw the Wolf's eyebrows lift when she got to the cadenza, his head nodding slightly as if giving his approval to the plan.

When she was done, she handed him the score.

TWENTY-TWO

~

Portofino, Italy
NOVEMBER 1935

As Angelo prepared to report for duty in Ethiopia, Dalia's pregnancy was confirmed. She had missed two periods, and terrible bouts of morning sickness soon overtook her. Angelo's mother brought her simple broths and loaves of bread to soothe her poor stomach, but Dalia could keep none of it down.

She wanted to enjoy as much time as possible with Angelo before he left, but she could hardly walk without vomiting. Pale and exhausted, she spent most of her time in bed. To be close to her, Angelo brought novels to her bedside.

The sound of him reading was still a sweet melody to her. He always kept his hand on top of hers, only taking it away when he needed to turn a page. Sometimes she would close her eyes and try to envision the characters with her and Angelo's faces. Every romantic kiss depicted was one of theirs. Any mention of a small child evoked images of the baby who grew inside her womb. She imagined being just like the maternal character in a story, tying the strings of the embroidered baptism cap, or cradling the baby in her arms.

She was so grateful to have this educated man who had brought her into the magical world of books.

And now that she could read with great fluidity, the words were no longer an impossible code she could not understand. She had learned so many things she never knew existed through the novels he brought to her bedside.

She particularly adored the latest serialized novels in **libri gialli**, which introduced her to the first translations of authors from abroad, their stories exposing her to en-

THE GARDEN OF LETTERS   233

tirely different landscapes beyond her small fishing village.

"You will never be lonely with a book at your side," he told her as he tucked his blooming wife into bed. From the collar of her nightdress, her breasts, now slightly swollen, peeked through. He had to do everything in his power to control himself, as he knew how fragile she was in the early weeks of pregnancy.

"**Limonina**," he whispered to her. "I think we've had enough reading today. Why don't you try and get some sleep?" He took his hand away from hers and placed both of his palms on her belly. She wasn't far enough along for him to feel even a soft bump let alone a kick, but just the thought of their baby growing inside her warmed his entire body.

"I'm going to miss you beyond words," she said, tears filling her eyes.

"I will write you every day, just as I did when I was in medical school. Did I break my promise then?"

"No," she said. "You sometimes wrote me twice a day, didn't you?" A small smile found its way to her lips and she giggled.

"Yes, so now that you're my wife, I will probably write you three times a day!"

"I can paper our bedroom with your letters," she said wistfully.

He had no idea that she would take this sentence to heart. That would come much later, only after he had returned.

Angelo left for Ethiopia the following week with little more than an army bag and his doctor's kit. In the latter, which he had purchased just out of medical school, he carried two sets of scissors, a roll of tape, a stethoscope, and a small hammer. He knew the doctors would be given more supplies once they set up camp, but he felt he needed to carry this bag with him to give him greater credibility with the soldiers.

Dalia had promised herself she wouldn't cry when Angelo left. But seeing him standing there in his army uniform, grinning at her, tore her apart. And even though she was still weak from the morning sickness, she took all the energy she had inside of her and ran to embrace him one last time.

When his first letter arrived a few weeks later, she felt as if she had stepped back in time and was still the young girl waiting for a letter to arrive from her love, away at medical school. But now she was a married woman with a child growing inside her, and the letter felt more precious than ever to her. She studied his careful penmanship on the envelope and the colorful stamps from Africa. She took her finger to the strokes of ink and tried to feel his energy coursing through. After a few moments to savor the anticipation, Dalia took the envelope to their bedroom, sat down on the coverlet, and began to read slowly.

My dearest Dalia, my limonina,

Every day, every hour, I think of you. We have just arrived in Tripoli, and will be moving toward Ethiopia in the next few weeks. I am keeping my spirits up thinking about you and our baby.

I have been keeping busy tending to small wounds, blisters, and infections. The men in my unit are an interesting bunch from all over Italy. My bunkmate, Carlo, also has a pregnant wife. We cross off the days on our calendars to reinforce that we are both one day closer to returning home.

**I go to sleep, darling, dreaming of
you. I imagine your belly growing
bigger every day, and I wish I could
place my palm on your skin and feel
not just one heart, but two.**

I love you.
Angelo

Dalia held the letter in her hands and
closed her eyes. She could feel his presence through his words, and the distance
between them fell away. In that rare moment of peace, Dalia suddenly knew exactly
what she was going to do. She would make
her passing remark to Angelo a reality. She
stood up and placed the letter on the bed.
Then, with newfound energy and a sheer
will of determination, Dalia went into the
kitchen in search of some flour and water.

The kitchen had many ceramic bowls. Dalia eyed each of them before settling on one
no bigger than the size of her palm. With a
few deft steps, she made a simple paste
out of some flour and water, stirring until the
consistency was pliable and sticky. Then

with a small pastry brush in hand, she returned to the bedroom.

Dalia knew immediately where in the room she would begin. She kneeled on the mattress, and there just above her nightlight, pressed Angelo's letter onto the wall, its back now sticky with glue.

Every day, Dalia waited for a new letter to arrive. When she had finished reading it, she took scissors and carefully cut around the edges to create small, unusual shapes. Sometimes, two or three of them arrived in one day. Each one she cut and then glued, so that eventually, a beautiful vine of love letters grew along her wall.

After several months, she had nearly covered the bedroom walls. She made small bursts of clouds with some of the letters and even a patch of flowers to accompany the vines. But she still left a few distinct pockets within the walls and ceiling, as if these were the moments of breath or heartbeat, that rested between them like two sleeping souls separated by the continents. In these patches of space, she took a brush and dabbed in bits of mica dust from the crushed stones of her village of San Fruttuoso, the one she kept in a jar beside her bed.

The bedroom was her special secret, for Dalia closed its door whenever family came to check in on her. She instead always received visitors on the terrace or in the little dining room near the kitchen.

Dalia was treated like a queen by everyone around her. To all those who gazed upon her, she was a beautiful woman with a life blooming inside her. She was told not to lift anything or strain herself in any way. If she expressed a craving, it was accommodated almost as soon as the mere suggestion of the food came from her lips. If she mentioned a cannoli, there would be an entire tray for her the following morning. If she wanted chicken, it was promptly prepared three different ways for her liking.

The coastal superstitions also applied in full force. No one was allowed to touch her face, for fear it would cause the baby to have an unseemly birthmark on the same place. And an amulet was waved in front of her belly to predict the child's sex.

She had seen this attentiveness to pregnant women throughout her own childhood.

It enabled Dalia to spend the day doing as she pleased. She spent a few minutes each day pasting Angelo's most recent letter and also enjoyed crocheting with her mother-in-law for the newborn baby's clothes or helping her with the cooking for the extended family.

Her most cherished part of the day, however, was once she retired to her bedroom for the evening. There she felt as though she were reconnecting with Angelo, even though he was now thousands of miles away. She savored lying on her bed and seeing his words everywhere. She knew if she rolled to her right, she could read his first letter, which was now just above the discussion of his travels and days in the desert. The letters near her headboard talked about a boy who had come to live in the camp and had become a special friend to Angelo. To the left of her bed was a poem he had written, one that never ceased to bring tears to her eyes:

You sleep with life inside you, your brightness illuminated in your eyes. I dream of your face, your smile, the clasp of your hand.

You are the waters between us, gentle,
   your own harmonious tide.
I am in the clouds, the wind that
   kisses you every night
A whisper of breath that hovers just
   above your sleeping lids.

By the last month of her pregnancy, she had papered all four walls of the room with six months' worth of Angelo's words. Dalia looked up at the ceiling and decided to decorate that as well. With her taut stomach now as large as a dome, she slowly made her way onto a ladder and began to glue Angelo's latest letters on the ceiling. She knew it was dangerous, so she moved as carefully and as slowly as she could. When she had also filled the ceiling, Dalia felt a sense of completion that welled inside her and fed both her own spirit and that of the baby. For all she had to do now was lie in her bed and look to any part of the room and there was Angelo's love. Written as if it were torn pages from a novel, spread like wings across every inch of their room.

In Ethiopia, daily life was more brutal than Angelo had let on in his letters to Dalia. The

camp he was stationed in was several
hundred miles outside Addis Ababa, in the
middle of the desert. The air was hot and
the dust storms were brutal on the men's
eyes. Although he had only done a bit of
surgery when he was in medical school,
these skills were quickly and repeatedly
put to use, as removing bullets and shrap-
nel kept him busy. Men were carried in on
stretchers with their flesh shattered from
the impact of bullets. He learned through
trial and error how far to dig, or how much
morphine they could spare. On the days
when supply shipments were delayed, the
men were strapped down and forced to
chew on a strip of leather while he ex-
tracted the bullet.

He rarely left the camp, and spent most
of his days in the surgical tent.

They were a motley group of men. As
most of them were uneducated, they at first
kept their distance from Angelo, thinking his
advanced degree and medical training
made him different from them. But over the
weeks, the close quarters of their cots, the
poor food, and their mutual longing for their
wives and girlfriends helped forge a cama-
raderie among all the men. Nicknames were

soon doled out. But out of respect, everyone always called him **Dottore** Angelo.

One day, two months into their encamp-
ment, there was a call for Angelo from one
of the soldiers.

"Dottore! Dottore!" Tancredi cried out
for him. Angelo sped outside the tent to discover a tall, emaciated African carrying a
boy in his arms.

The man could not have weighed more
than a hundred pounds. He carried his son,
equally famished, like a broken kite frame.
The skin on the boy's torso was as tight as
stretched canvas. His white bandages were
soaked brown with blood. The ebony of
both father and son's skin was camouflaged
by a thick coating of body paint, and from
underneath the stripes of pigment, the father's eyes were dark and wet like river
stone.

Both Tancredi and Angelo ran out to meet
the man, who collapsed as the others
reached him, the boy's body sliding weight-
lessly to the ground.

"Help me lift him," Angelo ordered Tancredi, and together they raised the boy onto
the stretcher that two other men had quickly
brought to the scene.

"We'll need to turn him over," Angelo instructed. They flipped him onto his back and the boy let out a small, muffled groan.

With deft hands Angelo placed one hand on the boy's scapula, and with his other hand, traced his finger across the bullet wound. A grape-sized entryway into the flesh of his shoulder was now crusted with blood and pus.

"Infection has already set in," Angelo said, more to himself than to Tancredi. He touched the boy's forehead. He was burning with fever.

"Go get the translator to tell the father we need to operate immediately," he instructed Tancredi. Angelo immediately followed the stretcher into the surgical tent, and within minutes he was preparing to operate on the boy. The instruments were sterilized by one of his assistants, and he had just begun to pull the morphine into the needle when Tancredi returned.

"Did you tell him?" Angelo asked. He did not bother to look up, his eyes instead firmly set on surveying the boy's wound, which now looked like a dark-ringed bull's-eye.

"I couldn't."

Tancredi looked pale.

"Why's that?" Angelo was impatient and just about to inject the boy with anesthetic.

"Because . . ." Tancredi stood there for a second like he had a stone in his mouth. "Because, **Dottore** . . . Because he was dead."

Angelo continued staring at the boy's shoulder and didn't answer Tancredi.

A great gust of wind entered the tent and lifted Angelo's surgical coat. He didn't move from his position.

He simply took out his scalpel and cut into the boy.

The boy survived the operation, but when he recovered, he had no one to claim him. The sight of the dying father—who had survived long enough to reach their campsite with his wounded son in his arms—was hard to forget for the other soldiers. They didn't have the heart to abandon the boy now that he was alone.

They learned his name was Nasai from the cook, Amara, who always made sure the boy was well fed. When other Ethiopians occasionally arrived, the men would always introduce the boy in a vain attempt to see if a distant relative could be found. But none came forward, and none were ever discovered. So Nasai remained with the Italians.

Grateful for the doctor who had saved him, Nasai dedicated himself to Angelo. He learned how to assist Angelo in the medical tent. He organized the instruments, folded the bandages, and helped clean up and disinfect after the surgeries. He always slept outside the tent, even though Angelo had offered him a cot. Some nights, Angelo would awaken and go outside the tarp only to discover the young boy, crouched like a protective lion, a small stick and flint blade in his hand.

Nasai learned to speak some broken Italian, to play cards with the men, and even to drink their coffee. But as many times as the men told him he could share a tent with them, he insisted he needed to sleep outside with the sound of the wind and the light of the stars.

The months passed, and Angelo and Nasai became more like father and son. Angelo taught him to read, and to eat with a fork and knife. To brush his teeth with baking soda, and to sing Italian songs.

He imagined his own child back at home,

growing larger every week in Dalia's womb. He continued to write her long letters and he tried to imagine how beautiful she must look, so ripe and full of life.

She wrote him letters on scented paper, sometimes tucking lemon blossoms into the envelopes so that even if it was only in scent, she could travel and be next to him.

At night, he would close his eyes and imagine his time in Africa as a distant memory, his world instead filled with Dalia and their many children scampering around the Portofino terrace. The surgeries in a dusty tent in the desert would be replaced by house calls to families he had known all his life. And at night, he would sleep deeply with his **limonina** curled by his side.

Dalia had tried not to think too much about the birth, but as the date drew nearer, her body seemed seized by a desire to prepare the nursery. Suddenly, nothing seemed clean enough, and the linen napkins for diapers all seemed like they needed to be refolded. As did the small dressing gowns her mother- and sisters-in-law had embroidered with her over the past several months.

She had been walking toward her mother-in-law's house, which was close to her and Angelo's, when she was suddenly struck with a terrible pain. She felt her entire torso besieged by a contraction.

Doubled over in agony, she somehow managed to get to the doorstep. Angelo's mother quickly ushered her inside.

"You're in labor," she told her. "We need to call the midwife." She placed one hand on Dalia's shoulder. "Don't worry, it's frightening the first time, I know . . ." She wrapped a shawl around Dalia, who was shivering. "The first time is always the hardest. Next time, you won't even blink."

She helped Dalia to sit and did her best to keep her calm. "I feel terrible to have to leave you, if even for a moment. But I need to get one of the girls to fetch the midwife. Vanna's house is closest. I'll run to her and come straight back."

Dalia whimpered that she understood.

"But don't worry, the baby won't come right away. It could take hours . . ."

Dalia let out another groan. The pain was excruciating. Moments after Angelo's mother left, she felt another sharp pain, so intense, she cradled her belly in her arms and begged for it to stop.

Just as she wondered how all the women before her had handled such pain, the contraction abated. The moment of reprieve was short-lived, though, and she felt the familiar sensation of her baby swimming inside her. The small fist of the child, pushing outward slightly from the corner of her abdomen. All of a sudden she felt another contraction, but now when she looked down, a flood of wine-colored fluid was pouring out of her.

When Angelo's mother returned, she found Dalia on the floor, white as a gull.

In a vain attempt to stop what she thought was bleeding, the old woman grabbed the first towels she could find, then lifted poor Dalia in her arms and tried to keep her warm.

Vanna, the sister closest to Angelo, arrived, ushering the midwife through the doorway. Each of them knew immediately that something had gone terribly wrong. The midwife, a wizened gray woman who had delivered hundreds of babies before, saw the pool of port-wine fluid beneath Dalia and felt her heart sink.

Vanna gasped upon seeing her sister-in-law laid out like a pale and suffering **pieta** over her mother's lap.

"Oh my God!" she cried.

Marina turned to Vanna and snapped into action. "This is not good. Start boiling the water, Vanna. Then get me a stack of clean sheets. We have to try and deliver the baby now."

With the water on the stove, the women draped a cloth on the long dining room table and lifted a semi-conscious Dalia on top, as this was the custom to prevent ruining the bed.

"Marina delivered all three of my babies. You're in good hands," Vanna whispered into Dalia's ear, in an attempt to soothe her. But she knew that when her water broke it had been cloudy like sea water, certainly not like diluted blood. She went to the bathroom and found a washcloth, soaked it in some water, and retuned to the dining room and brought it to Dalia's forehead.

Dalia looked like a frightened fawn. "Please, please tell me that the baby will be all right." Her voice was desperate.

Marina took her brown, papery hands and cupped Dalia's abdomen and went quiet. She looked at the young girl and saw her white pallor, her teeth clenched with pain. She did what she thought would bring the girl comfort without making a false promise; she took the girl's hand and gripped it in her own.

The blood continued to seep from between Dalia's legs, and Vanna tried to maintain a fresh supply of towels. Her two sisters had appeared, bringing every towel they had in their own pantries. Their mother was now wailing and calling out to God, Jesus, and the Madonna. To whoever might hear her supplication. Her fingers were wrapped over her rosary, her knuckles white from gripping the beads. From Dalia's lips there was a faint murmuring, for she was too weak to cry out. The only word she uttered was Angelo's name.

"When will this baby come?" Angelo's mother beseeched Marina.

"It's in God's hands. All we can do is wait."

Dalia slipped into unconsciousness, just as the baby was pulled from between her legs, pale and lifeless. Marina worked swiftly, cutting the umbilical cord and gave Vanna the dead infant to clean and swaddle, so that it could be prepared later for its wake and burial.

After Dalia's placenta was expelled she began to hemorrhage, and Marina looked for any tears that might be causing the bleeding, hoping she might be able to sew them shut. But there was nothing she could repair.

Her small, quick hands found the uterus, and she discovered what she feared the most. The uterus was lax and boggy. She desperately tried to massage it, but it refused to contract, and Dalia became blue underneath Marina's desperate fingertips.

After twenty frantic minutes, the girl was so cold to the touch that Marina knew the only decent thing to do was stop.

"She is with the baby now," she said, her eyes lowered and her heart heavy. Marina had delivered Angelo and had been looking forward to ushering his child into the world. But now there would be two funerals instead.

Angelo's mother began to wail and pounded her fists into her heart. Vanna, out of a maternal instinct, began rocking the lifeless baby in her arms. With her mother's cries in the background, Vanna found herself making a shushing sound, as she brought the porcelain-perfect infant up to her face. Even though she knew her nephew's cheek was cold and his skin china white, Vanna believed that the rocking in her arms and gentle humming could somehow ensure the infant a more blessed and peaceful sleep.

No one could believe the room that Dalia had kept hidden all these months. When they began to prepare the burial for her and the baby, it was Vanna who first discovered the room with all of Angelo's letters pasted inside.

"Mamma!" she screamed, running next door where her mother and Vanna's other sisters had already begun preparing Dalia's body for the wake.

Her mother was bent over Dalia's limbs, a soft washcloth in her hand.

"What is it, Vanna?" Angelo's mother had been weeping since the tragedy. Her grandson, swaddled and pale, looked like a frozen ghost. He was placed in a wicker basket on a table. Tall candles were already lit beside him.

"You must come! Immediately, Mamma. To Dalia's bedroom!"

Angelo's mother was trapped in a deep fog of sorrow and could not understand why her youngest daughter would be so disrespectful. The ritual of cleaning the body before burial was a sacred one.

"Vanna! Please stop this," she reprimanded her daughter. "We need to make sure that Dalia is ready to be received by God."

"No, Mamma. Please come. Please."

Her mother put down her cloth and washed her hands.

Then, with great fatigue and a grief-stricken heart, the old woman walked to Angelo and Dalia's house.

Just before he married Dalia, Angelo had taken over a small cottage walking distance from his parents. It had been the home of his grandmother, and was only a few steps away from where his parents lived. He had such wonderful memories of visiting his grandmother there. The house was always filled with the smell of fresh garlic and simmering tomatoes. After her death, it had fallen into disrepair. The vines of roses that she used to cultivate on the trellis near her patio had become wild and overgrown. The white walls of the living room were now a cloudy sepia. The whole house reminded Angelo of a faded postcard from a summer holiday long ago.

But in anticipation of bringing his new bride home, he had spent nearly two weeks throwing himself into every aspect of its repair.

He had brought Dalia home to a place where he believed they would make their own little family, and in which she would find comfort and beauty. The rooms faced out to the sea, their marital bed was made with crisp white linen edged in blue, and every wall in the house he had personally covered with several coats of fresh, white paint.

Now when the women walked into the house, a hush fell upon them. Dalia had maintained perfect order. The kitchen was spotless. The living room had one sofa and a small table with a few ornaments. There were several neat piles of books scattered throughout.

"Come," Vanna said. She spoke in a whisper to her mother and took her by the hand.

The two women walked toward the archway of the bedroom.

Vanna pushed the door slightly and led her mother inside.

Not a single word or a single breath passed between the two women for several seconds. Just as Vanna's had done minutes before, Angelo's mother's eyes widened with both wonder and disbelief. In between pockets of pale blue paint and bursts of shimmering white clouds, the wall and ceiling was papered with her son Angelo's words.

She turned to Vanna, her wrinkled fingers covered her mouth. "My God," she said. "How she loved him."

"And he her . . ."

The two women stood there looking at every corner, every crevice of the room, with their mouths half open. Neither of them could believe that Dalia could have undertaken such an enormous project during the months of her pregnancy. But right beneath their noses, she had created a room that was both a sky and a garden of letters. A place that was now frozen in time, the letters pressed to the walls like dried flowers. The plaster itself reinforced, by words from a heart that beat thousands of miles away.

They laid Dalia out in her wedding dress, with a garland of lemon blossoms in her thick, black hair. Her eyelids had been weighted so they would remain shut, giving the appearance that she was sleeping. Beside her slept the swaddled infant. His white face had started to become mottled, so that even in death it looked like a sculpture. But now instead of white porcelain, the infant looked as though it had been chiseled from blue-veined marble.

The crying in the house went on for days. An express telegram was sent to Ethiopia, telling Angelo the tragic news.

Angelo, however, did not receive the telegram until two weeks later. A week before, on an emergency trip to another camp several miles from his own, his jeep was ambushed. The driver was shot and lost control of the vehicle. It crashed and turned over on itself, pinning Angelo's leg under the chassis. Now, days later, he was in recovery from the surgery, his leg bandaged, one of his toes amputated, and his head in a fog of morphine.

Angelo's superior officer made the decision to wait to tell Angelo the telegram's contents until he had recovered from the immediate trauma of his accident, afraid that the news would affect his recovery.

Letting a few more days pass, the colonel eventually made his way into Angelo's tent. Angelo was sitting with his foot propped up and a book between his hands.

"Reading, as usual?" the colonel asked him.

Angelo put the book down and looked at his superior officer. "Yes. It's hard to concentrate on the words, though. My mind is still groggy." He pointed to his foot. "It's also hard to get around. I imagine I'm going to drag it around like a club, even once I'm off the crutches."

"I'm sure you'll figure out a way to manage it in no time. We need you in the medical tent . . ."

Angelo smiled.

The colonel hesitated for a second and Angelo, sensing something was wrong, suddenly grew serious as well.

"You've had a telegram from back home," he said, taking it from his breast pocket. The yellow paper shook slightly as he placed it in Angelo's hands.

Angelo looked at him for more information. But the colonel only lowered his eyes
and said, "I will let you read the contents in
private . . . but please know we are doing
our best to make arrangements for you to
go home as soon as possible."

The colonel quietly left the tent as Angelo
took his finger and opened up the telegram.
**"Come home for emergency. Terrible
tragedy. Wife and baby lost in delivery."**

Angelo's body began to shake. He tried
to get up to reach his crutches, but he fell
onto the tent's dirt floor, his body too weakened to get to the crutches. The men in
the camp heard his wails, and everyone
stopped what they were doing, their hearts
breaking to hear their comrade in so much
pain. But it was Nasai who reached him
first, who picked him up and held him.
Who brought him his crutches so that Angelo could eventually stand.

Angelo staggered out into the sunlight,
the dunes of Ethiopia stretching into the
horizon, and openly wept without shame.

From the moment he received the telegram,
Angelo felt as though his heart had been
torn from his body. Every motion he per-

formed was done without reason or emotion, but by a primitive instinct that kept his body moving toward the sole task at hand: to get back home.

"Three weeks and you can go back," the head of the camp told him. "We're sorry for your loss, but we need to get a replacement here first before you can return."

"They can't wait that long to bury . . ." His voice choked in his throat. "Sir . . . please . . ."

"I'm so sorry, Angelo. We feel terrible about what's happened. But I have my orders. There is nothing I can do."

When the replacement finally arrived, it was Nasai who helped Angelo pack his bags and organize his things.

They moved between themselves, without speaking. Nasai the fatherless boy, Angelo the widower and childless doctor.

Angelo still couldn't comprehend the contents of the telegram; the reality was too much for him. And now he would be leaving this boy who felt more like family than friend.

He had wanted to tell Nasai that he wished he could take him home with him. But he knew how unkind the villagers would be to this gentle boy from the desert plain, just because of the color of his skin.

Still, in the midst of his grief, Angelo looked straight into Nasai's eyes and told him: "I'm so sorry to have to leave you here." He knew this would be the last time he saw Nasai, as his foot injury had rendered him technically disabled and he would almost certainly remain in Italy once he returned.

Nasai smiled. "You are needed back home. You will save others just like you saved me."

Angelo fought back his tears.

"I will see you again soon," he told the boy. "You're my only son now."

But Nasai simply smiled, his eyes shining with tears. "You are here," he said, clutching his heart. "And at night, I will look up into the sky and know we are both looking at the same stars."

Angelo embraced the boy.

"I've left you all my books," Angelo told him. "You will find them near my cot." He struggled to remain composed. "And I have given Amara extra money to ensure you always have enough to eat. She didn't even want the money. She promised me she would always look out for you, that you can even come live with her family, if you like."

Nasai smiled. "Thank you, **Dottore**. You have given me so much already. I do not want you to worry."

Nasai stood there for a second, looking one more time at the doctor who had saved his life.

"I've made you something to remember me by . . ." Nasai opened up his palm and revealed a small wooden carving of a lion.

"To protect you, while I'm not there."

Angelo took the small piece of wood, which had been carefully carved, oiled, and smoothed by this young boy's hands.

"Thank you, Nasai." And he embraced him one more time.

"**Dottore**, we must get going!" the driver called out to him.

Angelo nodded. He went toward the truck, threw his crutches into the back, slid onto the seat, and took one last look toward the camp, where all the men had lined up to see him off.

And as Angelo's jeep began its way down the road, the last image he saw was Nasai running as fast as he could just to stay with him a bit longer.

TWENTY-THREE

~

Portofino, Italy
SEPTEMBER 1936

It took Angelo another ten days to finally reach home. His foot was still shrouded in bandages and he walked with crutches.

It was his father who met him at the port. The old man looked ancient. His face like driftwood, his eyes cloudy as fog.

His father embraced him without speaking. Then he pulled back to look at his son, who appeared completely ravaged by the tragedy. Angelo was rail thin, his face unshaven, and he was bent over on crutches with what looked like a club foot bandaged in a ball of linen strips.

"My son," his father finally said, the words

escaping from parched, lined lips. "I am so, so sorry."

The family had wondered if they should prepare Angelo for the sight of the room, which they now called "the Shrine." But there was no correct way to do it gently. He would have to discover it for himself.

He was first greeted by his mother, his sisters, and then his brothers, everyone hugging him and whispering words of condolence.

"It will heal," and "Yes, I will walk again . . ." became rote replies to the siege of inquiries about his foot, which he handled without emotion, his heart too battered to care.

After a long family meal, all the others departed, as his mother instructed. She stayed with him alone.

"I think I need to lie down now, Mamma. I'm so tired . . ."

"I know, Angelo," she said sweetly. She took her brown hands and clasped them over his cheeks, and kissed him as if he was her small, sweet child again. "I am so sorry this ever happened."

"I know, Mamma. I know."

"We did everything to save her and

the baby. We did. Marina said it was unforeseen . . . a **vasa previa**, but I don't know what that means." Her eyes were overflowing with tears, and she looked up to the ceiling to try and make them stop.

Angelo shook his head. "Let's not talk about this now, Mamma. I can hardly stand it."

She nodded. "I will sit in the garden while you sleep."

Angelo told her that she should go home.

"No, I will wait there," she said. "In case you need me."

He watched her as she walked to sit in the garden. Then he made his way to the room where he and Dalia once lay.

There was nothing that could have prepared Angelo for seeing the room Dalia had created with so much care and love.

From the moment he stepped through the arched doorway, his mind became a whirlwind of images he could barely comprehend. It wasn't just the sight of all his letters papered throughout the room, but the realization of what she had undertaken just to be surrounded by his words.

He stood there for several seconds, his

entire body hunched over his crutches. He craned his neck to see the ceiling. He turned in circles to see the letters he had sent to her and written with his own hand. He saw the shapes she had created through her scissors, the careful way she had used her small, nimble hands to paste together what looked like an intricate, flowing puzzle. The pockets of blue and white paint that shimmered in certain places, as though she had added her own magic to the pigment. It was as if Dalia had created her version of heaven before she died.

Angelo's mother had remained in the garden, expecting him to call out her name. But it wasn't "Mamma!" that he called out. It was Dalia's name chanted over and over, like a begging, a supplication, a hopeless wish for her to return.

He threw his crutches to the floor and fell to the bed weeping.

"Dalia. Dalia. Dalia." He said her name so many times that his own mother had to take her hands to her ears to block out a pain so intense and heart wrenching, it pierced like lightning through the air.

TWENTY-FOUR

Verona, Italy
JULY 1943

On July 25, the newspapers and radio stations report Mussolini's arrest in Rome. Still everyone in the north knows that even though Mussolini is no longer in power, the threat still exists that Hitler may use this opportunity to invade Italy and restore power to his old ally. Yet even with all the political uncertainty, life within the Liceo Musicale remains unchanged.

Lena tells Elodie she is considering dropping out of the music program.

"How can I play when tanks could be invading our streets any minute?"

Elodie shakes her head. "No one says

you can't be an anti-Fascist and also play your music."

She looks at Elodie. "I told Zampieri I will sell my viola to pay for the Morettis' fake papers. He promises he'll have them within a few weeks. What's the point of a piece of wood and strings when it could save three lives? I'd sell it in a minute if it could get them out of here."

"Do you really think they're not safe here? They haven't rounded anyone up yet. This is Italy. It's not Germany, and certainly not Poland."

"The minute the Germans enter Italy, the Morettis and every Jew here will be on a truck to Poland. You mark my word."

"And what about Brigitte? The Lowenthals are Jewish."

Lena shakes her head. "Berto clearly knows she's at risk, but I don't think she wants to leave him. And her parents trust him. Her father is supportive. After all, Berto is anti-Fascist and against the Nazis. It doesn't matter to them that he's not Jewish."

Elodie nods. "Perhaps it's even an advantage in these times."

"Exactly," Lena agrees.

Elodie knows so little about Brigitte. The woman strikes her as elusive, like a night cat; her movements almost skulking, her dark eyes piercing and suspicious.

"She seldom speaks to anyone except Berto."

"It's true," Elodie agrees. "I've never even seen her speak with Luca."

"Ah, Luca," Lena teases. She immediately notices that Elodie blushes at the mere mention of his name. "There's a meeting tomorrow at the bookstore. Will you be coming?"

It has been a few days since she last saw Luca and she is happy for any excuse to be near him.

"Yes, count me in," she tells her friend. But when Elodie returns home, she finds something far worse than she could have imagined.

Plodding up the stairs to her family's apartment, Elodie discovers the door ajar. There are two distinct voices: the desperate and tear-filled voice of her mother, and the careful and compassionate voice of Doctor Tommasi.

She does not hear the voice of her fa-

THE GARDEN OF LETTERS

ther, a fact that causes Elodie to be seized with alarm.

"Mamma . . ." She pushes the door open farther and enters the salon. She places her cello down by the desk.

In the hallway, she sees her mother's back, her shoulder blades visible through the silk of her dress. She has her palms to her face and her head is turning from side to side, as if insisting she will not believe what the doctor is telling her.

"Mamma . . ." Elodie approaches the two of them slowly, as if she knows she is entering a place where there is no joy.

It is not her mother who first turns to her, but Doctor Tommasi. His is a face she has known since she was a child. His white hair. His handlebar mustache. Everything about him is familiar and kind.

"Elodie, my child." He extends an arm to touch her shoulder gently, the first gesture in a dance that is informed in grief.

"It's your father . . . I'm . . ." He stops for a second. "I'm sorry."

She hears her mother's whimpering, the notes of anguish hanging in the air. Despite the precision of the doctor's words, she cannot believe what he is telling her.

"An embolism. Yes, I'm sorry . . . He went in his sleep. It would have taken him in seconds . . . I'm sure it was very peaceful. He felt no pain . . ." All the information is punctuated in staccato.

Elodie feels the floor fall out from underneath her. Her throat tightens and she can hardly breathe.

Her mother turns and embraces her violently, her tears soaking through Elodie's shirt.

For the first time in her life, Elodie hears no music in her head. The space in her heart and mind that used to be occupied by melody and song, is now replaced with the weight of sorrow. Not the kind of sorrow she is used to channeling into her cello, but a sadness that sweeps through her and takes with it every note.

Elodie and her mother receive the guests who come to their apartment to pay their respects. Every student and every professor her father knew from his years at the school come to kiss Orsina's hand and to tell her how sorry they are for her loss.

Elodie sits in the salon, her hands crossed and her eyes staring straight ahead. She sees her mother standing like a ghost, the black dress hanging on a frame of bones. She clasps the hands of people whose names she cannot recall and numbly whispers a few words of gratitude.

On the day of her father's funeral, when Pietro's prized violin students serenaded his casket with Bach's violin solo partitas, the reality of his absence strikes Elodie and Orsina. They can feel Pietro in every note. They can see his smile, his eyes closing as the music rises and swells within the church's vaulted space. Elodie can sense his hand moving alongside his students' bows, bringing their music to life. Hearing the music floating through the church, filling the air with both beauty and emotion, the two women are struck by the devotion and talent of his students. But their sorrow is all consuming, and the two women cannot stifle their sobs.

A week after her father's funeral, Elodie reluctantly returns to school. She had not seen Lena since the funeral, and she senses immediately that her friend is uncertain how to act around her.

"I'm sorry," Lena says embracing her.

"Your father was the kindest man. Everyone who had him as a professor adored him."

"Thank you, Lena." It is difficult for her to speak. Elodie grips the handle of her cello case in order to stave off the tears.

"I have a message from Luca as well." Lena pauses for a second, as if to weigh whether it was inappropriate to mention his name in the midst of Elodie's grief. "He wanted to come to your home to pay his respects, but he was concerned you'd think it was an invasion of your privacy. . . . He wanted to make sure I conveyed his condolences."

Elodie is relieved to hear the message from Luca. She had been wondering if he had heard the news of her father's death, and the fact that he had been thinking of her touches her deeply.

"I'm glad he and the others know . . . I wouldn't want them to think I had abandoned them. It's just been too hard to leave my mother and the house until now. We're still in such shock."

"We all know you need to take your time . . . But the Germans are approaching. The word is they will be here by the end of the summer. I'm just grateful Zampieri made good on his word and got fake papers for the Morettis. They will be leaving any day now. He's even found a smuggler to get them through the mountains, into Switzerland."

"It's nice to hear a bit of good news in all of this," Elodie says quietly.

"Yes, that's probably the only good news any of us will be hearing for some time." Lena sighed. "It's going to get a lot worse here once the Allies start bombing . . ."

"Bombing . . ." Elodie feels the word stick in her throat. "Don't they know we hate Mussolini as much as they do?"

"I don't think the people in charge care what we think. In the meantime, all we can do is get organized and prepared."

"I can't imagine things getting any worse than they already are." Elodie sighed. "Nothing seems real to me anymore, Lena. It's like I'm in a hideous dream and I can't wake up." She bites her lip. "I can't even move without thinking of the consequences to my mother . . . I feel trapped."

Lena nods her head. "We all live within cages, Elodie. The only way to survive is to find a way to navigate through the wire.

You are a resilient girl." She takes Elodie's hand and squeezes it. "Are you still in the September concert?"

"Yes. It's September third. We're lucky. We're getting a chance to perform at the Teatro Bibiena in Mantua . . ."

"The Bibiena . . ." She smiles at Elodie. "You're going to be the evening's star."

"I need to practice more," Elodie says quietly.

"Luca seemed interested in learning if you'd still be playing at the concert . . ."

"Yes, very much so . . . but I really have to get my playing back. The fact that Professor Agnelli hasn't cut me is a small miracle. He must feel indebted to my father."

"Everyone's in shock over your father. Your absence is completely understandable."

"Yes," she answers. "But I still should be practicing."

"I'll tell Luca that we spoke."

"Tell him I'll come to a meeting as soon as I can."

The approaching concert forces Elodie to refocus her grief and channel it into her cello. Just opening the case and peeling off the scarf reminds her of her father. She touches the wood, tilts the instrument, and applies the rosin to her bow. All these simple rituals, which she has performed nearly every day for years, are steeped in thoughts of her father. She closes her eyes and begins to play.

She finds him deep within the notes of the sarabande from the Bach cello Suite No. 6. There, her sorrow, stifled like a sob within her chest, is again released.

The cello welcomes her mourning. The sorrow it carried from its last owner joins with hers.

She closes her eyes as she plays, and sees her father. She feels him in her heart and in her cello.

"You are like me," he had once told her as he grasped her hand. She remembers the feeling of his fingers wrapped around hers, the way he traced her expansion, and how his palm had enclosed her hand. The pain of his absence softens. He had given her the gift of music, and as Elodie plays her cello, that gift and her connection to him feel eternal.

The September concert at the Teatro Bibiena is now a week away.

Elodie meets Luca at the bookstore, where he informs her that the Wolf will be coming to hear her play. "He says it's too dangerous to have you come play in his apartment now. He fears the neighbors are watching him. He wants you to play some-place public where he will remain unno-ticed."

Elodie looks at Luca puzzlingly.

"We have promised him a message. We just received new information and it needs to be transferred to him as soon as possi-ble. It must be delivered in your solo."

"That's impossible," Elodie tells him. "It's already been established that I'm playing the Grutzmacher cadenza for the Boc-cherini cello concerto. They will never let me play one that I wrote on my own. My professor decides what I have to play."

"I wouldn't ask you unless it was critical, Elodie."

"I need to think about the consequences of this. It's one thing to play an atonal code in the privacy of the Wolf's home. It's quite another to do it in a public theater."

"You will not have to play more than three unscripted chords, I promise you. The information will be transferred so quickly, no one will know but you and the Wolf."

"Why can't we meet in Mantua's Istituto Musicale? Can't the Wolf, with his many friends, organize that?"

Luca looks at her and shakes his head. "I wish I could tell you why. I myself don't fully know all the details. I'm only telling you what I've been told. The Wolf is one of our senior commanders. He knows things that even I don't. We need to do what we're asked, Elodie."

Elodie cannot sleep. The silence of the apartment is unbearable. She finds herself alone in the living room at night. She sits there with the bow on her lap and the instrument between her knees. She sees shadows on the floor, an impatient, invisible audience stretching before her. But she can't think of any notes to play.

She remembers listening to her father playing alone into the night and wonders what anguish had plagued him when he dove into the music like a phantom.

She goes to bed thinking of her father. She sees him at the kitchen table dressed in his robe, his body weak but his eyes burning into hers. She sees him mouthing the word **courage** to her.

And when she sleeps, she feelts her father's strength flow through her. His voice whispering to her, just as he did when she was beginning her studies of the cello, to reach down and find her fire.

The next afternoon, Elodie goes to the bookstore.

She is wearing a red sweater and black trousers. Her hair is pulled back and the angles of her face look as if they've been cut with glass.

"Luca," she says.

He is at one of the bookshelves when she approaches. She stands in front of him, before he's even had a chance to react to her voice.

"I will do it."

Her eyes focus on his.

She looks at him with conviction, her mind now full of the notes that had evaded her the night before. But it's the melancholy pull of strings. Rather, it's the clarion call of brass.

"I'm glad you've changed your mind." It

is as if a layer of skin has been peeled away and now she is burning in front of him like a flame.

"We can discuss the code the day after tomorrow," he whispers. "But tomorrow I must leave for Monte Comune."

"You're heading out to the mountains?"

"Not to stay. It will just be a day trip. I need to get a few things to my brother and his men."

"I want to go, too," she says.

"Your skills are better served on your cello. I'm not wasting them on a trip to the mountains."

"The fresh air will do me good. I'm the only **staffetta** who hasn't used her bicycle yet!"

Luca laughs. "Such a complex girl wrapped up in such a tight package. But don't you have school?"

"I only have a morning class. I can meet you straight after."

"Well, then, if you're dead set on going, there is something you can do to help me . . . I need you to pick up a package that we'll take to the mountains with us. Go to Zampieri's studio on Via San Guisto first thing in the morning before your class. He'll give you the package and instructions where to meet me later on."

"Okay," she says.

The light has changed in the bookstore's back room. From the small, narrow windows, Elodie remembers the words in French that her mother told her long ago. **Entre chien et loup**, meaning between a dog and wolf, the fleeting world of twilight. When light surrenders into darkness, or when innocence slips into danger. When one stands at a threshold between the calm and the call of the wild.

The next morning, Elodie arrives at Berto Zampieri's art studio, and Brigitte answers the door.

She does not greet Elodie by name, but rather gives a faint smile and ushers her into a large room where several sculptures are on display. In the corner is an abstract rendering of a woman reclining. Elodie looks at the figure's sharp hip and hollow pelvis and senses immediately that it's Brigitte.

She is standing alone with the smell of damp clay and plaster dust on the floor when Berto walks out to greet her.

"This is for you," he tells her. She glances at his hands grasping a canvas bag. His hands are clean and without traces of clay.

"No, I'm not sculpting," he says with a laugh. "No time for that right now . . . I have more pressing things to attend to."

Elodie smiles, embarrassed that he's read her mind so easily.

"Luca will meet you at the intersection where the two roads meet at the base of the Monte Comune. There, you will hike the roads together until you get to the camp. Take this package with you."

Elodie takes the bag from Berto's hand. "I understand."

"Good. Your work has not gone unnoticed, Elodie . . ." He squeezes her arm. "And Luca told me about your father's recent passing . . . I'm so sorry."

She stiffens slightly at the mention of her father. The grief is still raw inside her. "Yes, thank you. This is a good way to channel my energies."

Berto nods.

Elodie takes the bag and looks down at its contents. On the top is fabric for sewing, but it is so heavy that Elodie knows something more important lies beneath.

"Don't worry, it's not anything that can explode." He looks at Brigitte in the corner and smiles. "It's only some fresh food. If anyone stops you, just tell them you're going to a picnic."

Elodie places the parcel in her basket and begins pedaling. She travels through Verona's narrow alleys, past the Porta San Giorgio until the city streets become country roads and the farms and olive groves overtake the landscape. She stops midway, hot and sweaty from the day's unseasonably warm weather, to peel off her sweater. Beneath the layers, she has on a linen sundress. She places her sweater on top of the package in her basket and resumes pedaling. After nearly an hour, she comes to the intersection at the base of the mountain. Luca is already there.

He does not say her name, but merely watches her silently as she gets off her bicycle and hits the kickstand with her foot. She takes the package from her basket and walks over to him.

He reaches into his pocket to find a cigarette and lights it, blowing the smoke into the air.

When she approaches him, he feels the air escape from him. The white sundress and crisscross back reveal Elodie's smooth, round shoulders and slender arms. He has never seen so much of her skin before. Every time she comes to the bookstore, she always wears clothes that befit a serious music student: prim blouses and long skirts that cover her knees.

He wonders to himself, how many times can she transform in front of him. He had seen her morph from one creature to another when she played the cello. He had seen her as recently as yesterday, with her red sweater and black trousers, her eyes fierce as a lion's burning into his. And now, as she walks toward him carrying the package, she no longer seems like a lioness or an innocent young girl; she is something in between, and perhaps more dangerous. A beautiful, young woman.

He takes the cigarette from his mouth and throws it on the ground. And when she leans over to give him the package, he does what he was instructed never to do with one of the group's **staffette**: He pulls her into his arms and kisses her.

His kiss takes her by surprise. Though she imagined it—hoped for it—nearly from the moment she first saw him months before. She had wondered what the texture of his lips might feel like, the taste of his tongue, the sound of his breath merging with her own, and all she wants is for him to keep kissing her, to feel the grasp of his hands on her naked arms. To feel his fingers clasp her neck and run through her hair.

She places a hand on his chest, and the rhythm of his heart is a percussion that matches her own.

After several minutes, he pulls back to look at her again.

The straps of her sundress have fallen over her shoulders.

"As much as I shouldn't have done that, I had to . . ."

Again, she lifts her head up to his. "I'm so glad you did."

"I don't want to do anything else but kiss you again . . ."

She laughs and kisses him again on the mouth. "But we do have work to do . . ."

His fingers trace her breasts, the contours revealed to him through the sheath of white cotton.

"I don't want to work," he whispers into her ear.

Her eyes soften, communicating to him what she feels too embarrassed to say, that this is her wish as well.

His arms wrap around her one more time, lifting her slightly, pulling her to him so that she is forced to balance on her toes.

"Let's hide my bicycle," she whispers into his ear.

They discover a place thick with bramble and wildflowers and hide it there, covering it with as much brush as they can find. Then, before beginning their walk up the mountain, they used the opportunity of natural camouflage to steal another kiss.

The mountain paths were rough, and the sunlight flooded through the trees as Elodie walked behind Luca.

"My brother and Jurika are up here with six other men," Luca said. Elodie nodded, remembering the girl dressed in the men's clothes.

"They're setting up a camp, but they still need a lot of supplies.

Luca was carrying a large satchel of his own. Inside were more provisions for the men.

"My brother took over my father's blacksmith shop." He laughed. "You'll be surprised when you meet him."

She smiled and lifted her face to the sun. Halfway through their journey, she reached into her bag and found a small kerchief and tied it over her head, knotting it in the back, to keep the hair off her face.

"Now, I get the chance to see you in the role of a **staffetta**," he said. "The Wolf had told us you were unique. He was impressed with you."

"He said that? I had the impression my cello left more of a mark on him than my playing of the code did."

"You should never assume anything, Elodie. You should know that by now."

She nodded. "I assumed you were never going to kiss me. I'm happy I was wrong."

Luca smiled and let out a small laugh. Elodie was panting from the hike and stopped for a moment to catch her breath. She was beginning to tire.

"It's not much longer," he said.

"I just need a second. I've never been up this high before."

He nodded and readjusted the bag on his shoulders. She wanted to tell him it wasn't the mountain air that had made her feel faint. It was his kiss.

But she said nothing, preferring to remain silent. They both turned to look down at the valley beneath them, the walls of Verona now mere specks in the distance.

At the camp, they discovered a house and several shirtless men nailing new boards onto the structure. Jurika was with two other men, stocking guns in an arsenal hidden beneath a shed.

At least a dozen muskets were stacked in a low pile and there were several rounds of ammunition nearby as well.

"Luca," a man yelled out to him. He walked toward them. He was much larger than Luca and was wearing green trousers and no shirt. His skin was a dark chestnut color from the sun.

"Brother," he said and embraced Luca. "Thank you for coming. We're making great progress . . ."

"Yes," Luca answered, appraising the grounds. "I can see that."

"And who is this sweet thing you've brought with you? Clearly she's too delicate for the mountains."

"Dragonfly, meet Raffaele."

"Dragonfly?" Luca's brother grinned. "I like that . . . I like that a lot."

He appeared a wholly different animal than Luca. She could see the blacksmith in him even without the smock and iron in his hand.

"We brought you some things you said you needed . . . You know what's in my package . . . And underneath the sewing supplies in Dragonfly's bag are tins of food."

Raffaele's large hand squeezed Luca's shoulder. "You'll be coming up here in the winter with me, right? We're in for a hard fight."

"I will do whatever is needed. Right now, Zampieri and Maffini are planning our strategy. They tell me the Germans are already in the mountains burying their weapons."

Raffaele nodded. "We've heard that as well . . ."

"I'll try and come back in a few days. Do you have another list for me?"

Raffaele reached into his pocket and handed a folded piece of paper over to Luca.

"Read it and memorize it. Don't carry it with you, brother."

"I'll leave that to someone better equipped."

He gave the paper over to Elodie, who briefly looked it over before tearing it up into little pieces.

"I'll tell you what you need to get," she said with a small smile. "As soon as we reach home."

TWENTY-FIVE

~•~

Verona, Italy
SEPTEMBER 1943

When they arrive home, it's almost dusk. They stop just outside the Porta San Giorgio, knowing that when they enter the gates to Verona, the day's activities and the kiss between them must be another set of secrets packed away.

She stands with her toes braced to the pavement and her legs balancing the bicycle, the idle pedals pushing against her skin.

Her mind is ablaze with images: impressions that have their own flame and smoke.

She can still feel his hands on her shoulders; every one of their shared touches a haunting deep within her.

She does not want to go home, to the silence and to her mother now so strange in her widow's black. No, she just wants to go somewhere alone with Luca. She wants to stand naked and feel his touch traveling over her skin, a finely tuned bow moving across quivering strings.

Whether he is thinking the same things, he doesn't say. They stay perched on their bicycles, the arches of Verona in front of them, the warm day suddenly cooling and reminding them it's not summer at all, but fall.

She sees him reach into his pocket to find a cigarette, but he realizes he has smoked them all.

"Good thing you don't smoke," he says, smiling.

"I tried once, but I spent the next day coughing over my cello. It didn't sit well with me."

She can see him looking at her, trying to gauge what they are saying both with words and without them. The truth lay somewhere in the space between their words and in their eyes. It glimmered pale and radiant, like moonlight striking through ice.

He looks down at his handlebars, then back again briefly into her eyes.

"We'll need to meet tomorrow so I can put together the things for my brother . . ."

"Yes," she says. "I can come by after class."

"And we can discuss the concert then, too."

"Yes," she says.

"Then, until tomorrow." There is a softness to his voice, a thread of honey running through his words, and Elodie smiles.

"Tomorrow," she says, returning the sweet melody between them. They exchange one last look before placing their feet on the pedals and moving past the gates of the city as the blue-gray light swallows their figures whole.

That night, Elodie has no use for sleep. She plays deep into the night. She presses her chest against the red wood of her cello and plays with a newly mined passion for her music, for the strengthening Resistance, and for everything that she has become over the past four months.

The next day, after school, she arrives at the bookstore. Luca is busy with a customer, who is thumbing through a catalog. She sees him look up for a moment, a thin ribbon of smile crossing his lips, a signal in his eyes. She warms inside, interpreting their silent communication.

She walks to the back, where the new novels are displayed, and places her cello against the shelves. She scans the book spines before her eyes fall on one so tiny and slender, it seems almost invisible.

She pulls it out and holds it in her hands, the cover immediately charming her. A small boy leaping off what looks like the moon, his hands clutching the strings of a parachute pulled by fluttering birds. Around him are bright yellow stars and a ringed planet in the distance.

She begins to leaf through the pages, intrigued by the whimsical illustrations that are scattered throughout the text.

She begins to read when she hears Luca's footsteps approaching. Even before he speaks, she can feel his breath filling the air.

He takes the book from her hand and smiles. "That's a very special book."

"I can tell," she says.

"**The Little Prince**, by Antoine de Saint-Exupéry. Just translated from the French."

"**Il Piccolo Principe**," she says smiling.

"Take it," he tells her. "It's my gift to you. I think you'll love it . . . there is a lot of hidden meaning tucked within its pages."

"Really?" She can't help but sound intrigued.

"Yes." He places a hand on her shoulder and squeezes. "Don't be fooled by the childlike drawings. The story is a journey to discover one's inner truth."

She is quiet, looking up at him. She holds the book tightly for a few seconds. "I will begin reading it tonight."

"You'll finish it within an hour, then find yourself reading it all over again." He motions her to follow him into the back.

She follows, sliding the slender book into her bag.

In the back room now, she senses intuitively that there can be no room for flirtation. They must accomplish all their tasks as efficiently as they can.

She sits with her cello beside her, recalling every item on his brother's list. The food supplies, munitions, pots for cooking, and waterproof tarps, along with the smaller but no less important things, including matches for fires, warm socks, and gloves.

When they start to discuss the fall concert, she feels herself stiffening.

"I'm nervous about this," she says. "There are going to be a lot of people from Verona and Mantua inside the theater. People who know their music. People who knew my father."

She sees his eyes reading her in the light.

"**Carissima**," he says. "I do not want to sound harsh, but there is a hard reality to our work. You have a chance to perform an important task, sending information that could assist our men with the German's imminent invasion. But only you can decide if you want to do this or not."

She does not answer him at first. In her mind, she is carrying on a conversation he will not hear. Nor will he be able to sense it in her eyes, her breath, or in the silence between them. What **does** she want?

She wants her father back. She wants his face at the dinner table and his music in the living room. She wants her mother's Venetian cooking and her singing floating from the bath.

She wants another kiss from Luca. The chance to feel something other than wood against her chest, or strings against her finger pads. She wants to feel her age, not her responsibility. She wants to feel joy. She wants the pull of his hand and the sound of his voice saying her name. She wants to be able to play her music for the reasons she has always loved to play, not as a means to send a wartime code.

So no, she wants to tell him, rewriting the cadenza of the Boccherini concerto to slip an important message in for the Wolf to hear is not at all what she wants. But she does not tell him any of this.

She closes her eyes and utters five simple words.

"Yes, I will do it."

The program for the Teatro Bibiena is Marin Marais's "Bells of Geneviève," Boccherini's Cello Concerto in B Flat, and Saint-Saëns's "Dying Swan." It has already been announced to the public.

"Tell me how much information we need to reveal. I'm supposed to play the Grutzmacher cadenza in the Boccherini. It doesn't

have as much space as the Haydn that I
played for the Wolf before . . . but I suppose
there is some room for me to add a few extra notes."

He nods his head. "Apparently this code
is simpler than the first one. So the Wolf will
merely have to hear it, and there will be no
need to see a written score. We've been
told by one of our contacts with musical
knowledge that the coded information
should be inserted by adding a series of
longer chords. First some half-note triple
stops, followed by a few whole-note oc-
taves. Does that make sense? I'm not a musician, only a humble bookseller," he says,
smiling at her.

She feels her heart fluttering as he tries
to make sense of the musical instructions.
She wants to assure him that even if he
doesn't understand the use of chords, she
does.

"Well, the Grutzmacher cadenza is a fast
one. And I can even accelerate the speed
a little . . . so the new notes that we insert
shouldn't be too obtrusive."

Elodie pauses a bit to reflect. In her mind,
she plays the Boccherini notes mentally

and tries to insert the code as if performing.

"You have my full confidence," Luca says and his hand reaches out to touch hers.

Finally, Elodie feels her tension evaporate. His simple gesture of affection makes her come alive.

"It's easy enough to remember." She smiles.

"The specific amount of each kind of the triple-stop and double-stop chords, which we will know right before the concert, will indicate something important, relating to what we've learned about the German regiments scouted." He purposefully withholds the true meaning in order to protect her. "But can I hear you play the cadenza now, but just as it's written, so we can figure out where to put in the chords?"

She smiles at him as if he is inviting her to a dance where she is the one who will lead. She loves the fact that he has requested she play for him, even though he knows that she has fully understood the mission and doesn't need to practice. Still, she accepts his request and reaches for her instrument.

In the soft light of the bookstore, Luca closes his eyes and hears the notes rising from the cello.

Once again, he is struck by a change in her, a transformation he notices as soon as she starts to perform for him. Before she had played with a mastery of the notes, but now Luca detects another layer. A feminine, seductive pull moves through the music. Luca senses it immediately, with almost animal-like instincts: beyond their shared devotion to the Resistance and the intrigue surrounding the codes, she desires him as much as he does her.

He is entranced by her. He wants to take the bow from her and thread his fingers through hers. He wants to find her neck and expose the stretch of white skin that is hidden behind the curtain of black hair. He is taken not just by her beauty, but also by her talent. She is not like the girls who fill the air with pointless chatter, who laugh to cover their ignorance, who smile because they have no words.

Elodie has something that is completely her own. Her music is the root of her sorcery. She fills the air with it. She uses every part of her body when she plays: her fingers, her arms, her neck, and her legs. He simply cannot take his eyes off her.

When he can no longer hold back, he reaches for her. She feels his touch like lightning; she raises her chin and meets him with eyes lit and piercing.

Electricity runs between them, even before they touch. Luca leans into her. She feels his fingers move away the loose strands of her hair. When he places his lips over hers, she does not feel nearly as shy as the first time he kissed her. Her mouth is like an open envelope, her tongue an invitation.

He closes his eyes and kisses her again. And in the kiss, he finds himself moving. He discovers the shapes and tastes of each of her hidden corners. The sweetness of her throat. The peachlike flesh of her earlobe. In the circle of her collarbone, he discovers a small valley to rest his tongue.

In his hands he feels her narrow waist and the pianolike keys of her ribcage, before kneeling to the ground to find her again. This time, he traces her from her ankles, up through the taut length of her calves and the curve of her knees. Within the abundant material of her skirt he discovers the smooth softness of her thighs.

He is used to the sensation of paper between his hands, the perfume of leather and pulped wood. But Elodie comes with textures and scents all her own. In between her thighs she feels like velvet to him, while the bone of her ankle feels like polished stone.

And he finds the seasons woven through her. Her skin carries with it the fragrance of spring flowers. Her breath is like frost that warms with the heat between them. And her taste, the sweetest taste of fig.

It was the sensation of her fingers that he remembered first, before everything else fell away. He heard her slight whimper in his ear, a flicker of pain deep within her as she grasped him, as if to steady herself. In his arms, she shuddered, pulled away, then returned to him again. He wanted to hold her for a little longer. She was still wearing her skirt and blouse, but he could feel her whole body through the tracing of his hands over and under her clothes.

Now, he rested with knees bent, with one cheek in her lap as she gently stroked his curls, before taking a single finger to trace the shell-like curve of his ear. She caresses him with such tenderness, and Luca found himself looking up at this beautiful and mysterious creature he knew as Elodie, as Dragonfly, again lassoed by her gaze.

The first time he had kissed her in the mountains, it was he who had lifted her chin to bring her lips to his own, and it was his eyes that looked down at hers. Now she was the one gazing down onto him. He would never forget the sight of her eyes. He had never associated the color green with fire. But her eyes were indeed burning. Inextinguishable. And when she smiled, he felt almost blinded.

TWENTY-SIX

～✦～

Verona, Italy
SEPTEMBER 1943

Her head is full of Luca, not at all on the concert at the Bibiena, nor on the code she has promised to perform.

She takes the book out of her bag, hoping the story of **The Little Prince** will help soothe her restless mind. She finds herself smiling with each page; the little prince with his billowing scarf, his tousled hair, and his animal friends who speak in riddles. But when she approaches the end of the story, she realizes this is not a children's book at all, but one that is about the responsibility of love. And what is most important in life is almost always invisible to the eyes.

The next morning, the day of the fall concert, Elodie does not feel rested at all. She has spent the night either thinking of Luca or trying to decipher the hidden messages within the book. She now knows why Luca said she'd enjoy it. It, too, has its own secret code.

She can still feel his hands against her skin, his scent on her arms. Yet she forces herself to get out of bed and get ready. Luca promised that he would have the final chord numbers for the code, so she knows she has to get to the bookstore before rehearsal. As she pulls herself up from the covers, the very architecture of her body now seems different. It wasn't just the slight dull pain in her abdomen; there is a sense of an opening within her, a shifting of sorts. She always believed that music was the only thing that could fill the space inside her. Now she finds herself burning from the memory of his touch, the exhilaration of his breath, the brush of both his cheek and his hands, and she holds these strange and wondrous sensations in her own hidden place, where she can store all her memories of the previous night.

Attending to her morning chores, she no longer hears notes; rather, images of her and Luca flash through her mind. She feels as though she is watching a cinematic reel in which she is both a voyeur and an active participant. She can see Luca kneeling at the base of her chair, his hands deep within the folds of her skirt, yet also feel the sensation of his hands on her skin. She can see with perfect clarity the sight of their limbs entwined, the cotton of her blouse above her waist, his hands grasping her hips. She can taste and smell every memory. She recalls his scent of tobacco and dry paper. She can taste the salt on his neck, the warm flesh of his tongue.

She feels almost duplicitous, seeing her mother in the kitchen, smiling at her because she knows today is Elodie's concert at the Bibiena.

"You look radiant," her mother says, as Elodie swallows her coffee in one quick gulp. "I can't wait to see you on the stage tonight. I finished the alterations on your dress last night."

Elodie wonders, if beneath the schoolgirl uniform, her mother can see the change in her. That her daughter has discovered that it isn't only music that can articulate both the beauty and mystery of the world. That now she knows that the heart has its own rhythm and breath has its own pulse, and there is nothing in this world that can make you feel more alive than a simple touch of a beloved's hand.

At the bookstore, she doesn't find Luca as she had expected, but Beppe. He is standing in front of the cash register when she arrives. The brass machine has four white dials standing with numbers through its narrow top window.

"Dragonfly," he says when she walks through the door. Elodie has never heard Beppe call her by her code name, and it catches her off guard.

"I wasn't expecting to see you, but . . ."

"Yes, I know," he interrupts her. "Luca had to see his brother at the last minute. So much needs to be done now."

Elodie nods.

"Let's go to the back room. I'll shut the front door. It won't take us very long."

She lifts her cello and follows him to the back, where only a few hours before, she had been with Luca. The metal chairs and table look empty and almost skeletal without their bodies against them. A slight shudder flickers through her. She feels almost as if she is betraying Luca by being in this room without him.

Beppe is unaware of Elodie's mental gymnastics. As her mind leaps with the memory of Luca taking her bow from her hand, of her cello being placed on the ground, of his palms over the contours of her blouse, she struggles to regain her focus.

"Dragonfly?" Beppe waves a hand over her eyes.

Elodie blinks. "I'm so sorry . . . Yes. It's just that I have so much on my mind today with the concert . . ."

"I know you do. But you need the code, don't you?"

He walks over to one of the many bookshelves that line the room and pulls out a paperback edition of Italian court poetry. He fingers the pages, then stops at a page where Luca has written the number of chords she has to play.

"Somewhere in the cadenza, I need you to play three consecutive half-note triple-stopped chords. Then you need to do two double-stopped whole-note chords. Can you work this in somehow?"

Elodie closes her eyes and tries to imagine how she can best incorporate the code.

Inside her head, she can hear the music and she begins to weave the consecutive chords into the Boccherini cadenza.

After a few minutes, she opens her eyes as if struck by an epiphany. "I have it."

"So fast?" Beppe shakes his head, amazed.

Elodie smiles. "At the end of the cadenza, just before the orchestra joins back in, there are a series of repeated measures, all with the same chord. I can make three of them half-note triple stops and then the next two whole-note double stops. I'll make sure to play with a real flourish so they stand out." She began to speak as though Beppe was a musician himself, and that he could understand what she was creating.

"Well, you're the one playing it, so as long as you understand . . ."

"Yes, I understand perfectly. It won't be too difficult, Beppe. I can do it." She glances at the clock and begins to gather her things.

He comes over to her and squeezes her shoulder. His touch is hard, fraternal rather than sensual. And again she detects a difference within herself, as if she now has the capacity to decipher the different messages expressed even with a touch.

Beppe is wishing her well . . . wishing her good luck. His hands transfer no other sensations, as Luca's had the night before.

"I should be getting to school. I have rehearsal."

"Yes, of course." Already Beppe is walking her out of the back room and toward the front door.

"I'll see you soon. And good luck with everything tonight."

She smiles and lifts her cello higher onto her back, giving him a final wave as she heads out the door.

⌒

Elodie had chosen to wear a dress of her mother's for the concert over a week before. She had discovered it in a closet next to the yellow chiffon one. This dress, made of silk taffeta, was such a dark blue it appeared almost black. "Like the lagoon at midnight," her mother had said days before as she circled around Elodie, pinning the dress in the back to make it fit Elodie's narrow frame.

With the alterations made, Elodie slipped into the dress. Both women gazed at the sight of Elodie in the reflection of Orsina's long mirror.

"You look like a swan with that neck of yours," said Orsina. And it was true. Elodie's long, white neck stretched elegantly from the scalloped neckline of the dress. Against the material's water-streaked taffeta, she looked like she was emerging from the sea.

Elodie struggled to find her breath within the tight-fitting corsetry. She placed two hands on her abdomen. "I can hardly breathe with it on."

Orsina squinted at her handiwork; days before she had taken the dress in at the seams in order to fit Elodie's small torso. The girl was smaller than she had been at her age.

"Let me see . . ." Orsina came closer to Elodie, slipping two fingers between the blades of Elodie's shoulder and the gown's material. "You have plenty of room. Try and relax. It's just your nerves . . ."

Elodie struggled to take another breath. She lifted her arms, to make sure she'd be able to move freely with her bowing.

"There . . . see . . . It fits perfectly!" Orsina clasped her hands and smiled again at the sight of her daughter's elegant movements.

Elodie didn't answer her mother. Even if she could move her arms, the dress felt like a cage to her. And yet within the tightly fitting bodice, her heart was racing.

With the approaching concert, Orsina seemed to come alive. She had busied herself with Elodie's dress, her spirit happy to have something to channel her energy into. She knew how important it was for Elodie's debut at the Teatro Bibiena to be as perfect as possible. It was the most prestigious venue for the students of the Liceo to perform in and she only wished that Pietro had lived to see it.

The weather had turned cooler over the last few days, and the women wrapped themselves in long scarves. Elodie carried her cello; her mother carried a small purse that contained a tube of lipstick, a mirror, and a comb.

Traveling on the train to Mantua, Orsina marveled at the sight of her daughter. For months leading up to Pietro's death, she had noticed a change in Elodie's playing.

But she hadn't noticed her daughter's physical transformation. As the train wheels sped beneath Orsina, she had a chance to study Elodie in amazement. The girl was no longer a girl, but a young woman at the peak of her beauty.

Elodie seemed taller, thinner, even more angular. Her skin glowed. Her eyes were piercing. It wasn't just green that Orsina saw, but blue and gold. When she looked into Elodie's eyes, she couldn't help but think of the peacock feathers in her mother's hat shop.

She clasped her daughter's hand; the strong grip of her musician fingers was familiar. It reminded her of Pietro.

"Elodie," she said, "before the year's end, promise me one thing. Promise me you'll make me get on the train and go back to visit Venice, even if it's just for the day."

Elodie nodded. She had always wanted to see this city of her mother's childhood, this floating city that emerged from the sea. She never understood why they had never gone there.

Orsina looked out the window. She closed her eyes and saw the church where she first heard Pietro perform. She saw her

THE GARDEN OF LETTERS

mother in plum-colored silk, her own yellow chiffon dress fluttering over her knees. She saw the water underneath the canal and the window of her parents' hat shop filled with hats and exotic feathers.

She realized she had packed away so much of herself after she became a wife. As a child she had an almost incurable sense of adventure, a hunger for places far away. How many photographs of Paris had she pulled from her mother's magazine collection? Streetlamps and bridges, gardens full of flowers and automobiles instead of gondolas and **vaporetti**. Every feather she touched, she wondered not just which bird it had come from, but also which country. But her need to discover the world had somehow died alongside her parents. Looking at Elodie alight in her beauty and powers, she had the desire to find herself again. Even if her body was no longer young, her dreams were waiting to be rediscovered.

The two women held each other's hands during the short train ride.

Elodie wondered if her mother could feel just how nervous she was. The notes to the three pieces she was to play, she knew those by heart. She had played them for countless hours at school, at home, inside her head, but the pressure to deliver just the right new notes for the Wolf's perfectly tuned ear was taking all the breath from her.

"I'm nervous," she whispered, turning to her mother as they stepped with the others off the train.

"There's nothing to be worried about," Orsina said, hoping to soothe her daughter's nerves. "It's just a concert. Play with your eyes closed like your father taught you. That way you won't even see the crowds. You'll be able to focus fully on the music."

Her mother didn't understand. Her father would have never said such nonsense. Yes, she could close her eyes and perhaps tune out the faces of the crowd.

But that wasn't why she was nervous.

Her mind didn't feel as clear as it typically was. Every time she tried to concentrate and hear the music, she saw Luca. She saw the storeroom. She saw the two of them entwined.

She tried to take a deep breath, but the dress was like a second skin. Try as she might, Elodie couldn't get enough air into her lungs. Yet, in stark contrast, Orsina looked as though the train ride out of Verona had rejuvenated her. Her skin was luminous and her eyes were sparkling. "Train fumes are like oxygen for you," Elodie teased her as they came off the train. Orsina threw her shawl over her shoulder and brushed her daughter's cheek.

"Yes," she said. "I feel better from the trip . . . the rhythm of the train always helps me dream."

The Teatro Bibiena was Mantua's small but elegant theater, an illuminated vault of stone walls and velvet seats. Soft light flickered from candelabra-like sconces. Only a few people in the audience were related to the performers. The majority of seats were occupied by music lovers who wanted to see the next generation of performers.

Elodie had hoped that Lena would come, but the night before Lena had been wrapped up in more pressing things. Berto Zampieri had acquired the counterfeit passports for the Morettis.

"Forgive me, Elodie. But this will be their last night in Verona and I want to be able to say good-bye . . ." Elodie understood completely Lena's need to do this. The

Morettis' little boy was like a baby brother to Lena, and she had waited for months to get them passports.

Elodie nodded. "I understand; don't even give it a second thought. There will be other concerts."

Lena looked up to the sky, as if anticipating the buzz of airplanes, the threat of bombs. "I hope so. You've always been the optimistic one between us."

Elodie smiled. "Optimistic? I'll take that . . . better than being called naive."

Lena embraced her friend. "You are not naïve, you are stronger than you appear." She pinched Elodie's slender arm. "Goodbye, warrior, and good luck!"

At half past eight, Elodie walks onto the stage with the rest of the orchestra. She is seated closer to the front, near the conductor, so the audience can see her when she plays her cadenza in the Boccherini concerto and then her solo in the piece by Saint-Saëns.

She notices a slight shift in the breath of the audience as she appears. The sight of a beautiful young girl with a long swanlike neck, dressed in dark taffeta, and carrying her cello causes a stir through the audience. Elodie hears the gasps and feels a slight tremor run through her.

The musicians take their seats and focus their eyes on the conductor and his baton.

Marin Marais's "Bells of Geneviève" begins in perfect rhythm. The music is meant to simulate the ringing of church bells, both persistent and full of longing, rising to a crescendo. Elodie plays with increasing fury. Orsina sees that Elodie has yet to open her eyes since the piece began. The boys who play alongside her use their bows like swordsmen. They play with precision, but Orsina senses that they do not play like her daughter. Elodie is playing as though she has become one of the church bells. She is swaying back and forth, her body like a pendulum, her arms striking passionately with her bow. Still, Elodie's eyes remain closed. She does not look at a single face in the audience; she dances with the music alone.

When she finishes, the audience claps, some even stand and yell "Brava!" before they return to their seats and resettle themselves. After a small wave of silence returns to the theater, the students in the orchestra pick up their bows again. But a strange feeling overtakes Elodie. Within the first few rows of the theater, she sees Luca's face, his eyes radiant and shining, his complete attention focused on her on the stage. His smile curling like a cat's tail at the sight of her lifting her bow.

The orchestra begins the Boccherini and the music sweeps beneath her. Her fingers play the notes, but Elodie is not connected to the score. Her bow moves with perfect precision, but the sight of Luca's face is like a floodgate, a dam breaking inside her. She is seized by the images of the night before. His hands sliding over her; his fingers searching for her. She cannot stop the reel inside her head. It is as if he has taken possession of her mind.

Time and space suddenly fall away. She hears herself playing, but the notes are not what she wants. Her memory of the written score has taken control. The Grutzmacher cadenza, the one her teacher wanted her to play, emerges from her cello, and the small space she had to insert the code evaporates into midair.

No one but Luca and the Wolf—whom she cannot see, but whom she knows is in the audience—can detect her error. The cadenza was played perfectly, without a single note missing, but Elodie has failed her mission and she is seized with terror over her mistake. Her stomach is turning into tight knots. Her mind is racing. While moments ago her mind had temporarily been taken over, now every part of her is rushing to find a way to rectify her error. She wonders if she can add the code at the end, but she knows that it would sound out of place and set off an alarm with the others. If only there was a cadenza in Saint-Saëns's "Dying Swan."

She does not look again into the rows of the theater. She keeps her eyes on the floor, her cello firmly placed between her legs and her bow at her side. Part of her wishes that she could vanish from the stage. She does not want to find the searching eyes of Luca. She does not want to see the confusion or the disappointment on his face. Nor can she bear the thought of the Wolf's eyes. She imagines them bloodshot and furious, incredulous over her ineptitude.

Elodie tries to push the thoughts of both

men out of her mind. She tries to imagine
her mother instead. Orsina would have no
idea that Elodie had failed at her debut. Elodie straightens her neck, even as her gaze
remains fixed on the ground. She can feel
her mother smiling at the thought of her
daughter becoming the swan.

After the applause dissipates, a harp is
wheeled onto the stage for the final performance of the "Dying Swan."

The harpist, Francesca Colonne, arrives
on the stage, glorious in a long red silk
dress, her hair piled like a cornetto on her
head. Elodie is thankful that all eyes are no
longer on her but on the exquisitely delicate
Francesca.

Francesca sits down at her harp, the tall
instrument with its gilded scrolls and heav-
enly strings, and begins to seduce the audience into a dreamy sleep. She plucks and
strokes the strings with exquisite and celestial beauty. Elodie raises her head, her
long, white neck stretches from her blue
neckline, and it is she who channels the
beating wings of the swan, its heart on
the cusp of breaking.

When Elodie enters her own solo in the

piece, there seems to be no difference between the imaginary white bird she is evoking and her own death. She plays like a dying bird, her cello weeping with every note. When she is finished, she has collapsed at her cello, her white arms wrapped around its wooden body, her head hanging over its neck.

She hears Francesca whispering to her to get up to take her bow, her fingers gently pulling at her arm. But although Elodie hears Francesca's words in her ear, and feels her grasp trying to bring her to her feet, Elodie is so distraught over her own failure, she cannot move.

After the clapping has finally ended and Francesca has taken her bows, Elodie's wrapped fingers are pried from her cello's neck, her instrument is taken from her, and she is lifted onto her feet.

The audience is full of exclamations about the passion of her playing. "Incredible," several people shout. "She was the dying swan!" another voice bellows from within the crowd.

Orsina rushes from her seat to find Elodie, who is sitting on a small wooden chair near a vanity room, damp with perspiration and shaking.

"Elodie!" Orsina immediately takes the shawl that Elodie had dropped to the floor and wraps it around her daughter's shoulders.

"What happened? You gave me such a fright. I felt as though I was witnessing your death in front of me. You were delving into a river of blackness, and I wanted to leap from my chair and save you!"

Elodie pulls her shawl closer around her body and stares blankly at her mother. Elodie is so distraught she cannot mouth a single word.

"Elodie . . ." her mother says again. When her daughter doesn't answer, she swings around to the other performers and their parents.

"Can I get a glass of water? Please, somebody. Elodie is unwell!"

A glass of water is quickly fetched, and Orsina tries to get Elodie to take a few sips. She strokes Elodie's cheeks and tells her that she has played with not just perfection, but with incredible emotion. She tells her daughter that her father would have been so proud.

But those words have the opposite effect on Elodie. From the moment she says them, the anguish on Elodie's face only intensifies.

"Proud? Proud? He would have been furious with me, had he heard what I played . . . or didn't play."

She cannot think of her father now. She is imagining the Wolf furious over her mistake, and Luca needing to create a new means to convey the code in time.

But neither of the men appear backstage and Elodie surrenders to her mother, allowing her to take her from the theater. They push past the throngs of people who want to tell Elodie how extraordinary her performance was, the people who thrust their programs in front of her hoping for an autograph from a musician they expect to soon be starring throughout Italy.

Orsina lifts up her arm like a shield as she takes Elodie outside the Bibiena, pushing them into the darkness, until it's just the two of them in the back of a third-class carriage on a night train back to Verona.

TWENTY-SEVEN

Verona, Italy
SEPTEMBER 1943

On the train ride back to Verona, Elodie does not utter a single word. Orsina tries to rouse her from her waking sleep, reminding the girl of her beautiful playing that evening, how she played with such emotion and how proud her father would have been. But nothing can bring Elodie out from her trance.

As the train arrives at the station and the other passengers disembark around them, Orsina offers to carry Elodie's cello for her. But her daughter clutches the instrument so tightly to her chest that Orsina cannot free it from her embrace.

"Elodie, please . . ." She leans forward and puts her hands on her daughter's narrow shoulders. "You won't give me your cello, but I don't have the strength to lift you. We need to get you home."

Elodie rises like a wraith, all the while clinging to her cello, and walks down the carriage's steps to the platform below.

Orsina laces her arms through Elodie's and begins to steer the two of them through the cobblestone streets until they are safely inside their apartment. There, she unbuttons the beautiful dress and pulls a white nightgown over Elodie's body. Elodie lays her in her bed and brings the bed linen and blankets up to her chin.

She wants Elodie to close her eyes, but all her daughter does is stare at the wall.

Orsina cannot understand why her daughter has become so distraught. She wants to blame it on the music that evening, surmising that perhaps Elodie has connected Saint-Saëns's "Dying Swan" with her father's death to such an extent that it caused her to virtually collapse on stage.

All Elodie can think about is that she has failed. She is afraid she has endangered all of the men in the Resistance trying to fortify themselves in the mountains before the Germans invade. She is ashamed that the Wolf will think he made a major mistake relying on her with such an important mission. But most of all, she is despondent over what Luca must be thinking about her right now.

Her sense of failure is immobilizing. She cannot lift her arms or legs. Her entire body feels as though it's been weighted down with a sack of bricks. Orsina pulls a chair close to Elodie, takes her daughter's hand in her own, and grips it tighter than she should, wanting Elodie to feel the intensity of her grasp. And then she begins to sing.

What Orsina sings, Elodie cannot quite understand the words, for it is in the **dialeto del mar**, the old Venetian dialect of the sea. But she can feel the depths of the saltwater lagoon; the pull of the tide and the scroll of the fog.

And although Elodie could not reveal the true source of her anguish, she allows the ancient melody to enter her like water, permeate her skin and travel through her veins. It was a language she didn't speak, but Elodie still understood it somehow, like a rhythm that flowed between her and her mother. These Venetian melodies, songs of distant longing belonging to a mystical place, where ancient pathways, palaces, and dreams all floated. As she hears this music traveling through her ears into the fabric of her soul, Elodie closes her eyes and dreams of Luca.

When Elodie awoke the following morning, Orsina was still asleep in the chair. Elodie quickly washed her face and dressed herself in trousers and a blouse. There was no time to fix her hair, which was now half-undone from the night before.

Elodie quickly left the apartment, took her bicycle from the first-floor landing, and rode furiously in the direction of Luca's store.

It was only 8:00 in the morning, but she suspected he would already be there before the shop opened.

When she arrived, he was in the front. He opened the door. He looked grave.

"Elodie . . ."

She wanted to hear honey in his words. But what she heard was fear.

"I'm so sorry," she said. Her breathing was rapid. She had pedaled as fast as she could to the store and now she could hardly speak. "I'm so sorry . . . I'm so sorry. I became distracted . . . I swear to you I didn't do it on purpose. I had every intention of doing . . ."

"Stop," he said. He placed his hand on her shoulders. "I already know that."

She paused for a second and looked him straight in the eye. There she found the words, even though they remained unspoken, that she was looking for. She knew he had forgiven her. A sense of relief flooded through her and she tried to collect herself.

"But what about the Wolf? He must be furious at me."

"It's not about you or me, Elodie. All of this is far larger than any of us." He pressed his temples for a moment. She could feel his fatigue.

"Anyway, I haven't spoken directly with him. That was the point of the coded message last night . . . but we still have to find another way to get him the information he needs."

"There must be a way I can still get the code to him."

"Unfortunately, things are progressing far more quickly than any of us had imagined.

At most, we now have two days before the Germans arrive. To come up with a new code now, to get the message to the Wolf in time for anyone to be able to act on it, would be impossible."

Elodie started to tremble.

"You can't fall apart now . . . You just can't." He touched her arm. "So, yes, the code wasn't transmitted. There's a war on, things fall apart all the time. A message gets intercepted . . . or a contact is discovered and gets a bullet in his head. These things happen. You're not the first person in the Resistance to make a mistake, Elodie."

He reached for her cheek. "What does the Little Prince learn through his journey, Elodie? It's only with the heart one can see rightly; what is essential is invisible to the eye."

She smiled. "I marked that page when I read that," she said.

"Good. So you know that in life you must always follow your heart."

"Yes."

He covered his hand over hers. "There is so much to do now and we cannot lose our direction."

She nodded and his voice filled the air.

"Beppe is out with the others at Berto's studio now, trying to figure out what we need to do next. And Maffini and Zampieri are in Vicenza as we speak, with one of Berto's French contacts. I know from my brother that our scouts have already sighted several Germans moving through the mountains. Raffaele is requesting more ammunition. And now the delivery of that will unfortunately be affected by last night . . ."

Elodie's eyes flickered.

"There's going to be war, Elodie. What's happened can't be changed. We need to move on and fix it as best we can, as quickly as we can. It doesn't change what's in my heart. Nor yours."

Her eyes began to tear with gratitude. How happy she was that he had forgiven her for her mistake.

"It's so mysterious, this land of tears," he said, again quoting **The Little Prince**.

And hearing him speak another grain of truth, she couldn't help but smile.

◠

She follows him into the back of the store, where she discovers more guns—two boxes filled with Beretta M-34 pistols and three boxes of ammunition—than she has ever seen in her life.

"Beppe's been helping me all night. But there is still so much work to do . . ." He un-crates another box in front of her, one that contains only books. He pulls one out and opens it. In the center, just as Luca had shown her and Lena during the first meet-ing she had attended, a space had been carved to conceal a pistol.

He reaches to place a pistol inside, when she intercepts his hand and takes it in her own. She holds it for a moment. She knows there is no time for kissing, or exploring the curves of each other's body, but she still wants to feel the warmth of his skin and the sensation of his grip against her own fin-gers.

"We need to get all the pistols hidden into the books. I'm going to stack them on the storage shelves back here, so they'll be ready right when we need them." He smiles. "It's like a loaded library."

She laughs, but maintains her efficiency, quickly packing a pistol into each book. She's never held a gun before, and the weight of one surprises her.

"They should create a book large enough for a rifle," he says, as he watches her hold the pistol.

She does not particularly like the sensation of the weapon in her hand. She imagines Lena might enjoy the danger of something like that, but not Elodie. She simply places each one into a book and moves on quickly.

As she works, Luca takes each book and places it onto the shelf, occasionally looking at the clock. She knows the store officially opens by 9:30 A.M., so it is essential that every book is shelved with its secret weapon and that all evidence of their work has vanished by then.

Five minutes before the shop is due to open, Luca places the last book on the shelf. He picks up the empty crates where the pistols had been stored and the empty boxes that contained the carved-out books, and quickly carries them to the back alley, where he takes a hammer and breaks them up into small, nondescript pieces of discarded material.

When he comes in through the back door, he lifts an apron from one of the pegs and pulls her toward him.

"Come here," he says, wrapping his arms around her. "We've worked hard enough, I deserve one of these . . ."

He takes her in his arms and kisses her. And just like the Little Prince, she feels the layers that had once seemed steeped in shadow, suddenly sparkling with light. And for a brief moment, with his lips on hers, Elodie feels surrounded by stars.

Luca was right. There was no time to attempt another delivery of the coded information. That very evening, September 8, as Elodie and Orsina were eating dinner, the radio broadcast astonishing news: The king had publicly declared an armistice between Italy and the Allied forces. But even if the king's intention was to protect Italy from a German invasion, Mussolini had other plans. In order to restore his own power, Mussolini had made a pact with Hitler allowing him to send his troops into Italy through the north.

The Resistance had been made aware that the Germans would now be entering Italy any day. Unbeknownst to Elodie, Maffini and Zampieri had already boarded a night train to Verona and were rushing home to arrange an emergency group meeting.

While Elodie slept, the men conferred with Colonel Eugenio Spiazzi, a distinguished military officer whose allegiance was to the king, not to Mussolini. Believing the north had to be protected at any cost, Spiazzi corralled his own soldiers and established a strategy with Maffini and Zampieri. They needed to defend three bridges of Verona from the German tanks: Ponte Garibaldi, Ponte Nuovo, and Ponte Navi. The German army would be trying to enter Verona the next morning, when the fight to protect the city would begin.

At 7:00 A.M., there is a knock on Elodie's door. She looks through the peephole. It is Lena, her blonde hair wrapped in a long scarf.

"Elodie, I need to speak to you."

Elodie, groggy, opens the door and hears Lena giving her orders.

"You're needed at once. The Germans are already outside the city. They'll begin the attack on Verona within a few hours. Beppe says Colonel Spiazzi is telling us that we must wrangle every man and woman willing to protect Verona."

Lena's words are uttered like rapid gunfire. She is more alive than Elodie has ever seen her; Elodie can smell her adrenaline like perfume.

"I'll get ready right away," Elodie responds. She is about to turn to go to change her clothes, when she sees her mother in the threshold of the living room. She has heard every word Lena has said.

She looks at the two girls. Lena in her scarf, her blue eyes radiant and defiant. Her daughter, whose recent behavior she now understands, is a creature of incredible strength, a courage that runs far deeper within her than just her music.

Orsina feels a rush of energy permeating her body, as though the passion and courage of the two girls has surged into her as well. Her husband's death was caused by the Fascists, and she'll not let her daughter fight them alone.

"Lena," she says before Elodie can even speak. "Count me in, too."

Orsina and Elodie quickly change into their street clothes. Lena leaves them, telling her she's taken her bicycle and must inform all the other **staffette** about the situation. She tells them to go to Café Dante in Piazza dei

Signori, where they will be told what to do
next.

Just before leaping onto her bicycle, she
runs back to Orsina and embraces her.
"Thank you for helping us."

Orsina wraps her arms around Lena's
body. "My daughter is fighting and my own
husband died because of this brutality. How
could I not?"

Lena looks back at Elodie and Orsina
one more time before readjusting her scarf
and barreling down the stairs of the apartment house. The two women can hear her
footsteps as they slip on their own shoes.

There is shouting in the streets. Men who
have gone out for their early morning coffee at the bar and women who have gone
to the market to do their errands, are suddenly besieged with the terrifying news: the
German army has already started its as-
sault at the outer barracks and are making
their way closer to the city. For years, the
Fascists have ruled the city and no one
dared speak out against them for fear of im-
prisonment—or worse—from the Blackshirts. But no one wants to see their city
invaded by the Nazis. Even the Italian sol-

diers at the garrison do not want to find themselves under German occupation.

People flee back to their apartments and close their shutters, afraid of being arrested. The Fascists were brutal, but now with the looming threat of the Gestapo, nearly everyone is terrified of being sent to prison or shot. A few are willing to ignore the danger and volunteer to spread the information on how people can assist the Resistance; women whisper into one another's ears about where to stockpile food and clothing for the men who will need it. Elodie thinks she can tell with a single glance who is willing to help and who is not. Their eyes alone reveal their allegiance.

⌒

Elodie and Orsina arrive at Café Dante, where Brigitte is instructing all the **staffette** what to do. She is standing on a stool in what looks like borrowed military khakis and a white blouse. Her hair is pulled tightly away from her face, revealing her sharp features. Her expression is fierce and confident. Across her body is a long, heavy rifle and a rope of ammunition. "**Ragazze**!" she yells over the chatter. "Girls."

Suddenly the room falls quiet. No one is

used to hearing Brigitte speak, and her voice resonates with power and a sense of command.

"Today I need every one of you to forget you are women. Today there are no men and there are no women, only soldiers."

The women begin to cheer. Around the room, Elodie recognizes familiar faces from the meetings at Luca's bookstore, and also from around the city as well. There is the woman from the cheese shop and the young widow who lived on the floor below them who lost her husband in the Russian front. Every one of them is furious over losing her loved ones to Mussolini's campaign for power, and adamant she will not live under Nazi rule.

"Tell us what to do!" one of the women shouts. She is not a **staffetta**, but a matron eager to be useful.

"Berto is already with Maffini. The last report I've received is that they were heading toward the Caserma Ederle, where the 8th Artillery in Campofiore is set to join forces with Colonel Spiazzi and his garrison troops. So we need to be ready back here if the tanks enter the city." She gives a quick tap to the rifle on her chest.

"First of all, are there any nurses here?"

Two women raise their hands. Another says she has no formal training, but raised three boys so knows a lot about dealing with bruises and injuries.

"Go home and make bandages from sheets. Sterilize instruments if you have them. If anyone has an attic, start storing blankets and provisions in it. We need to be prepared for every outcome."

As Brigitte is giving out her orders, Elodie turns and sees that Lena has come through the door. She is soaked with perspiration, her hair wild, and her eyes are shining like two steel-blue bullets.

"The Germans have already passed through Brennero. They've attacked the barracks of Rovereto and Val Lagarina, and trampled our men on the outskirts of the city in Boscomantico and Parona. They are now going toward the Caserma Ederle, where our men are with Colonel Spiazzi." Lena reaches into her pocket for her scarf and mops her brow with it. "I have a special message from Spiazzi himself, telling us that it's absolutely essential that we delay the enemy's advancement. Brigitte, if you know where the spare weapons are, they want them moved to the Piazza delle Poste."

The room becomes completely silent. Brigitte lifts her chin and adjusts her rifle. She is still standing on the stool. "I do." Pointing to Elodie, Lena, and Orsina, she barks, "You three come with me."

Mother, daughter, and Lena all follow Brigitte to Berto's studio. A sense of déjà vu hits Elodie as she walks up the hallway to the apartment, having been there only a few days before. Brigitte adjusts the rifle on her back as she reaches to find her key.

The sculptures have been moved to a corner. On the table are four empty glasses, an empty bottle of grappa, a few scattered books, and some pens. Elodie can only imagine what sort of rushed activity happened last night, when Berto arrived home after his meeting with the colonel. If she and Luca were packing guns into books back at the store, then Berto's studio must have been filled with other unprecedented activity.

"Girls, quickly!" Brigitte orders them. Elodie shoots a look at Orsina. She can tell that being called a "girl" had invigorated her mother.

The women follow Brigitte to the bedroom. None of them look at the unmade bed or the messy end table. They stand there focused, waiting for Brigitte to tell them what to do.

"Come, we need to get these books off first . . ." She points to a large trunk at the foot of the bed covered with books. The four of them work quickly so that within seconds the books are on the ground. Brigitte turns toward the dresser and reaches deep into a ceramic pitcher to pull out a key.

She returns to the trunk and opens the lock, lifting its lid to reveal four ninety-one-millimeter rifles. On the side of the trunk are six hand grenades.

She orders Elodie and Lena to take a rifle. The gun is far too heavy for Orsina; Brigitte instructs her to take a canvas sack and fill it with the grenades.

The women do as they are told, their bodies weighted by the weapons. Brigitte takes the spare rifle and straps it to her chest, carrying the other one in her arms. She instructs Elodie to close the trunk, and all four women march out the door.

Elodie straps the gun across her body. For years, she has carried her cello in her arms or across her back, but the rifle has a wholly different sort of weight. It carries the weight of danger.

Elodie walks toward the Piazza delle Poste now not like a **staffetta** riding her bicycle or wielding her bow, but like a full-blown partisan. Nothing seems real anymore. She can hear the sound of gunfire and explosions throughout the city. The advancing enemy feels like a tremor running underneath the pavement. She cannot believe the sight of her gentle mother, slender as a reed, walking in front of her in a black dress, carrying a bag full of grenades.

Lena is walking beside Brigitte with a rifle strapped across her chest. Her blonde hair is the color of gold in the autumn sunlight, and her face is fixed with determination. For Elodie, this sight of her friend is the only thing she can fix upon. It is the only constant.

When they arrive at the Piazza delle Poste, they hear that three German tanks have already crossed the Ponte Navi and will be storming through the Piazza delle Poste any minute. There are forty Resistance fighters coming into the piazza. Like ants out of crevices, Elodie has no idea where they've come from.

"Orsina!" Lena shouts. "Go back to the café. Start organizing the older women. We're going to need to get food and water to the men. The fighting could last into the night."

Orsina looks at Elodie, a short, silent glance to see if her daughter would come with her so they could stay together.

"Mamma, go! I will be there as soon as I can to help. But leave me the grenades!" Elodie can hardly believe the words she is speaking. Never in a thousand years would she have thought she would be in a position to instruct her mother what to do with a sack of grenades. As Elodie dips down, her thin body already strapped with a rifle on her back and another in her arm, Orsina touches her daughter's cheek. "Don't let anything happen to you. You're all I have left."

Elodie pulls her mother closer, a gun now between their skin. "Listen, Mamma, you need to get out of here, right now. It's too dangerous. Get to the café!"

Her mother's eyes send a desperate silent message. She doesn't want to go.

"I'll be there as soon as I get these weapons to the men." She gives her mother a small push and turns to run as the sound of bullets fills the air. Her body is trembling from the weight of all the weaponry. Elodie runs for cover behind one of the small archways in the building across from the post office.

Lena has come out from one of the doorways and grabs Elodie by the sleeve. Brigitte is waving them to come behind the post office, and the girls run in her direction.

"Stand here!" she barks. "The men are coming. As soon as they come near, you give them your gun. Theirs will soon be empty, and ours are fully loaded."

Elodie and Lena nod their heads.

For the first time in her life, Elodie hears the sounds of grenades exploding. From the top of buildings and through windows, handmade bombs, furniture, heavy books lit afire, whatever heavy things the people can find, these invisible fighters are throwing them down on the Germans.

In addition to the approaching tanks, trucks with German officers and Fascist military commanders drive through the streets. Armed German soldiers pile out of the back of trucks and begin shooting blindly at the Resistance snipers, hidden among the roofs.

The men have come down from Campofiore and are now shooting directly at the tanks storming into the city. Giuseppe Bettero, a veteran soldier who joined the fight, places his rifle with two other fighters at the entrance of the bridge and starts directly shooting at the tank, which they succeed in immobilizing. Ironically, the enemy's bullet-riddled machine becomes an obstacle for others trying to pass through.

Within a few minutes, Elodie sees Luca and Beppe running toward the piazza.

"Get out of here." Luca is running into the piazza, carrying his rifle close to his chest. His face is covered with gunpowder and his hair is wild.

He pushes Elodie into a wall.

"Get out of here, Elodie! Now!"

Her eyes are wide. "Where the hell am I going to go?" She pushes back at him. He turns and starts shooting at some Germans in the street.

"Just get out of here!" he yells again. "You're going to get shot." In his eyes, she sees not only terror, but a desperate concern for her safety.

Elodie is still standing across from him, immobilized. Luca, frantic to get her out of harm's way, gives her a violent push, sending her in the opposite direction of the gunfire. Luca stands in the middle of the road, shooting into the oncoming tank, as Elodie runs toward Café Dante.

TWENTY-EIGHT

~

Portofino, Italy
OCTOBER 1943

The small room that Angelo has given Elodie is so white it appears almost monastic. The plaster walls are smooth like marble. The blue and white coverlet shows no wear.

Alone in her room, she hears the telephone ring and Angelo answer it, telling a woman that he will come and check her son's fever. In a soft, low voice, she hears him instructing the mother to keep a cool washcloth on the boy's head.

When he speaks, she hears kindness. The same lilting she had heard in her father's voice.

"I'll be there in a few minutes. Try to keep him comfortable," he says, hanging up the phone. He doesn't tell Elodie he is leaving. She just hears him open and close the latch on his medical bag and then shut the door.

For a few minutes, Elodie considers staying inside her room, but the chance to learn more about the man who has given her temporary shelter overpowers her. Over the past few months, she has learned to harvest as much information as she can, especially when no one is looking. She unlocks her door and comes to the small living room, where he had read aloud to her a few days before.

She walks past the small kitchen. The bowl of persimmons. The ceramic plates with the painted flowers. Above an end table, there is a small painting of the Madonna and child tacked to the wall. Underneath it is a miniature carved lion in a dark, exotic wood that seems out of place among the novels and seashells.

Soon she finds herself at the end of the main hallway. There the arched door is closed, like a secret. A clenched fist. But she cannot help herself. She puts her hand to the doorknob and finds it unlocked. She pushes inside.

Elodie has no words for what she discovers. The room is papered in words. Letters that are now yellow and faded, their edges coffee brown.

She feels like she has stepped into a tomb of lost love letters. She looks up; she looks down. She look to every side and to every corner. In between patches of blue and white clouds, yellowing letters have been glued to the walls. Between the two twin beds, each still neatly made and covered in a quilt of pale blue flowers, rests a wedding portrait.

Elodie picks it up and stares at the picture, which she knows must be Angelo and his bride. The features, although clearly younger, are surely him. She sees the thick hair and the arch of his brow. And finally his mouth, which is not full like Luca's was, but thin.

His bride is haunting in her beauty, especially her wide, doe-shaped eyes. She is wearing a dress that is sweet and innocent, lacking any sophistication. In her black hair, she has woven a garland of white blossoms.

Elodie places the photograph down gently and cranes her neck to the ceiling. There isn't a single patch of white plaster exposed, as every inch is covered in either glimmering blue paint or paper. She looks at one of the letters that is closest to her and observes the perfect handwriting. She reads the rolling sentences that talk of the desert heat, the longing for his bride, and the excitement to see his son.

Just above it, nestled like a leaf to the vine, is a poem. Above that is another letter that speaks of a man named Tancredi, a boy named Nasai, and a heart that is longing to see his **limonina**.

Elodie's heart is in her throat. She feels that she has now trespassed on something that was not meant for her eyes; a voyeur to a private dance that is meant for two people, not three.

She walks quickly to the arched door and passes through to the hallway, making sure to close it tightly behind her.

Even without Angelo at home, the house weeps in silence. She can hear the sadness, like a low moan sweeping through the hall.

She returns to her room and curls into her bed, trying to erase the thoughts of the room with the letters pasted to the walls. At the same time, she wishes she now had something written in Luca's hands. His scent on his sweater is now fading. Even now she isn't sure if it's the smell of damp wool or of his perspiration that she has carried with her for weeks, inhaling it every time she needed to feel close to him.

She wants to erase all of the other tragic thoughts that fill her head. She doesn't want to think about the notes crying out from the Wolf's wife's composition, or the woman who had gifted it to the man she loved. She doesn't want to think of her mother alone without her, or the fate of her cello.

She is still so tired, she can't think of escaping to another place just yet, or taking another boat to a place where she can try to become lost.

Instead, her hands begin mapping her body in private. She has missed her second cycle, and Elodie is now sure that a part of Luca grows inside her. She cups her breasts and feels their new fullness, the nipples so tender that even a graze from her blouse makes her flicker with discomfort. She has become used to the daily nausea in the morning, but the fatigue she feels is crushing. She has never felt so exhausted, even when she was running through the streets of Verona delivering weapons. Then her body felt strong and full of energy, not bone tired like it does now. All she wants to do is close her eyes, sleep, and awaken with everything from the past six months having been a bad dream.

Angelo returns home an hour later. Elodie can hear the sound of his medical bag dropping on the table, his footsteps walking toward the kitchen, and the strike of a match against the stove's gas stream. The sounds of his return are strangely comforting to her. She interprets them as a man who has come to terms with how to survive on his own.

She slides her hand away from her abdomen and straightens her blouse. She gets up and readjusts the waistband of her skirt and tries to smooth down her hair.

She walks toward the living room. She does not want to appear ungrateful to her host. She needs his shelter, his quiet oasis of calm; it's a place she'll accept with gratitude before her pregnancy begins to show. But when her body can no longer hide this particular secret, Elodie wonders if he'll ask her to leave.

The first week she stays with him, she refrains from asking too many questions. She is a guest in a house that contains stories, a history that she hasn't yet deciphered. So she tries to find clues in what she can glean around her. She studies him, trying to make sense of what she sees in his features and expressions, or his rhythms around his home.

What she knows for sure is that he is gentle. He walks softly. He touches things lightly. Even the way he stirs the sauce on the burner, he does with a gentleness that is surprising to find in a man.

They have quickly established their way of filling the space between them. In the morning when she walks out of her room for breakfast, he has already anticipated her preference for nothing more than dry toast and a coffee with so much warm milk it looks white when he stirs it.

She also strikes him as less restless than the others he has taken in, though he is unsure if this is merely a mask she wears to cloak something deeper he cannot yet see.

Angelo can tell she loves books almost as much as he does. When she thinks he isn't looking, he can see her out of the corner of his eye picking up the novels he has lying around the house. He has not read aloud to anyone since Dalia died, and the ability to now share a good book with someone gives his heart sustenance and breaks it at the same time. For years he has tried to lose himself in his books, to bury his pain by reading another person's story. Now when he picks up the pages of a novel, he finds he is no longer reading just to become lost, but to connect to this strange, new woman who sits across from him. The words, the sentences, weaving together not just one story, but a new one. One between him and Elodie.

TWENTY-NINE

~~~~

Verona, Italy
SEPTEMBER 1943

Elodie does not see Lena and Beppe being dragged into the Nazis' truck. She hears the news from Luca later on.

At the art studio, Maffini is lying on a wooden table. His trousers have been cut below the knee to reveal his bullet wound. Berto watches as Brigitte wraps strips of cut-up linen around his best friend's leg. He looks at her with amazement. At first, Brigitte does not want any of the other women to help her, even Martha and Giulia, who have both trained as nurses. She washes her hands in the basin and returns to Maffini's side.

"You need to get the bullet out," Martha tells her.

"Can you do it?" Brigitte asks her. Her voice is serious—calm and unflinching. Elodie struggles to reconcile her memory of Brigitte in a silk blouse and pearls with this warrior in front of her, who hours ago had strapped on a rifle, but who now is tending to battle wounds.

"No," Martha says shaking her head. "I have no surgical experience. We need to find a doctor right away. You don't want an infection to set in. If he gets gangrene, you're going to have to amputate."

Elodie can hear Maffini groaning. Berto and Brigitte are desperate to find ways to ease their friend's pain. Berto tries to offer him a sip of grappa, while Brigitte tightens the bandages to try and stanch the bleeding.

It had been Luca who carried Maffini, bleeding, up the stairs to the studio and ripped open his trouser leg to reveal where the bullet had entered. He had also been the one to tell Elodie that Lena and Beppe had been captured.

"Six dead and several of our group taken to the Edderle prison . . . And one of the

men saw Beppe and Lena taken in a separate jeep headed toward Palazzo dell'INA
near the Piazza Bra. We have to get them
out of there."

Elodie is shaking.

"We can plan that later," Brigitte says
above the chatter. "Right now we need to
find a doctor. We can't wait any longer."

Orsina approaches the dining room
table and looks at Maffini. His face is as
white as bleached cotton.

"How about Doctor Tommasi?" she whispers to Elodie.

Elodie knows that there was no one
kinder or more trustworthy than Doctor
Tommasi. He had delivered her, taken care
of her own father after his beating by the
Fascists, and been the one who told her of
his death.

"My mother can find someone to help,"
she tells Brigitte.

Brigitte looks up at her with firm eyes.
"Get him here as soon as you can."

Elodie turns to walk out the door, but Brigitte stops her. "Not you, Elodie. Have your
mother go. She's less suspicious. We can't
afford to lose anyone else after today."

While Orsina leaves to find Doctor Tommasi, Brigitte tells Luca to change his clothes.

"You're covered in blood," she says. Elodie stares at both of them. Brigitte does not weaken, even at the sight of so much blood.

"Elodie," she orders. "Go to the bedroom and give Luca some of Berto's spare clothes. He can't go outside like that."

He follows her into the back room, where the trunk has been emptied of its machine guns. Where the silver comb and brush belonging to Brigitte remain untouched on the side table.

In the wardrobe, Elodie finds a pair of dark pants and a white shirt. She sees Luca standing next to the table, his reflection cast in the long mirror that has been positioned across from the bed.

He is standing there shaking. His shirt is stained with Maffini's blood. Dark patches of stubble darken his face; his skin is covered with dirt and sweat.

"Come here," Elodie says gently. But he cannot move. It seems that because he has finally been given a moment to breathe and not have to shoot, to save someone, or to run, his body has momentarily shut itself down. So Elodie walks over to him.

She places Berto's spare clothes on the bed and begins to unbutton Luca's shirt. Her fingers move quickly and deftly. This is not the way she imagined undressing him for the first time, but the sight of his skin and the sculpture of his muscles sends a slight shiver through her all the same. She peels the shirt away from his shoulders, and he suddenly takes her hand and presses it to his heart.

"They took Beppe . . . they took Lena. They killed Luigi and Franco . . ." She doesn't know the men's names he is saying. But as soon as he mentions Lena, Elodie begins to cry.

"Lena . . . what will they do to her, Luca? I can't bear the thought of them torturing her."

"We can't think of that now, Elodie." He touches her cheek in a gesture meant to soothe her. "Vincenzo is already plotting a way to get the men the Germans captured out of the prison. So we will work with him to then save Beppe and Lena as well."

She feels protected by his touch, the
warmth of his skin against her own. Just
outside the doorway, she can hear the
others talking and scrambling. Brigitte is
telling them they all must scatter. Addresses
where the men can hide are whispered
to one another.

"Clean yourselves up in the sink. Comb
your hair and make yourself look like a good
Italian Fascist. Then lose yourself somewhere."

Luca slips into his new clothes, takes
Elodie into his arms, and kisses her one
more time.

"I have to go find Vincenzo," he says. "We
will figure out a way to get our men out of
the prison—and Lena and Beppe away
from the Gestapo . . . I promise you."

Luca leaves Berto's studio just as night is
falling. It is nearly curfew, and he knows the
Germans will be patrolling even more heav-
ily, searching for men who avoided being
captured.

Doctor Tommasi arrives, escorted by Orsina who, in her simple housedress and up-
swept hair, looks more alive than ever.
Elodie thinks to herself how much her

mother seems to have transformed over the past twenty-four hours.

Martha boils the water for the doctor, while Giulia places his instruments over a flame to sterilize them. Brigitte holds Maffini's head and tries to give him grappa, but the pain of extracting the bullet is excruciating. Brigitte takes a small washcloth, pours more grappa on it, and gives it to Maffini to suck on, hoping it will help quell his urge to scream.

After Doctor Tommasi has removed the bullet and stitched up the wound, he glances at Orsina and shakes his head.

"Every time you call me, I risk my life caring for the patient . . . You are lucky I've always had a soft spot in my heart for you, Orsina."

Orsina goes to him as the doctor washes his hands in the sink. "Thank you, Carlo," she says, and kisses him on both cheeks to show her gratitude. "We won't ever forget this kindness."

The next morning, Luca and Vincenzo lead a successful raid on the prison, where the remainder of the men are held. After they scale the walls, some scurry into the fields to be absorbed by peasants willing to hide them, while others head to the mountains to fight with the partisans.

"Maffini needs to be moved. It is already a small miracle that the Germans haven't knocked on the door searching for him here. They've probably already ransacked his apartment."

"We can't move him in the streets. He can't walk. His injury is obvious and will incriminate him and us right away." Brigitte is now becoming frantic. Her cool reserve is melting after the intensity of the past two days, and Berto has left for a secret meeting.

"I have an idea," Orsina tells her. "We need to find the clothes of an old man. A cap, a cane, even an old overcoat. I'm sure he can walk a few blocks that way, to a more secure place."

As Orsina and Brigitte work on the details to move Maffini to a safehouse, Luca tells Elodie she must go home and show up for class at the Liceo to maintain the consistency in her routine.

"It's essential you still appear the innocent music student," he tells her. "God knows what they're doing to Lena and

Beppe trying to get information out of them."
Elodie winces. Knowing Beppe and her
friend are captured causes a pain to run
through her. She knows from what happened to her father, the terrible measures
they use on prisoners during interrogations,
and it's difficult to bear the thought of Beppe
and Lena enduring such brutality. She
closes her eyes and silently prays for them.

At Palazzo dell'INA, Lena is brought into a
cement-block room with nothing in it except
a metal table, three chairs, and a lightbulb
that dangles from the ceiling. They have
tied her hands behind her and given her
nothing to eat or drink since they captured
her the evening before.
    After several minutes, two men appear.
Both are dressed in Gestapo uniforms.
    "Lena Galvetto?" one of the men asks
her. His Italian is thick with a German accent, and his face resembles a hawk.
    She doesn't answer, but just lifts her head
and stares at him. Her blue eyes are cold
as ice.
    She notices he twitches slightly at the
sight of her eyes.
    "Such blue eyes, such golden hair . . ."

he says as he comes closer. "You look more German than Italian," he says studying her.

Again she doesn't answer. She wants to spit in his face, but she is afraid of these two men. They could beat her, rape her. She has heard all of the terrible things they do to captured **staffetta** before they put a bullet to their heads.

"Do you know why you're here, Lena?" The German sits down on a chair and flips open a file. "So many things, Lena, we know about you, so many things . . ." He makes a small **tsk**ing sound against the roof of his mouth.

"It's too bad about the Morettis, Lena. You were such a good little girl to try and help them . . ."

Lena's eyes flicker. She feels her spine stiffen. Every hair on her body is standing on end.

"Did you hear what happened to the Morettis? Such a shame . . ."

She closes her eyes. She will not give them any shred of her pain. She will own her own grief.

The Nazi pushes his chair inches away from where Lena sits, her hands still tied behind her back. His face is so close to hers that she can smell the beer on his breath. He ignores her closed eyes, her bowed head. He knows she cannot escape and so, slowly, as if to maximize the pain of his delivery, he begins to detail the Morettis' fate:

"Thanks to your false papers, Lena, they did manage to get to the Swiss border."

She continues to keep her eyes closed. She doesn't want to listen to his words, but still they slice like a blade through the air.

"They traveled all night through the cold and the dark. And when the smuggler got them to the border, he told them to cut a hole in the barbed wire and to climb through. Ahhh, once they took a small step onto the Swiss soil, they'd all be safe." He walks around her, then begins circling around the room, smirking.

"But those Jews were not so smart, Lena. Not so smart at all. Papa goes first to pull little Luigi through. Then Mamma to follow. But Luigi gets caught in the wire. Oh . . . can you just imagine! You travel through the cold and the dark to get to safe, green Switzerland, with its cows and sweet milk, and at the very end little Luigi gets stuck in the fence."

Lena is shaking now. The tears are just behind her lids, but she won't open them. She refuses to let a single tear fall and give them the satisfaction.

"Well, the little boy lets out a little cry, which is almost imperceptible to the human ear, but is heard by one of our big, smart German shepherds. The sounds of those barking dogs running toward Mamma and Papa, and Luigi in the darkness. Can you just imagine the symphony, Lena?"

He begins to conduct in the air as if there is a full orchestra in front of him.

"Come on . . . you're a musician! Can you imagine the sound of the dogs barking, the boy crying, and the mother begging her husband to pull faster . . . to get the little boy through?"

Lena feels her stomach twisting inside her. She thinks she might vomit all over the table. She squeezes her eyes tighter trying to shut out the pain.

"Well, our dogs got there before the husband could get his son through. He was safely on Swiss soil, while his wife and son remained on Italy's." He pauses, contemplating the scene. Then, slowly he smiles revealing his gleaming white teeth.

"Are you shocked, Lena, that when the officer gave Signor Moretti the choice to leave his wife and Luigi and save himself, he crawled back through the hole to be with his family . . . Can you believe the idiocy of that bastard?

"We needed only three bullets to put them all out of their misery."

He turns to the second Gestapo officer and lets out a laugh. "Can you believe the stupidity of these Jews?"

Lena's interrogation lasts over three hours. The junior Gestapo officer leaves and soon another agent arrives—this one larger and stronger than the one already in the room. Within minutes of his arrival, he pulls Lena's hair to try and make her open her eyes and throws water in her face. When her eyes finally open, the senior Gestapo agent pushes photographs of the Morettis with bullets in their skulls under her nose, to prove to her they have told her the truth.

"Tell us the names of every person who attended your meetings and we will spare you the bullet that should end your life."

He is smiling. "Come on little Fraulein . . ."

He pushes a sheet of paper and a pen toward her.

Lena does not flinch.

The two men have all the time in the world. One tears off her blouse, while the other one takes off his belt. When the brass buckle hits her shoulder, Lena falls forward, her head hitting the table from the force of the lash. But her cry is almost imperceptible. She uses every bit of strength to try and mute herself. She will not give them the pleasure of seeing her in pain.

After two hours of being berated and beaten, Lena begins to transcend the pain. After the last whipping, she looks up at her torturers. Her glassy eyes shine with a resistance all her own.

"Those **eyes** of hers," the senior agent says. "I can't take the sight of them anymore."

"Tell us those names!" his cohort screams, pushing his face into hers. "Tell us now and we won't destroy those beautiful blue eyes of yours."

Her face is almost unrecognizable. They have slapped her with such force that her cheeks are a patchwork of scarlet and blue. And on her back, where the officer's belt had left her painful red welts, blood now leaked from the skin.

"Tell us the names!" Again they shout at her and pound their fists on the table.

"You have one more chance to save your eyes!"

Lena looks up at the senior agent and widens her eyes even further, even though her face is swelling larger with each passing moment.

She does not utter a single name as they bind her hands behind her back and bring another Nazi in with a bayonet that had been placed in fire. She fights with every ounce not to scream as they blind her, but the pain is too much, and the cry escapes her and shatters through the air.

When they are done with her, they tie a dirty bandage across the spot in which they gouged out her eyes and throw her into a van. They drive to Via Pelliciai and throw her bloody body in front of her family's apartment.

"You still have time to save your life, Lena Galvetto! Your parents are upstairs. They can still take care of you. Just tell us those names!"

Lena, now on the street pavement,

doesn't make a sound. Though upstairs, with the windows thrown open, her mother's screams pierce through the air.

Then, at the officer's nod, without hesitation, one of the soldiers lowers his rifle and shoots Lena in the head.

THIRTY

~

Verona, Italy
SEPTEMBER 1943

The men who have not been arrested or killed are now scattering through the city, trying to hide like hunted animals. Others try to make their way to the mountains. The next day, after the battle at the Piazza delle Poste, Luca's bookstore is stormed by the Germans. Although all the hidden guns had already been pulled out of the books in the storeroom, the remaining books with the incriminating holes and the anti-Fascist newspapers are discovered in the back, and a warrant is placed for his arrest.

Luca finds Elodie back at her apartment with Orsina. He does not have the heart to tell her that the Gestapo had blinded Lena before shooting her, and that Beppe had died in front of a firing squad.

Instead, he tells her the obvious. "It's too dangerous for any of us here now. They're hunting everyone down. It's time for us to get to the mountains."

Orsina is shaking her head. "We can't go to the mountains, Luca. Neither Elodie nor I could ever survive in the wilderness."

She looks at Elodie. "No, if we go anywhere, it'll be Venice. We can easily lose ourselves there."

Luca disagrees. "You two can't go anywhere now on a train with your own identity cards. Given her friendship with Lena, there's probably already a warrant out for Elodie's arrest."

"Well, what choice do we have?" Elodie says. "We can't just wait here for the Gestapo to knock on the door."

"There is someone up with my brother who can make false papers for you. Give me photographs of each of you and I'll take care of it."

"You're more likely to get caught coming back down into the city," Elodie says. "Let me go with you and get them, and then I will leave for Venice with mother."

The women exchange silent looks. Orsina does not want Elodie to go into the mountains, and Elodie does not want Luca to risk reentering the city once he's left.

Orsina is not budging. She is filled with a newfound strength that surprises her daughter.

"Mamma," Elodie says, her voice soft, yet insistent. "We don't have time to argue. I will get us the new identity cards. Then, Venice. I promise."

Outside, the sounds of gunfire still ricochet in the air. Luca walks past Orsina, who is standing rigid as a soldier in her own living room.

He pulls aside the curtain and peeks out to the piazza.

"I am worried about Lena and Beppe being held at the Palazzo dell'INA."

Luca looks at her and Elodie interprets his eyes.

"No . . . you don't think they . . ."

He doesn't answer her, and his silence pierces through her like an arrow.

Luca wants to take her into his arms and

soothe her, but Orsina has gotten to her first.

"They will execute us, too, if they find us," Luca tells Elodie and Orsina. "We need to leave today."

Luca cannot return to the bookstore, so he plans their escape as the women quickly pack a few things.

He tells Elodie to ride her bicycle to the base of the mountains where they had previously met. "If I'm not there, start hiking up to where we met Rafaelle and the others the last time. Bring photographs of yourselves."

He looks at Elodie, who is still shaking from the shock of Lena's and Beppe's deaths.

"Signora Bertolotti," he says. "I want to thank you for all you've done. You are incredibly brave."

"I am not brave, Luca. I have lost my husband to the Fascists, and I will not lose my daughter to the Germans." She looks at him with fierce eyes. "I am entrusting Elodie to you. Guard her with your life."

Luca nods. "That goes without saying."

Elodie embraces her mother and whispers in her ear to pack lightly. "We'll need very little now, so take just a few things. We don't want to carry too much on the train and draw attention."

Orsina nods. "Come back quickly, **carissima.** I'll have our things ready by then."

She pedals fast toward the gates of Verona, the air in her hair and her skirt lifted above the knees. Once she clears the city, she will still have many miles to go until she reaches the mountains. German soldiers are everywhere. They stand at each corner in their olive-green uniforms, their rifles leveled, and their hard eyes staring from beneath the rim of their steel helmets.

There is a roadblock when she gets to the Porta San Zeno, with several soldiers inspecting the papers of civilians who want to pass through.

She stops pedaling and pushes her feet to the sidewalk to halt the wheels.

"Papers?" a German asks her. He is staring straight into her eyes, and Elodie wonders if he can see the streak marks on her cheeks from her tears.

She doesn't want to give her identity card over to him, fearing her name might already be on a list from the Gestapo.

She smiles and reaches into her bag to feign a search.

Blushing, she turns to him and says, "It must be here somewhere."

Her face is flushed from pedaling. The top button of her blouse has come undone, and she can see the soldier trying to peek at her breasts.

She bends over her purse again, lower this time. "I know it's in here. Silly me. I rushed out so quickly . . ."

Elodie looks up at him and tries to channel Lena's spirit. She gives him her brightest smile and flutters her eyelashes demurely.

"I live just down the street. Let me go home and get it. I must have left it on the kitchen table."

She touches the button on her blouse slightly and smiles at him again.

"No need. But don't go far; you'll be searched again at every gate. We've been alerted to be on the lookout for traitors trying to escape today."

"Well, that's clearly not me," she said, saluting the German. He seemed delighted by her gesture.

"No, clearly not," he said, waving her through.

She continues riding on the path that leads to the mountains. She passes many Germans on her way there, but none of them bother to stop a young girl on her bicycle, pedaling away happily with the breeze in her hair. She cannot fathom how Luca will get past all of the soldiers. She prays he already has his own set of false papers.

After an hour, she arrives at the same spot she had met Luca nearly a week before. He is not there, so she stashes her bicycle in the bushes and begins the long walk up into the mountains.

All around her, the scent of the juniper and pine trees is invigorating. She had not yet had a moment to detect the scent of autumn in the city, with all the upheaval from the German invasion. But alone in the quiet of the woods, she now walks with the sun's golden light on her back and savors a moment of not having to be on her guard.

She finds her way without difficulty, using visual landmarks to guide her. She

remembers the rock where she had tied
her hair back with her handkerchief, and
next remembers where she had stopped
to gather her breath. She follows each
curve of the path, remembering where she
had gazed at Luca and he at her. Finally,
she mounts the last part, where she has
to push away branches and go deep into
the brush.

Suddenly from out of the woods, she
hears footsteps under the brush.

"Halt!" a voice shoots out at her.

She first sees the rifle. Then the body
who holds it. It's a tall, thin boy no older than
seventeen. He is dressed in faded green fa-
tigues, a worn V-neck sweater over his shirt
and a bandanna tied around his neck.
Elodie looks down and sees that he is wearing a belt studded with ammunition.

"I'm Dragonfly," Elodie says calmly. "I
work with the Dolphin." She has never called
Luca "the Dolphin" before, but she realizes
she must use battle names now.

He looks her up and down, acting as he
thinks a man, not a boy, would. She is unsure if he's trying to figure out if she is who
she says she is, or if he's just hungry to look
at a woman.

Elodie starts walking toward him. The boy lowers his rifle, turns, and begins walking farther. He says nothing, and she quietly follows.

After walking in silence for several more minutes, he brings her to a makeshift camp. Five men are sitting around a low fire, warming tins of meat.

She sees Rafaelle first; his large body and overalls are easy to identify. He has a long musket over his lap. Before she has a chance to speak, he looks up.

A smile crosses his face. "Dragonfly . . ." he greets her. He lifts his musket and drapes it over his shoulder, then walks over to her.

"Now, you're a welcome sight . . ."

The other men by the fire look in her direction, each of them smiling with appreciation.

Rafaelle places a hand on her shoulder. "I know my brother will be happy to see you."

She smiles, relieved that Luca has already arrived safely at the camp.

"He is out patrolling. Should be back in an hour. Did you bring the photographs of your mother and yourself?"

She nods, patting her bag.

"Good, then. Let me introduce you to our expert forger, Giorgio. Also known as the Falcon. He's in that tent over there."

They walk over to a pitched tent, which contains a table with a small wireless radio. Giorgio walks out, a cigarette dangling from his lips.

"Falcon, meet Dragonfly. A friend of my brother's and one of our **staffette**."

He extends his hand. "**Piacere.** A pleasure."

"She's brought the photographs for the new documents. Can you do it now? She won't be staying up here with us very long . . . unfortunately."

"No? What a shame." Giorgio smiles. "I think Jurika needs a little female company. That little blonde teacher who arrived the other day doesn't seem to be taking a shine to her."

Rafaelle lets out a big laugh and slaps Giorgio on the shoulder.

"Give him the photographs, Dragonfly."

She hands them over, and Giorgio takes them back into the tent. "Shouldn't take me too long," he says, winking. "Why don't you sit down?"

She watches as Giorgio withdraws two identity cards from a metal box. The Fascist seal is on their covers. He strikes a match to light a gas lamp and begins to work.

Elodie is sitting quietly. She begins to hum an Albinoni piece to distract herself from thinking about Lena and the upheaval of the previous few days. Elodie senses Luca's arrival before he walks into the tent.

He places his hands on her arms, and she feels herself grow warm just from his touch.

"Thank God you made it here safely," he whispers to her. "The Germans are everywhere, like flies."

"Take it outside," Giorgio grumbles. "I can't work with all your chatting! This has to be exact, or your girlfriend and her mother are going to get a bullet through their eyes."

"Yes. Yes, I'm sorry," Elodie apologies. "I'm so grateful for what you're doing,

Falcon." His name catches on her tongue like a nail caught on a piece of cloth.

Giorgio grunts, and Luca waves for her to join him outside the tent.

"Once he's done, I want you out of here. I want you on the next train to Venice."

"How will you find me there?"

"There is Resistance in Venice. Let your mother find a safe place for you both. And then wait for us to find you. Don't worry about anything else. I will find you. I promise."

They are still talking when suddenly three partisans arrive in the camp. A sense of commotion erupts.

Luca turns. "It's Rita and the others. They seem to have news."

Elodie turns and sees a blonde woman with two other men conferring with Rafaelle and some other partisans. The woman is young, in her early twenties, with a round face and small features. She, too, wears a bandanna around her neck and carries a musket that seems nearly as large as she is.

Elodie has never heard the name Rita Rosani before. She looks around to see if Jurika is close by, but doesn't see her in the group and assumes she is now out on patrol.

"We shot two Germans just some distance away. They're approaching. We need to get ready." She is breathless; her adrenaline lifting off her skin.

Elodie whispers into Luca's ear, "Who is she?"

He still has one ear listening to Rita, as he whispers, "She's a schoolteacher. Jewish. Family moved from Trieste to Verona. She just arrived in the mountains with a band of three other partisans who call themselves the Eagle."

Elodie looks at Rita's face and sees the Slavic features typical of people from the Trieste region.

"She was a schoolteacher?" Elodie can't contain her surprise. She looks at this young girl now draped with a musket rifle, and tries to imagine her instructing little children.

"She's a natural fighter, like our Jurika. She took out three Germans in Valpolicella. Let me introduce you," Luca says as he ushers Elodie in Rita's direction.

"Glad to see we have another woman joining our troop," she says to Elodie. She pushes her rifle over her shoulder and extends a handshake.

"She's not joining us," Luca interrupts. "She's just waiting for the Falcon to finish up with her papers."

Rita looks at Elodie to see if this is her decision or one that's been made for her. "Is that right?"

"Yes." Again Luca speaks for her. "Dragonfly has already completed several missions for the Resistance."

"I see," Rita says looking her over.

Elodie is about to say something when Giorgio walks over and hands her the two new identity cards.

"I present you with two of my best masterpieces. Dragonfly, you are now Anna Zorzetto from Venice."

Elodie studies the cards; she can't begin to tell them apart from the real ones. They are masterful. He has applied the embossed seal over her and her mother's photographs. Orsina is now Maria Zorzetto.

She hardly has time to thank him before she hears gunfire. Rafaelle orders the group to disperse in different directions.

A musket is thrust into Elodie's hands and Luca, now swearing, pulls her by the arm into the cover of the woods.

THIRTY-ONE

<ᴖ>

Portofino, Italy
OCTOBER 1943

Elodie has been a guest in Angelo's house for ten days. At night, she sleeps in the white room, the blue coverlet pulled to her chest. She dreams of people who are no longer beside her: Luca in the forest, his hair black as bramble, and her mother's voice floating from the bath. She also dreams of her cello, silent and pleading, desperate for her to bring out its song.

She feels the nausea lifting. The crippling fatigue has lessened, freeing her ability to move.

Angelo calls her Anna, and she feels her body stiffen. She lifts her head and meets his eyes. She wonders if he can read her like a map, or a sheet of music, knowing that this is not her real name. That somewhere beneath the skin and bone, her blood belongs to a girl named Elodie.

He notices her spine straighten. Her eyes flicker. She is like a cat, suddenly on guard. He wants to show her that she is safe here; that his offer to give her shelter is without obligation. He wants to tell her that it gives him comfort to help the person who is too scared to ask. That he's doing a form of penance for leaving behind the woman he loved, the child he longed to hold. He wants to tell her not to be afraid.

He sees that she is drawn to his books. He sees how she glances at the titles when she thinks he's not looking, and how she secretly tries to touch a cover, or trace a finger over a deckled edge. His Dalia had loved books, too. The paper, the smell, the texture, even the placement of the words on the page, all were forms of beauty to her. And he knew one thing: A woman who loves books has a dreamer's soul, with each story she has read woven into her own.

As she stands in the living room staring at the books, he pulls out two from the shelf.

"Do you like Moravia or Dante? Stendhal, or perhaps Fitzgerald?" He smiles, as the title **Gatsby Il Magnifico** slips from his lips. And, suddenly, with his list of names, Elodie feels as though she is back in Luca's bookstore.

"I have a favorite book," she says softly. "**Il Piccolo Principe**."

"**The Little Prince**," he says. "I know it very well. One must have experienced love to understand its hidden meaning."

She smiles. "Yes, I have my own copy with me."

She is surprised by how openly she answers him, but she finally wants to tell him at least one truthful thing about her.

"Do you?" he says. "May I see it?"

She walks back to her room and takes the book out of her bag. She sees the cover with the boy clutching the parachute made from birds, his feet lifting from the moon, and the sight of it makes her want to cry.

She returns and hands it to him.

He smiles, and the kindness on his face is overwhelming to her. "Come, let's find a place to sit. Zaccharia has a fever, but he's

just down the street. Francesca has a broken leg, but I've already plastered it and she
won't be going anywhere for several days.
Gherardo is ninety-two and has a head-
ache, but he's had it for the past fifteen
years." He lets out a small laugh. "Plus
there's the **kommandant**, of course, who
needs an insulin shot . . . but he likes me
to wait until five o'clock after he has his
schnapps to dull the pain from the needle.
A brave German he is, obviously." He smiles
again. "So, I can certainly take a few moments and read to you, Anna, before I have
to go."

He lifts his chin in the direction of the sun
streaming through the arched door that
leads to the garden.

"But I think you spend too much time in-
doors. It's not good for your health. You
need some fresh air and sunshine."

She smiles. Since she left her mother, no
one has been concerned for her care.

"Shall we go to the garden? I can read
to you there."

He senses her hesitation like a silent
movement that changes the air within the
room.

"It's private. No one will see us there. Think of it as therapeutic, if nothing else."

She nods, and Angelo feels as though he's accomplished a small victory as Elodie follows him.

In the sunshine, she finds herself squinting. Angelo is right, she hasn't been outside since she arrived, and the light striking her eyes and face is almost blinding.

She inhales the scent of gardenia and the now-familiar jasmine, and detects the sound of seagulls circling above. Below, she sees the stretch of the ocean and the port from where she first arrived. Viewed from high above the hills, it's now just a tiny spot.

As he lifts the book and takes a finger to the page, she remembers with gratitude how he pulled her out from the crowd and saved her from the German with the prying eyes.

"Where should I start?" he asks her.

"At the beginning," she says.

He nods. "As you wish. My wife used to like me to begin at the end of the books I read to her, so she knew if she had to conserve her tears."

Elodie ponders this for a moment. A card has been dealt, a revelation about his late wife.

"I have no more tears left now," Elodie says, looking out toward the sea. "With me, you can start from the beginning."

"As you wish, Anna," he says, and he turns back to the first page of **Il Piccolo Principe, The Little Prince**. "Allora . . ."

The hour passes between them quickly. He slips into a voice that sounds low and soothing. He reads about the little prince journeying through the first planets, where he meets the king, the vain man, the drunkard, and the man who makes maps. But he stops before her favorite part: the taming of the fox.

When her eyes close, he studies her in those quiet, stolen moments like a connoisseur of displaced persons. She is more complicated than the others that have come through his door. Simon, the Hungarian Jew, who arrived with a single diamond sewn into his pocket and stayed with him for only a few days before heading farther south. Guido, the eighteen-year-old soldier, who arrived at the port dressed as a seminary student after running away from his post, but who gave himself away by the military boots he still wore. It had been fortunate that the Fascist control at the port hadn't noticed them as well, but luckily they were distracted by an impressively large-breasted girl who had arrived on the same boat.

Angelo often recalled the first night Guido spent with him in his home. After drinking one too many glasses of **vino santo**, the boy could barely control his emotions. He insisted he wasn't a coward and that he loved his country, but he couldn't die on frozen Russian soil, where his papers ordered him to go. He would have preferred Ethiopia to Russia, the boy sobbed over his drink. At least there it was warm. Angelo winced. Thoughts of Nasai came flooding back to him. He felt the boy in the room like a ghost.

When he drank, Angelo's private hauntings returned. The two people he had abandoned were the ones who had most needed his protection, Dalia and Nasai. The midwife had insisted she had done everything she could to save her, but she wasn't a doctor. He couldn't help wondering where his predecessor, Doctor Pignone, had been when Dalia died? Drinking wine at his favorite café, or taking a nap in his hammock under the fig trees? He certainly was not with the midwife or his mother and Vanna as they struggled to save Dalia's life.

He would never show this boy, nor any of the others who came through his door, his room with the papered walls. Every night, he looked up and saw the words he had written to his pregnant bride, and he would sleep surrounded by the shadow of those letters. It wasn't the words that haunted him now, but the two hands that had cut them and pasted them to the walls with such devotion.

When Guido went down the hall to take his bath that night, Angelo noticed the boy empty his pockets onto the desk in the spare room, revealing a small rope cord with an amulet of San Giorgio. Angelo remembered so many of his fellow soldiers wearing a similar charm around their necks when he was in Ethiopia. The image of Saint George on his horse, a sword grasped to his side, was the gift so many fathers gave to their sons to protect them. Here in Porto-fino, one could see San Giorgio everywhere. He was the patron saint of the city.

Angelo had never been one to believe in superstitions or rituals even though he had grown up with his mother believing in the powers of saints. She prayed not only to San Giorgio but also to Saint Peter, the pa-tron saint of fishermen. And when Angelo had left for school, she added prayers to Saint Luke to protect her son from harm.

So he could not deny that things like am-ulets and good-luck charms gave people comfort. But Angelo certainly did not be-lieve these objects themselves held any special powers, but only connected people to the person who had given them. For him, it was the touch of his palm against his pa-tient's skin that created a seal between them.

He had watched countless times in hos-pital wards, even in the tents of Ethiopia, how a human touch could heal in a way that medicine alone could not. And so at night, when Angelo lay tormented by thoughts of Dalia, he often wondered if things might have been different had he been there to hold her hand.

Guido stayed with Angelo in his home in the terraced cliffs of Portofino for nearly two months. He helped the men in the family on the fishing boats, learning to repair their nets and their engines. Angelo was sure the boy was safe in Portofino, that no one had come looking for him among the lemon trees and ancient village roads that over-looked the sea. But then one morning, when Angelo woke, he found the boy was gone. He had disappeared without even leaving a note of good-bye. But he had left his trea-sured amulet for Angelo, placing it next to the carved-wood lion from Nasai.

The girl who calls herself Anna is now sit-ting across from him in his garden, her eyes closed, the wind slightly moving her hair. She didn't remind him of Dalia. No, his wife had been a book of abundant fresh pages, with eyes that were always hopeful and full of light. This girl was different. She reminded him of an old secretary desk he had once seen in his professor's office in Genoa, with its tiers of small drawers, its veneer like an intricate puzzle created out of an inlay of several different exotic woods.

Even her torso, which she always pro-

tects with two folded arms, was like a cab-
inet of secrets, brimming with stories yet
untold. He already suspects why she covers her belly, and why she has no appetite
in the mornings and sleeps for much of the
day. That was an easy diagnosis for him,
one he had concluded within her first few
days at his house.

But there was something far beyond this
feminine vulnerability that drew him closer
to her. It was as if he felt not like a doctor,
but rather like a watchmaker who wanted
to open the back of the dial to reveal all the
mechanisms, where he knew the true
beauty and intricacy lay.

After she has been with him at the cottage
for a few weeks, he begs her not to call
him **Dottore**, but by his given name Angelo.
They no longer move through the house as
strangers, but as two quiet souls who
have grown to understand each other's
rhythms.

When his sisters questioned Anna's arrival, he insisted that she was a daughter
of one of his old friends from medical school,
another one like Simon or Guido who temporarily needed shelter during the war.

It was Vanna who was the most suspicious of Anna. One afternoon in November, she stopped by the house to find her brother gone. Anna was sitting alone in the living room, her blouse untucked from her skirt and her gaze focused on her belly. Within an instant, Vanna felt certain about what she had suspected for the past two weeks: that the girl was pregnant. She was so thin in her arms and legs, but with each passing week she seemed to grow thicker in the middle.

Elodie heard the sound of Vanna's footsteps on the tile and looked up. Immediately she tried to tuck in her shirt and smooth down her skirt. But Elodie knew that Vanna had already seen her.

There was a part of Elodie that no longer wanted to lie, and with every day it became more difficult to conceal. She had been reading one of Angelo's books when she felt the first fluttering inside her. That was why she had untucked her blouse and placed her hands on top of her belly. It was so faint, so gentle, almost like a butterfly's wings caressing her from within, but she felt it and it took her breath away.

So when Vanna had caught her in this

moment of discovery, Elodie soon gave up her efforts to conceal her pregnancy and simply rose to stand before the woman.

"I'm sorry," Elodie said, her eyes glassy with tears. "I just felt a flutter for the first time."

Vanna, who was between the age of a mother and an older sister to Elodie, remained silent for what seemed like several minutes. She looked at the girl standing in her brother's living room, her hands now covering her belly, and it awakened her own maternal instincts to protect someone vulnerable. Elodie was pure despite her condition. And so there was no judgment in Vanna's voice when she came closer to Elodie and whispered, "I know."

Vanna had birthed three children herself and knew well the marvel of having a life growing inside you. It was hard to believe that it had been nearly fifteen years since she gave birth to her first child. Since then she had watched as her brother returned from Ethiopia, his heart broken, and wife and child already buried in the cemetery on the cliff overlooking the sea.

It would have been easy for Vanna to dismiss the young girl in front of her as a fallen, as someone who had no right to ask for shelter from her all-too-giving brother. But Vanna had seen the effect the girl had on Angelo. For the first time in years, he had begun to smile.

"Anna," she said, "how many months are you?"

"A little over three."

"So you have your energy back now?"

"Yes, too much. I want to clean everything for Angelo and show him how grateful I am for letting me stay here."

"And what about the father?"

Vanna could feel a shift in the room as soon as she asked.

"I see you don't have a wedding ring . . ."

Elodie shook her head.

"I have no ring." Her voice quivered. "I have many things from him. I have his sweater. A medal on a chain. A book with his words inscribed into it. But I have no ring." She paused. "And I won't be getting one."

She lowered her eyes and then raised them to meet Vanna's. She knew she should feel ashamed by this fact, that it revealed her immodesty, her lack of religious fortitude, and her inability to control her own

THE GARDEN OF LETTERS

desire. But how could one be ashamed for carrying something inside them that was conceived solely by love?

Vanna nodded and kept her face neutral and without judgment. She scanned Elodie to discover the girl's eyes flickering again. Without needing to ask, Vanna knew immediately that Elodie had felt another kick.

Vanna smiled and walked closer to Elodie. It made her feel young again to see this girl experiencing all the wonder and beauty of carrying her first child. Vanna had never stopped being amazed by every stage, but those initial movements were the first symbol that a mother and child were eternally entwined.

She had been relieved by the girl's honesty. Had Elodie tried to lie to her, Vanna would have been unable to trust her. But now she felt her heart warming to her. She knew the Virgin herself had been unwed and in need of shelter. What this girl needed now was kindness and nurturing. Her brother's life had already had so much sadness and loss, and she knew he was smart enough to already realize the girl was pregnant. It would be a blessing for him to have

the opportunity to see life brought into the
world after so much heartache.

"How old are you?"

"Nearly twenty."

Vanna smiled. "I was the same age when
I had my first son."

The two women were now only a few feet
apart. Against the backdrop of the garden,
Elodie looked beatific.

"I'll try and help you. Anna, you can trust
me. I will be your friend."

At that moment, Elodie wanted to tell
Vanna her real name and her whole story,
have it pour out of her like a stream of water that wished to run free.

But instead, she took Vanna's hand and
placed it on the center of her belly, then
placed her own hand on top.

The two women waited in perfect silence
until the sensation of a small foot fluttering
inside an invisible, watery world sealed
them to each other.

THIRTY-TWO

~~

Verona, Italy
SEPTEMBER 1943

The same way she had heard music as a child was the way she remembered her last moments with Luca. It came to her like a drowning.

She had been in the camp with Luca and the others for only two days. But within that short time, the north of Italy had exploded into war. The mountains, which had only known the sounds of birds before, were now shaking with the echo of explosions from the bordering cities. Elodie grew cold as she saw the plumes of smoke rising from the center of Verona. Even the sky had changed. The clouds were cut by the razor-sharp blades of airplane wings. And the sound of the engines was deafening.

She had left Orsina alone in the apartment to pack for Venice. She was supposed to have come home the following evening, but the incessant bombing had prevented her return. Elodie was sick with worry. She could only imagine how her mother must have been feeling alone in the apartment.

The first night she had slept in a small tent with Rita Rosani, on old sacks stuffed with straw. The schoolteacher's blonde hair looked angelic, but joined to her body, like another limb, was her rifle. During the night, Elodie saw Rita's hand reach for her musket like it was a lover whom she was afraid might leave her side.

On the second day, Luca was told to go farther into the mountains to look for a place to move their camp. Elodie insisted she would go with him.

She had not bathed for several days now, not since the morning after her recital, and she was self-conscious about the soot and dirt on her skin. She looked like a wholly different person from the girl who previously had been so resplendent on the stage.

Gone was the taffeta silk, the tight chignon—
all of the elegance of her debut.

The others looked like time-worn partisans. Rafaelle with his broad shoulders, his
brown skin, and hands that looked large
enough to be weapons themselves. Even
the other women, Rita and Jurika, had a so-
lidity to them that was foreign to her. Their
backs and shoulders were stronger. And
their breasts, so much bigger than Elodie's,
gave the impression that they were wearing armor.

She had not been thinking when she
jumped on her bicycle and pedaled to meet
Luca. She regretted not having worn trousers and a sweater, something that would
have protected her skin while she walked
through the bramble and thatch.

Luca was standing next to a small fire,
speaking with his brother and drinking from
a small cup of boiled acorn coffee.

"Want some?" he had asked her. "It's awful but it's warm."

She put her hand up and shook her
head no.

He walked over and wrapped a single
arm around her. "If I had known that you
would get stuck up here with me in this dirty

camp, with the Germans swarming the area, I would never have let you come."

She looked up at him and smiled. "I'm glad I'm here with you . . ."

He shook his head. "Your poor mother must be sick with fear. She expected you home yesterday."

"My mother is strong."

"We need a new camp." Rafaelle came over and interrupted them. "We've been here too long. Luigi discovered a German bunker last night, two miles east. I want to move our camp before we attack them."

Rafaelle pulled out a map and showed Luca where the Germans had been sighted. He moved his finger in the opposite direction and tapped a section of the map. "Try to find a safe place over here."

He started to walk away, but then returned. "And take Elodie with you," he instructed. "She shouldn't be left alone here, it's too dangerous. If we know about the German camp, they know about ours. I can't ensure her safety if she stays here."

Luca nodded. "Yes, you'll come with me," he said, looping his arm around her.

They began walking in the direction Rafaelle had indicated. There were no pathways, just spaces in between trees and vines. The smell of chestnut husks and oak leaves was heavy in the air.

After some time, there seemed to be a clearing in the woods. "What's that over there?" Elodie asked. In the distance, she saw what looked like an abandoned farmhouse.

Luca nodded. He, too, saw what looked like an old house. "If it has a roof and four walls, Rafaelle and the others will think we've found a palace for them."

Elodie smiled and reached to find Luca's hand.

They went over to inspect the structure more closely. When they arrived, they discovered that it was nothing but a skeleton of charred beams and stone. As they moved through what must have been the living room, their feet stepped over pieces of some family's former life: a child's cradle, a raggedy doll, four broken kitchen chairs, and a table covered in rubble and bits of the fallen roof. They trod on a carpet made of broken pottery and glass.

In the reflection of one of the old cloudy windows, Elodie saw her face.

"I don't think I've ever looked this tired . . . this dirty," she said as her fingers tried to adjust the strands of black hair that had fallen over her eyes.

She then extended her arms and showed the smudges of dirt and soot that at first glance might have looked like a series of bruises.

"What I would do for a warm bath right now . . ."

Luca nodded. He, too, was covered in a thick veil of gray.

He wanted to give her what she wanted, a beautiful bathtub like the English had in their manors. Deep, white porcelain, bear-claw feet, and steaming water up to her chin. The thought of her emerging from it was in itself a heady dream for him.

Through one of the broken windows, he saw a large washing basin in the backyard, certainly deep enough for a girl Elodie's size to bathe in. In the kitchen were several copper pots. Luca was sure he could make a fire, with sticks and the pieces of scattered wood around the house.

"Do you see a water pump, Elodie?"

Elodie shrugged. "No, but I'll check outside."

They both found their way to the outer garden, where they discovered a pump buried in the tall grass.

"You're going to get your bath," Luca said. He had begun to grow a beard over the past few days, and through the shadow of his stubble and dirt-smudged face, his eyes were shining. In the sunlight, they were the color of honey.

"But how?"

"You'll see," he said. "Just wait."

"Let me help," she protested. She lifted her hand to move her hair from her eyes.

"No, just go inside and rest until I call for you."

Luca looked up at the sun and saw it was midway in the skyline. They still had time before it got dark and cold. Still, he moved quickly and with great efficiency. He gathered small, dry twigs for the kindling and searched for larger pieces of dry wood, knowing they wouldn't create any smoke.

When he was satisfied, he took out his lighter and shoots of fire soon flickered in front of him.

He took the copper pot to the water pump

and washed it, then the larger, deeper
washing bin as well. After each was clean,
he filled the copper pot with water and
brought it over to the fire, and fashioned
some old rope over the makeshift harness,
so that it could be heated from underneath.
He lugged the large washing bin closer,
so he could eventually pour the hot water
into it.

When he had finally heated enough
water, he called to Elodie in the farmhouse.

"Here is your bath, **carissima**!"

She stood there shaking her head and
lifted a single hand to cover her smile. "Luca,
how did you manage such perfection?"

"Come on, quickly now!" he said. "I want
you to tell me that I got the temperature of
the water just right, too!"

She smiled coyly. "If you insist."

Elodie walked to the corner of the garden and, with her back toward Luca, slowly
began to remove her clothes.

She started with her blouse. Unbutton-
ing the row down her front, she slipped it
off her shoulder. And although it was already quite dirty and not expensive at all,
she couldn't bear to put it on the ground.
She found a tree branch and carefully

draped it across. Then, she unzipped her skirt and stepped out of the material, placing that, too, on the branch.

With her body sheathed in nothing but a simple cotton slip, Luca could feel his heart pounding. She seemed to wait an eternity, standing there with only the angles of her shoulder blades revealed above the backline of the slip, her lithe arms reaching to undo the already loose pinning of her hair.

She then turned around to face him, walking over to the steaming basin of water he had prepared for her.

When she had gotten so close that he could touch her, only then did she lift up her slip and reveal her nakedness in its entirety to him.

He could not believe his eyes. This was the first time he had seen her naked. In the bookstore he had discovered her under the canopy of her clothes, his hands finding her underneath the curtain of her skirt and the cotton veil of her blouse. But now she stood in front of him, completely revealed.

It was as if he had been given a gift; the rare glimpse of something that had never been exposed before. She was porcelain white, opaque and luminous at the same time. Her breasts were two small globes of perfection, her buttocks like the curve of a mandolin.

He watched, transfixed, as she lifted a single leg and entered the makeshift bath.

Elodie now stood knee-deep in the water, her arms crossed to cover her breasts. She turned her head, looking at him over her shoulder. A thin ribbon of hair fell over one of her eyes, and she smiled at him in a way that paralyzed him.

"Did you see that pitcher by the old stove?" she asked. "If you bring that here, it would be helpful . . ." The small ribbons of muscle in her back sprung up in high relief.

Again, he could barely breathe. She looked like a living sculpture.

"Yes, of course . . ." he stammered. "I'll get it right away."

Luca returned quickly with the pitcher and dipped it into the water. He stood up and poured it over her body, long, fluid streams reflecting off her glistening skin.

Neither of them could remember who kissed the other one first. She knew he had placed the pitcher down. That he had stood up and taken a step closer to her so that the length of his body was parallel to hers. She, still naked in the tub, he standing just against her, his shirt becoming wet as he pressed into her. She felt herself shiver and reached to touch his chest. She sensed the rhythm of his heartbeat, the music just beneath his skin. She fingered the amulet and leather cord around his neck before he reached for her fingers, pulling her closer, bringing her mouth slightly upward toward his own. In her nakedness, she wanted him to cover her with his body, his touch. And so she waited for him to come to her fully.

He took his hands first to her hair, then to the bell shape of her shoulders, and then up again to cup her face in his palms. When he held her cheeks in his hands and kissed her, he felt himself weaken as if there wasn't an ounce of fight left in his heart or body.

With every touch, she shook slightly in his arms, like a small bird that was trying to take flight in the cradle of his hands. His thumb felt the contrast between her breast and nipple, his fingers the narrow of her waist, then on to to the curve of her hips. She was now out from the tub and against him, drawing her with him to the ground, pulling himself so close into her that he heard her expel just the faintest, smallest cry.

He looked into her eyes and they were shimmering with a light like he had never before seen. He felt himself traveling between time and space, where nothing mattered now but the pull between them.

The fear, the exhaustion of war, and the threat of death dropped away. The only thing in Luca's mind at that moment was that he loved Elodie.

He inhaled every part of her as if she were his own breath. She was like air, fire, and water all at once—every element that he needed to exist in this world.

They had used their clothes to dry themselves off. They kissed again, lovers who couldn't get enough of the other's touch. She remembered the sensation of being clean, the clear spike that ran from her head to the bottom of her feet, and of feeling alive.

She remembered that once she had pulled on her skirt and buttoned her blouse, she had turned to Luca and looked at him deeply in the eyes, and thought that nothing else mattered in the world except him.

And although they were no longer entwined, and their limbs now moved freely and separately, she still felt him as if his body was imprinted inside her. It was like music that penetrates and still moves within you, even after the melody has ceased playing.

As they walked, she remembered him looking up at the sky, his neck stretching out from the collar of his shirt as he searched for the sun in order to learn the direction they needed to go.

They headed back to the camp holding each other's hand. She saw her delight in his eyes; her happiness mirrored in his smile. Both of them felt as though their discovery of a new camp would make everyone cheer.

She remembered the sight of the small bellflowers beneath her feet, how careful she had been not to step on them and crush their petals. That was her last memory before the sound of bullets ricocheted through the air. She had not wanted to harm the delicate blossoms. But then there was the sound of shouting, the chaos of the ambush. The sound of Luca turning to her and saying, "Not now! Jesus. Please not now!"

They were steps away from the camp,

but already Elodie could hear gunfire as though she were in the line of fire. Luca pulled her into a thicket and told her to make herself into a tight ball.

"Stay here, Elodie," he ordered. His face was the same as when he had pushed her against the wall in the Piazza delle Poste and ordered her to get inside the café.

Now, she was even more afraid. She begged him not to leave her alone in the woods. But she knew she couldn't fight; she had no gun and would be useless in battle.

"I need to go!" He leaned over and kissed her one more time, the amulet of St. George dangling from his throat.

"I'll love you forever, Elodie. Remember that. From beyond the stars." He kissed her one last time.

She felt herself trembling. She did not want him to quote **The Little Prince**. They were too young to have a love that existed beyond sight or touch.

He pulled his necklace of San Giorgio from his neck, breaking the leather knot in the back. "Hold this. It will protect you."

She hadn't wanted to take it. But he had tapped his rifle and told her he already had protection. That she was the one who needed the amulet more than he.

As the sound of gunfire laced the air, she clasped his amulet like a rosary. She heard the horrible screaming of soldiers in German. It was only hours later, after the sound of bullets had ceased, and she no longer heard a sound coming from the camp, that she stood up from the mass of thicket and broken tree boughs and went in search of Luca and the others.

She saw Rita first. Her face was covered in black dirt and her blouse had been ripped down the length of her sleeve. Blood soaked the kneecap of her trousers.

Luigi was standing above two dead Germans, pulling their rifles from their lifeless bodies.

To the left of the tent, Elodie spotted the Falcon on the ground, his chest soaked with blood and his eyes motionless, staring up at the sky.

Another body was slumped over a trunk that some of the others had used for sitting. Elodie could see by the slender build and kerchief around the neck that it was the young boy who had just the day before brought her up to the camp. Elodie felt her stomach rising within her chest. She was sure she was going to retch.

Rita looked at her; her eyes conveyed everything.

"We were ambushed," she finally managed to say. "We lost Raffaele, too."

Elodie shook her head. She felt her fingers tighten around the amulet. The small disc with the saint in the center cut into her skin.

She did not believe Rita. Without the sight of his body, she believed there was still a possibility Luca was alive.

"They attacked while you were away. It was Raffaele who heard the first footsteps while he was out on patrol. He killed the first two, but another five followed."

"We had found a new camp . . ." Elodie's voice trembled.

Suddenly, Elodie saw two men carrying a large body from the brush on a stretcher made of vine poles. She did not need to look at the face to know it was Raffaele's. She saw the overalls and knew immediately it was him.

She shut her eyes tight, not wanting them to see Raffaele being placed, lifeless, on the ground.

Rita came over and embraced her. "We will move there after we bury the dead. And we'll have to do that quickly, before more Germans arrive. They will be looking for their men when they don't return."

She then saw Jurika and another young partisan, Carlo, bringing Luca's body back to the camp on another makeshift stretcher. Elodie knew it was him, even before she saw the soles of the boots, the dangling of a thin arm.

When they lowered him to the ground, she felt every part of her sink into the earth. Her own blood drained from her head and from her heart. There was no breath, no music, left inside her. She felt Rita's arms tighten around her. The teacher knew better than to call him a fallen **partigiano** to the trembling girl; she referred to him as Elodie's **amato**, her love. And then so softly did her mouth whisper the words her father had once blessed over her: **"Hasten thoughts on golden wings. Hasten and rest on the densely wooded hills."**

Elodie said the two lines as if they were a prayer.

THIRTY-THREE

Verona, Italy
SEPTEMBER 1943

Elodie stood there motionless, her face pale with shock. She was cold and shivering. She could not believe that Luca now lay beneath a mound of hastily dug earth. Only a few hours ago they had been together, their bodies wet and entangled, nothing separating their beating hearts but a thin sheath of skin. But now the only trace of him was a makeshift cross marking his grave.

It was Rita who insisted that Elodie leave the camp. "Get your mother and go to Venice." She was staring at Elodie, her blonde hair pulled tightly behind her ears. Rita had yet to wash the dirt from her face. "That is what Luca would have wanted . . . certainly not staying here in the mountains to die. They say a partisan's life span is no more than six months," Rita said, shaking her head.

It was hard for Elodie to imagine the young woman who stood before her as a schoolteacher. Rita looked every bit the warrior. Her body was strong and muscular; her blue eyes were hard like river stones. "This is no place for you. You have your mother waiting at home. My family was put on a truck bound for a concentration camp." Rita's voice was like flint. "At least here I get to choose how I will die."

"I don't want to leave him here . . ." Elodie was still wearing Luca's sweater, and his amulet was still wrapped around her hand.

Rita looked up at the sky. The sun was already midway in the horizon. "There isn't a reason to stay here. You are not a soldier. You need to go now."

If Elodie did leave now, she might be able to get home before curfew. So in a daze, she followed one of the remaining partisans down the wooden path.

"I can't take you any farther than this," he

said as they came close to the base of the mountain. He had taken her nearly to the end of the dirt path. Between the trunks of the pin oaks, Elodie could see the stretch of the road below. "Be careful . . . There are Germans swarming around everywhere."

She nodded.

"Good luck," he said, casting one last look in her direction before he began his ascent back up into the hills.

She found her bicycle in the brush, its black frame still covered in the branches. She had camouflaged it in the same way she had with Luca the first time they met in the mountains. Now, as she began to move the pine limbs, clumps of leaves, and dried grass, she saw that her hands were shaking.

It had only been a little over a week since she and Luca had stood there in the wilderness collecting leaves to cover her bicycle. She had marveled at how different he seemed since the battle in the Piazza delle Poste. His muscles moving beneath his canvas shirt, his sleeves rolled to show the length of his arms.

In the bookstore, Luca had moved like a

quiet mouse. But here in the woods, he moved like a lion.

She still could not believe he was gone. Every part of her fought to erase the image of him and his brother being carried into the camp, lifeless and soaked in blood. She pretended it was not true, that she would see him shortly in the back room of his store on the Via Mazzini. Where she would again play her cello for him, and his eyes, his touch, and every part of him would spring forth and come alive.

She was afraid that if she began to cry, she'd never be able to stop. But the tears welled inside her, and no matter how much energy she put into ensuring they didn't fall, she felt them all the same. Painful as bits of swallowed glass.

Once on her bicycle, her body took over. She pedaled for forty minutes before she was stopped by two Fascist policemen who asked to see her identification.

She handed them her new papers. In her mind, she had already memorized her new name, Anna Zorzetto, as well as her new birth date and all the other details. Fortunately, her dirty appearance after days in the woods did not pique the guards' interest, and she was allowed to pass through.

When she finally arrived at the gates of the Porto San Giorgio, the German officers were busy pulling over truck and cars, focusing their efforts to investigate the male drivers entering the city. They barely noticed a girl with her heart torn out of her chest, her eyes wide and unblinking as she held back her tears.

THIRTY-FOUR

Verona, Italy
SEPTEMBER 1943

When Elodie reached her family's apartment building, she struggled to pull her bicycle inside. It took every ounce of her strength to make it up the stairs.

Orsina was only three steps from behind the door when she heard Elodie's knock. She had been waiting there virtually from the moment Elodie had left with Luca days earlier. She threw her arms around her daughter.

"I expected you back two days ago . . . When you didn't return . . ." Orsina's voice cracked. "I thought you were dead!"

"I couldn't get back home . . . there were

explosions in the streets. The Germans are everywhere . . ."

Orsina shook her head. She looked at her daughter, who by now had found a seat on one of the living room chairs. Elodie looked beyond exhausted.

"When do we leave for Venice?" Elodie was so weak that she could barely manage to get the words out. All she wanted to do was crawl back into her childhood bed and sleep.

"We'll leave as soon as you feel strong enough." Orsina hesitated for a moment. "But after you left with Luca, I started to wonder how we could manage to make a new start there." She took a deep breath. "Your father gave us such a good life while he was alive, but we have to think how we'll find money to live without his income from teaching."

Orsina scanned the room. "There are a few things we could try to sell. The dishes, the silverware." She stopped herself mid-thought. "But who would even buy them? No one has extra money to spare now, and they're not of any real value . . ."

Elodie was barely listening to her mother.

She cupped her face in her hands and began to sob.

"Luca's dead, Mamma."

Orsina's face turned pale.

"A group of German soldiers discovered his brother's camp. We . . . We . . ." She was trying to find her breath through her tears. "We had just scouted a new location and were returning to tell the others when the shooting began . . ." She knotted her hands together, her knuckles draining from pink to white.

"He insisted I stay hidden in the bushes . . . I begged him to stay . . . but he wouldn't."

Orsina wrapped her arms around her daughter. Elodie's cheeks were so wet now that Orsina could feel the tears soaking through her blouse and onto her own skin.

She continued to hold Elodie for several minutes until her daughter's tears stopped.

"I want to leave here, soon." She was trying to regain her breath and peeled herself away from Orsina's arms. "I have our new papers." She stood up, went to her bag, and fetched the new identity cards. "One of the partisans made these for us, only a few hours before he was killed." She handed Orsina's over to her. "We're Anna and Maria Zorzetto now."

Orsina took her new identity card and studied the new name.

Elodie tried to smile. "Seriously, Mamma, you must remember this . . . It's important in case we're ever questioned."

Orsina closed her eyes and etched the new date into her mind. "Your memory comes from me, **carina.** I will remember it."

Elodie touched her temples with her fingers. Her face was streaked with red from crying. "I wish I didn't remember so much . . . I can still see Luca's body . . . his fingers blue . . ." Her voice cracked and she stopped.

Orsina came over and embraced her, but Elodie pushed her away.

"I just want to leave here and forget everything."

Orsina tried again to soothe her daughter. She searched for her fingers and squeezed them. "We will make a new life in Venice. We will drown our painful memories in the lagoon and start anew."

"It's strange for me to envision us picking up everything and going to Venice."

Elodie bit her lip and searched to focus on her mother's eyes. "It's so close by train but you and Papa made it seem like it was a door to a city that it was best to keep closed."

Orsina became quiet. A strange light came over her face.

"As much as I love Venice, I've associated it with death. I buried my parents there, I lost my first pregnancy there . . . So after I had you, and your father and I made a new life in Verona, I just could never manage to return."

"Then why now?" Elodie was trying to understand her mother's inner mind.

"Because Venice is a maze. It's a place where you can both lose yourself and also reemerge. Especially for those who know it well." She took a deep breath. "And it's not safe for you in Verona anymore."

Orsina reached to pull back Elodie's hair. She wanted to see her daughter's eyes and anchor herself to them. These were eyes she had watched since the moment the girl had come into the world. She had seen them transform from innocence into maturity. Now even through her daughter's grief, she saw the strength within them.

"You're right, though. We will need money, Mamma."

Orsina nodded in agreement. "Yes. We must figure out a way to sell what we can."

Elodie lowered her eyes. "Father did leave me something valuable." She reached for her mother's hand. "But it never really belonged to me. It's now time for someone else to continue its story."

She turned her head and looked at the cello resting in the corner. Its red varnish was glimmering.

Orsina shook her head. "No. I won't let you. It hasn't come to that yet."

"I have a buyer in mind," she said, her decision already made.

She briefly imagined herself without her cello and felt a crushing sensation inside her chest. But perhaps she needed to rid herself of everything she had before she arrived in Venice. To let the lagoon she had yet to see swallow her whole and then spit her out, new and transformed.

The next morning, Elodie woke up and held the instrument one last time. She unwrapped it from its yellow scarf, stroked its long neck, and ran her fingers up and down the strings.

She had no doubt who the right person to buy the cello would be. She needed someone who knew its history and appreciated its provenance. She also wanted to be sure that the new owner would take as great care of it as she and her father had. Only one person she knew fit this description, and she knew exactly where to find him. She just had to hope that he was still there. And so the next morning, Elodie, or rather Anna Zorzetto, was on a train to Mantua to see the Wolf.

She boarded the train to Mantua and found a seat on one of the third-class wooden benches. Holding her cello closely between her arms and legs, she scanned her fellow passengers. Everyone had the same weary expression. Blank faces that conveyed only the simplest message to anyone who pondered them for a moment too long: "I know nothing. I have nothing of value. I only ask that you let me travel undisturbed."

In these times to be left undisturbed was truly a gift. So when the German

pass-kontrol barged into the train compartment, demanding papers and scrutinizing identity cards, it caused nearly every heart on board to stop momentarily.

Elodie watched the woman next to her let her toddler suck on a piece of stale bread that was no bigger than her thumb. Everyone looked so thin, their hollow faces ghostlike and grave.

The woman seemed to find Elodie and her instrument a curious addition to the compartment. Her eyes slid over the curve of the case and the lock of Elodie's fingers around its middle.

"It must be heavy," she finally said.

Elodie nodded. The child reached to touch the case, his tiny fingers gently caressing its inner curve.

Elodie heard his little voice above the din of the locomotive's wheels. "What is it?"

She felt his finger graze against her own, its warmth cutting through the chill that had run through her since Luca's death.

"It's a cello, **carino**," she said quietly. "And it makes the most beautiful music."

Since the Germans had arrived, it was impossible to travel on the rails without any significant delay. A typical forty-minute trip from Verona to Mantua could now take over two hours.

As Elodie looked out the window and saw the outskirts of Mantua, the city majestically rising in the distance, she felt as if she were traveling back in time. She could see the church bell tower and the medieval walls, and she tried to remember how long it had been since she was last in the Wolf's apartment, playing the encoded cadenzas within those peacock-blue walls.

It had been nearly three months. Even in that short time period, so much had happened. Her father had died. She had failed her mission at the Bibiena. The Germans had invaded Italian soil. There had been the bloodshed at the Piazza delle Poste. Lena and Beppe were murdered. And now the heartache of losing Luca. Elodie wrapped her arms around the cello case even more tightly and shut her eyes.

She wondered what the Wolf would say when she arrived at his apartment. Whether he'd greet her warmly, or say he wanted nothing more to do with her after she had bungled the code at the Bibiena. She tried to imagine him instead bringing her into the apartment, sitting her down calmly, and asking why she had come.

She practiced in her head how she would ask him whether he would be interested in buying her cello. She would never forget the sight of the Wolf's eyes when she first pulled it out of its case. He looked as though she had walked in with something more valuable than gold.

As she exited the train and made her way toward Mantua's central square, she told herself that this would probably be the last time she would hold the instrument in her arms. She stiffened under her sweater, her spine as straight as a rifle. She wanted to feel like stone, to no longer feel the river of grief that flowed just beneath her bones. In her life, she had held two things that she loved more than anything else: her cello and Luca. And within the next hour, she knew the last of these would be gone.

Her memory did not fail her. As soon as she alighted the train, she began to maneuver through the streets toward the Wolf's apartment. She entered the city through the Piazza Sordello, down the cobblestone street past Saint Andrea. But with so few pedestrians on the street, Mantua now seemed like a ghost town.

As she walked, she noticed three German soldiers smoking cigarettes outside of a local bar. One of them called out a leering remark to her. She maintained a face of neither disgust nor amusement, but one of indifference, as if his crude words were just another particle permeating the air.

When she arrived at the Wolf's apartment building, she found the large wooden front door slightly ajar. A small boy had just come in with his mother, and they were looking through their mailbox. They didn't even notice the girl with the cello who slipped in behind them and made her way up the stairs.

She knocked twice at his door. When no one answered, she turned the doorknob and, to her surprise, found it unlocked. Elodie walked inside.

A flood of memories from the last time returned to her. The long, narrow hallway. The wooden pedestal table with unopened letters stacked high. But unlike her first visit, there was no music floating through the apartment. The only thing she heard now was her own footsteps against the tile floor.

It was in the white room in front of the music salon that she first realized something was very wrong. The room had always been pristine when she had visited before. But now the sofas were sliced open, their stuffing pulled out and strewn on the floor. The glass vase that she had admired previously was shattered into pieces. The coffee table had been overturned, and the Oriental carpet that had first enthralled her was no longer there.

By the time she walked into the music room and put down her cello, Elodie was shaking. What she saw then was even more shocking than she could have ever imagined.

The peacock-blue walls looked like a desecrated tomb. The silk panels were slashed and cut open. The strings of the grand piano had been severed and brutally pulled out like weeds. Elodie looked at the wall where the painting of the girl in the kerchief had once been. But that, too, was gone.

Around the Wolf's desk, papers littered the ground like snow. She knelt down, her hands fumbling to neaten the scattered papers.

Her heart was racing. Every sound she heard, every creak in the rafter, every rustle of paper, sent a wave of panic through her.

Nearly everything about the apartment that she had once found so beautiful had been either confiscated or torn apart. And the Wolf? What had they done to him? She felt a terrible lump in her throat as she tried to imagine his fate.

The desk was filled with traces of him: a small red lacquer pen, a tin of pastilles, and a wand of half-melted sealing wax. Against a ceramic lamp, there was a framed photograph of a young woman, which Elodie had not noticed before.

The black-and-white image was of a young woman seated at a piano. She couldn't have been older than twenty in the photograph. Elodie studied her as though she were looking at herself. The woman's posture was as straight as a razor, her gaze unflinching. She was dressed in a simple, white sheath with her legs neatly crossed. Her eyes, dark and fierce, looked as though they knew something the photographer did not. They radiated an inner intelligence and a certain preternatural wisdom she was content to keep to herself.

Her hands, which were folded on her lap with long, slender fingers, showed clear evidence that she was a musician. The two middle fingers had loosened from the woman's clasp. Elodie could almost hear them tapping against the woman's skin. Beneath the tight smile and the crossed legs, Elodie could see what no one else except the Wolf probably saw, that music was clearly dancing through her head.

Elodie sat down at the desk and pulled out the center drawer. There she found something else unexpected: handwritten sheets of music. As she read the notes, she could hear the melody and feel the urgency and undulations of emotion contained within the score. Almost immediately she realized that this was the music the Wolf had been playing when she arrived at his apartment for the first time.

They had taken everything of value. And they had destroyed anything else of any beauty. But they could neither see nor understand the hidden treasure that sat resting inside this simple wooden drawer.

She had not heard music in her head for several days, not since before she left to go to the mountains and Luca. Even after she returned home and was ensconced in the living room where she had played her cello ever since she was a small child. But now the score, written by a woman she never met, penetrated her entire body. Elodie felt as though it was composed solely for her. She could hear the sadness contained in the notes, as if the composer was writing her own requiem. She heard the grief. The longing. But in between the valleys of notes, a legato of light and hope ran throughout.

She took hold of the score and instinctively placed it in her cello case.

Elodie walked quickly back toward the train station, still carrying her beloved cello. She had failed to sell it to the one person she knew who could fully appreciate it. But she was returning to Verona with something that transcended monetary value; the music composed by the Wolf's wife. Like her cello that once belonged to Enrico Levi, a man whom she had never met, she felt this music was also now entrusted to her care.

Over the next week, Elodie and her mother sell Pietro's violin and piano to a friend from

the conservatory. Orsina also quietly sells
her gold necklace and the black beads
that had been her mother's. For all their
trouble, they now have just enough money
to get to Venice and live there for a few
months.

Orsina now calls Elodie "Anna." They
memorize their new birthdays and repeat
their new last name over and over. Into her
red valise, Orsina packs to begin her new
life, while Elodie packs to forget her old one.
Her mother folds her dresses and her black
skirt with care. She takes her cotton summer dress that even in her now middle age
sets off her narrow waist and toned calves.
She packs a single silk flower for the sake
of beauty, and the wedding portrait of her
and Pietro for the sake of love.

Elodie's suitcase contains only dark blue
and gray clothes. In her rucksack, she
packs the music she has taken from the
Wolf's apartment, carefully placed in a paper folio and tied with a leather cord. She
does not wear the medallion from Luca, for
it is the amulet of a soldier. She instead
tucks that into a small pouch and drops it
into her bag. And among her other belongings, the bar of soap, the toothbrush, and

her cherished copy of **The Little Prince**, it sinks like a small pebble cast into the sea.

"Where will we stay?" Elodie asks her mother the night before they leave.

"There is someone I know who will give us shelter," Orsina assures her daughter. And so they leave. Elodie holding a single suitcase and her cello, her rucksack on her back, Orsina clasping the same red valise she had carried when she had left Venice years before.

At the Verona station, German soldiers stand guard near every platform. The green uniforms, the metal helmets. In one corner, there is a woman in a black coat clutching the hand of a young child. Her face is frozen and pale. One German is shouting to another that she is a Jew with false papers. His language slices through the air, brutal as a blade of steel. Elodie's blood runs cold just hearing it.

She does not dare alter the direction of her eyes, even though she wants to stop and help them, as she knows Lena surely would have done.

Elodie walks symmetrically, one hand

carrying the cello, the other her suitcase. On her back, she wears her rucksack. In the past three months, she has perfected her public walk and now she moves slowly and methodically, as though she were incapable of distraction.

Orsina does not move like Elodie. She does not understand the movement of stealth. She is slower and more easily distracted than her daughter. She does not know how to focus her eyes straight ahead, to avoid turning around if she hears the slightest noise or others speaking. To ignore everything around you except getting to the place you need to go.

The two-hour train ride to Venice takes more than five hours. In the compartment, the men and women sit tightly on the third-class benches that are hard and offer little comfort. Women unwrap heels of stale bread from handkerchiefs and drink water from canning jars used to store summer tomatoes.

Elodie and Orsina hand their papers over when asked. **Yes, we are Anna and Marie Zorzetto**, they say to every German officer who questions them along the way.

Yes, she is a student. Yes, we have family in Venice. Yes, thank you. Danke.

Elodie does not ask Orsina where they will go to once they arrive in Venice. Instead, she intends to do nothing but blindly follow her mother. She remembers her mother telling her that Venice is a maze, and Elodie closes her eyes, counting the hours until they arrive and she can finally become lost within it.

⌒

She had imagined many things about the city, like the gondolas, the mist, and the lagoon. And I Gesuiti, with its celadon and gray marble walls and dark pews, where Orsina had first heard Pietro play.

What she could never have fathomed, however, was the sense that they had arrived at the end of the world. Waterways stretch like blue carpets waiting to be sailed, and pastel palazzos emerge magically from the sea. Beauty and decay seem to coexist, creating a sense of integrity that is both defiant and uniquely its own.

The facades of the palazzos had remained splendid, even though their yellow and red pigments had faded and become pitted over time. The great buildings were like ancient trees whose rings came not from age, but from the incessant rising and falling of the tide. It was as if the city bore a unique wisdom: it knew it was wiser to live amid the ever-moving currents than to do battle against them with mere bricks and stones.

"You're carrying too much," Orsina tells Elodie. "Let me carry your cello, at least. Let me . . ."

Elodie shakes her head and tells her mother she is fine. A bag in one hand, her cello in the other, and the rucksack on her back. "Don't worry," she instructs. "I promise I won't tip over."

"Where are we going?" she asks Orsina.

Orsina pauses to look at her daughter. "Someplace safe."

They dip into small alleyways and re-emerge into the light. They walk across bridges and see starving cats in the corners and iron balconies draped with bougain-villea and laundry lines.

Up in the sky, the sun is beginning to set.

"Castello," her mother finally says. "We will find Valentina there."

Above a small, shuttered shop that read "Hats for Sale," they find a buzzer with the last name "Scarpa." Orsina rings the bell. It is now almost dusk, and a woman opens the shutters from above. She looks down and searches among the shadows.

"Who's there?" she asks. She does not recognize the older woman with the red valise or the girl with the cello.

"Orsina Moriani," Elodie's mother replies, looking up toward the window.

"My God," Valentina utters. "Come up . . . I can't believe you're finally here."

On the top flight of the stairs, an old wooden door creaks open and a small, delicate woman embraces Orsina.

"Come inside, you two," she says, and waves for them to enter.

Elodie scans the room, amazed. Inside, it is a crowded den of scraps of material, wooden heads wearing felted hats, jars with feathers, and open boxes stuffed with beads and fake pearls.

"It's like old times, Valentina," Orsina says, setting down her valise. "I can't tell you how good it is to see you . . . It's a relief to see some things never change."

"Oh, they have, Orsina. Don't let all the ribbons and velvet fool you." The woman smiles and her face softens.

Her age is difficult to pinpoint, though Elodie knows she is younger than her mother by the way the two women speak of the past. She notices Valentina's hands as they flutter through the air punctuating her speech, like two little birds aloft.

"I can't believe you're back in Venice after so long . . . Let me take your coat, your bags." She speaks with considerable warmth and looks at Elodie with affection. "And your instrument, my dear . . ." She smiles at Orsina. "I see she takes after Pietro, no?"

Orsina lowers her eyes. "Yes. Very much."

"And how is he?"

Orsina doesn't answer and Valentina crosses herself.

"I'm so sorry. May God rest his soul."

She offers them what she has: some water boiled from the well. A bowl of unsalted polenta. "I'm sorry I have so little. The rations . . . We all have to get by now on so little here," she says, again apologizing. "Some days it seems we exist on nothing but water and air."

"Like our city," Orsina says smiling.

"Yes, if we are to die of starvation, at least we will float away with grace."

Elodie watches as her mother and Valentina try to merge the last images they each had of the other from years before with the person now standing before them. They discreetly scan each other. The lines of the face, the condition of the hands, the wisps of silver in the hair. These are all clues to a life. Valentina's hands are lined and rough, and show years of work and toil. And although her mother is older by a decade, the comfort of her life in Verona has made her look nearly the same age as Valentina.

"It's been over twenty years," Valentina finally says. "Yet looking at you now, I still can see so many traces of your mother. She was beautiful in every aspect of her life."

"Thank you," Orsina replies with tears in her eyes. "And she would be so proud of you, to see how you've managed to carry on with her work."

Orsina looks around at the apartment, cluttered with so many odds and ends. She remembered that Valentina had a unique gift. While some people could only see beauty when it was perfect and whole, Valentina could also see it in fragments. She was the rare person who could pick up a shattered piece of porcelain and find the art in it.

"After the war began, I couldn't keep up with the rent on the store. But I've managed to make some extra money with a little imagination. Venetians still want to be fashionable, even in hard times."

Elodie's eyes travel to a black coat thrown over a chair near Valentina's sewing machine. The inside of the coat was lined in a beautiful red silk.

"Ah, you like that one, **carina?**" She walks over and lifts the coat from the chair to show Elodie. "You know where I got the lining for that?"

Elodie shakes her head, her fingers reaching to touch the silk. The red was beautiful. It reminded her of the color that Francesca, the harpist, wore the night of the concert at the Bibiena.

"From an old Italian flag! I found one in the trash heap; can you believe it? Probably some **kraut** tore it down and threw it in the garbage bin." She clicks her tongue. "I've still got two more panels of the flag left.

And I certainly can't let them go to waste!"
She lets out a small laugh. "I'm going to sew
another coat with a green lining."

"You were always so clever!" Orsina says,
complimenting her. She, too, took her fingers and reached to touch the lining of the
coat. She was amazed that her friend had
the resourcefulness to create something
beautiful from something she had taken
from the trash.

"Oh, thank you!" Valentina says, her voice
clearly showing her happiness in what her
handiwork had produced. "If only I had access to more flags, we could all be wearing our secret allegiance in the linings of our
clothes."

THIRTY-FIVE

{~~~}

Portofino, Italy
OCTOBER 1943

Ever since Dalia's death, Angelo had grav-
itated toward fragile things that needed extra care. He rescued the half-dead potted
flowers from his sisters' gardens. He fed
stray cats. He sprinkled seeds for the birds.

For every patient whom he knew had no
money to pay him, he would still wake up
in the middle of the night and go to his side.
He never denied a single person—rich or
poor, mean spirited or kind—his attention
or his care. Even now, he still visited the
German **kommandant** every evening with
a small vial of insulin, injecting him so skill-

fully that the man had vowed never to return to Germany.

"Here I've got the air, the lemon trees, the
roll of the sea. And a doctor with a touch
so light, I don't even feel the needle!" He
spoke Italian, but though his vocabulary
was rich and his choice of words precise,
his intonation still lacked the melody of a
native.

"We all want to return to the place where
we're born, sir. It's part of the cycle of life,"
Angelo said as he pushed up the **kommandant**'s sleeve and quickly injected him with
the needle. The man didn't wince.

"No," the **kommandant** said, rolling down
his sleeve. "Dusseldorf or here? I chose
here, thank you very much!" He reached for
another sip of **sciacchetra** and licked his
lips.

On a large marble commode was a
gramophone. Classical music filled the air.

"Do you like music, **Dottore?**" The liqueur had loosened him.

"I'm not an expert. But I did go to the The-
atro Carlo Felice a few times when I was
in medical school."

The **kommandant** smiled.

"And whom did you hear play? Do you remember?"

"I don't, I'm sorry. It was a string quartet visiting from Austria, but their name escapes me. I just remember that my friend and I could only afford standing-room tickets."

The **kommandant** laughed. "I excuse you. You didn't get the full experience then."

"Well, my feet did."

"I'm sure. But music should be savored amid comfort." He gestured to the paintings on the walls, the gilded furniture. Angelo knew the red house that the **kommandant** had taken for his personal quarters had once belonged to the Bassani family, and he wondered how much of the sumptuous belongings were actually theirs.

But the gramophone was unmistakably German. The heavy wood case. The dial with the brass fittings. The best Italian versions looked like music boxes you opened, their covers inlaid with designs of mother-of-pearl in intricate designs. The **kommandant**'s looked like it would resemble a humidor with its lid closed.

The music continued to flood the room.

"Do you recognize this, **Dottore?** It's by one of your country's great composers."

Angelo couldn't hide his lack of musical knowledge. "No. I'm afraid not. I plead ignorance on my own musical knowledge."

"Rossini's Fifth String Sonata." The **kommandant** smiled again. "You know, he composed that when he was only twelve years old."

"Incredible," Angelo said, listening to the intricacy of melodies and instruments intertwined.

"Indeed. Prodigies like that are few and far between."

Angelo nodded his head.

"I played the violin for years, but my father played three instruments. We moved around as children and I always remember my father warning the movers that his instruments were more precious to him than the furniture."

"And what did you tell the movers when you were sent here?"

"I told them 'Heil Hitler!' Of course."

"Of course."

The mentioning of Hitler's name made Angelo's blood turn cold. More than seven hundred kilometers south, in the boot of Italy, the Allies had already started liberating Salerno. The fighting in Rome was escalating. He wondered if the bloodshed would reach Portofino. He knew the boys in Cinque Terre were already joining the Resistance. He looked at his hands as the needle began skipping on the gramophone. No more notes floated into the air, only the sound of an ended recording. He was still holding the empty vial of insulin he had used for the **kommandant**'s shot. He placed it into his medicine satchel and clamped the bag shut.

"I will see you tomorrow, **Dottore**."

"Yes, tomorrow. Of course. Do you need anything else?"

"As a matter of fact . . . Might I have a few more of those sleeping pills . . ."

"You are still having insomnia?"

"Yes. I end up spending the whole night listening to records."

Angelo reopened his bag. "I will give you just a few . . ." He tapped out three tablets and handed them to the **kommandant**. "Only use them when necessary. They can easily become a habit."

The **kommandant** grunted.

"How's your cousin?" he suddenly asked Angelo, the words catching the doctor by surprise. "One of my men told me you had

THE GARDEN OF LETTERS

another visitor staying with you. This one's quite pretty, I hear."

Angelo smiled, maintaining an outward appearance of calm. "She was not feeling well for some time, but the sea air is helping her recover." He forced a smile on his face for the sake of appearances. "So she's doing much better now. Thank you, sir."

The **kommandant** nodded and reached for his silver cigarette case. "How close a relation is she? A first cousin? A second?" He laughed.

"Third, actually," Angelo replied without any inflection. Inside, however, he could feel his adrenaline rising.

"Well, that's good," the **kommandant** said, a grin coming over him. "It's getting to be wintertime, and a pretty girl is always the best thing to hold when the weather gets cold."

Angelo left the **kommandant**'s villa unnerved. He hated to think that he was the subject of any village gossip and certainly did not want to rouse the suspicions of the few Germans who were assigned to patrol the area. Not that there were so many of them now that the high season had come to an end. Portofino was morphing into the ghost town it typically became after October. The German soldiers who came for their leave and filled the hotels the way the English tourists had for nearly a century, had since left to return to their units. The shopkeepers that kept embroidered linens and other souvenirs had since shuttered their windows. All that remained of the village activity was the one bakery and the grocery store, and even they kept limited hours.

Angelo did not believe there was any suggestion on the part of the **kommandant** that he was harboring a war fugitive. If anything, his remarks smirked of sexual overtones. One benefit was that if the villagers were gossiping about him and Anna, no one had seen the girl outside of his house since she arrived. And thus, no one but Vanna and he had noticed her thickening waistline.

Angelo had suspected her pregnancy from the first morning she stayed with him. He noticed how she could barely eat anything for breakfast except for a few morsels of torn bread, despite the fact that she clearly had been on the run from something and thus lacked access to food. How she fatigued easily. How she held her hands protectively over her belly, how her skin was luminous like a deep sea pearl.

But it was Vanna's sudden maternal overtures to the girl that confirmed his medical suspicions. She seemed to visit his house daily now, more often in the past few weeks than she had done in the past several years. Vanna now came almost as frequently as she did when he first returned from Ethiopia to the unfathomable news that he had lost his wife and child.

THIRTY-SIX

~

Venice, Italy
SEPTEMBER 1943

They are eager to leave. Valentina has been generous in giving them shelter, but she has little room to spare for long-term guests. A foot-pedaled sewing machine takes up most of one corner, along with a table piled high with bolts of material, patterns, and tins full of needle and thread. And while Orsina shares Valentina's bed, Elodie has slept on the couch.

"I need to stretch my legs and to get some air," she tells her mother. Valentina cautions her to be careful. "The Germans are swarming the city. And it's so easy to get lost if you're not from here."

"Yes, let me go with you," Orsina implores her. Orsina knows that, after a few walks, Elodie will be able to memorize the paths and bridges she would need to return back to the apartment. But until then, Orsina does not want Elodie out alone.

Elodie agrees, and the women change their clothes to go out. Elodie, into a simple navy dress, and Orsina into a black one.

Valentina looks at the two of them and frowns. "I'm not even going out," she says, pointing to a pile of work she has to do, "and I still look more fashionable than the two of you."

Dipping into the back of the apartment, she returns with two cloche hats.

"Here," she says, handing one to Orsina made of burgundy felted wool with a black ribbon sewn around its edge. For Elodie, she selects a navy one stitched with a scattering of translucent beads.

"Your mother would never have forgiven me if I didn't offer you one of her hats for a walk in Venice with her granddaughter."

Orsina takes the hat between her hands and is comforted by it. The contrast between the stiff felt construction and the delicate plumage instantly takes her back to her childhood, when she loved to touch all the beautiful things that flowed in abundance in her mother's workshop.

"Are these ones salvaged from the store?"

"Yes," Valentina replies. "I still have a few that I could never bear to sell. You should each have one. Elodie, in particular, should have something made by her grandmother's hands."

Elodie goes to the oval mirror above the side table and places the hat on her head. She never wore a hat in Verona. When she was cold, she simply wrapped a scarf around her head. The hat makes her looked older, more sophisticated.

"You look beautiful, Elodie," Valentina says as she approaches. Orsina had already positioned her hat on an angle, like a natural. She goes to grab her purse.

"You two should be careful," Valentina cautions. "The Gestapo shot two gondoliers just a few nights ago. They claimed they were running guns for the Resistance."

Valentina clicks her tongue. "The poor boys. They were brothers. I don't know how their mother will manage now."

Elodie's eyes shift to the window just beside Valentina's sewing table. A pale flash of light is streaming in through the narrow opening, which gives the dark, cluttered apartment the air of a Tintoretto painting.

"Orsina, Venice will come back to you," Valentina promises. "I'm sure as soon as you start walking, the pathways, all the hidden spots of beauty, will return to you as if you were here only yesterday." She smiles. "But use caution. The Germans are patrolling in full force." She shakes her head. "And avoid going through the Ghetto. There is terrible suffering everywhere in the city, but especially for the Jews. We should be helping them more." She let out a deep sigh. "But fear has made everyone blind."

Several days have passed since they ventured out into the streets of Venice. Fall has cast the city in a veil of soft light and everything around them sparkles. The dome of the Salute church glimmers in the harbor. And the palaces on the Grand Canal are a bouquet of soft pastels against the chalk-blue sky.

They walk through the small, snaking **calles** of Castello and toward the harbor, their beautiful hats pulled over the rims of their eyes.

In the center of San Zaccharia, three German officers struggle to ask for directions in broken Italian, and an Italian woman gestures in the direction of the Rialto. Orsina dips her head and whispers just low enough that Elodie can hear.

"Resistance can come in many forms, it seems," she says, her lips curling into a slight smile. "In this case, she's sending them the completely opposite way."

They walk past the near empty Hotel Danieli and the Bridge of Sighs with its windows carved with stone bars.

She inhales the air, damp and briny lifting off the harbor. The mist, so intoxicating, fills her lungs. The buildings of Giudecca emerge in the distance and the sound of church bells and ferry horns fill her ears. Elodie's eyes struggle to differentiate between the sea and the sky.

And then past the marble arches of the Doge's Palace and the brick tower of the Campanile, she is suddenly in front of San Marco.

As she lifts her head toward the basilica, Elodie hears the sound of fluttering wings.

Hundreds of dark pigeons, with iridescent necks, taking flight.

It is a place of wings and starbursts. High above San Marco's ramparts, a winged lion looks over the square, its majestic gate flanked by a parade of Etruscan horses. Glimmering mosaics sparkle underneath gilded arches, and a cobalt blue frieze is studded in gold stars. And in the pale, afternoon light, trapezelike shadows fly across the piazza like another dark, exotic bird.

But at the outdoor Café Florian, the pianist is playing **Die Wacht am Rhein** for a few German officers. Elodie's body stiffens at the sound of the German melody, her mother sensing the tension in her daughter's arm looped tightly within her own.

They cross through the Square and dip into another side street until they reach the **vaporetti.**

And as they begin to wander home, they avoid passing through the stone gateway that leads to the Ghetto, the ancient neighborhood that the Jews of Venice had lived in for centuries. Two shops flanking the archway are already shuttered closed, both marked by large swastikas and an ordinance

ALYSON RICHMAN

announcing that they were "**Verboten**," having once been owned by Jews.

Elodie's eyes search for any signs of life within the damp, stone buildings. In a tall narrow window, she spots a child staring with half-hollow eyes, her head wrapped in a scarf as gray as an oyster shell. The girl's eyes meet Elodie's for a brief moment, before falling back into the shadow of her apartment.

In a few steps, the women suddenly find themselves facing two large German soldiers.

"Halt!" they call out to the women. Orsina and Elodie stop in their tracks like a pair of hunted deer. "**Ausweis.**"

The women reach to find their papers.

"Where are you going?" one of the men asks in German. He takes their papers. When neither woman answers, he tries again in broken Italian.

Orsina responds in Venetian. Her vowels elongated, her tongue rolling each word.

"She's speaking in bloody dialect," the soldier curses. "I can't understand a word." They each cast an eye on Elodie, who has yet to lower her eyes under the brim of her dark red hat. On the contrary, she stares directly, unflinching. Lena would have been proud.

The German hands their papers back. "Go! Get yourselves home!"

Elodie can feel her mother's pace quicken, her chest inflating and her breath slightly halting. Only after they are steps away from Valentina's apartment, does her mother finally let go of her arm.

Over the next week, Elodie learns to glide through the city like a native Venetian. She memorizes the small, narrow passageways and the bridges with only a few steps, even the ones that don't have names. She avoids the large, populated areas like the Rialto or the Piazza San Marco, where German officers frequent in groups, their boots marching against the cobblestones, their battle songs and anthems filling the air.

In the evenings, as Elodie tries in vain to fall asleep, her body sagging against the couch's weak springs, her mind replays over and over every moment she spent with Luca. And one night, a sentence he had said only in passing when describing his past returns to her. He had mentioned a friend in Venice who owned a bookstore with a funny name. "La Toletta," he had said, and laughed. "The name means 'the vanity table.' Pelizzato and I used to sell books together on the streets in Milan. Our carts stood side by side." A sense of longing fills her heart as she remembers the intimacy of being in the back room with Luca, the smell of paper, and the thrill of telling each other stories filling the air.

The next morning, she tells Valentina and Orsina she wants to find a new novel to read. "I'm getting restless and need something to do, but I'm afraid to disturb the neighbors with my cello." She has taken it out of its case several times since arriving in Venice, to stroke the varnish and rub rosin into her bow. Sometimes, when the other women were busy with their sewing, she had quietly plucked the strings, just to let the instrument know she had not forgotten it.

"Yes, as much as I'd love to hear you play," Valentina agrees, "since everyone around here knows I've lived alone for years, the sudden arrival of a cellist would bring suspicion." She walks over to Elodie and touches her shoulder lightly. "A few

bookstores are still operating. I could certainly suggest a few . . ."

"A friend once told me about a shop in
Venice that had a good selection of Amer-
ican novels in translation." Elodie pauses.
"La Toletta . . . I think that was the name."

Valentina nods, pulling a pin from between her pursed lips and fastening it to a
piece of fabric in her hands.

"Yes. Of course. It's not far. Close to Accademia." She places her sewing down and
draws Elodie a quick map with landmarks.
Elodie looks at it intensely for a moment and
then reaches for her coat.

"Don't you need the map?" Valentina
asks her.

"Oh no," she says, delighted to have the
chance to put her good memory to use. "It's
already in here . . ." She taps her finger to
her temple.

Orsina smiles. She knows exactly what
Valentina is thinking: that even though
Elodie is not a native to this city, she has
still inherited her memory from Orsina's
bloodline.

Walking down the Calle del Magazen,
Elodie crosses the Ponte dei Greci near the

gothic Palazzo Zorzi, with its rose-colored facade and tall windows, before walking through the Campo San Provolo. Her stride is quick and efficient, a form of camouflage in itself. When she finds herself in the Piazza San Marco, always densely populated with German soldiers, she doesn't linger for a moment. Instead, she slips into the shadow of the Procuratie, where she tries to be invisible and avoid any eyes, Venetian or German.

She continues walking past the Baroque church in Capo San Moisé, quickly memorizing the statue in Capo San Stefano as a landmark to guide her return. She crosses a wooden bridge, the Ponte dell'Accademia, and upon reaching the other side, turns right and passes another small square and bridge until she finally sees the long black and gold sign reading "La Toletta: Libri."

Dozens of books are in the window. She sees Dante and Bocaccio. She sees Chaucer in translation, as well as the newly popular Pearl S. Buck. She pushes through the door of the shop and pulls down her scarf. Inside, the perfume of pulped wood and tanned leather overpowers her. It is the scent of Luca, his essence captured in the fragrance of paper and ink and in the stacked crates filled with books. She feels her heart breaking, for the scent carries her back to a place where Luca was very much alive.

"May I help you?" A voice emerges from behind a bookshelf.

Then a slender figure with a head full of thick black hair appears. She notices the apron, the rakish grin, and the eyes that are neither hazel nor brown but something in between. At first glance, he could easily have been Luca's brother.

"Looking for a book, I gather, signorina?"

"Well . . . I . . ." she is stammering. She doesn't know where to begin. Even deciding how to introduce herself presents a challenge: If this man knew Luca, does she go by Elodie or Anna? Will he even know that Luca is dead?

"A friend told me about this store . . ." Her voice is soft and she can hear her nervousness laced throughout the words. "He had a shop just like this . . . in Verona . . . we were good friends . . ." She feels her voice falling away. "I have just moved here and I . . ."

He has moved closer to her, so that their

ALYSON RICHMAN

bodies are only a few feet apart now. He has taken his hands out of his apron, and his eyes scan her. She can see in his squint, in his now-intense gaze, that he is hardly listening to her words, but instead focusing on the other things she is communicating beyond her control: the inflection of her voice, the pauses of her breath, the slight tremor in her movements.

"And I remembered he had mentioned your store . . ."

"Is that so?" he says. He unties his apron and places it on a table of books. "What is the name of your friend, and the name of his store?"

She does not believe there is anything to be lost by being truthful now. Luca is already dead. The bookshop, ransacked by the Germans, is now no doubt shuttered and closed.

"Luca Bianchi, and his bookshop was called Il Gufo. It was on Via Mazzini."

He takes a kerchief from the pocket of his trousers and wipes his brow. Still, she can feel him studying her. Her face. Her eyes. Even her hands.

"And you?" he asks. "Did you work in the store with him?"

"No," she says slowly. "I studied music there."

To this, he smiles, as if the pieces of a puzzle are suddenly making sense.

"Yes, Luca was a friend of mine. One of my best, in fact." By speaking of his friendship in the past tense, she realizes he knows that Luca is dead.

"He was mine, too." There is a quiver in her voice, like a finger that has momentarily slipped off its string.

"May I sit down?" she says, gripping the edge of one of the tables in the store. The image of Luca's limp body suddenly flashes before her. She feels the floor coming out from beneath her.

"Please . . . Yes, of course," he says, rushing to find her a chair.

When she catches her breath, she looks up and discovers he is offering her a glass of water. His kindness is so heartfelt, she feels it like an embrace.

Under damp timber, the walls lined with books, they share stories of Luca. Pelizzato tells her he had met Luca when he first started selling books from a cart in Milan.

"We traded stock. He always preferred

the modern writers, while I was building up my collection of the classics." He laughs. His teeth are a shade paler than coffee, and his eyes are filled with light. "We were also reading Marx, debating the pros and cons about Communism, smoking too many cigarettes, and trying to flirt with pretty girls like you . . ."

She finds solace in his memories. She can see Luca with his back against his cart of books, a cigarette between his lips. And everything about this store—the scent of paper, the half-uncrated boxes, the crowded shelves—it all reminds her so much of Luca.

After a few moments of silence between them, Pelizzato's voice reemerges. "May I ask you something?"

"Of course," she says, shifting slightly in her seat.

"You said you're a musician?"

"Yes . . ."

"What instrument do you play?"

"The cello." She is studying him now as intensely as he is studying her.

"Luca told me about a cellist with an extraordinary mind. I can put all the pieces together now. Your eyes, your hands, even the way you move." He takes another breath and scans her again.

"It's an honor to meet you, Dragonfly," he says extending his hand.

Given all of Pelizzato's similarities to Luca, it does not surprise Elodie that he, too, has been running supplies for the Resistance through his bookstore with the assistance of the Wolf.

"There are several booksellers involved in the Resistance, Dragonfly. But it was Luca who really emphasized to all of us how much could be hidden within a book."

She nods. "Yes, I saw him demonstrate it with a Beretta."

"Ahh, the gun tucked within its pages is not such a new idea . . ." He laughs. "That one is an eighteenth-century invention. But using the pages to conceal messages is rather genius. It almost always got past the controls . . ."

"I remember he used Tolstoy when he demonstrated the codes . . ."

"**War and Peace**?" He laughs.

"Yes," she says. She was happy he knew Luca so well.

"There were certain things that the Wolf

insisted he didn't want written down at all. Even if hidden in books. That's why Luca was so excited by your ability to transmit codes and information through your music."

She looks down and bites her lip. "Until I blundered it all."

He doesn't acknowledge her remark, but rather focuses solely on the facts of the bungled mission. "Yes, we were hoping to coordinate our intelligence information with Zampieri's contacts within the French Resistance . . ."

He clears his throat and fumbles into his shirt pocket to find a cigarette. Between their two faces, blue rings of smoke waft into the air. "The Wolf had his hand in many operations. He was intrigued by you because there was no way anyone would know there was a code locked inside your music." He takes another puff.

"You were an asset. An original one. And he appreciated it."

She feels shame creep over her, like a daughter who has disappointed her father and knows it. "I had every intention of transmitting the code that night. For some reason, I lost control of my mind as I was playing . . ."

"Mistakes happen. It's unfortunate when they do, but the Wolf is a resourceful man. He takes risks and sometimes they pay off and sometimes they don't. He's the best type of man to have in the Resistance. He moves like smoke . . . and he's not afraid to die."

Elodie felt herself shiver.

"You mean because they took his wife?"

"Yes . . . Isn't it a fact that when you lose the person you love most in the world, you no longer fear death?"

She looks at him, her confidence returning. The discovery of this store and its owner, a man to whom she can talk freely, is a relief. It is like a rope tethering her to her old life.

"Yes," she says. "I know this feeling well."

He withdraws the cigarette from his lips and twists it into the ashtray.

"I know you do, Dragonfly. That's why I said it." He smiles at her. "But maybe in your case, you can still try and stay alive a bit longer."

Over the next few days, Elodie watched her mother and Valentina settle into each other like sisters who had not been particularly close as children, but had found each other late in life. Each of them happy to have each other and to share many of the same memories.

To Elodie's surprise, Orsina came alive working with all the scraps of material cluttering the apartment. Although it was far from the abundance of exotic and luxurious materials that she remembered from her mother's studio, Orsina enjoyed the challenge, much like Valentina, in creating something beautiful out of another person's castaways.

Valentina had found an old handbag and was unstitching the leather and pulling at the pieces to see if she had enough material to make a pair of children's shoes.

She stood up to search for a stiffer needle and stronger thread.

"The two of you are amazing," Elodie said, looking at the workshop the women had made of the living room. "I could never imagine making a pair of shoes out of an old leather handbag."

"When you get to be our age, you learn the art of reinvention," Valentina said with a small laugh. "It helps to keep you young."

"Actually, I think I need a little of that myself," Elodie said, as she found herself needing to sit down in one of Valentina's old velvet chairs. Her fatigue was so suddenly intense, she wondered if she might be ill.

She was desperate to sleep. A long, deep slumber that she hoped would cure her of her recent constant exhaustion, of her stomach feeling queasy all day. But her sleep was always restless and fitful. She missed her old bed, its smell of starched linen and the adjacent living room, where for years she and her father would get up in the middle of the night and play.

And her dreams were more like hauntings, fitful ones that depleted her energy instead of restoring it. She would see Luca behind her eyes, dressed not as a bookseller, but as a partisan. The bandanna wrapped around his neck, the gun in his arms. She would wake up with her hand balled into a fist, as though his amulet was still placed between her fingers.

Restless, but not wanting to awaken Valentina and her mother, Elodie would sometimes unlatch her cello case and caress the instrument, as if it were the last thread that connected her to her old life.

Afterward, as she wrapped it back into its silken scarf and laid it back in its case, she would touch the music that the Wolf's wife had written. As she tried to fall back asleep, her mind would be filled with thoughts of this woman whom she had never met, but to whom she somehow felt connected. Each of this woman's notes sounding like a requiem inside her head.

During the day, she challenged herself with walks around the city, trying to memorize each landmark so that she could navigate her way home. There seemed to be a hundred different ways to reach the Piazza San Marco, and every day she took a new path and discovered another secret passage or another hidden spot of beauty.

She learned to interpret the sounds of footsteps. The light tread of a Venetian, who sprang with ease over the bridges, in contrast to the heavy sound of a German's boots on the pavement, which penetrated her bones like percussion. And she learned to find places where there was no sound at all, tiny pockets of the city that maintained a perfect and exquisite silence. It was in those spaces that she closed her eyes and heard only the sound of her own breath interlaced with the beating of her heart; a music that was utterly private and wholly her own.

She visited La Toletta bookstore as often as she could. Every time she sat with Pelizzato, she asked if there was news about the Wolf or whether there was some way she could again help in transmitting a code. Every time, Pelizzato shook his head, no.

Then one afternoon, he nearly leaped from his chair when she walked through the door.

"Finally, you've come!"

He bounded to the door and turned the sign on the window to "Closed."

"We do need you, now." He guided her into the back of the store.

"Some things I didn't want to say earlier, because I was waiting for more details. But today, just today, I got the word."

She pulled the scarf from her hair and sat down. "Yes . . . what is it?"

"The Wolf is in Genoa now. He fled Mantua just after the concert at the Bibiena . . ." He paused, pondering the right words. ". . . After you didn't transmit the code."

She felt a flicker inside her as if he had

burned her with his cigarette. The wound was invisible, but it singed her all the same.

"I did not want you to blame yourself, so I didn't mention it before. But the Gestapo ransacked his apartment shortly afterward. He's still active throughout the north, though, moving information through different channels as best he can. As of yesterday, he was working for the Genoa command."

She took each piece of information as though it were small bits of bread that nourished her. She had been so worried after she had seen the state of the Wolf's apartment, and now she knew, at least, that he was alive and unhurt.

"We have essential information for him that must get to him by Tuesday, but we've been struggling to find the best way to transmit it. When he learned I had made contact with you, he requested that you play the message **col legno**." He smiled at her. "I'm not a musician, so I'm not even sure what that means . . ."

She smiled, knowing exactly what it meant. "It means he wants me to play with the wood of the bow, instead of with the hair."

"Ah, I see." He smiled. "So the Wolf basically wants you to tap out the message for him, as though it's a Morse code."

"It seems that way. But you'll need to give me the beats."

"Yes." He stood up and came back with a book. He opened it up to the center.

"The code was written by a violinist. But he says it will be easy for you to transmit."

Elodie smiled. "So I'm not the only musician working for you . . ."

"No, but certainly the prettiest . . ."

She laughed at him.

"All right then," he said, his voice regaining its focus. "Let me see what it says: 'Two beats, then one. A pause, then four quick beats, a longer pause, then one beat followed by three short and louder strikes.' Do you have that?"

"Yes. I have it." She repeated it verbatim and then tapped it out on the counter with her hand. He smiled.

She repeated it one more time with her hand, so that he could hear that she had indeed pressed it into her memory. "Not that my bow is going to like it . . ."

"Well, it's for the greater good, right?"

"Yes," she said, smiling.

"Good." He appeared satisfied. "Your

story, if you're questioned on the train, is that you're auditioning to be a music tutor for a wealthy family in Genoa."

She nodded her head to show she was listening.

"This is your cover. The family's name is Fiorello. They're at nineteen Via del Porto. The Wolf is being put up there secretly. But he will come out and listen to the code when you arrive."

She nodded, absorbing the address into her memory.

"You just need to get yourself from here to Genoa without being questioned. That's the dangerous part. Your papers are good?"

"Yes," she said. "I've been stopped a few times, and no one's seemed to suspect they were false."

"Perfect. Go get yourself ready. Pack just a few things in a rucksack. Anyone who travels with a suitcase these days attracts suspicion. There's a ten A.M. train tomorrow leaving from Santa Lucia. Can you be ready by then?"

"Yes," she said.

"And you remember the address?"

"Yes. I'm positive. You needn't worry about my memory."

"The Bibiena was an aberration, I take it."

Just the mentioning of it caused her to feel a stabbing pain. "Yes. I have nothing to distract me now," she said as she pulled her scarf up around her face. "I'll look forward to seeing you when I return."

"Travel safely," he said. As the bell hit the door as she left, she felt as though he was channeling the words of Luca.

THIRTY-SEVEN

Portofino, Italy
DECEMBER 1943

"You need to tell my brother before Christmas," Vanna tells her. "It's the right thing to do."

Elodie nods. She is sitting on the sofa with a spool of white yarn in her lap and two long knitting needles that Vanna brought her a few weeks ago, hoping to give her something to do to pass the time.

"You hide it well, but in a few weeks' time, it's going to be quite clear there's a baby growing inside of you. Trust me."

"I know," Elodie agrees.

The knitting has been good for her hands. Her fingers have felt stiff since she arrived.

Even in Venice, she pretended to silently play her cello, her fingers moving across the strings, her bow lifting and swaying without ever touching the bridge. But everything changed in Genoa. She shudders just thinking about her last hours before she caught the boat to this village, which seems to be the only place in Italy to have evaded the war.

"I will tell him this week," she promises Vanna.

Vanna looks at her with compassion. "Somebody sent you here for a reason," she says as though she's looking at an angel or a saint. "You didn't know what Angelo was like before his wife died. He walked around the village as though he had swallowed the moon. He glowed like starlight just at the mention of her name." Vanna shakes her head. "When she died, he went dark. There was nothing that could bring the light back inside him."

"I know," Elodie answers.

"So then, you've seen the room . . ."

"Yes," Elodie tells her. "When he was out . . . I didn't mean to, but I entered it by accident."

"So then you know how he's kept

ALYSON RICHMAN

everything intact." Again, she shakes her head as if her brother's tragedy never gets easier to talk about. "I imagine the letters must be yellowing and cracking like bits of old parchment by now."

Elodie nods. "Once inside, it's like you've entered an ancient tomb. I felt like I was violating him by being there. Even talking about it now makes me feel as though I'm betraying him somehow."

"You're a good soul," Vanna says as she begins packing up her needles and yarn. "But he's thirty-eight years old. He has been in mourning for eight years now. He should not sleep in a room of memories. He should be building new ones."

"Don't we all sleep entombed in our memories?"

Vanna raises an eyebrow. "I know I certainly don't. I'm asleep from the moment my head hits the pillow."

Elodie looks toward the garden.

"Some nights I feel as though I'm drowning in mine." She takes the point of the needle and presses it slightly to her forefinger, just to feel the pain run through her.

That night, underneath her pillow, Elodie now hides a baby's bonnet and two booties made of pure, white wool.

She knows Vanna is right in saying that she needs to tell Angelo about her pregnancy. But what Vanna doesn't realize is that she is keeping other secrets more hidden than the baby.

The simplicity of her life here, sheltered in a remote cottage, is so far removed that she could easily erase her past and forget the war outside the granite cliffs. Angelo keeps the **kommandant** and his soldiers far away from his house. The only traces she hears from the war are the engines of the planes overhead.

She knows that there are fewer Germans here than when she arrived; the officers who came for a week's reprieve and checked into one of the colorful hotels in the harbor have since left. "It's empty now," Angelo informs Elodie one night when the candles flicker between them and he gazes at her with soft, kind eyes while she finishes the simple pasta dish he has prepared for her. "It's just the locals and a handful of the **kommandant**'s men on patrol, now," he says as he lifts their plates and brings them to the kitchen sink to clean. "From November until March, Portofino is finally allowed to sleep."

The ability to sleep deeply eludes Elodie and she thinks of Angelo's words wistfully. It would be a gift to be able to forget, to sleep unfettered by fear or nightmares, but her mind refuses to. Elodie closes her eyes and wonders how long it had been since she left Venice for Genoa. On her fingers, she counts out seven weeks. The memory of her departure that day still makes her blood run cold.

She had come close to death in Genoa. That morning, as she quickly placed a few belongings in her rucksack, including the sweater from Luca, his amulet, and the music she hoped to return to the Wolf's hands, her mother had begged her not to make this journey. Orsina suspected that it was another mission that was taking her daughter away for a few days.

"Please," Orsina had pleaded with her. "We are finally safe here. We can make a new life, and no one will know about the Piazza delle Poste. Here you will simply be the daughter of a Venetian."

Elodie took her mother's hands in her own. "I will always be the daughter of a Venetian and I will come back to you, but, in the meantime, a friend needs my help . . . and it's very important that I go."

Orsina shook her head. "Do you not hear the airplanes overhead? Do you not see the Nazi brigades walking the streets?"

"They are virtually all I see, Mamma." She pulled the drawstring closed on her rucksack and went to reach for her cello. "And that's why I'm going."

Valentina stood there without speaking, understanding the position of both women. She held out a quiet, unornamented hat for Elodie to take on her journey.

Elodie took it and walked out the door.

She took the **vaporetto** to the station and bought herself a third-class ticket to Genoa. She looked like the simple music student she had been before the onset of war. Her white blouse and navy skirt revealed no skin. Her instrument gave her a certain air of seriousness. And under the brim of her hat, her eyes shone like sharpened steel.

On the train, she slipped into her new role as Anna Zorzetto. She held her papers in her pocket, and her rucksack and instrument sat beside her. She could hear the tapping of the code in her mind. Her bow would once again play with precision for the Wolf. She would redeem herself and also help the Resistance. She would honor the memory of those this war had so cruelly taken from her.

Before the war began, the train from Venice to Genoa would have taken close to six hours. But now, with all the delays caused by constant security checks, she was told by Pelizzato it could take more than ten. She put her head against the window and tried to get some sleep until the conductor and the German customs agents again passed through the train carriage.

It was when the train stopped in Verona that she first felt herself panic. The platform was filled with what looked like nearly a hundred people, all hoping to board.

"We're going to be here for some time, I'm afraid," she overheard the man next to her say to his seatmate.

His friend nodded. "I heard that the partisans hijacked one of the trains in Genoa last night. They shot fourteen Germans and took all of their munitions. They'll be extra vigilant on the trains today . . ."

Elodie looked out the window and feigned sleep. Her fingers clasped her cello, but she felt as if she had just swallowed ice.

The train stopped and started, and she fell in and out of sleep. The nausea sometimes welled inside her so intensely that, at times, she feared she might become sick in front of her fellow passengers.

Every smell bothered her immensely. Things that never disturbed her before, like the scent of tobacco or garlic, now made her feel ill. She took Luca's sweater from her bag and tried to find his scent somewhere buried inside the wool. But all that did was to make her ache even more for him.

She tried to imagine herself in front of the Wolf again, pulling out her cello and redeeming herself in his eyes. She would hand him the music written by his wife and tell him that she had discovered it in his apartment when she went to look for him.

She pictured in her head every scenario of playing for him now in a room in Genoa,

whose address she had of course memorized. She heard the code beating inside
her head. She saw his white hair, his glacial-
blue eyes.

What she had never imagined was what
she actually found when her train finally
pulled into the Genoa station. That was
something she could never have foretold.

As she managed to get herself off the train,
hoisting her rucksack over one shoulder
and her cello over the other, Elodie heard
a large commotion close to the train platform. As the other passengers pushed past
her, some dragging small children, others
towing large trunks and valises for the next
part of their journeys, Elodie could see in
the far corner of the platform a large group
of men.

German soldiers were forcing a parade
of manacled prisoners, each of them shack-
led by handcuffs and linked together by an
iron chain. They were being pushed toward
a cattle car on one of the tracks. The Germans, in their green uniforms and with
rifles draped over their shoulders, were
shouting obscenities to the men and telling
them to move faster toward the cattle car.

Somehow Elodie sensed that she knew one of those men.

And so she drifted, as if by instinct, closer to the chain gang rather than toward the station's exit signs.

As the men walked with their heads down, and their feet shuffling slowly beneath them, her blood suddenly went cold and her feet became frozen to the station's floor.

She noticed his trousers first, the expensive wool of the tweed fabric and the tear at the knees where it looked as if he had been forced to kneel. His pants contrasted with those of the men on either side of him, who all wore the overalls or dark canvas clothes of factory workers. And this man's shoes were those of a gentleman. Not the industrial black boots of the other prisoners, but shoes that were handcrafted, their color, the shade of a fine cognac.

Her eyes scanned from his shoes to the cuffs, traveling upward until she saw the man's pale blue shirt, which was torn and covered with blood. She could see that his face had been beaten, with one eye swollen shut. So by the time he fully turned to face her, she instantly knew who he was.

It was, without a doubt, the Wolf.

She looked at him wide-eyed. And, suddenly, as if he felt something shift in the air, he, too, looked up and saw her. They then each, almost instantaneously, tried to look away from the other. But by then it was too late.

Out of nowhere, she felt a painful clamp on her arm as a tall officer in full German gear pulled her nearly out of her shoes.

The last she saw of the Wolf, he was being pushed with a rifle to his head onto a cattle car, which was already crowded with poor, starving Jews.

What happened next was so brutal and terrifying that even when she recalled it weeks later, it felt like a violation, one that penetrated her body with a terrible force.

She remembers the German's face. His flint-colored eyes. The waxen skin. The hands that gripped her like an animal being taken to its slaughter.

He leads her to a small room within the station and tells her to sit down. She notices the desk with its stack of papers, the cloudy water glass, the lack of light except for the single bulb dangling from the ceiling.

He looks at her papers. "Well, Anna Zorzetto from Venice, you knew that old man, didn't you?"

She does not answer him. So he comes so close to her that she can smell the cigarettes on his breath.

"I don't feel well," she tells him. "I might be sick."

He smiles at her; his teeth are the color of newsprint. His hands are eerily white; his fingernails, meticulously groomed.

"I'm not afraid of sickness . . ." he says. "Do you know how many people I've seen vomit just before they're pushed in front of the firing squad? Too many to count."

She feels her body becoming almost weightless, as if she no longer senses her feet in her shoes. As if her body is not connected to anything except her cello now wrapped within her arm.

"Where were we?" he starts again. "So that man, in the manacles . . . you knew him?"

Again she doesn't answer.

"Empty your bag."

She places her cello against the wall,
goes back to the table, and unlatches the
buckle on her rucksack. One by one she
begins taking out its contents: the slender
copy of **The Little Prince** from Luca, his
sweater, the pouch with his amulet, the tin
of toothpaste, and her brush. The extra pair
of underpants and clothes. And finally the
sheets of music.

He walks over to examine her belongings. He lifts the sweater, opens the tin of
dentifrice, and snickers slightly when he
touches her flimsy underclothes.

She is about to return to her cello, feeling as though she's somehow left it vulnerable by leaning it against the wall, when she
sees that the German officer has already
started toward it.

Within seconds, he placed the case on
the floor and opened it. She watches with
horror as he pulls off the silken scarf.

"And what do we have here?"

She is so afraid that she has bitten
through her lip. The taste of salt and iron
flickers over her tongue.

She says nothing, but instead stares hor-
rified as his fingers, as long as icicles, slither
across her cello's strings and caress its

wooden curves. His touch is like a predator's.

"This looks quite valuable . . ." He looks up from examining the cello and tries to find Elodie's eyes, but she quickly closes them.

She cannot bear to see her instrument being touched by someone so loathsome. She feels as though she's being forced to watch something she loves being violated.

"Please . . ." she says. Her voice escapes her like the sound of a small child pleading. "Please, it's only a cello."

"Why," he says, "I can tell that this is no common cello. I'm certain of it . . ." He pulls it out from the case and begins examining it more carefully. As his hands move over the instrument, she feels as if he's touching her own skin and she is overcome by revulsion.

"It's not special," she says. "Please, just put it back."

He turns to her and smiles again, like someone who has just discovered a hidden treasure that will soon be his own.

"This is a very rare instrument. Even I can see that."

He takes a single finger and draws it across the red varnish.

"What's a young girl like you doing with such an expensive cello?"

"It was a gift," she says quietly. "From my father."

He lifts the cello up and stands it on the floor. He takes his hands to it, mapping it as she has done so many times. He places a finger on the bridge before inserting another finger into one of the intricately scrolled sound holes. He closes his eyes, as though touching the cello brings him some sort of ecstasy, which once again revolts her.

"You could have a grenade in there, for all I know." Again, he continues to search the cello with prodding fingers.

She doesn't say anything, but allows him to study the instrument. She knows that the truly important item she is carrying—the code inside her memory—is something he will never find.

Having discovered nothing to incriminate her, he places the cello back in the case and snaps the latch closed.

For a second he seems to hesitate, as if pondering what to do next.

Suddenly, she can see that a decision has come over him. His eyes ignite.

He comes to Elodie, his skin nearly touching her own. He smiles and caresses her cheek. He takes her chin in his hands and gently, almost tenderly, raises her face to meet his eyes.

"I will give you something of great value in exchange for your cello," he says so softly she feels as though he is blowing each word into her ear.

Elodie fixes her gaze. "What's that?" she whispers, trying not to tremble.

The officer smiles.

"Your life."

He lifts the cello from the floor and opens the door.

"This is your one chance to get out of here. Now go."

THIRTY-EIGHT

~

Portofino, Italy
DECEMBER 1943

Angelo returns home that afternoon, quieter than normal. Elodie can hear the anguish in the silent way he moves. There is pain in his step and in the dropping of his keys on the table, even in the way he puts his medicine bag down by the door.

Elodie places the book that she is reading down beside her and walks toward the kitchen, where he is now washing his hands.

She stands behind one of the white columns that separate the rooms.

"Is everything all right?" she asks quietly.

He shakes his hands, and sprinkles of water fall onto the tile floor like rain.

"Yes," he says, his eyes softening at the sight of her. "I just had a very bad day. Three girls and their mother had been combing the woods for mushrooms when one of them stepped on a land mine. The father had to be pulled away from the site." Angelo's voice cracks midsentence. "He refused to leave until they had found every limb."

Elodie shudders. She remembers her mother telling her, just a few days before the battle at the post office, about a girl who had gone strawberry picking a week before her wedding and had treaded over a mine. Her mother said that the family buried the girl in her wedding dress.

"I'm not sure if you're hungry," she asks him. "Vanna came by with some squid her husband caught today. And I picked some zucchini from the garden. I could fry them with a little garlic and oil."

He manages a weak smile. "No, I think today's events have stolen my appetite. But thank you."

"I can't imagine how terrible it must have been . . . looking for the bodies."

"You have no idea." He shakes his head. "The Germans are claiming it was a partisan mine."

"Really?" She is careful not to reveal any sort of expression on her face, but the mention of the partisans startles her.

"Yes. I hear there's a group living in the cliffs in Cinque Terre, some even in caves. They're doing all sorts of things to sabotage the Germans."

Her stomach turns in knots. In seconds, her mind flashes to the mountains outside Verona, the sight of Luca's body lifeless on a stretcher made of vines, and of the partisan Rita Rosani with a gun strapped to her side.

"I had no idea . . ." The words fall from her mouth, but her mind leaps between her own memory of being in the mountains and the fear that she might not be as safe in Portofino as she had thought.

"But it doesn't do any good now to blame the partisans, or even the Germans. The women are dead. Nothing will change the fact that there will be four needless funerals next week."

Elodie glances at the clock on the wall. It is half-past six.

"And the **kommandant**? Did you already give him his injection today?"

"Yes, just before I came home. Why?"

"Did **he** mention the mine incident?"

Angelo walks into the living room, pulls up the legs of his trousers, and sits down next to her. "He did mention it, in fact. And he was very irritated by it."

She raises an eyebrow.

"Yes. He'd already had what looked to be his third **sciacchetra** by the time I gave him his shot. Not the best thing for a diabetic. Nor a man who needs strong sleeping pills . . ."

Elodie tries to choose her questions carefully. She needs to know if the **kommandant** is more of a threat to her than she has previously thought.

"I'm surprised they allowed a diabetic into the army. I thought the Reich only promoted men in perfect, Aryan health to such a position."

Angelo is bemused by her mental alacrity. "Oh, he didn't know he was a diabetic when he first arrived in Portofino." He shakes his head. "I was the one who diagnosed him. I'm not sure how they missed it at his physical. A simple urine test would have shown the results. And his symptoms were as clear as day. He was thirsty all the time, going to the bathroom constantly. Losing weight. He thought he had cancer, so when I told him he'd be fine with just a shot of insulin every day, he nearly gave me a medal." As he answers her, he can't help but smile; it is clear how intently Elodie is listening to him, and her attention flatters him.

"Still, none of his men know about his medical issue. We have an unspoken agreement. I quietly take care of his health, and he lets me take care of my patients without interfering."

"Your patients? Why would he interfere with you taking care of children or old people? I'm sure there aren't even a handful of men left in this town who could possibly be a threat to the German command."

"Well, I consider you one of my patients," he tells her. "You're someone who needs my care. It was clear as day that afternoon I first saw you coming off the dock."

"I am not sick, Angelo," she says.

"I never said you were sick, Anna." He looks out the window before returning his gaze to her. "I just said you need my care."

When he calls her "Anna," it always makes her feel as though she is somehow betraying him, and she dislikes that feeling immensely.

"I am grateful for your kindness," she says, folding her hands over her lap. She wonders if he already suspects what she feels obligated to tell him. That underneath this tired, white blouse is a stomach that is growing more taut with each passing day. He is a doctor, a man whose profession is rooted on his powers of observation. If Vanna has already sensed it, then perhaps she is the only one maintaining this facade of chastity.

They return to the living room, where an open window brings fresh sea air into their lungs. He reaches into the coat of his suit jacket, rumpled from the day and soiled with what looks like mud from the woods.

From his pocket he withdraws a small volume, a book of poetry a friend in the village has lent him.

"Eugenio Montale, a poet native to this part of Italy . . ." He places a hand on the cover. "Do you know him?"

She shakes her head no. "I've been reading one of your books by Moravia when you walked in just now . . ."

He pulls off his coat and stretches his

legs. "This one is even better," he says, smiling. He licks his finger, turns to the first page, and begins to read aloud.

**Be pleased if the wind that enters the orchard
brings back the surge of life:
here where a dead tangle of memories
sinks and founders,
there was no garden, only a reli-
quary . . .**

Around them the poetry, the breeze, and the sound of his finger touching the edge of paper all feel like a protective embrace. A shield against the world and the war outside.

**The commotion you hear is not flight,
But a commotion in the eternal
womb . . .**

"Eternal womb . . ." and as the words lift off his tongue, she hears his voice crack.

There is a brief pause between them. Elodie looks at Angelo, his face seemingly etched between two worlds: his past

and the possibility of a shared future between them.

She is moved by the sight of his fragility.
A vulnerability that makes her want to reach
out and touch his hand.

She has an urge to be transparent with
him. To tell him the truth about who she really is. To confess her real name and to tell
him the story of what brought her to the
Portofino dock that afternoon, when he
picked her out from the crowd and saved
her.

But, after all this time, she doesn't even
know where to begin.

She lifts her eyes up to him slightly, questioning if he has selected this poem for a
particular reason. She wonders if it contains
a code like the ones embedded within the
music she played in her former life. But his
was a message that had nothing to do with
weapons, but rather of something growing
between them.

Her hands fall near the folds of her skirt.
She sees his eyes fall to the small mound
above her waist, no bigger than a wheel of
bread.

He doesn't say a word. She looks at him.

Notes and words, things that float on a page, are easy to read. But the interpretation of eyes is an ancient code. She studies his quiet focus; the blue-gray softness of his pupils. She wants to believe that his gaze is a benediction, a silent dialogue between them; an acknowledgment that he already knows the secret Vanna has pressed her to confess, and is not upset by it. But the potential danger from the mine incident and her new fear of the **kommandant** undermine her confidence. Suddenly, she finds herself very afraid.

That night, after dinner, she walks out to the garden. The December air is cool, but not enough to cause the flowers or lemons outside to frost. The bees have all left and the mosquitoes are asleep. She imagines for a moment her mother now entrenched in Venice and wonders if up north there is already snow.

Beside the small wooden bench, where small pots of herbs grow, she sits down to gather herself. Inside she feels a thousand things—fear, vulnerability, and a desperate urge to tell this man who has given her shelter that a life now grows inside of her.

When she looks up, she sees Angelo standing underneath a trellis of roping green vines. She is suddenly struck in a way that both softens her and terrifies her. Her secrets have the potential to destroy him, and this creates an almost instinctual urge within Elodie to flee.

"Anna," he says. "May I sit with you?"

"Yes," she whispers. They rest for a moment side by side.

"I never finished that book of poetry this afternoon. Would you like me to read you the rest?"

She nods. As he begins to read, she is struck by the difference in his voice from the other times he has read for her. Angelo now reads not like a storyteller, but like a musician. She hears the melody of his voice, like the memory of her long-lost instrument. She hears the unmistakable sensation of wanting to keep certain words suspended in the air.

"Bring me the sunflower so I can transplant it here in my own field burned by salt-spray . . ."

She hears the beauty and sadness in his voice. The pull of his heart. And it haunts her. Blindsides her. She hears it as though he is channeling the ghosts of her cello and bow.

That night, she lets him read to her until he reaches nearly the last page. He brings her a blanket, and she allows herself to receive this act of kindness from him for the last time. She has a desire to touch him, to feel the warmth of his fingers and the grip of his hand. But her fingers instead twist inside the cotton blanket.

"Angelo . . ." She whispers his name with great tenderness. There is so much she wants to tell him, but "thank you" is all she manages to say.

When she says these words to him, she feels her heart breaking. She places a hand on her abdomen, knowing full well she must now leave him before it is too late.

THIRTY-NINE

~

Portofino, Italy
DECEMBER 1943

The next morning, she hears his movements in the kitchen. The withdrawing of the plates from the cupboard. The placement of the cutlery on the table. The sound of water coming from the faucet. It is a familiar melody to her, but now Elodie hears it like a dirge.

When Angelo leaves for his rounds in the village, she starts to pack the rucksack she held so carefully when he picked her out in the port months before. Now she replaces the contents inside it in reverse order. She places Luca's sweater like a cushion on the bottom. Then she puts her own clothes directly on top of his.

She pauses briefly to open the pages of **The Little Prince** and for a moment, the memory of Luca washes over her so strongly that she finds herself closing the book and resting it for a moment on her belly. She feels the sensation of movement inside her once again. It's like a trapped wing beating within her, but the music of this fledgling life is like nothing she has ever known.

She picks up Luca's medal of San Giorgio. She places it on top of the book and the sheets of music she still hopes to one day return to the Wolf. With all of her remaining worldly goods now safe inside her rucksack, she laces it tightly and then silently makes her way out the door.

⌒

She has not left the safety of Angelo's home in the entire time she's been in Portofino. From the height of the cliff, she can see the port below. The brightly colored fishing boats. The water, the color of a dissolving jewel. As she starts to walk down the steep hill, her legs feel as though she herself has spent too much time at sea as they shake beneath her.

She knows that she is fleeing out of fear and has no clear plan for leaving Portofino. She hopes she can at least find one fisherman willing to take her someplace west. Like to an island as remote as Elba, a place where people go to forget, to live quietly and unnoticed like grains of sand.

The same sense of panic sweeps over her as it had when her cello was taken from her in Genoa. From the very moment the German said "Anna Zorzetto from Venice . . ." she knew she couldn't go back to her mother and Valentina. She might place both women in danger if the officer decided to pursue her connection to the Wolf. Now, she feels a similar sense of panic wash over her. All she knows is that she needs to get away, to take the first boat leaving the port and protect the people she loved.

She glances at the sky, a dull shade of pewter, and prays the village will now be as empty of Germans as Angelo has told her it is in the off-season.

Midway down the hill, she is stopped by a German officer on patrol. His jacket is green, his jodhpurs the color of bark. Across his chest is a rifle that makes her blood grow cold.

"Where are you going?" His Italian sounds wooden, as if he has learned the language with only half an ear.

"I'm just going into town to buy some bread," she answers without offering any further detail, as she was taught to do by Luca and Beppe.

"It's three o'clock. The bakery is now closed." He glances over her, studying her carefully. "I haven't seen you before. Do you live here?"

"Yes," she lies, thinking he would be more inclined to let a local girl move on her way.

"Where?"

"Just up the hill." She gestures abstractly in that direction.

"Why are you carrying such a big rucksack just to buy bread?"

She does not flinch. Instead she looks straight into his eyes, as if she were aiming a revolver at him.

"You'd better come with me," he says, grabbing to take her by the arm.

They walk for only a few minutes, down the path then up another hill toward a yellow church. Right before it stands a large red house with a tower, protected by an imposing metal gate.

"Here," the German says as he momentarily lets go of Elodie's arm. She pauses as if suddenly stuck by an arrow. On the side of the wall, pressed into the cement pillar, she sees a marble plaque with the words **San Giorgio** etched into the stone. And above the door of the villa there is a marble relief of San Giorgio thrusting his sword into a dragon.

"San Giorgio," she whispers involuntarily, like a single breath escaping. Inside her rucksack, she can feel the flame of her medal, as if the satchel now contains its own fire.

"Yes," the German says, as he hears her murmur. "He's the patron saint of this village. Or didn't you know that already, living here as you claim to?"

Music is playing inside the red house as they enter. It is a piece Elodie has performed many times in her life, the prelude from Bach's Cello Suite No. 1. It rises off the Victrola like a lullaby from Elodie's past.

"This way," the German orders her. They

walk through a marble hallway. Large pieces of baroque furniture rest against the walls. When they arrive in the main receiving room, Elodie looks up to see a large tapestry woven in green and gold, the image of San Giorgio emerging through the threads like an apparition.

She suddenly senses Luca all around her. The revelation that the patron saint of Portofino is the same one he had chosen for his own protective talisman makes her feel as though Luca is sending her comforting signs from beyond the grave.

"**Mein kommandant**." The German salutes. From behind, Elodie makes out the **kommandant**'s thin blonde hair and the thick, pink fingers, which grip his armchair.

"Just a moment," he says without turning. "It's almost finished."

Elodie closes her eyes. The music is unmistakable. She hears the cello strings as though they were strung as tight as twine across her heart. It has been months since she's heard the instrument played, and the record reminds her of her family, her past, and her cello that was taken from her. The pain is raw and piercing.

"Yes, please . . . let it finish," Elodie utters, even with the German's hand still gripping her arm. "I adore the Bach cello suites."

The **kommandant** turns his head, and suddenly the air changes within the room. He looks at Elodie not as prisoner brought in for questioning, but as something unexpected: a fellow Bach connoisseur.

Neither Elodie nor the **kommandant** speaks until the conclusion of the piece. But the **kommandant** watches Elodie carefully. Her body remains rigid under the other soldier's grip, but her eyes are alive, her pupils registering every nuance of the music.

When the music ends, the **kommandant** stands up and goes to the Victrola. He lifts the needle off the record with a careful hand.

The soldier comes over and whispers something into the **kommandant**'s ear. The elder man dismisses him from the room and then approaches Elodie. She can see the pores of his skin and the gray of his eyes.

"What a curious girl you are . . . You recognize the Bach Suites?"

"Yes. I, too, love Pablo Casals's recording of them."

"Hmm . . . Why?"

She thinks of making a comment about

Casals's well-known anti-Fascist politics, but refrains. "Well, to start . . . he's a master of the cello."

She is not sure if she has revealed too much. But the presence of San Giorgio throughout the house has bolstered her confidence.

She knows little about the **kommandant** except for what Angelo has told her. His proclivity for liquor. The diabetes, and their daily arrangement for his late-afternoon insulin injections. But she also recalls that Angelo has mentioned how the **kommandant** often needed strong barbiturates to fall asleep. His need for pills and a diagnosis of diabetes were private matters he didn't want made known.

"Yes, Casals," the **kommandant** says. "I can't say the men in Berlin would approve of my listening to someone who has given their friend General Franco such a hard time. But he is indeed a virtuoso beyond compare." As he walks closer toward her, she realizes he believes he is more than just a connoisseur of music, but also a master of detection.

Her back stiffens like a cat. Her eyes

flash, and suddenly she sees in the corner of the room several shapes that are so familiar to her. The dark case of a violin and the large, almost womanly shape of a cello.

"You are not from Portofino," he states as he stares at her up and down.

She returns his gaze. They are both players in a game of chess. "No, I am not . . . I've been staying with a distant cousin of mine. Angelo Rosselli, the village doctor . . ."

The **kommandant** grunts, a small smile appearing on his lips.

"Do you know him?"

"Yes, I know him very well. I was told there was a young, pretty cousin staying with him." He considers Elodie again, inspecting her even more carefully than before.

"My colleague said it looks like you're packed to leave Portofino. Yet you claim to merely be going out for bread."

"Yes," she answers, her voice carefully measured. "Is this now a crime?"

"I'm not sure . . . Let me see your papers, and then we can decide."

Elodie feels her fear ignite inside her. She fishes into her rucksack, touching her medal of Saint George as she searches to retrieve her forged papers.

She hands them over to the **kommandant**, who reads them with a quick glance.

"Anna Zorzetto. From Venice?"

She merely offers a slight shrug in response.

"That's a long way from here. I had no idea our village doctor was partially Venetian."

"It's a distant relation."

"I see. And you left Venice because?"

"The threat of bombs, of course. My mother felt it would be safer here."

"Of course." The **kommandant** nods his head as if humoring her. "Have they bombed Venice? I thought it was only Verona."

The mention of her home makes Elodie feel as though he is dragging a shard of glass across her back. But she stifles her urge to reveal her discomfort.

"Every night there was the sound of sirens. I couldn't sleep. Here it is peaceful."

"A long way to journey just for a better night's sleep, Anna."

"Insomnia is a plague," she answers, already aware of his weakness. "If you don't suffer from it, you wouldn't understand."

THE GARDEN OF LETTERS 519

Her words register with him immediately. She can see his eyes come alive as though they speak the same language. "I actually do understand. Quite well, in fact."

She does not answer.

"So, Anna . . . I see we share two things in common. Insomnia and a love of music." He reaches for the decanter next to the Victrola and pours himself a small glass of liqueur.

"I'm not terribly curious about your life in Venice. I don't want to hear about your mother nor the suffering you endured from the sound of the sirens. What I would like to know—before I decide what to do with you—is how you could recognize Casals's playing of the Bach."

Elodie remains quiet. Her eyes focus for a moment on the instrument cases in the corner. She is like a drowning woman now eyeing a life preserver.

"That's easy, sir," she finally answers. "I have played the cello for years."

He offers her the cello, as if it were a pawn he can spare in their chess game. The black case is placed on a table and then unlatched. The glimmering instrument is more golden than the one taken from her in Genoa, but its beauty nonetheless captivates her.

"**Bello**," she says as her finger reaches to touch its varnish.

"It was my father's," he says. "The violin is mine."

She doesn't respond. She doesn't want to waste her breath with words. If she is going to save herself, she knows it can only be done by her bringing this instrument to life.

"May I?"

He nods. "Yes. Please."

He offers her a chair. Sitting down with the cello, she expertly positions it between her knees. To buy some time to further calm herself, she searches the case for a piece of rosin, which she applies to the bow as she has done thousands of times in the past.

She pulls the cello to her chest and notices her abdomen is thicker than when she had played at the Bibiena months before. For the first time, there is now something separating her and the cello she is playing on.

There is another life.

This new life buoys Elodie. It gives her a new motivation. It is not only herself that she must now save, but the child as well.

Elodie grasps the bow and, by rote, slides it over the strings to tune the instrument. In her head, she can hear her father plucking a perfect A to help her, as though he, too, were now standing there waiting to hear her play once more.

When she feels she is ready, she takes a deep breath and lifts her bow. To anyone looking at the living room, the resemblance between the girl wielding her bow and the image of Saint George raising his sword to slay the dragon, is uncanny.

The pieces she chooses to play probably have little significance for the **kommandant**. But for her, they are the most meaningful ones she could possibly have selected. She re-creates her final performance at the Bibiena. First the "Belles of Genevieve," and then the "Dying Swan." When she finishes, she lifts her head and sees the **kommandant** standing with his mouth open, his eyes almost wet with tears.

"Beautiful," he murmurs. "**Exquisito**."

He reaches for the glass of **sciacchetra**

he has poured for himself, and extends his arm to take the bow from her.

"I'm not finished," she says boldly. "I still have one more piece."

He raises an eyebrow. "As you wish . . . I will not stop you."

Elodie begins to play, again impassioned, the notes of the Boccherini concerto rising from her cello like stitches of a quilt being plucked and released into the air. When she arrives at the place where she had once mistakenly played the Grutzmacher cadenza, she does not now pause. Instead, she increases the fervor of her playing. She is like a diver thrusting herself deeper into the water. She plays the code that she faltered on months before. She plays it this time for the ears of the Wolf and Luca, and she plays it with perfection. She plays it just for them. A tribute to them alone.

The **kommandant** is speechless. He places his drink down and begins to clap. He is surprised by this gifted girl in his living room, brought to him like a stray dog with a dirty rucksack and a face that looks like a fox.

Elodie does not look up right away. Had she lifted her gaze then, she would have seen the second figure that had just entered the room.

Angelo had arrived to administer the **kommandant**'s injection before making his way home to her. He stands at the threshold to the room, amazed by the beauty of Elodie's music, hidden from him until now.

Before he can speak, the **kommandant**'s voice fills the air:

"What a talent your cousin has, **Dottore**. Knowing my love of music, why have you kept her a secret from me?"

Angelo stands at the threshold, seeing Elodie's head lifting from the scroll of her cello. For a second, her eyelids are still partially closed, as though she is waking from a long sleep. When her eyes finally do open, it strikes him straight to his heart, as though he is seeing her true self for the first time.

He notices her rucksack against the leg of the chair and reads her more clearly than he has ever before. He doesn't care what trouble first drove her to Portofino, or what has caused her to leave in haste from the shelter of his home. He will now do anything in his power to save her.

"**Kommandant**," he says walking into the room. His fingers whiten around the handle of his black medicine bag. "I'm so glad you've had the chance to hear Anna play. I've been meaning to mention her to you for some time now. She's been a great pride to the family for many years. Isn't she wonderful?"

"Indeed, she is," the **kommandant** says. "A veritable virtuoso. So unexpected here in this hidden corner of the world."

"Isn't it the nature of Portofino to keep its beauty for a chosen few?"

The **kommandant** nods. Another chess game begins, this time between the two men. One with a gun in his desk. The other with a leather bag filled with syringes and pills.

"Yes. How fortunate we are here compared to the rest of Italy. No one's bombing us, while Milan and Salerno burn to the ground. Your cousin traveled a great length to get here, just because she couldn't sleep with the sirens blaring in Venice."

Angelo glances at Elodie, who is frozen. Her arms grasp the cello toward her belly like armor.

"It's terrible not to be able to sleep, as you well know, **Herr Kommandant**."

"Yes. I've told Anna how we share this affliction. So many things we have in common, she and I . . . music, sleeplessness, and a desire to be left here alone."

Angelo's bag contains the sole source of his power. The needle and syringe that he can administer without the **kommandant**'s ever feeling any pain from his touch, and the white tablets of Nembutal, which enable him to sleep.

He walks closer to Elodie and the **kommandant**. He looks to Elodie, his eyes reassuring her with a glance. On the long wooden table, he places his leather bag and unlatches it, the sound of the metal snap filling the air in one sharp note.

"Your insulin, **Kommandant**. It shouldn't be administered too late today."

The **kommandant** walks over to his chair and rolls up his sleeve. His authority suddenly yields to Angelo, who swabs the man's bicep with cotton soaked with alcohol. He pushes the needle into the glass vial and pulls back the syringe.

"Another artist in the family," the **kommandant** says, rolling down his sleeve. "I didn't feel a thing."

"And how's your sleep been?" Angelo says as he reaches his hands down into his bag. Elodie can hear a faint jangle of pills. A temptation. She hears it like windchimes.

"I'm happy to keep helping you with your problem," he says as he measures out just a few pills and places them in a spare glass bottle. He prudently doesn't leave too many. He wants to keep the **kommandant** hungry for more. He needs to preserve their arrangement. He needs to protect himself. And Elodie, most of all. His and the **kommandant**'s arrangement, much like the cello she now holds to her belly, is a shield.

FORTY

~

Portofino, Italy
DECEMBER 1943

The **kommandant** tells them to both go home. "I have no need to hear any war stories about Venice, Anna," he tells her. "Or anywhere else, for that matter. But don't think you're not going to be playing for me again. You're my secret now, too." There is an understanding made between them that requires no further conversation. His eyes communicate their agreement between the two men.

"Take her and go home, **Dottore**. I'll see you tomorrow."

Elodie packs up the cello in silence and returns it to the corner. Angelo waits for her at the steps that lead to the hallway. When she approaches him, her rucksack now strapped to her back, he takes her by the hand.

They have never touched before and the sensation of his fingers wrapped in hers, feels like a promise. She no longer feels alone. She no longer feels afraid.

Hand in hand, they begin to walk up the hill toward his house.

This time when he asks if he can carry her bag, she slips it off her back and gives it to him without any trepidation. When they arrive at the archway, it is Elodie who lifts the tangle of vines, so Angelo can get to the heavy green door with ease.

They enter the house in silence, their movements are those of a couple who have returned from a long journey and are thankful to be home.

He places down her rucksack and leaves his medicine bag on a chair.

She is already in the kitchen peeling an orange. He takes a pitcher and fills it with water. He brings it to the living room. She places the plate of orange wedges down. Then two glasses for the water.

"Sit," she tells him softly.

He lowers himself into the worn sofa. His eyes are blue as a gull's. His mouth soft like the lip of a shell.

"I need to tell you a story," she says as she, too, sits down.

He looks up at her.

"I've been waiting," he says. And his words finally release her.

⌒

Elodie starts off slowly. "This is not a story like in your novels," she tells him. "Nor is it as beautiful as the poetry you read yesterday, which warmed the air. This is a story that is full of heartache and will make your blood run cold."

He stares at her. He is full of wonder, the music that she played an hour before is still in his ears. "Anna," he says. "I am happy that you are here. No matter what you tell me, please know that I will always give you shelter. You are safe with me."

She wonders if this is the first seedling of love, the embrace of protection. She feels it like a blanket of warmth covering her limbs and penetrating her bones.

"You are so very kind . . ." But she holds her breath, not yet fully believing him. Soon he will learn the truth that she is not Anna Zorzetto, but Elodie Bertolotti. A cello student from Verona, a **staffetta** for the Resistance, and a pregnant woman whose lover—not even her husband—died on the soil of the Monte Comune.

"When I first arrived, you said you picked me out from the crowd because I looked the most afraid." Her voice quivers. Her hands are like a folded dove over her belly. Her eyes lift from the floor to meet his own.

"Two months ago, I left Venice, telling my mother that there was someone in Genoa who needed my help. She begged me not to go, saying that it was too dangerous for me to travel. Already the sound of sirens was deafening, and we slept every night fearing a bomb might drop on our heads."

Her heart is racing inside her. She looks again at Angelo, who has not taken his eyes off her.

"A few months before, I had fallen in love with a man in Verona. He loved books like you do, and working together with him, I carried hidden codes for the Resistance," she said, her voice lowered to a whisper. "In my music, through my cello playing. And

I made a mistake one night that possibly caused the loss of several lives."

She takes a deep breath. "This man who loved books. I heard music in his heartbeat; I came alive just with the grazing of his hand. I loved him in a way that was so new, I discovered a part of me that I had never known existed . . . And then one day in the mountains, where we were hiding with the partisans after we had all fought together at the Piazza delle Poste, he was shot by a band of Germans." Recalling the violence of Luca's death, the light in Elodie's eyes becomes engulfed in shadow. To Angelo, it is like watching an eclipse.

Angelo sits quietly listening to her confessional, never once interrupting her. There had been countless times he sat beside the dying, particularly when he was with the army in Ethiopia, before a priest could arrive to perform last rites, and his patient began reciting the very things that haunted his soul. Now Elodie's words spill forth in a similar way.

"**Carissima**," he says, finally interjecting himself. "You need not do this to yourself." He moves his chair closer to where she is sitting. "Certainly not for my benefit. I gave you shelter because I sensed you needed it, and because my own heart is heavy with loss . . ."

His eyes are pale and wet like oysters, shucked and raw. "Anna, you have filled the empty spaces in my home. You have no idea how grateful I am that you are here."

She lifts her hand, as if to stop him from saying any more words of kindness.

"Angelo, I am not Anna . . . My name is Elodie Bertolotti. My papers are false."

"You thought I believed Anna was your real name, **carissima**? Please. Every time it came from my lips, your face seemed surprised." He lets out a small laugh. "The only thing that has caught me off guard was your talent with the cello. That, I was not expecting."

His lack of surprise startles her, but now she cannot stop until she has revealed everything she has kept from him.

"There is one other thing." She pauses gravely. She tries to catch another breath. "What you don't realize, is that you didn't save just one person that day at the port. You saved two."

She unlocks her hands, and her fingers

stretch to pull taut the fabric of her blouse around her belly.

"I'm at nearly four months." She looks straight into his eyes, which have become wet with emotion.

"I'm sorry I never told you earlier. I promised Vanna I'd tell you before Christmas." She looks down at her belly. "That's one of the reasons I tried to leave today. I don't want to cause a scandal in the village and do harm to your good name here as the pregnancy becomes more pronounced." Her voice begins to tremble and she struggles to release the words inside her.

He wants to speak, but his words, too, are caught in his mouth. Didn't she understand that she had saved him, too? That she had repaired the places of his heart that he had believed were permanently cracked, like shattered glass?

Didn't she realize that she was beginning to restore him? That her very sounds soothed him. The echo of her footsteps on the tile floor. Her preparing the water for her bath. Her fingers turning the pages of one of his books. Her breath. Her laugh, when she allowed it to escape. She had enabled him to feel alive again for the first time in years. She had offered him light and air.

"Elodie . . ." He says her real name for the first time. It flies through the air pure and singular. A truth.

"You have given me so much since I arrived," she continues. "You let me regain my strength and to come to terms with all that I'd recently lost." Her fingers grip the edge of the couch. She takes a deep breath. "You gave me space to breathe. To recover. To come to terms with this child that now grows inside me."

"I did it because I sensed you needed kindness . . ." he says. "And it was easy to extend it to you." He had not expected his hand to travel toward hers, but he soon found himself moving even closer to her. He places a hand on top of hers, the swelling of her child beneath, now protected by each of their cupped hands.

She feels his hand over hers like a coverlet, a tarp that could shield her from all harm.

There is a silent looping between them as their eyes meet and they touch. Beneath his hands, he feels the life growing just beneath her skin. It strikes him so deeply, he feels it like a wound that has been unbandaged and finally allowed to meet the sting of the air.

"You will never know how beautiful I find you now."

She feels as though she has become all water. That her bones have dissolved. The sharp edges of her heart soften like beach glass.

Their two faces hover between them for a few seconds.

He does not kiss her first. Instead he waits until he feels the pull of her hands bringing his face so close to hers that he can inhale her breath like vapor.

She feels a cry well inside her. The struggle to maintain her secrets has taken so much energy and now, without them, her heart opens. She feels simultaneous loss and hope. She sees Luca flash before her eyes, before finding herself again in Angelo's touch.

His kiss is soft and careful. He caresses her cheek, then the edge of her ear. And when he kisses her she feels weightless. Her desire to be loved again, her happiness of having finally shed her secrets; Elodie feels she could take flight.

She places his fingers on the buttons of her blouse and helps him unfasten her.

He cups each breast. Traces each line, every curve and each plateau. Her body is so full of life that in her embrace, he feels the broken parts of him beginning to heal.

He wants to make love to her properly on a bed, but he knows that his room, with the letters from his lost wife on the wall, is not an option. So he gathers the pillows from the sofa and lays one behind her back, opening her gently like a flower from his garden, her hair soft as a bird's feathers in his hands.

When her blouse falls away to reveal her belly, so small and taut, he feels his body freeze for a moment from the sheer beauty of her. Her skin glows, almost opalescent.

He feels the hardness of her nipples. The pregnancy has made them dark as chestnuts, and he feels their texture stiffen as he runs them under his tongue.

He waits before he enters her, not wanting to rush. He is just so grateful to have her in his arms. But she wraps her legs around him even more tightly, and he finds himself traveling into depths unexpected, the power of their coupling striking both of them to their core.

⌒

When Elodie awakens the next morning, she discovers herself in the small bedroom with her body warm under the blankets and a flower by her bed.

She listens for sounds, but hears nothing but the chirping of crickets.

When her eyes come to focus, she sees Angelo in the doorway, smiling and dressed.

"How did you sleep?" he asks her.

"I hardly felt you carry me to the bed," she answers. "That's how deeply I slept. I certainly didn't need any pills."

He smiles and she feels a sense of warmth again flood through her.

"I hope you slept just as deeply."

"I did not sleep, but I still had dreams . . . They were so beautiful, almost like visions."

Elodie pulls the covers off her legs and reaches to find her clothes. Although her hair is not yet brushed and her face is not yet washed, to Angelo, Elodie's radiance is blinding.

As she walks over to him, he is struck by

how different she now appears. She now moves with a sense of weightlessness. Her protective armor has been shed.

In the living room, amid the piles of books and keepsakes he has collected over the years, he searches to find his own copy of **The Little Prince**. He suddenly feels the desire to read to her while she nestles in his arms.

He hums while he searches and smiles when he finally finds his copy, the familiar cover, with the migrating birds and the little boy clasping the strings.

"So we have two copies of this book in this household . . ." She smiles as he slides next to her on the couch.

"Yes," he says, as his fingers reach to gently touch its cover. "It is a very special book."

"To think it was written for a child," she says. She rests her head on his shoulder and closes her eyes.

"Reading some of the passages to you the other day, I found myself discovering things within the story I hadn't noticed when I read it the first time." He reaches for her hands and kisses her fingers. "There is so much hidden wisdom within such a slender book."

With her head still against his chest, she can feel the rhythm of his heartbeat change. The tempo has quickened.

"Yes," she whispers. "When you have lost someone you love, the message that love still exists even when we cannot see it or touch it, makes the pain almost bearable."

Her fingers tighten around Angelo's. The memory of Luca's last words, that he would be "smiling at her even from beyond the stars," returns to her. She always wondered if he had foreseen his own death that day.

"It is very much a guide," she says, and she can feel a hard lump in her throat like she's swallowed a stone. "On how to survive after a heartbreaking loss."

She feels his thoughts shift. And she suspects it is the memory of Dalia returning to him. She closes her eyes and opens her heart.

She feels his rib cage swell underneath her. She reaches for his fingers and squeezes his hand.

He takes a few moments to gather his words and then begins to speak.

"Just like you told me your story last night, I think it's important you know mine."

She looks at him and nods. Although she has already heard bits and pieces of his past from Vanna, she knows how important it is that she learn this story from him.

"As you fell in love with a boy who loved books, I fell in love with a girl I taught to read. I saw her one afternoon walking with a basket of lemons and a gardenia in her hair, and just the sight of her caused me to lose my heart.

"She became my wife." He took a deep breath. " She died when I was a continent away, in Africa. She died and our baby died. And they buried them in the little cemetery behind the Church of San Giorgio before I was able to get home."

He chokes on his words. She takes her hand and cups it behind his head and strokes his hair and then his cheek, until her palm, too, is damp from his tears.

"I should have been there with her when she delivered. I should not have left her here alone."

"It is no more your fault than Luca's death is mine," she says in a whisper.

His arm reaches to grasp her waist, and

he holds it there for a moment until his breath returns to him.

"To think, you didn't suspect I knew you were pregnant all along. What kind of doctor would I be if I didn't notice your symptoms?" he says, smiling at her. "You have given me a gift, Elodie. You have allowed me to right a wrong. You have enabled me to care for a woman and a child who need my protection."

She feels herself trembling. She knows that what he says is like another message lifted from the book. She has become his rose.

FORTY-ONE

Portofino, Italy
DECEMBER 1943

When Vanna arrives that afternoon, she finds both Elodie and Angelo still nestled on the couch where they'd been since the morning. There were still untold parts of their stories, like the threads of an unfinished carpet that would still need to be finished off and tied.

Angelo had felt Elodie's anguish as if it were his own as he listened to her describe how her cello was stolen from her, how the Wolf's arrest had caused her to believe that if she returned to Venice it might threaten her mother's safety. She had wandered the streets of Genoa for what seemed like hours until she eventually found herself at Genoa's enormous port. The harbor was crowded with all types of boats. The larger ones were surrounded by German officers, but she had noticed there was a sign for a few ferries departing to the coastal villages of Liguria and beyond. She wasn't thinking clearly, only that she wanted to get somewhere safe. Rapallo, Portovenere, the boats destinations were all a blur to her. She chose the boat to Portofino simply because it was the first one leaving from the dock.

"I sat on that boat and I felt I was half dead," she told him. "I had just seen a dear friend carted off in manacles, and then the German took my cello . . ."

Angelo looked at Elodie's hands differently now that he knew she was a musician. The strength and elegance of her fingers held a deeper beauty to him. But more than anything, he wanted to start a new life with her.

"When the war is over, I will take you to see your mother again," he promised. "And we will find you a new cello. But until that, you must write and let her know you are safe. And we will visit Venice together after the baby is born."

When he spoke with such tenderness for the child she was carrying, she heard a new melody inside her. Music that was not mournful, but rather full of hope.

Vanna placed down her basket and looked at their hands, now like two trees whose roots had become entwined.

"I took your advice, Vanna," Elodie said. "He knows everything now."

Vanna eyes flickered. "For once, I was the smart one."

Angelo smiled. "Yes. And now you need to tell her that she has nothing to worry about meeting the rest of the family."

"Of course not. They will be relieved to see your gloom has finally lifted. And don't worry about the rest of the town, either. There is too much sadness from the war, for anyone to be unkind to a beautiful pregnant girl. They'll be happy the village doctor has finally found a wife.

"I expect to see you both tomorrow at my table for Christmas Eve," Vanna said before she left them. "You will be seen as a gift."

That night, Angelo led her to the room where Dalia's letters had for years papered the walls. "I can't bring you here to sleep. It doesn't seem fair," he said as he studied her eyes. "Perhaps we can paint over it? There's a can of white paint in the shed."

"No," she said softly. "It's part of your history and should be respected."

She was not afraid of the room. On the contrary, it moved her deeply. She, too, still carried Luca's love inside her. She could recite his words as if they were love letters papered onto her heart.

If she were to stay with Angelo, and build a life with him and Luca's child, the past layers of their story needed to be respected, not erased.

She was silent for a moment and then began to move about the house. Through the windows, moonlight streamed into the rooms as Elodie worked in the kitchen, pulling down a canister of flour from the shelf and mixing it with water to make some glue.

She found a pastry brush in the drawer and slipped it into her pocket, and then walked to her little room where she had slept for the past two months. There, she

found her cherished sheets of music and
her copy of **The Little Prince.**

He watched transfixed as she did what
he had imagined Dalia had done years before. Elodie quietly found a pair of scissors
and began to cut bits of the written music,
so that now the score appeared almost like
clouds of floating notes. When she was
about to take her scissors to her beloved
book, Angelo stopped her and offered her
his own.

She did not speak, but she accepted his
copy, keeping the one from Luca pristine.
She took her scissors and began cutting
the colorful watercolors of the little prince
landing on the different planets and of his
parachute made from flying birds. She cut
out the images of the friends he met along
his journey: his beloved rose, the elephant,
the snake, and the fox. She cut out the magical baobab trees, the asteroids and the
stars. She thought of the child that grew inside her, the way the baby might one day
gaze at the ceiling. And she smiled as the
walls suddenly sprang to life.

The sight of her cutting and kneeling with
a bowl of glue, papering the walls with bits
and pieces of her own history, and carefully

pressing them in the open places that did not cover the letters he had sent to Dalia, touched Angelo so deeply. He felt as though his memories and his future were merging into one.

After she had finished adding her own pieces to the walls, Elodie slid next to Angelo in bed.

"Now we will sleep under a shared story," she said. "It's only right."

Angelo's hand reached to touch her growing middle, and his body flooded not only with warmth, but with gratitude as well. For now the wound in his heart had finally been mended.

And they fell asleep under a new canopy, one created from sheets of faded letters, suspended notes, and paper stars.

AUTHOR'S NOTE AND ACKNOWLEDGMENTS

The Garden of Letters began after I heard an extraordinary story one night at a dinner party about a friend's father. As a young man, he was trying to flee to safety during World War II when he was saved by a barrel-chested man in a small village on the Italian coast. Like the character Angelo, the stranger emerged from a crowded dock just as my friend's father was about to hand over his forged identity card to a German control officer. The man called out, "Cousin! Cousin! I've been waiting for you all week!" and saved him from further scrutiny by the officer, and also subsequently provided him shelter during the war. Thank you, Judy Goldsmith, for telling me the story that became the genesis for this novel.

After hearing this story, I immediately

envisioned the opening scene of a novel. I was fascinated by the intersection of two strangers meeting that afternoon at the dock: one person who is on the run and has a secret, and the second figure who innately senses the other's deep fear. From there, I began to imagine the two main characters in **The Garden of Letters**: Elodie, a woman who is in need of a safe harbor for reasons that unfold during the course of the book, and Angelo, the haunted doctor who desperately wants to help others because of his own tragic past.

For most of my career, I've woven themes of painting and art into my novels. This time, though, I wanted to write about another form of art: music. Not only did I want to write about how a musician experiences the world, but I also wanted to explore a more mystical element—how we as human beings are able to communicate without the use of words. Although much of **The Garden of Letters** centers around the use of hidden codes by the Italian Resistance during World War II, it also explores how we as people communicate with only our eyes and our body language, making us capable of telling a story without uttering a single word.

As with all of my novels, many of the secondary characters in this book are based on true-life historical figures. During my first research trip to Verona, I was taken to the city's synagogue by my wonderful translator and guide, Katia Galvetto. It was there that I noticed the commemorative plaque for the Jewish schoolteacher turned partisan Rita Rosani, who led a small squad that fought numerous battles against the Germans. Although an exhaustive search by Ms. Galvetto turned up little information about Rita Rosani, I wanted my readers to learn about her courage and her heroic death at the age of twenty-four on the Monte Comune in September 1944, a year after she appears in my novel.

Brigitte Lowenthal, Berto Zampieri, and Darno Maffini were also historic figures, all active in the Veronese Resistance. With the help of Katia Galvetto, I was able to meet Professor Vittore Bocchetta, now a spry ninety-year-old, who worked alongside Zampieri and Maffini in the Veronese Resistance. The novel came alive after that meeting with Professor Bocchetta and the amazing research done by Ms. Galvetto. I later learned that Brigitte Lowenthal married Berto Zampieri after the war. Brigitte's family, however, took cyanide pills, taking their own lives rather than being sent to a concentration camp.

The story of the character Lena's death, how she was first blinded and then shot in front of her parents' apartment, was inspired by the torture and murder of the real-life partisan Irma Bandiera, whom I read about in Leon Weckstein's book **200,000 Heroes**, about the Italian Partisans and the American OSS in World War II. The book is filled with many fascinating stories about brave Italian citizens and American soldiers who fought against the Germans during the war, and I'm indebted to the book for my research about this exciting time period.

I also am extremely grateful to several other people who helped me along the way. Many Italian friends went above and beyond to help ensure that the book is historically accurate and also reflects a realistic portrait of wartime Italy. Rita Annunziata of Bellagio, Italy, who my young children still call "Nona," provided me with essential information on the life of a doctor in Italy during World War II. Michela Cocchi graciously met me in Bologna and translated an exhibition on the writer Laura Orvieto, giving me an invaluable lens on life of a young girl during Fascist Italy and its eventual descent into war. A special thanks to Emanuela Negri and Raffaele Coluccino at the Verona Music Conservatory for helping me understand the musical instruction for a young cello student during the war, Deborah Venditti for her knowledge on the Teatro Bibiena, and Elena Gatz and Lucia Roditi Formeron for illuminating stories about the Veronese Jewish community.

I also owe a great deal to Costanza Bertolotti, who was able to illuminate the experience of the Mantova Resistance and other details that made the book richer as a whole. The warmth and general support by Count Gherardo Scapinelii Di Legugigno, who shared many stories of his family's life during the war and also graciously introduced me to several helpful contacts, most notably Vanna and Marina Magrini and the Venetian Patrician Family, Zorzi, and the particular assistance by N. H. Pieralvise

Zorzi, who shared with me many of his own family's photographs and stories that shed light on the Italian Resistance. And a special and heartfelt thanks to Giovanni Pelizzato who is now the proud owner of his grandfather's bookstore, La Toletta, in Venice, and who, after sharing stories of his grandfather's involvement with the Italian Resistance, in particular, how books were used to send codes and store pistols, was the inspiration for Luca in this novel.

Vivienne Courtney was instrumental in sharing her early experiences as a young cello student, and Stewart Wallace provided helpful information on musical composition. Tina Josinksy shared helpful anecdotes of her childhood in Italy during the war. Thanks to Stephen Gordon and Howard Fox for their musical expertise and assistance in devising/inventing several of the musical codes within the book and my father, Paul Richman, who also assisted with musical questions. I am also grateful to Charles Goldstein, Countess Enrica Rocca, James Mondex, and his staff at Mondex Corporation, for their knowledge and contacts of art stolen by the Nazis for the initial research for the book.

Thank you to Antony Currie for his dutiful and careful editing, which has followed me with each book; and Nikki Koklanaris, for your medical expertise, all-around editorial feedback, and helpful contacts: Doctors Alice Cootauco and Judith Rossiter. For helping me with my research, I thank Maryelizabeth Koepele. I also would like to thank those who were kind enough to read earlier drafts of the novel, including Marvin Gordon, my friend and fellow author Martin Fletcher, Robbin Klein, Victoria Leventhal, Jardine Libaire, Tina Spitz and my parents, Ellen and Paul Richman. Your thoughtful comments were always welcome and instructive. And also a special thanks to Melanie Lawless, who offered a welcome place for my children when I was knee-deep in finishing the book.

Stephen Gordon, sweetest of all husbands, saint of all saints, and husband and father extraordinaire, who reads every draft and is happy to serve as a sounding board when

I need clarity, none of my books would be possible without you. Sally Wofford-Girand, my wonderful and supportive agent, I thank you once again. You have helped bring my books to a worldwide audience of passionate readers, and I'm incredibly grateful for your early support since I was just over twenty-five years of age. To Sam Fox, a special thank-you for finding the title for this novel. Finally, a special thanks to my editor, Kate Seaver, and the rest of the staff at Berkley/Penguin, who have always worked with me to create the best book possible.

READERS GUIDE

~

The
GARDEN
of
LETTERS

QUESTIONS
FOR DISCUSSION

1. The book moves between several time periods, weaving together Angelo's and Elodie's pasts, as well as their present together. How does this enrich the storytelling?

2. A major theme of the novel is how we communicate without words, most notably through the power of music. How else do the characters communicate nonverbally?

3. How do Elodie's feelings about music change throughout the book? How does this reflect her shifting worldview?

4. Elodie's father tells her that "you sense what's hidden beneath the music." How does this foreshadow her work for the Resistance movement? How else is foreshadowing used in the novel?

5. Elodie often says that her extremely precise memory is "the Venetian in me." Do you think it's possible to inherit traits from your ethnicity?

6. Lena seems more alive after attending the Resistance meetings, and later on, Elodie observes the same in her mother as she aids in the fighting. Why does this happen?

7. Do you think that Elodie, on some unconscious level, purposefully leaves the Wolf's code out of the cadenza during her concert at the Bibiena? Or is she truly lost in the music? How might the events that follow have changed if she had performed the code?

8. As the Germans enter Verona, average citizens step up to fight: "'Tell us what to do!' one of the women shouts. She is not a **staffetta**, but a matron eager to be useful." Would you have joined the Resistance if you lived in wartime Italy?

9. The account of the Wolf's ransacked apartment—"The silk panels were slashed and cut open. The strings of the grand piano had been severed and brutally pulled out like

weeds"—is disturbing, despite its describing only objects. Why? What do you think ultimately became of the Wolf and his wife? Could they have survived?

10. The first line of the book reads "Her rucksack contains her life reduced to small pieces." Later on, Dalia produces a box filled with small trinkets that she replaces with Angelo's letters. What would represent your "life reduced to small pieces?" What objects do you consider sacred?

11. Why does Angelo gravitate toward things that need extra care? Considering his history with Dalia and Nasai, has he always done so?

12. Valentina can find beauty and value in items that others see only as trash. What are the parallels between her and Venice itself, a city where "beauty and decay seemed to coexist?"

13. Why does Dalia paper the room with Angelo's letters? Why does Angelo leave them intact "like an ancient tomb"? And why does Elodie add to them? What does the "garden of letters" represent to each of them?

14. The characters often refer to passages from **The Little Prince**: "It's only with the heart one can see rightly; what is essential is invisible to the eye." What is the significance of these passages? How does it apply to Elodie's life in Verona, and later on, in Portofino?